BOOK THREE OF
THE PATH OF PATHOS TRILOGY

SIMON SHUGAR

Copyright © 2025 Simon Shugar
All rights reserved

The characters and events portrayed in this book are fictitious. Any similarity to real persons, living or dead, is coincidental and not intended by the author.

No part of this book may be reproduced, or stored in a retrieval system, or transmitted in any form or by any means, electronic, mechanical, photocopying, recording, or otherwise, without express written permission of the publisher.

ISBN: 9798306674803

DEDICATION

For Thomas.

Chapters

Chapter 0 - A View of The Sky (Recap) 5
Chapter 1 - Awake 12
Chapter 2 - Tracks 23
Chapter 3 - Clash at the River 41
Chapter 4 - The Bridge 57
Chapter 5 - Village of Kyrne 72
Chapter 6 - Hunting 82
Chapter 7 - Drowned River 93
Chapter 8 - Nixie 105
Chapter 9 - Riding 115
Chapter 10 - Time to Scout 128
Chapter 11 - Whitestone 141
Chapter 12 - Fire's Hymn 162
Chapter 13 - No Longer Home 170
Chapter 14 - Break In the Wind 191
Chapter 15 - A Lesson 203
Chapter 16 - Inkling 211
Chapter 17 - Hide 223
Chapter 18 - Father's Book 241
Chapter 19 - Berries 251
Chapter 20 - Horse Thieves 262
Chapter 21 - Disguise 274
Chapter 22 - Spring Soldiers 292
Chapter 23 - Replacements 301
Chapter 24 - Marching On 317
Chapter 25 - Battle Begins 333
Chapter 26 - Prince's Duel 345
Chapter 27 - Royal Ride 358
Epilogue 371

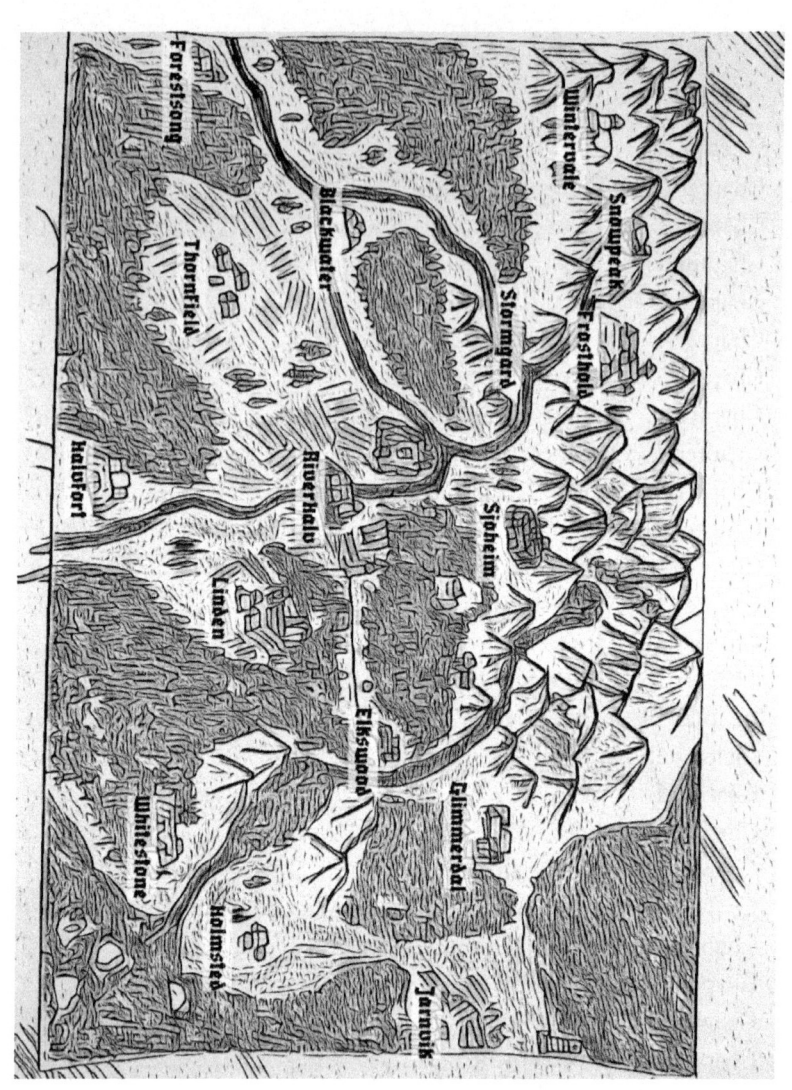

Chapter 0 - A View of The Sky (Recap)

"We've just helped someone start a war"

That was the last thing I heard before darkness took me. The words echoed in my mind, even as the world blurred into silence.

War. It always came back to war.

It started long before me, long before I even knew what war truly meant. The old king was dead, and his three sons had turned on each other. The youngest princes, Harlan and Erik, refused to let their elder brother, Eldric—the rightful heir—take the throne. They split the kingdom in three, tearing it apart, dragging everyone into their fight. I never wanted to be part of it.

But war doesn't care what you want.

It reached my home, the village of Linden, like a storm. My father went off to fight with the other men, leaving my mother and

I to fend for ourselves. Life was hard, but we managed—until the day it all unraveled.

Tensions rose within the village.

My mother—strong, unshakable—was wounded by Pedar, a boy both too old to be a child and too young to be a man, his mind twisted with rage he couldn't control. And then, as if that wasn't enough, she was hurt again—this time by Captain Varek, the leader of a visiting brigade. He dealt with Pedar swiftly, but what he took from my mother was far worse. The soldiers left us broken, taking half our harvest with them.

Her wound festered. No one in Linden could help her. So we left for Riverhalv, where my aunt Linette lived with her husband, Garret, and their son, Lars. We thought maybe the healers there could save her. But Riverhalv wasn't a refuge. It was soon a city under siege. War followed us like a plague, its shadow growing darker by the day.

While my mother's condition worsened, I tried to stay strong. But I felt like I was drowning in it all—until the day my father saved me.

My father had received our message.

He heard of my mother's illness and deserted the army to reach us. He gave up everything—his duty, his safety—just to come back. I didn't understand it then, but later I would see the weight of that choice, the consequences waiting for him in the shadows.

He made it just in time. Just in time to save me from drowning, to spend one precious day with my mother, and to see her pass. I'll never forget that day. We danced by the river, the three of us, while the siege raged beyond the walls. For a moment, it felt like the world had stopped, like the war couldn't touch us.

And then it ended.

When my mother passed, my father took me away from it all—away from the city, the siege, the memories. He helped me through my grief, not with words but with time, teaching me how to hunt, how to survive. In the woods, he gave me something to hold onto, something to focus on. He gave me back a piece of myself.

We did try to return home.

Back to Linden, back to what was left of the life we had before. But the past has a way of catching up. We ran into Captain Varek—the same man who had taken so much from us. My father took his revenge, severing Varek's hand, but the cost was steep. We had to flee, the fields burning behind us as the past was reduced to ash.

Eventually, the running stopped. We found a place at the base of the mountain, deep in the woods, where the world seemed quieter. It was there, surrounded by the stillness of the forest, that my father began teaching me about pathos—our gift. The ability to sense the life around us, to feel what others were feeling, was both a blessing and a burden. He taught me to control it, to quiet the flood of emotions that could overwhelm me, to use it as a tool rather than let it use me.

We built a cabin, made a home out of nothing. For a while, it was ours. For a while, we thought we'd escaped the war.

But the war found us.

Captain Steen, a friend of my father's, came looking for him. He brought promises: a way to end the fighting, a clean slate for my father's desertion. All we had to do was find the prince's heirs—Sanne and Niklas. My father agreed, though I wish now he hadn't.

We found the heirs. The war ended—or at least paused. But the cost? My father's life. He fought until the end, taking Captain Varek with him. Varek had been there under orders from Fief Lord Cedric, a man whose ambitions ran as deep as the war itself. Even with Varek gone, it didn't feel like a victory. The kingdom wasn't whole again—it was just split into two instead of three.

And I was alone.

For a while, I was content to be alone.

Living off the land, surviving in the mountains and the glens between them—it felt like enough. But eventually, my bowstring snapped, my supplies dwindled, and my clothes became little more than rags. I was thirteen summers or so by then, and I knew it was time to return to civilization, to face people again.

I sought out Sjoheim first. The city was overwhelming, loud, and crowded, and I wasn't ready for it. My state drew stares and insults at the gate. I traded pelts for what little I could—a restrung bow, a bit of food—and took my first hot bath in years. It felt good, but I wasn't used to people, to their sharp words and quicker tempers. Things went sideways, and before I knew it, I was stealing clothes from the same young man who'd insulted me. My escape was messy, but it was helped along by the first bard I'd ever heard—a voice I'd never forget.

After Sjoheim, I went back home to my father's cabin, my cabin. I wasn't looking for just shelter, though. I was looking for the one thing my father had left for me—a book. A book I hadn't even known existed until his dying breath. I didn't know he could read or write. He was a woodsman, a scout. Who would have guessed he'd be learned?

But when I got there, the book was gone. Stolen. And I had to find it.

I'd heard rumors from traveling merchants—bandits and highwaymen roamed the lands since the end of the Three Prince War. It had to be them. They were the ones who'd ransacked my cabin and taken my father's book. I decided I could use my ability—my pathos—to sense people and track them down.

I scouted the woods, following the lessons my father had taught me. I hunted, mapped the land, and pieced together their possible movements. My search took me south, back into the Elkswood and to the town of the same name.

In Elkswood, I joined a hunt for a boar. It gave me a reason to be there, a way to stay without drawing attention. I even managed to best the creature, dragging it back to town in triumph. It wasn't just about the hunt, though—I met new people. Viktor, the kind tavern keeper; Rolf and the other hunters who treated me like one of their own; Oliver, who became my rival; and Anni, a scribe who helped me expand and complete my map. For the first time in a long time, I started to feel like I belonged somewhere.

We celebrated.

Oliver and I took down a boar that plagued the town and in return were promised a boon from Fief Lord Cedric, a meeting I dreaded. But before Cedric could arrive, news came of a bandit attack. I didn't waste any time. I left the celebrations abruptly and followed their trail. Using my map and my pathos, I tracked them deep into the forest.

I was wrong. Naive. Young.

They weren't bandits—they called themselves the Forsworn. Refugees, outcasts, and remnants of the last war. Like me, they were just trying to survive. And they didn't have my father's book.

They were led by Commander Crosse, a man of quiet authority, and his second, Wulfric. At first, they captured me, took my map, thinking I was a spy for Cedric. But Jory—someone I'd once shown kindness to years ago—convinced them otherwise. He also convinced me they weren't the bandits I'd been chasing.

Through the winter, I helped them. I hunted so they wouldn't need to raid as often, and I taught Jory to make traps as he couldn't hunt to save his life.

In return, Commander Crosse repaid me in the only way that mattered. Using his resources, his fences and contacts, he found my father's book. He gave it to me as I prepared to leave their group and head back to Elkswood.

I had hoped to find Anni, to take her up on her promise to teach me to read and write.

I made it to her father's shop and handed her the book, explaining what it was—what it meant to me. But that's when Fief Lord Cedric's men found me. They dragged me away and threw me into the gaoler's cell.

They locked me up, and I realized too late what had happened. Anni had made a copy of my map. Cedric's men had it now. The Forsworn had once thought I was a spy for Cedric, and now Cedric believed I was a bandit because the Forsworn had used my map to raid. He questioned me brutally, demanding answers I didn't have. But even if I did, I wouldn't betray the Forsworn's trust.

During my time in that dark cell, Oliver and Anni visited me from outside the barred window. I explained everything to Anni, and she believed me. Despite the danger, she kept her promise, teaching me to read and write through the window bars. It passed the time.

That, and the rats that scurried through my cage.

Even without my help, Cedric had plans. He told me of them with a sneer, mocking me, calling my father a deserter and a traitor. It was then he revealed the truth—that my father and I had ruined his schemes three years ago when we saved the prince's heirs. Sanne and Niklas were never supposed to survive. Cedric wanted them dead so the war could go on. That was why Captain Varek was there. That was why my father died.

Cedric left me humiliated, beaten down, and told me of my fate—a grim end to match his hatred.

I was furious, desperate. I couldn't let him win. I did something I hadn't thought possible—I used my abilities to communicate with the rats. They were my allies in that moment, helping me slip free of my cell and escape.

I ran, faster than I'd ever run before, even though two seasons in that prison had left me weak and stiff. My legs burned, my lungs screamed, but I didn't stop. I reached Jory first, warning him of Cedric's trap, and then pushed on to Commander Crosse.

But it was too late. Crosse had already taken the bait—Princess Sanne, the heir to the throne and now the spark of another war.

And so, the cycle begins again.

Chapter 1 - Awake

The world jostled, sharp and uneven, rattling through my body like loose pebbles in a tin pot. My head swayed forward, then back, like a puppet on strings. Something pressed against my cheek—rough, scratchy, and warm. I tried to pull away, but the rhythm kept nudging me, relentless.

A hard bump sent me lurching fully awake, my head snapped back. Pain shot through my skull as it connected with something both solid and fleshy. A grunt and a string of curses followed, the voice rough and too familiar, but I wasn't ready to place it yet.

My neck craned as I blinked into a sky so blue it might've been painted. White clouds drifted lazily, their edges blurred like they'd been smudged by a careless hand. High above, a dark shape cut through the light, a bird gliding with effortless grace. It wheeled once, its wings spread wide, silhouetted against the sun's sharp glare. The air trembled with a high-pitched caw, the sound slicing through the quiet like a razor.

And then, like someone had popped a soap bubble, the world crashed back in. Hooves thudded against packed earth, a steady rhythm that jarred my teeth. The leather saddle beneath me creaked with each stride. Somewhere nearby, trees whispered secrets to the wind. My shoulders ached, muscles stiff from some indignity I couldn't yet recall.

"Spirits below Tomi, you've got a head like a stone," the voice muttered again, low and dripping with irritation. Wulfric. I'd have known that gravel-and-iron tone anywhere.

But that voice—close enough to feel the heat of his breath—wasn't what made my pulse pick up. It was the way he said my name once, a single syllable, like a curse he couldn't swallow.

Wulfric's arms caged me in, broad and corded with muscle, hands gripping the reins. His knuckles were scarred and dusted with road dirt, fingers twitching slightly as the horse shifted under us. I craned my neck, squinting down. The saddle leather creaked, warm and worn, its smell mingling with sweat and damp wool. My own legs dangled, feeling useless and too light, like they didn't belong to me.

"Where are we?" My voice cracked, dry as autumn leaves.
"Riding south," Wulfric said, his tone gruff but not unkind. "You've been out the better part of a day, boy. Must've run yourself dry. Surprised you didn't keel over sooner."

The words pricked at me, sharp and familiar, but I pushed past them. My chest tightened, and panic climbed my throat like ivy. "We need to go. Now. It's an ambush!" My hand jerked toward the reins, but his arm didn't budge.

"Alright, lad. Steady." His tone softened, the roughness gentling like a whetstone on steel. "You're with friends. You're safe. We got your warning. You did good. Just breathe, yeah?"

I swallowed the knot rising in my chest, the air harsh in my lungs. Looking ahead, I caught sight of Commander Crosse, seated tall on his horse like a statue carved from iron. His fur cloak hung heavy on his shoulders, and his head turned slightly as if sensing my gaze. A few more riders flanked him, their mismatched armor catching the weak sunlight, gleaming dully where it wasn't rusted or dented.

Behind them, the rest of the Forsworn moved on foot, their ragged line snaking down the trail. Faces smudged with dirt, weapons strapped to backs and belts. Fifty, give or take. They moved like tired men, silent except for the rhythmic crunch of boots and hooves. My breath evened, but something still pressed at me. My chest felt too small, my pulse too loud.

Closing my eyes, I reached out. The world around me sharpened into clarity. The Forsworn buzzed with muted emotion—fear, determination, fatigue. Sanne's presence stood out, jagged and vivid, even as her face betrayed nothing. Her unease pulsed against me like a heartbeat, steady and cold.

I stretched further, beyond the line of men and horses, into the woods on either side. Animals moved in the underbrush, their focus flickering toward us, quick and curious. The scent of damp earth and pine clung to the edges of my senses, grounding me. But further still—past the trees, through the hills—there was something else. Heavy, deliberate. Men. Hundreds of them, their emotions a distant roar, one force split in two. The shape of them clawed into my mind, closing like a set of jaws around prey.

"They're coming," I said, my voice barely above a whisper. My hand gripped Wulfric's arm as if it might keep the jaws at bay. "North and south. Both sides."

The weight of Wulfric's chest shifted against my back as he rumbled low, a sound like stones grinding under a heavy wheel. His breath stirred my hair. "Aye, lad. We know. Sent out scouts. Found the northern army. That's why we're heading south, deeper into the forest. Long way 'round."

"No, you don't understand!" My voice cracked, my throat dry and raw. The reins under his calloused grip creaked as the horse shifted beneath us. "They're south too! They're trying to trap us!"

Wulfric stilled behind me, his chest a solid wall of muscle, rising and falling in measured rhythm. "You sure about that?" he asked, his tone sharpened by suspicion but softened by something else, something that made my stomach lighten, trust. He knew my answer before I spoke.

"Yes. They're coming. I warned Jory, warned the others, but they're not waiting at the hideout. They're coming for us—now!" My words tumbled out too fast, my heart hammering hard enough that I was sure he could feel it through my back. His hands tightened briefly on the reins, then one moved to the pommel of his saddle, the leather groaned under his grip.

"Hold on, boy." His voice turned gruff as he kicked the horse into motion, the sudden jolt sending me lurching forward. The beast surged ahead, the creak of its tack and the dull thud of hooves swallowing any reply I might have made.

We closed in on the head of the column, where Commander Crosse rode with the kind of authority that could quiet a room without a word. His fur cloak swayed with the horse's gait, catching the faint sunlight filtering through the canopy. His broad shoulders loomed, his groomed beard shadowing his weathered face, but his eyes were alert, constantly sweeping the path ahead and the men behind.

Beside him rode Sanne, her braid catching the light like a golden thread. She sat with a rigid grace, her hands resting lightly on the pommel of her saddle. Two guards flanked her—one with a spear across his lap, the other with a sword, both watching the forest with hawkish intensity. Her mouth was pressed into a hard line, her expression unreadable, but the tension was unmistakable.

Wulfric drew alongside Crosse, his horse snorting as it slowed. "Commander," Wulfric called, his voice rough as bark, "we've got a problem."

Crosse turned his head slightly, his sharp eyes narrowing as they flicked to Wulfric, then to me. "What sort of problem?"

Wulfric's grip on the reins tightened, his shoulders stiff against my back. "Tell him," he said, his voice low and gruff.

The words stuck in my throat for a beat, the weight of Crosse's stare pinning me down. I forced them out. "It's a trap," I said, each word rough against my dry throat. "There's a brigade to the north—the one your scouts saw—but there's another one to the south. They're trying to pin us between them."

Crosse's sharp gaze didn't waver. The lines of his face seemed carved deeper, the weight of decisions pressing heavy on his broad shoulders. "You're sure?"

I nodded, swallowing hard. "I warned Jory and the others. The fort isn't safe. They're coming for us. Now."

Crosse's lips pressed into a tight line, his eyes narrowing as he glanced toward Wulfric, who gave a small nod. Before he could say anything more, a voice cut through the tension.

"Tomi?"

I turned as the sound of my own name threw me off balance. Sanne sat straighter in her saddle, her pale braid catching the sunlight, her expression both surprised and cautious. She looked different—older, more composed than I remembered. The regal way she held herself made her seem untouchable, yet her voice carried a thread of familiarity that pulled me back to the past.

I fumbled for a response, bowing awkwardly from the saddle. "Sanne," I managed, feeling the weight of her gaze on me.

Crosse's head tilted as his sharp eyes darted between us. "You two know each other?" he asked, his tone pointed.

I opened my mouth, but he raised a hand, cutting me off. "Never mind. I'll get the story later," he said brusquely. "Right now, we've got more pressing concerns." He turned in the saddle, barking orders. "Send runners. One north, one south. Confirm the boy's story."

Two riders broke off from the column, their mounts kicking up clods of dirt as they rode hard in opposite directions.

"Wulfric," Crosse called, his voice steady and commanding. "We're moving west."

Wulfric grunted, his jaw tightening. "West? You're sure about that? Lad could be wrong."

Crosse's eyes flicked to me, then back to Wulfric. "I trust him," he said firmly. "He hasn't led us wrong yet. If they plan to squeeze us, we'll move out of the vice."

Wulfric hesitated, then nodded sharply. "West it is." He turned, shouting commands to the line, his voice booming over the rustle of horses and creak of armor.

Both men raised their voices, shouting orders down the line. The tired shuffle of the Forsworn shifted into hurried movement. Men adjusted their packs, weapons clanking as they turned westward. Sanne and her guards moved off ahead, the princess's braid swayed with the motion of her horse.

The thud of hooves and boots filled the air as we began to move again. The forest pressed close around us, the sunlight dimmed beneath its canopy. The steady sway of the horse beneath me lulled my mind into a dull rhythm, Wulfric's arms solid at my sides. But the dry air scratched at my throat, and before long, a cough started low, a rasp deep in my chest. It clawed upward until I couldn't hold it back anymore. I doubled forward slightly, hacking into the crook of my arm.

"Here." Wulfric's rough voice came from behind me. His arm brushed my shoulder as he offered a water skin over my head. "Take it. Brave thing you did, coming to us like that. I bet there's a story in it too. I'll have that once we slip Cedric's grip."

I took the skin with shaking hands and tilted it back, the cool water sliding down my throat in desperate gulps. Relief came slow, but it came, washing away the raw sting that had settled there. My stomach churned, a reminder of how far I'd pushed myself. I'd run nearly all night and into the morning, my legs burning, lungs screaming, just to give them my warning. I didn't know how long I'd been out after that, but the rest was sorely needed.

"Thanks," I said, handing it back. My voice was clearer now. "I'll be glad to share it—once we're safe."

Wulfric took the water skin, tying it back to his saddle. His silence felt heavy, not from judgment, but from the weight of knowing too much. The horse shifted beneath us, and my stomach churned as it jolted me side to side. I clutched the saddle horn, trying not to lose what little composure I had left.

"Can I get down?" I asked, my voice hesitant.
Wulfric's laugh rumbled low and deep, shaking against my back. "You sure you're up to it, lad? You ran yourself ragged."
"I'd rather walk on my own feet," I said, my stomach flipping again.
He leaned back, and I felt his head dip in a nod. "Never ridden one, have you?"
I shook my head, feeling the motion sway my balance even more.
"They're magnificent beasts." He patted the horse's neck, the creature flicking its ears in response. "This one's called Halder. We took him in a raid a few seasons back. Stubborn as a mule at first, but he's got heart."

Wulfric swung his leg over the saddle and hit the ground with a thud, dust rising around his boots. He straightened, his broad, scarred hand gripping my arm as he steadied me and helped me down. I caught a proper look at him for the first time since waking.

His head was shaved close to the scalp, the smooth skin

catching faint glimmers of sunlight. A deep scar ran down the side of his neck, jagged and pale against his weathered skin. His eyes, sharp and steady, caught mine for a moment before he gave me a grin, full of teeth and wit.

"There. No more seasick on land, eh?" he said.

I managed a weak chuckle, though my legs felt wobbly beneath me. Halder snorted, his large, dark eyes watching as I moved closer. I reached out, resting my hand on the warm curve of his neck. The horse twitched his ears, then leaned into the touch.

"He's glad to be rid of the extra weight," Wulfric said with a smirk, his voice lighter now.

I stroked the coarse hair, the tension in the animal's muscles easing under my palm. His relief hummed against my hand, as though he were thanking me for sparing him the effort. The sensation settled something in me, too.

The thought of talking to Sanne tugged at me like a loose thread. She rode ahead, her braid swinging lightly with each step of her horse. Her shoulders were stiff, her guards flanking her on either side like iron gates. I wanted to ask her about Niklas, about what had happened after they got away from Varek in the mountains, how they'd been caught by Captain Steen and what had happened after. But the weight of the moment, the guarded way she carried herself, told me it wasn't the time.

The scouts returned not long after, their horses kicking up clumps of earth as they pushed through the line. Both men dismounted quickly, their faces grim and lined with sweat. They approached Commander Crosse, voices low but urgent.

"They're not far behind," one of them said, his words clipped from exhaustion. "Hundred men in each brigade, at least."

Crosse's expression darkened, his brow furrowing. He stood silent for a long moment, his jaw tightening as he processed the news. The forest seemed to press in around us, the weight of the trees adding to the tension.

"What'll we do?" Wulfric's voice broke the silence, his tone rough but steady.

Crosse glanced at him, his eyes narrowing. "We can't fight. We've spent too much on this raid already." He gestured toward the men behind him, their ragged armor and tired faces. "We're not equipped for a stand."

He turned to the line of riders, raising his voice. "Bring the princess here."

Sanne was guided forward, her horse stepping carefully over the uneven ground. Her gaze met Crosse's as she drew near, calm but unyielding. It wasn't the first time they'd had this conversation; his tone carried the weight of repetition.

"What were Prince Erik's men doing with you?" Crosse asked, his voice sharp but even.

Sanne folded her arms, her voice calm but lined with iron. "I've told you. I was to be given to Harlan. My brother Niklas was to stay with Erik. Each prince would keep one of us as an heir."

Wulfric snorted, shaking his head. "Until one of those stallions manages to stud a foal of their own." His crude tone carried a grim humor.

The princess turned her gaze on him, steady and cold. "Yes," she said, her voice cutting through the air like a blade. "Until we were no longer needed."

The silence that followed was heavy, the weight of her words hanging in the space between them. Wulfric shifted but said nothing more.

Crosse's gaze lingered on her for a long moment before he

asked, "Where was this meeting to take place?"

Sanne met his eyes, her tone unwavering. "Near the Halv river. Just outside Halvfort."

Crosse's face hardened as he considered, the weight of the decision dragging the air down around him. Finally, he straightened, his shoulders squaring as if bracing for impact. "We have no choice," he said, the words cutting through the murmur of the men. His eyes locked on Sanne. "We'll hand you over to Harlan."

The words hung in the air, heavy and sharp as the snap of a bowstring.

"You can't do that!" I blurted, my voice cracking. A cold weight settled in my chest as I stared at Crosse, disbelief clawing at my insides. "You just rescued her."

Crosse turned his sharp gaze to me, his jaw tight. "Rescued?" His tone cut like a knife. "We weren't rescuing anyone, boy. This wasn't some grand act of valor. It was a raid. We were after a resource—a bargaining chip."

I opened my mouth to argue, but the words faltered. My eyes darted to Sanne. "But… she's free now."

I waited for something—a spark of defiance, a sign that she agreed with me. But her face remained calm, a mask of unshakable resolve. When she finally spoke, her voice was even, almost detached. "He's right, Tomi. If we want to avoid a war, I need to be handed over to Harlan. That was always the plan."

The weight of her words sank in like a stone in deep water. "But you won't be free," I said, my voice quieter now, the fight draining out of me.

Sanne's gaze locked onto mine, her eyes as cool and distant as the Halv river. "I am a princess, Tomi," she said softly. "I'll never be free."

Her words lingered, echoing in the pit of my stomach. Wulfric let out a low growl behind me, his scarred neck twisting as he shook his head. "Spirits take him," he muttered. "Cedric's a real bastard if he planned all this. What's his game, Commander?"

Crosse's expression darkened, his shoulders stiffening. "Same as always. Rising through the ranks, solidifying his power. He's been clawing his way up since the Three Prince War."

Wulfric spat onto the dirt, his lips curling into a snarl. "Bloody worm."

Crosse didn't acknowledge the curse. He squared his shoulders, his voice rising above the murmur of the men. "So be it. We make for the river Halv."

The sound of horns shattered the brief silence, distant but unmistakable. A low, mournful cry that carried a weight of urgency. The brigades weren't far behind.

"With haste," Crosse barked. "Let's go!"

The column lurched into motion, boots pounding against the forest floor, horses snorting and tugging at their reins. The sound of the distant horns grew louder, each mournful wail a reminder of the forces closing in behind us. My legs burned as I hurried alongside Halder, the horse's breath hot and sharp against the cool air. The forest seemed to tighten around us, the shadows deeper, the undergrowth thicker, every branch clawing as if trying to slow us down. The weight of Crosse's decision clung to the air, heavy and suffocating, as if even the trees understood the stakes. The pursuit was no longer distant—it was a thunder at our backs, relentless and unyielding.

Chapter 2 - Tracks

The next two days chewed through me like dull teeth. Commander Crosse drove the Forsworn hard, pushing the column south toward the Halv River. Every muscle in my body protested as I walked alongside them, sweat stung my eyes, my legs trembling with exhaustion. I wasn't one of them—not really. I was just there, caught in their current like a broken branch dragged downstream.

It felt strange to be surrounded by people again. For so long, it had been just me, my pack, my bow, and the quiet rhythm of survival. Now, I had none of those things. My pack, stripped from me back in Elkswood. My bow, gone. All the tools that had been my lifeline since my father's death were out of reach, leaving me to depend on others. It didn't sit right. I missed the weight of the bowstring in my fingers, the solid heft of my pack slung over my shoulder. I missed the certainty of self-reliance.

Wulfric had handed me a dagger and an axe the morning after we'd set out. "Better than nothing," he'd grunted. "I'll find you a bow. Give me time." So far, he hadn't made good on that promise. I felt the emptiness at my back like a phantom limb.

The days were hard on everyone, but especially on my weakened body. Months in a cell had sapped the strength I'd once carried in my legs and lungs. The days blurred into a constant struggle to keep pace, every step reminding me of how far I'd fallen. Wulfric had offered to let me ride Halder more than once, but I'd refused, even though my stomach turned at every jostling step.

"Halder's a good beast," Wulfric had said, his bald head gleaming under the sun as he walked alongside the horse. The long scar running down the side of his neck twitched with the movement of his jaw. "Strong and steady. Won't throw you like some skittish mare."

I shook my head, resting a hand on Halder's warm flank. "I need my strength back," I said, my voice rough from exertion. "I can't afford to lose what little I've got."

Wulfric had laughed at that, a low rumble that seemed to shake his massive shoulders. "Stubborn as a mule, aren't you? Suit yourself, lad." He patted Halder's neck before falling back into the line, his deep voice rising to bark orders at one of the younger men.

Despite my aching legs and the pull of exhaustion in my chest, I kept going. It wasn't just pride that drove me forward—it was the need to feel capable again. To stand on my own feet, even as they dragged against the unrelenting earth.

Nights came like a heavy curtain, pulling down over the forest and swallowing the light. The air turned sharp and cold, the dampness creeping through every layer of clothing. We collapsed in clusters, no fires allowed under Commander Crosse's strict orders. The risk was too great. Cedric's men were less than half a day behind us, their pursuit relentless. A stray flame could be the spark that ended us.

I lay on the ground, the packed dirt unforgiving beneath me. Every muscle ached, my body worn thin from the march. The sounds of the forest shifted with the night—branches groaned under their own weight, leaves rustled in the faint wind, and somewhere far off, an owl called into the darkness. The warmth of Halder's breath on my neck was a small comfort, the horse dozing quietly a few paces away.

The days blurred into one another. I rode with Wulfric just behind Commander Crosse, the rhythmic thud of Halder's hooves lulling me into a kind of half-awareness. Conversation was rare; none of us had the energy to spare. Even Wulfric, usually quick with a jab or a wry comment, stayed focused, his gaze fixed on the road ahead. The tension in the air was like a rope pulled too tight, ready to snap.

It wasn't until the third day that something broke the monotony. Crosse's voice cut through the hum of hoofbeats and labored breaths. "Tomi."

I blinked, startled to hear my name. Ahead, Crosse had turned in his saddle, his sharp eyes catching mine. There was a seriousness in his gaze, something that made my chest tighten. Wulfric slowed Halder, his broad hand steady on the reins as we drew closer.

"Commander wants a word," Wulfric muttered, his voice low.

Commander Crosse dismounted, his boots crunching against the loose gravel on the forest floor. He tugged at his gloves, his movements slow and deliberate as he turned toward me. His gaze bore into mine, it was the kind that made your insides squirm even if you hadn't done anything wrong.

"We're still days out from where Prince Erik's men are supposed to meet Harlan's at the Halv River," he said, his voice low and measured, like he was calculating every word. "Cedric's forces are closing in. Closer each day. I need your advice, Tomi."

My mouth went dry. "My advice?"

"You're a huntsman, aren't you? A tracker?"

I hesitated, then nodded, though the term felt too complimentary for what I was. "I tracked animals," I said. "Not people."

Crosse tilted his head, his eyes narrowing slightly. "But your father did."

I nodded again, this time slower. My chest tightened, the

mention of my father always hitting like a rock to the ribs.

Crosse didn't press further. He waited, the heaviness of his silence urging me to speak. I thought about the question, turning it over in my mind. Hunting was hunting, wasn't it? Tracks, trails, the way things moved through the woods—it couldn't be that different.

"Because there's so many of us," I started, my voice hesitant, "fifty or so with twelve horses, it'll be tough to hide. We could use the horses to double back, lead a separate trail away, but any scout worth their salt will figure out there's no men on foot with them. It might buy us time, but not much."

A woman standing nearby shifted, her voice cutting in. "Won't that tire the horses?"

Before I could respond, Wulfric spoke up, his voice rough but certain. "The horses are restless, keeping this pace with the men. They'll take to the run. Be better for 'em, actually."

Crosse nodded, his expression thoughtful. He didn't look at her or Wulfric, his focus still on me. "Anything else?"

I glanced down at the dirt under my boots, at the faint traces of the path we'd been carving through the woods. "If we can get to the river, we can lose our trail. Water doesn't hold scent or footprints, not like soil does."

Crosse smirked, just a little, like I'd confirmed something he already knew. "Working on it," he muttered, then straightened. His voice came sharper, cutting through the quiet. "Go with Wulfric. Help him hide our tracks."

Relief mingled with nerves as I nodded. The thought of doing something—anything—felt like a breath of fresh air. "I'll do my best."

Wulfric clapped a heavy hand on my shoulder, the weight of it grounding. "Good lad. Let's see if your 'best' can keep Cedric's hounds off our heels a while longer."

I followed him, already trying to piece together the best ways to mask fifty people moving through a forest when in truth I'd only ever done it for two.

Halder shifted under me, muscles coiled tight as Wulfric urged him forward with a sharp nudge of his heel. The wind rushed past, tugging at my hair and clothes, and for the first time in what felt like forever, I let myself smile. Halder's power rippled through me, each hoofbeat sending a surge of energy up through the saddle. His breathing was deep and steady, his body warm under my legs.

Wulfric glanced over, his bald head glinting in the slivers of sunlight filtering through the forest canopy. The scar running down his neck twisted slightly as he grinned. "Feels good, eh, lad? Better than trudging through muck on foot."

I nodded, gripping the reins tighter. "I didn't think it'd feel this… alive."

"Alive's a good word for it," he said, patting his own mount's neck. "Halder's a damn fine beast. You've got yourself a good one."

Halder snorted as if agreeing, and I reached down to run my hand along his neck. I could feel his pulse, strong and steady, under the damp coat of sweat. "He likes this," I said, half to myself.

"Of course he does." Wulfric's laugh rumbled low. "Better than crawling along at a man's pace. Let him stretch his legs a bit, and you'll see what he's made of."

We surged forward, the horses tearing through the trees with a rhythm that felt almost wild. I leaned into it, gripping Halder's mane lightly with one hand, letting him guide me as much as I guided him. Though Wulfric, who sat behind me, guided us both. It was freedom, a fleeting moment of it, and I drank it in.

The ride didn't last. We pulled up near a bend in the path where a scout was waiting, her figure shadowed by the trees. Blae was her name—lean, wiry, with short-cropped hair that stuck out at odd angles and a sharpness in her green eyes that cut deeper than any blade. She raised a hand in greeting, her bow slung low across her back. I ached for that bow.

"Cedric's scouts will pass through here soon," she said, her voice quick but calm. "They're moving faster than I expected."

Wulfric cursed under his breath, his hand tightening on his reins. "We'll make it work. Tomi, what do you think?"

My mind stuttered, then raced. "We… we need to lead them somewhere believable. Somewhere it looks like we'd camp or regroup. Somewhere with tracks leading in every direction, like we're trying to throw them off."

Blae raised a brow. "We are. Still, that's a lot of tracks."

I swallowed hard. "We can't make it perfect, but it just has to look convincing enough. They're looking for us, not perfection."

Wulfric grinned at Blae. "He's got a point. You heard the boy. Let's make it messy."

We worked fast, circling the horses back to lay heavy prints into the dirt. I directed the others to trample the underbrush in places, break branches in others. Sweat trickled down my back as I stepped off Halder to scuff up the ground with my boots, leaving prints where a scout might think a man had knelt. My mind raced as I pieced it together, like a puzzle I'd never seen before.

"Over there," I called to Wulfric, pointing at a patch of soft soil. "Make it look like we stopped. Have the horses leave deeper prints."

"Got it," Wulfric said, his tone sharp as he swung Halder around.

Blae was already moving, her wiry frame weaving through the trees as she snapped twigs and scattered leaves with practiced ease. "You sure this'll fool them?" she asked.

"Not for long," I admitted, wiping sweat from my brow. "But

long enough, I hope."

We didn't have time to make it perfect. Blae motioned us back just as the faint sound of hoofbeats reached our ears. We hurried up a rise, crouching low behind a patch of thick brush. Halder huffed quietly beside me, his breath warm against my neck as I laid a hand on his shoulder.

Blae crouched by my side, an arrow already nocked in her bow. Wulfric settled on my other side, his broad chest rising and falling in steady rhythm. "Let's see if they take the bait," Wulfric muttered. "Blae, you see them?"

"Coming now," she whispered, her eyes narrowing as she scanned the path below.

The scout emerged, his silhouette sharp against the dappled sunlight breaking through the canopy. Dark leathers clung to his lean frame, the folds of his hood casting shadows over his face. The horse beneath him moved cautiously, its ears twitching at every sound, its steps muffled by the forest floor.

He slowed as he neared the false trail, pulling the reins with a practiced ease. The horse snorted softly, pawing the ground once before stilling. The scout leaned forward, his movements deliberate, studying the earth. A gloved hand brushed over the tracks we'd made, fingers pausing as if deciphering a code left in the soil.

I crouched lower, my breath caught in my throat. My senses stretched toward him, not to hear his thoughts—that wasn't how it worked—but to feel. pathos wasn't precise; it was a net cast wide, pulling in emotions, ripples in the unseen. The scout's feelings ebbed and flowed like the tide. Confusion. Suspicion. A flicker of worry that pulsed like a muted heartbeat.

He didn't trust what he was seeing.

My chest tightened. It wasn't panic I sensed from him—no, this was something sharper, colder. Doubt. Not just in the tracks. In himself. *Was he doing this right? Was this good enough?*

The sensation was unnerving, like standing too close to the edge of a cliff. My palms grew damp against the cool bark of the tree I was leaning on. The scout shifted in his saddle, tugging his hood back slightly, revealing sharp cheekbones and eyes that flickered with intent as they scanned the scene again.

His horse snorted and stomped, but he pulled it back, his gaze lingering on the tracks as if searching for something that didn't fit. My heart pounded harder, matching the rhythm of Halder's breath beside me.

He wasn't buying it.

The scout lingered, his head tilting as he studied the tracks. His hand hovered near the hilt of a short blade strapped to his side. I flicked my eyes to Wulfric and Blae, their faces shadows in the brush beside me. Blae's lips parted, her voice so low it was almost swallowed by the forest.

"He's not buying it."

She'd said what I was already thinking. My throat felt dry, my heart pounding harder than it had any right to. The scout's doubt was like an itch I couldn't scratch, his unease gnawing at my own. We couldn't just sit there. He'd figure it out.

I hissed through clenched teeth, keeping my voice low. "Get the horses. Make noise. In the direction we chose to lead them."

Blae turned her head sharply, her green eyes narrowing. "You're mad," she whispered. "That won't—"

"I'm going," I said, cutting her off as I slipped lower, edging toward the brush.

Wulfric's hand shot out, his fingers brushing my sleeve. "Where do you think you're going, lad?"

"Closer." The word was out before I could second-guess it. The plan wasn't even fully formed in my head, but the weight of the scout's doubt pressed harder. I couldn't ignore it. "I need to get closer."

"Closer?" Wulfric's whisper was sharp, edged with disbelief. "Are you stupid, boy?"

The last thing I heard as I ducked into the undergrowth was his low muttering, gruff and exasperated. "Spirits save us, he's got no bloody sense."

The brush clung to me as I crept forward, each step feeling slower than the last. The scout was just ahead, his dark leathers blending into the shadows beneath the trees. Every movement I made felt amplified—the rustle of leaves, the faint crunch of soil under my boots. In the distance, I could sense Blae and Wulfric moving toward the horses, their presence faint but reassuring.

Then I stepped on a twig.

A sharp snap shattered the quiet. The scout's head jerked up, his hand flying to the hilt of his blade. I froze, muscles coiled tight, my breath caught in my chest. My fingers drifted to the shaft of the axe at my side, the weight of it grounding me.

The scout scanned the forest, his hooded gaze narrowing as he swept the area. My heart pounded against my ribs, but something in me stirred, a desperate idea I didn't have time to question. I reached for the sensation I'd felt before—the connection I'd made with the rats in the cell. It wasn't the same. The distance, the complexity of a man's mind—it all felt harder, heavier. Still, I closed my eyes and pushed.

Images, fragments, feelings. Men moving through the trees. The press of hooves on soft soil. Voices muffled by the wind. I focused everything on sending it toward him, letting it flow out of me like smoke curling through the forest.

The scout stiffened. His hand twitched near his blade, confusion rippling across his face. His emotions hit me in a chaotic rush—anger, suspicion, frustration. He shook his head sharply as if trying to clear it, his expression darkening.

Then, in the distance, the horses neighed.

The scout's head snapped toward the sound. I held my breath, watching his face shift. Confusion melted into something sharper—certainty. His shoulders straightened, his grip relaxed, and for a moment, he stood still, his gaze fixed in the direction of the noise. Then, with a muttered curse, he turned his horse and rode off, heading back the way he came.

I sagged against a tree, my legs trembling. My head throbbed, the effort leaving me feeling wrung out and hollow. I let out a shaky breath, falling back into the brush. Had it worked? I wasn't sure. My pulse thundered in my ears as I sat there, staring at the empty trail.

Some time later, I heard familiar voices approach, Blae's low and steady, Wulfric's gruff and irritated. They found me slumped against the tree, still trying to catch my breath.
"You absolute fool," Wulfric growled, his shadow loomed over me. "What were you thinking? You could've gotten yourself killed."

Blae crouched beside me, her sharp green eyes studying my face. "But it worked," she said simply, her voice carrying a thread of reluctant admiration. "The scout's gone. He bought it."

I met her gaze, still unsure. "You're certain?"

She nodded. "I saw him leave. We pointed him the right way."

Wulfric muttered something under his breath, shaking his head. "Lad, you've got a death wish. Next time, use your head."

I swallowed hard, the exhaustion pulling at me like a weight. "I think I did," I murmured, more to myself than to them.

Relief washed over me as I climbed back onto Halder. My legs ached, my arms felt heavy, but for the first time in days, I felt like I'd actually done something. We turned back toward Commander Crosse and the others, the forest closing in around us as the tension began to lift—if only for a moment.

The sun hung low in the sky, its golden light bleeding through the canopy, casting long shadows across the forest floor. The Forsworn had gathered in clusters, their voices low and movements careful as they settled for the night. Wulfric led Halder and I back to the group, his broad hand resting briefly on my shoulder.

We found Commander Crosse near the center of the camp, his fur cloak marking him with a quiet authority that seemed to ripple out in waves. Wulfric stepped forward, his boots crunching against the dry earth. His voice rumbled low, heavy with both praise and something unspoken. "Scout took the bait. Their lot's headed off in the wrong direction." He glanced at me briefly, his scar catching the dim light, before adding, "The lad did good. Damn good… though I'd like to know exactly *how* he managed it."

Crosse's mouth curved into a faint, approving smile, though his sharp gaze flicked between Wulfric and me, as if measuring the weight of Wulfric's words. "Good," he said, his tone clipped. "You've bought us some time."

His eyes settled on me, piercing and relentless, sharp enough to strip away any pretense. "Join me," he said simply, his voice leaving no room for argument, as he turned toward the sparse camp.

The Forsworn's "camp" was more a scattering of bodies than anything organized. Men lay on their cloaks or patches of dry ground, their weapons close at hand. There were no fires, just the lingering smell of smoke from earlier raids clinging to their clothes.

Crosse gestured to a rough circle where rations were being handed out. Smoked meat, hard bread, and a few bruised apples made their way around. I sat beside Wulfric, the ground cold and unforgiving beneath me, while Blae perched on a fallen log. A few of the other Forsworn leaders joined us, their faces lined with dirt and fatigue.

Crosse didn't waste time. "We make for the Halv river," he said, breaking a piece of bread and speaking between bites. "If we keep pace, we'll reach it in two days."

One of the leaders, a wiry man with a patch over one eye, frowned. "And then what? We make it to the river, but what about our families? The ones we left behind?"

Crosse's gaze didn't waver. "Once the princess is handed over, we'll go back. We'll find them."

A knot tightened in my chest. Hand her over. The words burned in my ears, but I kept my mouth shut, clenching the hard bread in my hands until it crumbled.

Crosse gestured toward me with a slight tilt of his head. "The boy gave them a warning. They've had time. They'll know to move."

I swallowed hard, the guilt settling like a stone in my chest. I hoped Jory had gotten away in time but I wasn't so sure.

The rustling of leaves and the sound of boots on dry twigs

pulled my attention. Sanne emerged from the shadows, flanked by her guards. Her braid swung with each measured step, her chin lifted high despite the weight of her circumstance.

Crosse stood, brushing crumbs from his hands. "Just in time."

He waved the others off with a sharp motion. "Go. Rest while you can."

The leaders dispersed without complaint, their voices fading into the quiet murmur of the camp. Only Crosse, Wulfric, Sanne, and I remained.

Commander Crosse rested his forearms on his knees, his sharp eyes fixed on Sanne. "Apologies for the... accommodations," he said, his voice low, almost gruff. "Not exactly fitting for someone of your station."

Sanne tilted her head, her lips curving into something like a smile but colder, sharper. "I've endured worse," she said, her gaze sliding toward me for the briefest of moments. "Haven't I, Tomi?"

The weight of her stare pressed on me like a stone. I nodded, unsure if it was the right response. "You have."

Crosse raised an eyebrow, leaning back slightly. "Do tell," he said, gesturing for her to continue.

Sanne's voice didn't waver. "At the end of the war, when my father saw there was no winning, he had us smuggled out of Sjoheim. The city was under siege, and we were to cross the mountains, escorted by loyal men."

"I remember hearing rumors of that," Crosse said, stroking his beard. "Never thought they'd be true."

"They were," Sanne said, her voice sharper now. "But we didn't make it far. Cedric's men found us. Hunted us."

Crosse's eyes flicked to me. "That where you come in, lad?"

I hesitated, but Sanne's steady gaze seemed to pull the words from me. "My father was one of the hunters. Recruited by Cedric himself. He didn't want to join, but there wasn't much of a choice.

Two squads went after her and her brother."

"Two squads?" Wulfric interjected, his scarred neck catching the firelight as he leaned forward. "Seems excessive for two kids."

"One of them was led by Captain Varek," I said, the name like ash on my tongue. "His orders weren't to capture. They were to kill."

Crosse straightened, his brow furrowing. "And Cedric sent both after the same prize. Interesting."

"He wanted them dead," I said, my voice steady now. "If my father hadn't stopped Varek, they wouldn't be here."

Wulfric let out a low whistle. "So Cedric wanted the war to keep going." He rubbed a hand over his bald head. "Spirits' breath, why?"

"Opportunity," Crosse said, his voice flat, as if he'd pieced it together already. "A fractured kingdom is easier to climb. With the princes too busy killing each other, Cedric could move into their gaps, gather influence, and build his power base."

"Bastard," Wulfric muttered, his voice low and dark. "Always had a stink about him."

Sanne's jaw tightened, her gaze fixed somewhere past us. "And we were just pieces in his game."

The conversation fell into silence. The crackle of the night around us grew louder, the shadows pressing in. Crosse stared into the darkness, his expression unreadable, but his fingers tapped once against his knee—a signal of thoughts churning behind his steady exterior.

I shifted on my feet, the silence heavy enough to smother the air. I glanced at Sanne, her profile rigid, her gaze pinned to the distance. "I'm glad you got away," I said, the words fumbling out before I could think better of them.

She turned slowly, her eyes sharp as glass. "I'm not sure if I should be thanking you for that," she said, her tone cutting. "Or demanding they put you to the headsman's axe. Not that I could anyway." Her gaze swept over the gathered Forsworn, the corners of her mouth twisting into something bitter.

My chest tightened. "Why?"

Her voice softened, but it didn't lose its edge. "If it wasn't for you and your father, we wouldn't have been found. My father might still be alive."

Crosse leaned forward slightly, his hands clasped between his knees. "That's unlikely," he said, his voice calm but firm. "Prince Erik and Prince Harlan wanted Eldric dead. They collaborated to kill their brother. Even if you hadn't been found, you and your brother may have died in those mountains for nothing."

Sanne's lips thinned, her jaw tightening. "It's easy to say that now."

I wanted to shrink under her gaze, but instead, I forced myself to meet it. "What happened when Captain Steen found you?"

She hesitated, her hands folding tightly in her lap. "He was respectful," she said at last, her voice low. "Stern, but not cruel. He brought us back to Sjoheim, as ordered. By the time we arrived, my father was already defeated. The city was silent, like it had been drained of life. Erik's banners hung from the walls, and my father's body..."

Her voice faltered, and I saw the faintest tremor in her hands before she steadied herself. "They took us to the palace. Niklas and I were locked away in separate wings, guarded day and night. We were kept alive, but only because we were useful pawns. That's what they've called us all these years—pawns."

A knot formed in my stomach. "I'm sorry," I said quietly. "The last few years... they must have been—"

"Tough?" she interrupted, her voice soft but brittle. "They were. But we're still here."

I wanted to tell her about my father, about how he'd fought to save them, but the words felt tangled in my throat. Before I could untangle them, she looked at me again, her expression gentler now.

"I know," she said. "Captain Steen told me. I'm sorry about your father, Tomi. For what it's worth, he was a good man." Her lips twitched, a faint ghost of a smile. "You too, for rescuing us."

The words hit me harder than I expected, and for a moment, all I could do was nod.

Wulfric leaned back, his scar catching the flickering light of the moon. "You do get around a bit, boy, don't you?" he said, his voice rich with amusement. "Every story that comes out of your mouth makes me feel like I've been living under a rock."

Commander Crosse's lips curved into a faint smile. "He's not wrong," he said, glancing at me. "You're making a name for yourself, Tomi. Just like your father did."

I shifted uncomfortably. "Did you know him?"

Crosse shook his head. "Not personally. But I've heard the tales. Reading the first few pages of his book made me realize exactly who he was. He was a scout under Aldwin, wasn't he? A captain. Betrayed by Cedric. That was Cedric's first step in his rise to power. Your father deserted after that, didn't he?"

I nodded, the words heavy in my throat. "He did. To find my mother and me. She was dying."

Sanne, who'd been quiet, looked up. Her voice softened. "Did he find her?" she asked, her gaze steady but tinged with something I couldn't place. "Before she passed?"

"Yes," I said simply. "Just in time."

For a moment, no one spoke. The crackle of branches in the distance and the faint rustle of the wind filled the silence. Then Crosse cleared his throat and shifted the conversation. "And you, boy? Have you read that book of his?"

"Not yet," I admitted. "But I've learned to read and write a little. A friend has it. After this... I'll go back and get it."

Crosse nodded, his expression serious. "We'll see to it. But you'd best be careful, Tomi. Cedric holds grudges like a wolf on a scent. After this, I have no doubt he'll see you as a fugitive."

The words landed heavily, like stones sinking in my stomach. I looked away, my fingers brushing over the dirt. Fugitive. The word clung to me, dragging me down with the weight of all it meant. I thought of Elkswood, of Anni, of Oliver, of the life I'd scraped together before it all unraveled. It wasn't much, but it was all I'd had.

And now, it felt further away than ever.

The crack of a branch snapped the quiet. Blae burst into the clearing, her hair sticking to her damp forehead, her breathing heavy. "They've been spotted," she said, her voice urgent. "A force. Not far."

Wulfric stiffened beside me, his scar catching the low light. "Spirits damn it," he muttered, his hand resting heavily on the hilt of his blade.

Commander Crosse's gaze swung to me, sharp and accusing. "Your plan didn't work."

"It's not them," Blae cut in, her tone clipped. "It's the other force. The one from the north."

Crosse froze for a moment, his face hardening. Then he swore, a low growl that rolled out like thunder. "We're being squeezed," he said, his voice like iron. "Damn Cedric and his ambition."

Wulfric glanced at me, then back at Crosse. "What now?"

"We march," Crosse said, his voice steady but grim. "Through the night. We don't stop."

The men began moving before he'd finished, a ripple of urgency running through the camp. The air thickened with tension as I scrambled to my feet, falling into step beside Wulfric. The scrape of boots on dry earth, the creak of leather straps, and the muted murmurs of men preparing for a long, dark trek filled the space around us.

    The shadows seemed to press closer as we set off, the forest swallowing us whole. Behind me, Blae muttered something under her breath that sounded like a prayer. Ahead, Commander Crosse's figure loomed in the gloom, his shoulders square, his pace relentless.

Chapter 3 - Clash at the River

The night swallowed us whole, the only sound the rhythm of boots crunching against dry leaves and the occasional stumble of someone too tired to lift their feet. Shadows clung to the forest, dense and heavy, broken only by the faintest silver of moonlight slipping through the canopy. It wasn't enough to see, not really. Most moved blind, trusting the figures ahead to keep them on course. I fortunately had my senses to guide me.

A man in front of me tripped, his curse muffled as he collided with the next in line. They both stumbled, barely catching themselves before the entire column faltered. "Keep moving," Wulfric barked from up ahead, his voice low and sharp, a tether pulling us all forward. The man muttered an apology, his voice raw, before staggering back into place.

I tightened my grip on Halder's reins, the horse plodding beside me with steady steps. Every muscle in my body ached, my legs screaming with each movement. The others fared no better. Shoulders hunched, heads dipped, we looked like revenants, dragging ourselves through the trees.

Somewhere in the distance, a branch snapped. I froze, my pulse racing, but it was only one of the scouts. Blae emerged from the shadows, her wiry frame barely more than a silhouette. She leaned toward Commander Crosse, her voice a whisper that didn't carry back to us. Whatever she said made him glance over his shoulder, his gaze sweeping the column.

We pressed on.

By the time the first rays of sunlight pierced through the trees, the air was thick with exhaustion. A man to my left staggered, catching himself on a tree, his face pale and drawn. Another fell, his knees hitting the dirt with a dull thud before someone hauled him back to his feet. By all rights I should have been just as exhausted or more but freedom drove me; as it always has.

"Daylight," Wulfric muttered, pulling Halder's reins to a stop beside me. His scarred neck glistened with sweat, his breath fogging in the cool morning air. "About damn time."

Commander Crosse raised a hand, halting the group. "Switch out on the horses," he called, his voice firm but worn. "Those on foot, take a moment to drink and eat. Scouts—keep moving."

There were murmurs of relief as people slumped against trees or sank to the ground. I stood still, letting the weight of the moment settle over me. My fingers brushed Halder's neck, his coat slick with sweat. His breathing was steady, though I could feel the exhaustion in him too, a faint tremor in his legs.

"You're not taking a turn, lad?" Wulfric asked, his brow raised as he handed his reins to a man too tired to protest.

I shook my head. "I'll keep walking."

He huffed a laugh, clapping me on the shoulder. "Stubborn, aren't you?"

I didn't answer, too focused on Blae as she returned from another scouting run. Her short-cropped hair stuck to her forehead, her green eyes sharp despite the shadows beneath them. She approached Crosse, gesturing with quick, efficient movements. His jaw tightened, his lips pressing into a thin line.

"What is it? Hear what she's saying?" Wulfric asked, his voice quieter.

"North," I said, the word heavy on my tongue. "They're closing in."

The tension in the camp was clear, every breath, every glance weighted with the knowledge that time was slipping away. The rest offered by the horses was brief, fleeting. The moment Crosse's hand signaled, we were moving again, the forest stretching out endlessly ahead.

The sun climbed higher, but it didn't bring relief. It only cast long shadows across our path, the light mocking the weight dragging us down. Every now and then, a scout would return, their words quick and clipped, each report darker than the last.

"They're gaining," Blae said at one point, her voice low but sharp enough to cut through the morning haze. "Half a day behind, maybe less."

Crosse's expression didn't change, but his pace quickened, his fur cloak billowing behind him like a storm cloud. Wulfric muttered a curse under his breath, gripping his blade's hilt like it was the only thing keeping him upright.

I felt it too—the urgency, the fear pressing against my ribs. The army to the north wasn't just growing closer. It was hunting us, relentless as wolves in the dark. And we were running out of time.

We trudged through the endless day, the sun beating down like a cruel overseer. Every step felt heavier, the forest swallowing us whole as if it meant to trap us. No one spoke unless it was necessary, the silence broken only by the shuffle of boots on dirt and the labored breaths of the weary.

When word came back that the pursuing army had stopped to make camp, a ripple of exhausted relief swept through the column. Crosse raised his hand, signaling the Forsworn to halt, and his voice cut through the stillness. "We rest here."

The words were barely out before people collapsed where they stood, dropping onto cloaks or bare patches of earth. The relief in the air was thick, but it wasn't enough to drown out the low groans of aching bodies. Men and women stretched out like broken marionettes, their faces pale and hollow under the fading light.

I couldn't sit. The moment my legs stopped moving, the exhaustion would take me, and I wasn't ready for that. I pushed past the tightness in my chest, the dull ache in my calves, and reached for something useful to do.

Grabbing a skin of water from one of the packhorses, I started moving through the camp. "Here," I said, offering it to a woman lying against a tree. Her hands shook as she took it, her lips dry and cracked. She nodded once, her voice too spent for thanks.

I moved on, finding a boy no older than I was slumped near his father, both of them staring blankly ahead. I handed over a strip of smoked meat, then a hunk of bread from the ration pack slung over my shoulder. The boy's eyes widened for a moment, but he said nothing as he broke the bread in half and passed it to his father.

"Good lad," Wulfric muttered as I passed him, his voice hoarse. He was seated on a fallen log, his broad shoulders slumped but still carrying that quiet, immovable strength. "Keep at it. These folk need more than just their commander shouting at them."

I nodded, the weight of his words sinking in. Moving through the camp, I passed out what I could, a quiet rhythm that kept my legs moving and my thoughts from spiraling. For once, I didn't feel like I was just a shadow trailing behind the Forsworn.

I moved to the next huddle, handing out bread and a half-empty water skin. The forest felt heavier, the air thick with quiet exhaustion. Shadows stretched longer as the last light of day gave way to dusk. I noticed her before I saw her guards—the princess, moving through the camp with her chin high, her braid trailing down her back.

Princess Sanne crouched near a woman lying against a tree, handing her a piece of cloth to pad a blistered foot. Her guards hovered close, their eyes sweeping the camp like wolves circling a den. I blinked at her, unsure if I'd imagined it, but when she stood and dusted off her hands, her gaze caught mine.

"You're helping!?" I blurted before I could think better of it.

Her lips quirked, something between a smile and a smirk. "Is that so strange?"

I hesitated, shifting the rations on my shoulder. "A bit. You're a princess."

She stepped closer, her guards mirroring her movements. "I've been locked in a tower for years, Tomi. Handing out bread is the closest thing to freedom I've had in a long time."

I handed her a strip of meat. "Yeah, well... I was locked in a cell. No tower. Just rats."

Her eyebrow arched. "A cell? What did you do?"

"Cedric," I said simply. "Wrong place, wrong time. He thought I was with the Forsworn. Turns out he wasn't far off." I shrugged, forcing a smile. "And you? Why the tower?"

She took the strip of meat, rolling it between her fingers as her gaze flicked toward the fading sky. "To keep me safe, so they said. I think my uncle Erik just wanted me out of the way."

I nodded, falling into step beside her as we moved through the camp. "So, a princess in a luxury tower and a hunter in a damp cell. Sounds like the start of a bad story."

She laughed softly, a sound that felt out of place among the weary silence. "Luxury, sure. But try being guarded day and night, every letter read, every word watched. My world shrank to those walls."

"And mine was stone," I said, feeling the weight of it all over again. "Cold, wet. My only friends were rats. I even named one."

Her lips twitched. "What did you call it?"

"Muck," I said, grinning despite myself. "Fitting, right?"

"Charming," she said dryly, though her smile lingered. "At least you had company. Mine were maids who barely spoke and guards who wouldn't dare look me in the eye."

"They didn't talk to you?" I asked, surprised.

"Not unless I spoke first. Even then, they answered like they were scared of me." Her voice softened. "I wasn't a person to them, just a symbol."

We stopped near a small group, where she handed bread to a young boy and ruffled his hair. He looked at her with wide eyes, then darted off to share the bread with his sister.

"You're a person now," I said, quieter.

Her gaze shifted to me, her expression unreadable. "And you're free."

"Yeah," I said, though the word felt hollow. "For now."

She looked back at the camp, her guards edging closer as if they sensed the conversation was nearing its end. "You're not what I expected, Tomi of Linden."

I chuckled, shouldering the ration pack again. "And what did you expect?"

"Someone quieter," she said, turning to leave. "Someone... simpler."

Her words lingered as she moved, a soft echo in my mind. I watched her for a moment, the shadows playing across her face, before the thought I'd been holding onto broke free.

"What about your brother?" I asked, handing her another ration to pass along.

Sanne hesitated, her hands pausing mid-motion. "Locked in a

different wing," she said quietly. "They kept us apart. We saw each other once a season if we were lucky."

I frowned, the weight of her words sinking in. "That must've been hard."

"It was," she said, her voice steady but tight. "I worried about him constantly. Still do. Prince Erik…" She trailed off, her gaze turning distant. "I think he's grooming Niklas to be his heir."

"Grooming him how?" I asked, though I wasn't sure I wanted to know.

"Teaching him to think like a prince," she said, her tone sharp. "To see people as tools. It's subtle, but it's there. Niklas is smart, though. I just hope he doesn't lose himself."

I nodded, the words catching in my throat before I forced them out. "And you? Won't Harlan try to do the same to you?"

Her lips twisted into a bitter smile. "Not quite. I'll be married off to one of his loyal men, someone who'll keep me in check. A pretty pawn in his game."

"Or worse," I joked, trying to lighten the mood. "The prince's bride."

Her smile vanished. "Don't joke about that," she said sharply, her tone like a slap.

I raised my hands in apology, my cheeks burning. "Sorry."

We worked in silence for a while, passing out rations and water. The quiet gave me too much time to think. I glanced at her, her expression unreadable as she moved from person to person. Guilt twisted in my stomach, coiling tighter with every glance.

It was our fault. My father's and mine. If we hadn't helped Cedric, if we hadn't tracked them down, Sanne and Niklas might never have been captured. They might've been free.

I caught her escorts a little farther off, talking among themselves, their backs turned. The idea hit me hard and fast. I leaned closer to her, lowering my voice to a whisper. "If you want freedom," I said, "I can help you. We can go now. I know how to slip away."

Her eyes flicked to the guards, then back to me. I could see the wheels turning in her head, her fingers tightening on the water skin she held. "Come on," I urged, my voice barely audible. "We can make it."

She remained silent, her lips pressing into a thin line. I could feel her thinking about it, the pull of the idea tugging at her like a current. For a split second, I was tempted to push her, to nudge her thoughts the way I had with the scout. But then she shook her head.

"No," she said firmly. "I have to keep to my responsibilities."

Her words hit harder than I expected. I started to say something, but she cut me off, her voice softer now. "I know you feel guilty about it."

I froze, her words pulling me up short. "What?"

"I can see it," she said, her gaze steady. "You and your father... you did what you thought you had to. I don't blame you."

The lump in my throat grew tighter. "I'm sorry," I said, the words barely a whisper.

"It's okay," she said, a faint smile flickering across her lips. "Things will work out."

Her words grated against me, leaving something raw behind. "How?" I asked, unable to keep the edge out of my voice. "How does any of this work out if we hand you to Harlan? You'll be locked up again!"

She didn't answer, instead reaching for another skin of water and passing it to an older man slumped against a tree. I swallowed my frustration and bent to help a woman struggling to unwrap a bandage, my hands working as my thoughts spun. Her words clung to me, sharp and barbed, like a splinter lodged too deep to remove.

The camp gradually slowed, the murmur of voices and shuffle

of tired feet giving way to a heavy stillness. Sanne handed off the last of the rations, her fingers lingering on a loaf of bread before she turned back toward her guards. They flanked her as she walked away, their figures tall and silent, their armor catching the last glint of light.

I lingered where I stood, watching her retreating form. Her stride was steady, her back straight, every step measured, as if each one carried the weight of a kingdom. Something in me twisted. She seemed untouchable, unshakable, but I couldn't help but wonder what it would take to break that calm.

The night deepened, and I returned to my bedroll, the cool ground pressing against my back as I lay staring at the stars. Exhaustion pulled at me, but my mind wandered before sleep could claim me.

I dreamed.

My mother's laughter rippled like sunlight on wheat, her hands soft against my face. Then the image blurred, the fields of Linden fading into the smoke and chaos of Riverhalv. My father's strong voice called out orders to a faceless crowd, his silhouette framed by the glow of distant flames.

Lars appeared next, my cousin with his awkward grin, flanked by Bryn, Colm, and Dael. They'd been boys, playing at soldiers with wooden swords, laughing as if war were just a game. Was that what I was doing now? Pretending? I saw myself back then, sparring with Egon and Erland as Freya perched on a rock, smirking at our clumsy moves. Those days felt like they belonged to someone else, a boy I could barely remember.

The crack of a branch jolted me, the dream splintering into darkness. Shouts echoed through the camp, snapping me fully awake. I sat up, heart pounding, reaching for my axe out of instinct.

The camp was chaos. Figures darted through the dim light, scrambling to pack what little they had. The hum of urgency pressed against my chest, a low current pulling everyone into motion.

"Tomi!" Wulfric's voice boomed, cutting through the noise. I turned to see him striding toward me, his bald head catching the faint glow of the moon. "The northern army's moving. They rose early."

"What?" My voice came out hoarse, my mind struggling to catch up. I gripped the axe tightly, its weight grounding me. "Already?"

"Aye." Wulfric's face was grim, his scar twisting as he spoke. "Crosse says we're moving now. Can't let them close the gap."

The sleep had helped, but my legs still felt like lead as I stumbled to my feet. Around me, men and women groaned under the weight of their packs, their faces drawn with exhaustion. Horses stamped and snorted, their handlers tugging at reins to get them in line.

The tension was thick, choking. Weary but unwilling to stop, the Forsworn pressed forward, ready to march again.

The air was thick with urgency as we pushed through the forest, every step biting into the damp earth. The Halv River was close, less than half a day away, but the news Blae brought back from the scouts turned every mile into an eternity.

"They're closing in," she said, her voice low but sharp. "No more than an hour behind us now."

Commander Crosse's face hardened, the lines around his mouth cutting deeper as he glanced at Wulfric. "We're not going to make it to the river."

"Spirits damn them," Wulfric muttered, his hand resting on the pommel of his sword. "We need to stand."

Crosse nodded, his gaze scanning the dense forest. He raised his arm, signaling the group to halt. "We find higher ground."

The Forsworn stumbled to a stop, men and women leaning on each other, their breaths coming in ragged gasps. I swallowed hard, the weight of their fear pressed into my chest. It wasn't just mine anymore—I could feel it bleeding off them, a tide threatening to drag me under.

Crosse and Wulfric moved quickly, their sharp eyes picking out a rise in the forest just ahead. "There," Crosse said, pointing. "We make our stand."

The Forsworn surged forward again, driven by the sharp bark of orders. We climbed the rise, the earth uneven beneath us. At the top, the trees thinned slightly, giving us a view of the winding road below and a glimpse of the Halv River in the distance.

Crosse wasted no time, his voice cutting through the rustling leaves and murmured fear. "Form ranks. Spears at the front. Swords and axes in between. Shields at the ready."

Wulfric moved through the group like a storm, his booming voice pulling the Forsworn into position. "You heard him! Keep it tight. No gaps!"

The clatter of weapons being readied filled the air as men and women scrambled to their places. Their movements were stiff, weary, but the sharp tone of Wulfric's commands kept them steady. I hovered near the edge of the rise, clutching my axe, the weight of it unfamiliar and unwelcome.

Blae appeared again, her face pale, her short-cropped hair clinging to her damp forehead. "They're moving fast," she said, breathless. "They'll crest the other rise in minutes."

Crosse turned to her, his expression unreadable. "Then we'll make sure they don't get past this one."

He moved to me, his eyes sharp and assessing. "Tomi," he said, his voice low but firm. "You stay with the princess."

"What?" The word slipped out before I could stop it.

"If this goes south," he continued, ignoring my outburst, "you're to leave. Take her, Wulfric, and the scouts, and get out of here. Understood?"

I nodded, the motion stiff and jerky. My hands clenched around the axe, the wood biting into my palms. "Understood."

Crosse held my gaze for a moment longer, then turned away, his cloak billowing as he moved to join the others. I looked toward Sanne, standing a short distance away with her guards. Her expression was calm, almost detached, but I could feel the tension radiating from her like heat off a fire.

The Forsworn settled into their positions, the air thick with the rustle of armor and the murmur of quiet prayers. My chest tightened as I felt the anxiety building, a wave of fear that wasn't just my own. It clawed at my throat, stealing my breath.

The minutes stretched, each one heavier than the last. Somewhere beyond the rise, the sound of boots and hooves on packed earth grew louder, the enemy closing the distance. We waited, the forest holding its breath with us.

The sharp snap of a twig broke the heavy silence. Blae crouched near the edge of the rise, her bowstring taut, her eyes locked on the distant road below. Beside her, Wulfric stood with one hand resting on the hilt of his blade, his scar catching the faint light as he frowned toward the forest.

Then we saw them.

Another brigade, their armor glinting in the patches of sunlight that filtered through the trees. They moved with precision, their banners snapping sharply in the breeze. The river shimmered faintly in the distance behind them, marking their destination.

Wulfric's hand tightened on his sword. "Spirits, another force," he muttered, his voice a low growl. "That's Harlan's lot. You think we can make a break for it?"

Commander Crosse didn't look at him. His gaze stayed fixed on the movement below, sharp and unyielding. "No."

"No?" Wulfric shot him a glare, his voice rising just enough to turn heads. "They're right there, Crosse. They could buy us time, a way out."

"And if they see us now?" Crosse's voice was quiet, but it cut through Wulfric's like a blade. "We look like invaders. A vanguard, maybe. Either way, we'll be stuck between two armies, and they won't care who we are."

Wulfric fell silent, his mouth pressing into a hard line.

Crosse didn't waver. "We stand here. Then, we go to Harlan's men."

No one argued. The weight of his words pressed down on us all, solid and immovable. We shifted into position, bracing ourselves for what came next.

The minutes stretched, each one heavier than the last. The second force—the same one that had been pursuing us from the north—moved into view, their boots crunching against the dirt road, banners fluttering sharply as they rounded the bend. As they passed, their backs were already to us, their formation fixed on the river ahead, oblivious to the rise where we waited, weapons poised.

Everyone tensed. Spears lowered. Fingers gripped hilts. Breath caught in throats.

But the men didn't turn.

They kept moving, their formation holding steady as they marched down the road toward the river. The banners disappeared over the rise, and still, no one came. The forest held its breath with us.

The sun climbed higher, burning away the shadows. Still, no horns sounded. No one shouted. The men below continued on their path as though we didn't exist.
Wulfric let out a low, disbelieving breath. "They didn't see us."
I could feel the tension around me easing, but my chest stayed tight. My fingers twitched against the haft of my axe, unwilling to relax.
The forest remained still, save for the faint rustle of leaves and the distant murmur of the brigade moving toward the river.

No one moved. No one dared speak.

We waited for a span, until the sun shifted in the sky as the two forces came within reach of each other.

The clash came suddenly.

The first line of soldiers from the northern force surged forward, a wave of steel and leather colliding with the disciplined ranks of Prince Harlan's men by the river. From the rise, I could barely hear the first impact over the pounding of my pulse.

"What's happening?" I asked, my voice dry in my throat.

Wulfric, standing beside me, narrowed his eyes, the scar along his neck catching the light. "They didn't know we were here," he said, voice low and taut. "They weren't after us."

Blae, crouched with her bow resting on her knee, shot Wulfric a glance. "Then who were they after?"

Commander Crosse's voice cut through the air like a blade. "Them." He pointed, his fur cloak stirring slightly in the wind as his finger directed our attention to the melee unfolding on the road below. Swords clashed, shields splintered, and bodies pressed together in a desperate, brutal rhythm.

I stared, confusion tightening in my chest. "I don't understand—Erik's men? Why would they come after Harlan's force? We were going to give Sanne to him, weren't we?"

"It's not that simple, lad," Wulfric muttered, his tone grim. "But damn it, why the rush? They were going to get the girl."

Commander Crosse didn't take his eyes off the battle. "It's one thing to hand something over willingly. Another thing entirely to take it by force. This isn't about Sanne. This is about control." His jaw tightened. "Erik must have thought Harlan took her, so he sent a brigade to cut him off. A preemptive move. And that bastard Cedric... he beat us to it."

"Cedric?" Blae said, her voice sharp, almost disbelieving.

Crosse's eyes darkened as he let out a low growl. "This was the plan all along. Cedric doesn't need an army—he just needs chaos. If Erik thinks Harlan betrayed him and Harlan thinks Erik is challenging him, the war restarts. He's done it. War's started again."

The words hit like a blow to the gut. I glanced at Sanne, standing nearby with her guards, her expression stony and unreadable, her fists clenched at her sides. The din of battle below carried on, distant and relentless, as if the world itself had turned against us.

Wulfric cursed under his breath, his hand resting heavily on his blade's hilt. "Spirits damn him. What do we do now?"

Commander Crosse's gaze didn't waver. "We don't hand her over, that much is clear. It's too late for that." His voice hardened. "We find another way."

His words hung in the air, heavy and uncertain, as the screams and shouts of war echoed from the road below.

Chapter 4 - The Bridge

The clash of steel and the distant cries of battle filled the air, carried up to us on the wind. I crouched near the edge of the rise, my hands gripping the cool earth beneath me. Below, the battle raged by the Halv River, the wide expanse of the bridge dominating the scene. On one side, Harlan's men stood with their banners held high—a crimson heart pierced by a sword. On the other, Erik's forces pressed forward, their black-and-silver raven banners rippling like storm clouds over a field of steel.

"They're taking a beating," Wulfric muttered beside me, his arms folded as he leaned against a tree. His scarred neck caught the light as he tilted his head, watching Harlan's forces falter under the relentless assault. "Ravens fight like they've got the spirits themselves pushing their blades."

Commander Crosse stood on my other side, his sharp eyes locked on the chaos below. His expression was unreadable, but his fingers tapped against the hilt of his sword. "They're holding the bridge, barely," he said. "But Erik's men are better trained, better armed."

The heart banners wavered as Harlan's front line buckled. Men fell into the water, their screams cut short as the river swallowed them. The sound of Erik's forces shouting above the din reached us even there, a triumphant roar that sent a chill down my spine.

Wulfric shook his head. "They're going to lose it. One good push, and those lads'll be swimming."

Crosse didn't answer immediately. His eyes flicked to the rear of Harlan's forces, where a surge of movement caught my attention. More men, clad in the crimson-and-gold of Harlan's colors, emerged from the tree line. They marched onto the bridge, their arrival bolstering the faltering line. Harlan's banners swayed but didn't fall.

"Reinforcements," Crosse said simply, his tone flat but heavy with meaning. "They're not done yet."

The tide shifted. Harlan's men pushed back, driving Erik's forces toward the far end of the bridge. The raven banners wavered, their confidence faltering under the renewed strength of their opponents. From our vantage point, I could see Erik's forces regrouping, their formation tightening as they began to retreat.

"Smart," Wulfric grunted. "They're pulling back before they lose too many. Erik's lot might be bastards, but they're not fools."

Crosse nodded, though his gaze remained sharp, wary. "They'll regroup. This isn't over."

I swallowed hard, my throat dry. The distant sounds of the battle began to fade as Erik's forces pulled away from the bridge, leaving Harlan's men to stand victorious—for now. The banners of the pierced heart rose higher, crimson streaked with blood as the soldiers below rallied, their cheers echoing faintly up the ridge.

Wulfric let out a low whistle. "Well, that's a turn. Thought for sure the ravens would take it."

Crosse's hand tightened briefly on his sword. "The question isn't who won today," he said. "It's what comes next."

I stared at the field below, the bodies scattered like broken toys across the bridge and the riverbank. The sight of victory didn't feel like relief. It felt like the start of something worse.

The bridge below had grown quiet, the battlefield eerily still save for the distant cries of the wounded. I turned to Crosse, the question burning in my chest. "What do we do now?"

Blae crouched beside a tree, brushing dirt from her hands as she spoke. "Can't go north. We could maybe take what's left of Erik's forces, but it'd be a bloody mess, and he'll have more out there

soon enough. Roaming the countryside, stirring up trouble."
Wulfric snorted, his hand resting on the hilt of his sword. "Riverhalv's going to turn into a battlefield again, mark my words."

The impact of those words struck me like a wave crashing against my chest. My aunt and uncle. Lars. The last time I'd been there, the city was under siege, and the memory was still sharp in my mind. I could see their faces, hear their voices. My cousin Lars, bright-eyed and eager, playing soldier in the yard. The thought of them caught in another war made my stomach twist.

Blae's voice pulled me back. "And south's no better. Cedric's lot might be further behind, but they're still coming."

Crosse nodded, his expression carved from stone. "We can't go back. Not yet." He looked at the bridge, its bloodstained stone stretching toward a fort in the distance. "We'll have to cross."

Wulfric's head whipped toward him. "Not that bridge," he said firmly. "It leads straight to Halvfort, where Harlan's men are waiting. Marching into their camp's a death sentence."

Blae stood, brushing her hands on her trousers. "There's another way. Smaller bridge downriver. Leads to an old burnt-out village."

Crosse's sharp eyes fixed on her. "Is it safe?"

"Should be," she said. "We were chased out of there during the last war. Not many know about it, and the woods nearby are good for hunting and foraging. We could lie low for a while, regroup."

Crosse crossed his arms, considering her words. His silence stretched, the weight of it thickening the air around us. Finally, he nodded. "We move. Quickly. Before Harlan's men spot us."

He turned to Blae. "You'll lead. Take us to this bridge. I want another scout keeping tabs on Cedric's position."

Blae nodded, already moving to organize the others. The brigade stirred into motion, tension humming in every movement. Wulfric shot me a look, his scar pulling tight as he scowled.

"Another long march, lad. You ready?"

I swallowed the knot in my throat and nodded. I didn't know if I was ready, but we didn't have a choice.

The forest pressed close around us, the undergrowth crunching beneath tired boots. The Forsworn moved in near silence, save for the occasional grunt or whispered word. Even the horses seemed subdued, their steps measured as if they, too, felt the weight of exhaustion. I fell into step beside Commander Crosse, his tall frame hunched slightly as he rode his horse.

He glanced down at me, his beard shadowing the curve of his mouth. "You're faring well enough, boy," he said, his voice low and steady. "Better than most who've been through what you have."

I shrugged, adjusting the strap of the axe on my belt. "Getting my strength back," I said. "Cell didn't do me any favors, but... it could've been worse."

Crosse's mouth tightened, a flicker of something like regret crossing his face. "What Cedric did to you, locking you up like that... you weren't even one of us. It wasn't right."

"It doesn't matter," I said quickly. "In a way, I am. My father was a deserter. That's close enough, isn't it?"

Crosse tilted his head, his sharp eyes narrowing. "I don't blame him. I deserted too, once. Only I wasn't as lucky as your father. Went to find my family. By the time I reached them..." His voice dropped, the words left unspoken but heavy in the air. "They were already gone."

The weight of his words hit hard, and I looked away, my gaze fixed on the ground ahead. "I'm sorry. I know how that feels."

Crosse nodded, his hand briefly brushing the hilt of the sword at his side. "Too many villages burnt in a war no one wanted. Too many families left with nothing but the spirits of the dead to guide us."

His voice grew quieter, more measured. "We need a leader who can stop this. Who can avoid wars like these altogether." He paused, his eyes scanning the forest ahead. "We might just have to side with Harlan."

The thought made my stomach twist. "Is he any better than Erik?"

Crosse didn't answer right away. Instead, his gaze drifted ahead, his face carved from stone. Finally, he said, "Have you kept up with your drills?"

I laughed softly, a bitter sound. "Only to keep from going mad in the gaol. I'm better with a bow."

He raised an eyebrow. "Think you could kill with a bow?"

"I... I have," I admitted, the memory of that terrible moment tightening my chest. "Not on purpose."

His gaze was heavy, unflinching. "Killing's a hard thing, lad. Facing a man, aiming to take his life—it changes you. You may need to find out what you're made of before this is over."

I swallowed hard, the weight of his words settling over me. "I hope I don't have to."

Blae's voice cut through the quiet, sharp and clear. "Bridge just up ahead."

Crosse straightened in the saddle, his hand resting on the hilt of his sword. "Good. Let's keep moving."

The tension in the air didn't lift as we marched forward. If anything, it thickened, settling over us like the shadow of the war that seemed closer with every step.

Soon, the river opened up before us, carving a wide gorge through the landscape, its rushing waters far below an ominous murmur against the forest's quiet. The air was thick with damp and the faint tang of moss. Up ahead, Blae stopped and pointed. The bridge loomed, a spindly structure of rope and weathered planks swaying faintly in the breeze. It looked like it might snap under the weight of a bird, let alone a horse.

Commander Crosse rode closer, his sharp eyes narrowing as he studied the bridge. "Form a line," he called, his voice carrying over the murmurs of the group. "Horses first. They'll give us the most trouble if this thing gives."

Men muttered their agreement, though their faces were drawn tight with doubt. Wulfric strode forward, his broad shoulders squared. "You heard him. Let's move, one at a time. Keep 'em steady."

The first horse balked at the edge, its nostrils flaring, hooves stamping the dirt. Its handler murmured low, pulling the reins taut, inching it forward. The planks groaned under the weight, and everyone held their breath as the animal took its first hesitant step.

Halder stood beside me, his ears flicked nervously. I laid a hand on his neck, feeling the taut muscles quiver beneath my palm. "Easy," I murmured. "You'll be fine."

The line moved slowly, each horse crossing with painstaking care, their handlers clinging to the ropes as the bridge swayed. The Forsworn waited in tense silence, eyes darting to the forest edges as if expecting shadows to emerge.

A prickle ran down my spine, a low hum in the back of my skull. I froze, my senses reaching outward, brushing against the vast expanse of life surrounding us. Then I felt it—something sharp, something wrong, cutting through the forest like a knife. Hoofbeats. Close, rapid.

"Someone's coming," I said, my voice tight. My gaze snapped to Crosse, who turned to me, frowning.

"Who?" he asked, his tone clipped.

"I don't know," I said, straining to focus. "But they're riding hard."

Wulfric clapped a heavy hand on my shoulder, his bald head catching the faint light. "Good ears, lad," he muttered, unsheathing his blade.

The hoofbeats grew louder, the pounding rhythm echoing off the trees. Then he emerged—a lone rider, bent low over his horse's neck. His cloak flapped behind him, the fabric dark with blood, and an arrow jutted from his shoulder like a cruel thorn. The horse stumbled as it reached us, the rider barely clinging to the saddle.

He raised his head, his face pale and drawn, lips trembling as he gasped out the words. "They're here."

His body slumped, slipping sideways from the saddle, and hit the ground with a thud. Dust rose around him, the silence broken only by the frantic snorting of his horse.

Commander Crosse's voice cut through the thick tension, sharp and unyielding. "Blae! Get him up. Now."

Blae darted forward, her wiry frame moving with purpose as she knelt beside the fallen scout. Blood darkened his tunic, pooling beneath him as she grabbed his arm and hauled him upright. His head lolled, but his eyes fluttered open just enough to take in her face.

"Bran, get that horse across the bridge!" Crosse barked, pointing toward the riderless beast, its flanks heaving. Bran, a broad-shouldered man with a streak of gray in his beard, lunged forward, grabbing the reins. The horse tossed its head, resisting, but Bran held firm, his voice low and steady as he coaxed the panicked animal toward the bridge.

The air felt tight, like the world itself was holding its breath. I could feel them now—Cedric's men—pressing in like a stormfront, the pressure building, suffocating. My skin prickled as my senses stretched outward, brushing against their anger, their resolve, their bloodlust. It felt like drowning in an ocean of noise.

The horses on the bridge struggled too, their ears pinned back, hooves skittering on the planks. They could feel it—the menace approaching from the shadows, growing closer with every heartbeat.

Wulfric's voice rumbled through the chaos. "Form ranks!" His broad frame moved among the Forsworn, shoving men into place, his scarred neck flushed with exertion. "Spears up front, axes behind! Keep the damn line tight!"

I stood frozen by the bridge, my hand brushed against the haft of my axe. Sanne was beside me, her face pale but her chin lifted, her gaze fixed on the trees. The guards flanking her whispered to each other, their hands gripping their weapons so tightly their knuckles turned white.

"Tomi!" Crosse's voice snapped me back to the present. He was at my side, his sharp gaze locking onto mine. "Your job is the same. Once the horses are across, you protect her. Stick with her guards." He nodded toward Sanne, his voice steady despite the tension in his frame. "Get her over the bridge. The others will follow."

I nodded, my throat dry. The weight of his command pressed on my shoulders, heavier than any weapon I'd ever carried.

The forest shifted, and then they appeared—men pouring out from between the trees, tabards of green with a red dragon stark against the backdrop of leaves and bark. Cedric's men. Their swords gleamed in the dim light, their shields braced as they charged.

The Forsworn braced too, a rough, ragged line of spears and blades. The clash was inevitable, but for a moment, everything seemed to pause—the world balancing on the edge of violence. Then the first shout rang out, and the line surged forward.

The forest exploded into chaos as Cedric's men surged from the tree line. They moved as one, tabards with the red dragon on a green field catching the faint light as their boots pounded the ground. A guttural war cry cut through the air, making my grip tighten on the haft of the axe until my knuckles ached.

Crosse stood at the front of the Forsworn line, his fur cloak whipping behind him, heavy with sweat and grime. His sword moved with brutal efficiency, each strike landing with the wet crunch of metal biting flesh. Blood spattered his face and arms, and he didn't flinch, his focus locked on the chaos ahead. His shouts were raw, not just commands but a challenge to every man charging at him.

A soldier lunged, blade aimed at Crosse's chest. He twisted his body, the attack glancing off his shoulder guard with a grating screech. Crosse responded instantly, his sword driving into the man's stomach with a sickening squelch. He didn't wait to see him fall. With a guttural snarl, he yanked his blade free, turned, and cleaved into the neck of another who had gotten too close. Blood sprayed the ground, and still Crosse pushed forward, each step deliberate, his boots grinding over loose dirt and splintered bone.

"Hold the line!" he bellowed, his voice cutting through the clash of steel and the screams of the dying. He didn't just lead—he was the wall they pressed against, the reason the Forsworn hadn't broken yet.

Beside him, Wulfric fought like a man possessed. His broad axe came down with a meaty thud, splitting a man's helm as though it were nothing more than rotten wood. Blood streaked down Wulfric's bald head, mingling with the grime caked along the scar on his neck. He swung again, his roar a wordless defiance that sent Cedric's men staggering back. One soldier thrust a spear at him, the point skimming his ribs. Wulfric let out a pained grunt, caught the shaft in one massive hand, and wrenched it free, splintering the wood in the process. Without pause, he rammed the jagged edge into the man's throat, the soldier's gurgling scream lost in the noise.

Blae moved like a forest spirit behind them, her bow singing as she loosed arrow after arrow. She ducked low, barely avoiding a wild swing from an enemy blade, then rolled to her feet, nocking an arrow in one fluid motion. The soldier who'd swung at her staggered back, clutching his throat as blood poured between his fingers. Blae didn't even watch him fall; she was already aiming at another.

The stench of blood and sweat hung thick in the air. Bodies piled at their feet, the dirt turning to mud under the steady drip of life pooling into it. The Forsworn line wavered but held, their faces pale with exhaustion and terror. Crosse turned to them, his sword raised, his voice raw and commanding.

"Hold!" he roared again, his blade coming down to block an incoming strike. Sparks flew as the clash jarred his arm, but he didn't falter. He shoved the attacker back with a savage kick, his boots slipping briefly in the gore underfoot. "Hold, damn you!"

I crouched near the bridge, my body thrumming with tension as the horses clattered onto the planks, their hooves slipping as Bran fought to guide them across. The princess stood just behind me, her guards flanking her with weapons drawn, their faces pale but set.

I wished for my bow. The axe in my hands felt foreign, heavy, and wrong. I knew the drills—I could hear Crosse's voice barking instructions in my head—but drills weren't battles. My heart pounded as I watched Cedric's men crash into the Forsworn line. The clash of steel and the cries of the wounded echoed, sharp and relentless.

Three of Cedric's men broke through the line. They moved fast, too fast. The princess's guards met two of them, steel clashing as blades sparked. The third—a man with a scar across his cheek and a sword gleaming in his grip—locked eyes with me. My stomach turned to ice as he charged.

I raised the axe awkwardly, stepping back as he swung. The blade sliced through the air, missing me by a hair as I stumbled, bringing my own weapon down in a wild arc. He blocked it easily, the force of the impact jarring my arms. His movements were fluid, confident, while mine were clumsy and desperate.

I swung again, my grip slippery with sweat, but he caught the axe's haft with his sword and twisted. The axe flew from my hands, landing with a dull thud in the dirt. He kicked me hard in the chest, and I hit the ground, the breath knocked from my lungs.

He stepped past me, his sword gleaming as he moved toward the princess. My vision swam, my chest burning as I struggled to rise. The princess's guards were still locked in their own fights, too far to help. My gaze fell on the axe lying just out of reach. I stretched, fingers brushing the wood, and grabbed it.

With a shout that was more fear than fury, I hurled the axe. It spun end over end and struck him in the arm, the blade glancing off his armor but biting at the exposed flesh below. He cried out, his sword dropping as he turned, his face twisted in rage. He stormed toward me, blood dripping from the wound, murder in his eyes.

I scrambled backward, my hands scrabbling in the dirt as he

raised his blade, and then Wulfric was there. His weapon came down like a thunderclap, cleaving through the man's side. The force of the blow sent Cedric's man to the ground in a lifeless heap.

Wulfric turned to me, his scarred face flushed and furious. "Get up, boy! Take the princess and cross that bridge now!"

I staggered to my feet, my legs shaky beneath me, and reached for the princess's arm. Her remaining guard disengaged from his fight and followed as we hurried toward the bridge, the chaos of battle roaring behind us.

Princess Sanne was the first to step onto the bridge, her braid whipping in the wind as her guard ushered her forward. The other guard—the one who had fought to protect her moments ago—lay motionless on the ground behind us. Blood pooled around his body, his sword still clutched in his hand. I gritted my teeth and turned away, gripping my axe tightly as I followed.

The bridge swayed underfoot, each step accompanied by the creak of strained ropes and the groan of aged planks. The river below roared, a churning torrent of foam and froth that threatened to swallow anyone who fell. I froze as I approached the first plank, my stomach lurching. The rush of water seemed deafening now, drowning out the scrape of the wind through the trees. The thought of that seething current reaching up to claim me sent a wave of cold through my chest.

I clutched the rope railing, its rough fibers digging into my palms, and stared at the path ahead. The planks, weathered and slick with moss, blurred in my vision. My axe felt impossibly heavy in my grip, pulling me downward, as if the river itself were already tugging me into its depths. My pulse hammered in my ears. For a long, trembling moment, I couldn't move.

I can't swim.

Sanne was nearly halfway across, her steps sure and deliberate. The guard behind her hesitated briefly but continued. Somewhere inside, a flicker of shame mingled with the fear, hot and acrid, spurring me forward. One step. Then another. The bridge groaned beneath my weight, the ropes pulling taut against the wind's push. I focused on the weave of the ropes and the slick gleam of the wood, refusing to look down again.

"I don't think this thing was built for so many people," I muttered, my voice tight.

"Then don't stop moving," Sanne shot back, her tone sharper than I'd expected. She didn't look at me, her focus locked on the other side.

I hesitated before answering, the tremor in her voice telling me more than her words. "You doing okay up there?" I asked, gripping the rope railing as the bridge swayed dangerously.

"Are you?" she countered, finally glancing over her shoulder. For the first time, her mask of composure cracked, just a little.

"Not even a little," I admitted, my words chased by a weak laugh.

Her lips twitched, almost forming a smile, but then the bridge lurched again, and the moment passed. "Then keep walking," she said, her voice steadier this time.

We reached the other side, and I grabbed her arm to help her down as she stepped onto solid ground. She didn't pull away, and for a moment, our eyes met—hers full of something I couldn't quite place, something that made my chest tighten.

Relief washed over me, sharp and overwhelming, leaving my legs trembling as I released the tension I hadn't realized I was holding. The steady, unyielding firmness of the ground beneath my boots felt almost foreign, like a long-forgotten comfort rediscovered. My breaths came in shallow bursts, my grip on the axe loosening as my fingers ached from holding on too tightly. Behind us, the bridge swayed in the wind, its groans now distant, no longer a threat.

Behind us, the remaining Forsworn battled on the other side of the bridge. Commander Crosse and Wulfric led the defense, their weapons flashing in the uneven light. Blae stood slightly behind them, her bow snapping arrow after arrow into the fray. The Forsworn were fewer now, their numbers almost halved, but they held, retreating step by painful step toward the bridge.

"Move, damn it!" Crosse barked, his voice cutting through the chaos as he slashed at an oncoming soldier. Wulfric shoved another Forsworn man toward the bridge, his axe swinging wide to hold back Cedric's soldiers.

One by one, they crossed, their faces pale and drawn, their clothes torn and bloodied. When Wulfric and Crosse were the last to cross, Crosse's command rang out: "Cut the bridge!"

I didn't need to be told twice. I raised my axe and swung hard at the ropes, the blade biting deep into the fibers. Another man joined me, his hands shaking as he hacked at the other side. The ropes frayed, snapping one by one, until the bridge gave a final, wrenching groan and collapsed into the raging water below.

The soldiers on the other side had just reached the bridge, their faces twisted in fury as the planks disappeared into the rapids. Several of them plunged into the water, their cries swallowed by the torrent.

"Arrows!" someone shouted, and I turned just in time to see the first volley darken the sky. They struck the ground around us, splintering against the rocks and trees. One man fell with a cry, clutching his shoulder as blood seeped between his fingers.

"Into the woods!" Crosse shouted, his voice like iron. "Now!"

We didn't hesitate. The Forsworn scrambled into the forest, their steps uneven and desperate as arrows continued to rain down. I stayed close to Sanne, keeping her within reach as we ran. The sound of the river faded behind us, swallowed by the shadows of the trees.

Chapter 5 - Village of Kyrne

The forest stretched out before us, dense and shadowed, swallowing the light as Blae led the way. Her movements were sharp, purposeful, but there was no hiding the slump in her shoulders. The Forsworn trailed behind her like broken branches dragged along by the wind. Every step was heavy, each breath labored. The forest floor, soft with pine needles, muffled the sound of our boots, but the weight of loss was loud enough to drown out the silence.

I walked near the middle of the group, Halder's reins in my hand. He snorted occasionally, his breath misting in the cool air. I could still feel the trembling exhaustion in his muscles, mirrored by my own, though he carried no one now. My legs burned, and my ribs ached from where I'd been struck in the earlier chaos, but I kept moving.

We'd lost too many at the bridge. I didn't need to count the faces to know how many were missing. It was in every glance, every hunched figure dragging one foot after the other. We didn't talk about them. The dead felt close enough to touch without saying their names.

Commander Crosse rode near the back, his fur cloak dark with dried blood. He said nothing, his gaze fixed ahead, but his presence anchored the group. Wulfric was close by him, walking beside his horse, his axe slung low at his side. His face was streaked with dirt and blood, his bald head shining faintly in the muted light filtering through the trees. He didn't look like a man who'd rest soon.

I helped where I could. Carrying a pack for one man, a blade for another. Holding out a waterskin to a woman whose hands trembled too much to drink on her own. It wasn't much, but it was something to keep my hands busy, to push back the emptiness gnawing at my insides. Each act of kindness felt hollow in the face of the despair I could feel leaking from everyone around me. It sat in my chest like a stone, pulling me down.

Blae's voice cut through the quiet, low and clipped. "We'll stop soon," she said without looking back. "There's a clearing ahead. Small, but hidden enough."

The only response was a murmur of acknowledgment, and even that felt weak.

I glanced around as we moved, catching snippets of faces in the line. Sanne, flanked by her single remaining guard, her expression unreadable, her shoulders stiff with exhaustion. The others—some limping, some clutching wounds, all wearing the same haunted look—were strangers to me but not to each other. They moved as one, even as they faltered, bound by a shared grief that hung over us all.

The river lay behind us, marking the line we'd crossed—from Prince Erik's fractured domain into Prince Harlan's. It had bought us time, but not peace. The weight of the chase clung to us like a storm cloud, Cedric's men a shadow stretching longer with every step, refusing to fade.

The forest seemed endless, the path ahead swallowed by thick undergrowth and towering pines. My feet dragged, but I forced myself to keep pace, to match the rhythm of the Forsworn around me. I couldn't let myself fall behind.

The clearing was a reprieve, but only barely. We stopped long enough to gulp down water and catch a few breaths before Blae urged us onward again. No one complained. The weight of what chased us hung heavy in the silence.

The forest thinned as we pressed forward, the trees giving way to blackened stumps and patches of overgrown weeds. The air changed too, carrying the faint, acrid scent of old ash. Blae led the way with Commander Crosse and Wulfric close behind her. Sanne and I followed, the rest of the Forsworn trailing in a ragged line.

We crested a rise, and the village came into view—or what was left of it. The charred skeletons of homes slumped against one another, their timbers rotted and splintered from years of neglect. A few structures still stood, stubborn against time and fire. Two wooden homes leaned precariously, their walls patched with moss and creeping vines. A third sat further back, its roof partially caved in. At the center of it all was a circular stone dun, its entrance sealed with jagged rocks. The remnants of life hung there like revenants, clinging to the broken earth.

Commander Crosse dismounted, his boots crunching against the scorched ground. He surveyed the ruins, his face unreadable. "What is this place?"

Blae didn't look at him. Her voice was low, rough at the edges. "Kyrne," she said. "It was my home."

The silence that followed felt heavier than the air. Even Wulfric, usually quick to quip, stayed quiet as Blae stepped forward, her gaze sweeping the ruins like she was seeing memories instead of rubble.

"When the Three Prince War started, Fief Lady Gudrun Stormrider came here," Blae continued, her words slow, deliberate. "She demanded we join her army—men, women, anyone who could hold a blade. My father said no. So did the others." Her eyes locked on the stone dun. "She burned us for it."

The words were full of loss. I felt it before she said it, the searing weight of her grief pressing through the air. My chest tightened, and I had to focus on my breathing to keep the feeling at bay. Blae's voice didn't waver, but I could feel the fracture in her steady tone.

"She took my husband and my boy," Blae said, her eyes still fixed on the dun. "Dragged them to her army. They died at Riverhalv. I didn't even get to bury them."

Wulfric let out a low growl, his hand tightening on the haft of his axe. "Stormrider," he muttered. "She was a spirit-damned butcher. Burned her way through half the kingdom and called it justice."

Blae didn't respond. Her gaze stayed locked on the village, her shoulders taut like a bowstring. I could feel the depth of it now—rage, sorrow, and a hollow ache that I couldn't even name.

Commander Crosse stepped forward, his voice soft but firm. "I'm sorry for your loss, Blae," he said. "For all of your losses."

Blae's lips pressed into a thin line. "It doesn't change anything."

"No," Crosse agreed, his tone carrying the weight of his years. "But maybe we can build something here. Rest. Recover. Then build something that lasts. Something that no one can burn down."

I glanced at him, surprised by the steadiness in his voice. He wasn't just talking to Blae. He was talking to all of us. I could see it in the way the others held themselves, their exhaustion mixed with a faint, flickering spark of hope.

Wulfric stepped closer to Blae, his broad hand resting briefly on her shoulder. "We'll make sure no one else lives through this," he said, his voice like gravel. "Stormrider's kind. Cedric's kind. They don't win."

Blae nodded, a small, jerky motion. Her hand brushed her bowstring, and she let out a slow breath. "We use the village for now," she said, her tone soft but resolute. "But don't make promises you can't keep."

Crosse looked at her, his expression unreadable for a moment, then nodded. "We'll see to it. Rest while you can. We've got work ahead."

The Forsworn began to spread out, their movements quiet, almost reverent. I stayed back, watching as Blae stepped toward the dun, her figure small against the ruins. The weight in the air pressed down, heavy as stone.

Commander Crosse barked orders, his voice cutting through the heavy air. "Search the village. Anything we can use, anything still standing. We'll sleep in the two wooden structures and set up a latrine near that old outhouse. Keep it orderly."

The Forsworn moved sluggishly, their weariness plain in every step, but the weight of Crosse's voice kept them moving. I lingered, watching Blae as she stood near the stone building at the village's center, her bow still in hand. Her eyes hadn't left the dun.

"What's that?" I asked, stepping closer, nodding toward the sealed-up structure.

Blae glanced at me, her green eyes shadowed. "A shrine," she said simply. "We weren't much of a village, so we leaned on the spirits for help. Kept us fed. Kept us safe. Or so we thought." Her voice faltered, softening. "I think we forgot them, boy. Took more than we gave. And when the fire came, they let us burn."

Her words sat heavy between us, sinking into the ash-streaked ground.

Sanne strode over, her steps as measured as always. "Is that why it's closed up?" she asked, her gaze locked on the crude rock barrier sealing the shrine's entrance.

Blae nodded, a sharp movement. "We blocked it ourselves. After the fire, those of us who were left thought maybe it was cursed. The spirits angry with us. No one dared go inside after that."

I looked at the shrine, trying to imagine what might linger behind the stones. My mother's voice stirred in my memory, soft and lilting as she told her stories of the spirits: of the Wind Spirit that danced through the trees, of the Fire Spirit that watched over the hearth, and of the Water Spirit that carried messages in the river's flow.

"My mother believed in the spirits," I said quietly, my fingers brushing against the smooth, cool stone of the necklace she'd given me. It hung around my neck on a thin cord, one of the few things I'd managed to keep from the gaoler. The green-blue stone seemed to hold its own light in the fire's glow. "She used to tell me stories about them. Said they watched everything, listened to everyone, but only helped the ones who asked nicely."

Blae let out a low, humorless laugh. "Your mother was a smart woman." Her eyes shifted to the necklace for a moment before meeting mine, softer now. "My son would've been just a bit older than you now."

I froze, her words hitting harder than I expected. The raw edge in her voice made my stomach twist. I glanced down at the stone again, its cool weight grounding me. "I, uh… I should go help the others," I said, my voice fumbling.

Blae gave a faint nod, her gaze lingering on me for a moment longer before turning back to the shrine. The wind rustled through the trees, carrying the faint smell of charred wood, and I turned away, walking quickly toward the others.

The shell of the village came to life, if only barely. The Forsworn moved through the remnants of what once was, patching together a camp from the remains of wooden walls and smoke-stained beams. The buildings weren't much—a leaning hut here, a half-collapsed longhouse there—but they were enough to shield us from the cold. It wasn't Linden, not even close. No fields stretched to the horizon, no sense of permanence. This place had been carved out of the forest, lived off it, and when the forest couldn't give anymore, the fire had come to take it back.

A stream wound near the edge of the village, the sound of it rushing over rocks soft and constant. People went in shifts, careful not to linger. Water was fetched upstream, the blood washed away downstream. The trail of red and dirt that swirled into the current felt like a wound opening in the earth. I stayed upstream, filling skin after skin, avoiding the others' eyes.

That night, they lit a fire in the center of the village. Its light flickered over tired faces, hollow and lined with dirt. The flames made everything sharp—blades of grass, shadows of trees, the edges of men and women beaten down by too many battles. The air was thick with the smell of smoke and exhaustion.

I sat toward the edge, knees tucked close to my chest, feeling the weight of the group press on me. We hadn't lost many, but every absence felt sharp, like a missing stone in a crumbling wall. Mostly men with a scattering of women like Blae, who carried bows and blades not out of choice but necessity. Their movements were steady, practiced—not born to it, but forged by it. Voices rose and fell around the fire, low and uneven. There were no stories of triumph, no songs to lighten the dark. Just murmurs, raw and frayed, like threads barely holding the group together.

Across the fire, I saw her—Princess Sanne. She sat straight-backed, her face calm, her hands resting on her lap. Her guards flanked her, what was left of them, their armor dented and dark with blood. She didn't meet anyone's eyes, her gaze fixed on the flames. I couldn't tell what she was thinking, but I could feel it—like the rest of them, like me, she was carrying too much.

One of the men broke the quiet. His voice, sharp and bitter, cut through the air. "It's her fault," he said, nodding toward Sanne. "If

we'd known, we'd never have raided that damn caravan."
Heads turned, the firelight catching tired eyes and furrowed brows. Sanne didn't move, her posture rigid, but I saw her fingers twitch—just once, then still again. The man stood, his shadow long and jagged against the flames. He pointed at her, his hand trembling with anger.

"She's accursed," he said, louder now, his voice heavy with frustration and grief. "Brought nothing but death down on us. On our friends."

I felt the air shift before I saw Commander Crosse rise. He moved with the kind of authority that didn't need to be loud. His hand closed around the man's wrist, firm and unyielding. "Sit down," Crosse said, his voice low, even. It wasn't a request.

The man hesitated, his anger simmering as he glanced at the commander. For a moment, I thought he'd push back, but then he met Crosse's gaze. Something in Crosse's expression stopped him cold. Slowly, the man sat down, his shoulders slumping as if the fight had drained out of him.

The fire crackled, filling the silence that followed. Sanne hadn't moved. Her face was still calm, her gaze steady, but I could feel the tension radiating off her like heat from the flames. She wasn't going to defend herself. She wasn't going to say a word.

And neither was anyone else.

The firelight flickered across Commander Crosse's face, his fur cloak casting shifting shadows as he stood tall, already commanding the circle with his presence. He looked around the fire, his sharp eyes meeting each of the Forsworn in turn. The crackle of the flames filled the silence, echoing the tension in the air. Each face was drawn, worn hollow by loss and exhaustion, waiting for something—anything—to hold onto.

Crosse's voice broke the silence, low but steady. "We've been through worse. And if you're here now, it's because you've survived. That's what we do—we survive. Even when princes tear the kingdom apart, when lords send their men after us like hounds, we endure. And we will again."

He let the words hang in the air, his sharp eyes cutting through the group. "What happened out there wasn't because of her." He turned, his gaze falling on Princess Sanne. She met his eyes, her shoulders stiff, her face calm, but there was a flicker of something deeper—a quiet pain she kept locked away. "No, this wasn't her doing. It wasn't ours, either. Cedric, Erik, Harlan—they're the ones to blame. Their ambition, their greed, their hunger for power. They're the ones who have made pawns of us all."

Murmurs rippled through the group, heads nodding, fists tightening. I could feel the shift, the weight in their postures lightening, if only slightly.

Crosse's voice grew stronger, rising over the murmurs. "But we aren't pawns. We are the Forsworn. We've lost people, yes, but we haven't lost ourselves. Not yet. And we won't. First, we'll find our people—the women, the children, the injured, everyone left behind. We'll bring them here, to this place. This village will be ours. We'll rebuild it with our own hands. We'll make it strong, a place no one can take from us."

The firelight danced in his eyes, his voice filling the clearing like the beat of a war drum. "Let the princes fight their wars. Let them burn their fields and send their armies to die. We'll endure. We'll carve out a life worth living, here, together. For ourselves. For our families. For every damned soul who's been crushed under the weight of their crowns."

A cheer broke out, raw and defiant, as if it carried the weight of everything they'd lost and everything they still clung to. The sound washed over me, filling the hollow spaces in my chest with a flicker of hope.

Crosse raised his fist toward the flames. "For the Forsworn!"

The cheer roared louder, a collective cry that shook the night. For a moment, the weight pressing on me felt lighter, as if the fire itself had burned it away.

Chapter 6 - Hunting

The morning sun barely touched the clearing, but the Forsworn were already at work. Voices called out across the village, steady and determined as debris was hauled away, trees were felled, and rudimentary tools hacked at the overgrowth. Commander Crosse stood in the center, directing each task with sharp, purposeful gestures, his voice carrying over the chaos.

I leaned against the cool stone of the dunn, its rough surface pressing into my back. My fingers idly traced the cracks running through the ancient structure as I watched the camp take shape. The energy from the previous night's fire seemed to fuel everyone, their movements filled with a purpose that had been absent for days.

A whisper brushed the edge of my senses. Faint, almost like a sigh, it came from the dunn behind me. My hand paused, resting against the stone, and for a moment, I felt it again—something distant but insistent, like a voice I couldn't quite hear. It wasn't the wind or the echo of the camp. It was something deeper, quieter, and it pulled at me, demanding my attention.

"Thought I'd find you skulking about."

I whipped around to see Wulfric standing a few paces away, his bulk unmistakable. His scarred neck caught the morning light as he grinned, holding something long and familiar in his hand.

A bow.

"Not the prettiest thing," Wulfric said, giving it a shake. "But it's better than nothing." He tossed it toward me, and I caught it awkwardly, my fingers closing around the worn wood. It was rough, patched in places, and the string looked like it had seen better days, but it was a bow.

"You found one?" My voice came out breathless, and I realized how much I'd missed the weight of it in my hands.

"Thought you'd be pleased," Wulfric said, his grin widening. "But don't thank me just yet. You're gonna have to make it sing again."

Blae stepped into view, her bow slung across her back, and gave me a nod. "Wulfric figured you and I could head out. The dried meat's getting old. Something fresh would do the lot of us good."

I straightened, clutching the bow tighter. "You're serious?"

"Does this face look like it jokes?" Blae said, deadpan, though her lips twitched like she was fighting a smile.

Wulfric chuckled, crossing his arms. "I'll take that as a yes, then." He gestured toward the edge of the village. "Go on. Blae knows the land. She'll show you the ropes."

I nodded quickly, my pulse quickening. I glanced at Blae, and she motioned with her chin toward the trees. "Let's see what you can do, boy."

As I followed her, the bow in my hands and the weight of Wulfric's grin at my back, I couldn't help but feel something else stirring inside me—a flicker of purpose. For the first time in days, maybe even weeks, I felt like I could do more than just survive.

The forest stretched around us, thick and green, the air damp with the scent of pine and moss. Blae moved with the ease of someone who had known those woods her entire life, her footsteps silent on the soft earth. I followed close behind, scanning the ground for trails. Every so often, Blae would pause, bending slightly to trace her fingers over broken twigs or pressed grass, her sharp eyes catching details that my father would have noticed more swiftly.

I missed my map. My fingers twitched for it, the familiar parchment that had been my constant companion in Elkswood. But I didn't miss the crowd—the weight of so many bodies, so much tension. Out there, with just Blae and the endless stretch of trees, I could breathe again. The bow sat comfortably in my hand, a reminder of what I'd been without for too long.

"Your village must've been good at this," I said, watching her as she studied the faint mark of a hoofprint in the mud. "Hunting, I mean."

She straightened, giving me a small smile. "Nearly everyone was. We didn't have fields like those on the outskirts of Thornfield or Blackwater. It was the forest or nothing. My husband—" Her voice faltered for a beat. "He was better at it than me. My son liked to tag along. Thought he'd become a better tracker than either of us."

"You taught him?" I asked, surprised.

Her smile softened. "Bits and pieces. He was little, but he had the patience for it. Always said the spirits whispered to him, showing him where the deer were."

I nodded, watching her carefully. There was something raw in her voice, a sharp edge beneath the words. "When did you join the Forsworn?"

"Not long ago," she said, moving forward again, her gaze sweeping the forest floor. "After the village burned, I wandered. Tried to find work, safety—anything. For a while, I fell in with a bandit gang." She glanced back at me, her expression unreadable. "Times were tough. They'd take what they wanted to survive."

I felt a flicker of surprise. "How'd you end up with the Forsworn?"

Her voice turned colder. "Crosse found us. Killed some of the bandits, but the rest of us... he gave us a choice. Join or be left for the crows." She shrugged, her movements tight. "I chose the Forsworn. Turned out, they weren't so different—just better at knowing where to draw the line."

"Times are tough," I said quietly. "I thought the Forsworn were bandits at first too."

She laughed, a sharp sound that broke the quiet. "No surprise there. We do what we have to, same as anyone. But bandits? No. Bandits don't care who they hurt. We're different." She paused, her gaze catching mine. "They, we, have to be."

I nodded, her words sinking into the stillness around us. The forest felt heavier somehow, the weight of survival pressing in from all sides. I tightened my grip on the bow and followed her deeper into the trees.

Underbrush stretched out before us, dense and shadowed, the air cool under the canopy. My fingers curled around the bow, rough wood smooth against my palms. It wasn't my father's bow—not the one I'd grown up watching him string, not the one I'd carried with me for years—but it was enough. For the first time in too long, I felt a flicker of myself return. A hunter, not just a boy running from the past.

Blae crouched low, her hand brushing against the damp earth. "Tracks," she whispered, pointing to a faint indentation in the soil. "Doe. Small herd, maybe."

I nodded, stepping carefully to her side. The tracks were light, barely visible under the layer of fallen leaves. My heart quickened, the familiar rhythm of a hunt settling into my chest. "How far ahead?" I said, not telling her that I could feel them, their presence.

"Not far," she said, straightening. "Stream up ahead. They'll be drinking." She glanced at me, her sharp eyes narrowing. "You ready for this?"

I nodded again, the bowstring taut under my fingers. "I've been waiting for this."

She didn't say more, just gestured for me to follow. We moved silently, weaving through the trees, our breaths shallow and measured. The forest felt alive around us—the rustle of leaves, the distant call of birds, the faint trickle of water growing louder with each step.

Then I saw them.

Three deer, heads bowed to the stream, their coats glinting dully in the filtered sunlight. My breath caught, and I instinctively reached for an arrow, nocking it carefully. Blae stayed still beside me, her own bow raised but not drawn. She watched, waited.

I focused, the world narrowing to the doe in the center. Her ears twitched, her muscles tense, but she hadn't seen me yet. My fingers grazed the string, the wood of the bow creaking faintly as I pulled it back. It wasn't perfect—nothing like my father's bow—but it held steady.

The release came almost without thought, the arrow slicing through the air. The doe jerked, stumbling forward before collapsing with a soft thud. The other deer scattered, their hooves pounding against the forest floor as they vanished into the trees.

Blae stood, lowering her bow. "Good shot," she said, her voice even but laced with approval. She moved toward the doe, kneeling beside it to inspect the kill. "Clean. Quick."

I followed, the rush of the hunt still pulsed through me. I bent to help her lift the deer, its weight solid and heavy between us. The bow hung across my shoulder, the string brushing against my back with each step. It wasn't just a tool—it was a piece of me I'd been missing, and I swore I'd get my own bow back someday.

Blae glanced at me as we carried the deer. "You've been taught well. Whoever trained you knew what they were doing."

"My father," I said quietly, the words grounding me. "He taught me everything I know."

She nodded, her expression softening. "He'd be proud. You're good at this."

I didn't respond, but her words stayed with me as we moved through the forest, the deer heavy but not unwelcome. By the time we reached the village, I felt more whole than I had in weeks.

We returned to the camp as the sun began to dip, casting long shadows over the clearing. The village looked a little less like ruins and more like something living, though only just. A few of the wooden structures had been cleared of debris, the jagged edges of broken beams chopped into manageable pieces. Smoke curled lazily from a makeshift fire pit at the center of the camp, and the air carried the tang of sweat and freshly cut wood.

The deer on our shoulders drew attention immediately. Heads turned, and murmurs rippled through the Forsworn. A few smiles broke out among the weary faces, and for the first time since the bridge, it felt like hope had managed to creep in.

Wulfric strode over, his broad frame casting a shadow. He whistled low, eyeing the deer. "Good work, lad. Blae." His gaze shifted to me, and a grin tugged at the corner of his scarred mouth. "Didn't think you had it in you."

I shrugged, trying to hide the flicker of pride. "Had a good teacher."

"Don't let it go to your head," Blae muttered, smirking as she adjusted her grip on the deer.

We brought it to the largest clearing near the center of the camp. A few others joined us, helping to lay the carcass on a flat slab of wood someone had fashioned into a crude table. Blae grabbed a knife, her movements precise and practiced as she set to work dressing the deer.

The first cut was deep, splitting the belly open with a wet sound. The sharp smell of blood filled the air, and I wrinkled my nose but didn't look away. Blae pulled out the entrails, tossing them into a bucket nearby. "Make yourself useful," she said, nodding toward the bucket. "We'll bury this after."

I grabbed the bucket, my hands sticky from the blood on the wood. Around me, others gathered, watching with interest or passing tools back and forth. Someone handed Blae a second knife, sharper and smaller, and she worked quickly to skin the deer, peeling the hide away in one smooth motion.

It was messy work. The blood soaked into the dirt beneath the table, and the smell clung to my hands even after I wiped them on my tunic. But as the meat was cut into sections and handed off to be roasted over the fire, A murmur of anticipation rippled through the camp.

The fire crackled, and the scent of roasting meat filled the air, overpowering everything else. Stomachs growled, mine among them, and people gathered closer, drawn by the promise of something warm and fresh.

By the time the first pieces were ready, the sun had sunk low, leaving the camp bathed in the orange glow of the fire. Plates were passed around, wooden and mismatched, and the deer was divided as evenly as they could manage. I sat cross-legged near the edge, a chunk of meat on my plate, still steaming.

The first bite was rich and gamey, the juices dripping down my chin. It wasn't perfect—cooked a little too fast in places, still pink in others—but it was the best thing I'd tasted in weeks. Around me, others were eating, talking, even laughing. The tension that had wrapped around the camp since the bridge seemed to loosen.

Blae settled beside me, a plate balanced on her knees. "Not bad for a day's work," she said, her tone dry but warm.

I nodded as I watched the firelight flicker across her face. "Think we'll catch another one tomorrow?"

She grinned, sharp and quick. "If we're lucky. But don't get used to this, boy. Dried meat's still on the menu." Her words stirred a ripple of laughter, faint and brief, but it spread through the camp like sparks catching on kindling. For a moment, the weight of exhaustion lifted, the air lightened by a shared, fleeting sense of camaraderie.

The laughter stilled as Commander Crosse's voice cut through the low murmur of the camp. "Wulfric, Tomi, Blae—over here. Toric, Lenna. You too." His tone left no room for delay. Faces turned toward him as the named leaders rose, their movements steady but heavy with the day's wear. I was surprised to have been called with them along with the princess.

Crosse stood by the fire, the glow flickering across his face and casting sharp shadows that seemed to deepen the lines of weariness etched into his features. Wulfric took his place at Crosse's right, broad arms crossed over his chest, the jagged scar along his neck catching the firelight like a brand. Blae hovered nearby, her sharp green eyes flicking between us, the bow slung low across her back giving her an ever-ready appearance.

Sanne sat slightly apart, her expression unreadable but her presence as steady as a stone in the river. Toric, wiry and quick, shifted on his feet, his gaze flicking toward Lenna, who stood silent and firm, her cropped black hair brushing the edges of her angular jaw. Each of us brought something different to the firelight, but the weight of what was coming settled on all shoulders evenly.

Crosse let his gaze sweep over us before he spoke. "We've made a start here, but this isn't enough. We need the rest of our people—our women, our children, the injured. They're out there, scattered, and we don't know where. Jory and his group should have moved by now, but we've no way of knowing where they've gone."

The words hung heavy in the air. My stomach twisted at the mention of Jory. I hoped he'd made it, that the warning I'd given him had been enough.

"Cedric's men are still out there," Crosse continued, his tone hard. "And with Erik and Harlan lighting the kingdom on fire, the roads will be even more dangerous. We can't send everyone, but we can't wait, either."

Wulfric nodded, the motion slow and deliberate. "I'll go," he said, his voice like the scrape of a whetstone. "Take a few with me. We'll bring them back."

"I'll go too," Blae said, stepping forward. "The boy can hunt in my steed."

Crosse shook his head, the weight of his authority pressing into the space between them. "No. We need you here, Blae. Hunting, scouting, keeping us fed and safe. You know this land better than anyone."

Blae scowled, her lips twitching as if biting back an argument. "The boy's a good hunter," she said, her tone clipped.

Crosse's sharp gaze landed on me, pinning me in place. "He's not one of us," he said, his voice steady but not unkind. "I imagine he wants to get back home. To his father's book, his belongings."

The truth of it stung, though I wasn't sure why. I shifted under the weight of their stares, feeling my awkwardness like a heavy cloak wrapped tightly around me. "I... yeah. I do."

"Then you'll go with Wulfric," Crosse said, his tone leaving no room for debate. "But be careful. You're a fugitive now. If they catch you, it's back in a cell—or worse."

Blae leaned forward, her voice sharper than the edge of her blade. "The bridge is out. You'll have to head south, near the old ford where the River Halv becomes the Drowned River. It's dangerous, but there's a rope crossing there. I'll give you the details."

Toric's face darkened, and he shifted on his feet. "The Drowned River," he muttered, his voice low. "They say it's cursed, where the waters swallowed a whole army during the Three Prince War. Spirits linger there, pulling at the living who dare cross."

Blae rolled her eyes, brushing off his superstition with a wave of her hand. "And they'll keep pulling if you can't swim. It's just a river, Toric. Dangerous, sure, but no worse than anything else we've faced."

Commander Crosse's voice cut in, calm but firm. "We'll work on getting the bridge back in place by the time you return. If Cedric's men cross before we're ready, we'll have a bigger problem than dark spirits." His gaze swept over the group. "The ford might be tricky, but it's our best option for now. You'll handle it."

Wulfric grunted, his tone dry. "We'll manage."

Sanne, who had been silent until now, suddenly straightened, her voice cutting through the murmurs. "What about me?"

Crosse's jaw tightened. "For now, princess, you stay with us. Until we figure out what to do."

Her laugh was bitter, her eyes cold as they locked onto his. "So I'm still a pawn."

"Yes and no," Crosse said, his voice steady but with an edge that silenced any retort. "It's for your safety as much as ours. We need to work out what's happening. Once we do, you'll be free to go."

"And where would I go?" she asked, her tone sharp, her chin tilted high. "To my brother. To free him."

Crosse's gaze hardened. "Then no. Not yet. We won't let you go into that."

Sanne's mouth tightened, her anger palpable even from where I stood. She rose abruptly, her guards following as she stormed into the shadows without another word.

Crosse sighed, the sound heavy with exhaustion. He turned back to the rest of us. "Does everyone understand the plan?"

We nodded, the gravity of his words sinking in. There wasn't much room for discussion or dissent.

"Good," Crosse said, his voice firm again. "You move at dawn. Get some rest while you can."

As the group began to disperse, I caught a glimpse of the commander, his shoulders bowed slightly, the firelight painting his face with lines of weariness. For all his strength, the weight of this war hung on him, heavier than I'd ever realized.

Chapter 7 - Drowned River

Wulfric's hand on my shoulder dragged me from the shallow pool of sleep, the faint light of pre-dawn filtering through the trees. His voice, rough and low, rumbled in the stillness. "Up, lad. It's morning. Time to move."

I groaned, rubbing my eyes as I sat up, the cool morning air biting through my cloak. The camp was quiet, the faint snores of the others blended with the rustle of leaves overhead. Wulfric didn't wait, turning and moving toward the next bedroll.

I followed, my boots crunching softly against the ground. Wulfric crouched near a stocky man with a thick mop of reddish-brown hair. He gave the man's shoulder a hard shake. "Peter, on your feet."

Peter groaned, rolling onto his back and glaring up at Wulfric. "Spirits take you, can't a man sleep?"

"Not today," Wulfric replied with a grin. "Tomi, meet Peter. Grumpiest bastard in camp, but he's got a nose for trouble."

Peter sat up with a scowl, rubbing his face. "Wonderful. A boy. Just what we need." His tone was sharp, but his eyes didn't hold malice, just weariness.

The next bedroll belonged to a younger man, fair-haired and wiry, who stirred before Wulfric could nudge him awake. "I'm up, I'm up," he muttered, pushing to his feet and shaking out his cloak.

Wulfric smirked. "That's Svend. Always eager, but don't let it fool you. He'll whine about the walk before midday."

Svend grinned, his teeth flashing in the dim light. "And you'll complain the rest of the way."

The four of us gathered our belongings quietly, rolling up cloaks and securing what little supplies we had. Wulfric led us toward the center of the village where Halder waited, already saddled. His breath puffed out in the chill air as he shifted his weight, the reins tied loosely to a post.

Wulfric ran a hand down the horse's neck. "Halder's coming with us. He'll carry what we can't and run back if there's trouble." The horse snorted as if understanding, his ears twitching.

We moved through the sleeping village, our footsteps careful against the debris and uneven ground. The remnants of the Forsworn lay scattered around what little shelter the ruins provided. I caught glimpses of faces half-hidden by blankets, their breathing steady in the dawn light. Sanne's guards sat watch near the stone dunn, their figures outlined against the gray sky.

Wulfric kept us moving, his pace steady but quiet. Peter muttered something under his breath about being dragged out before first light, but Svend only smirked, his steps light and eager. The cold nipped at my cheeks, and the weight of the bow slung across my back felt heavier in the stillness.

We reached the edge of the village, the forest looming ahead. Wulfric paused, his gaze sweeping over the group. "Keep sharp," he said, his voice low but firm. "This isn't a stroll. Let's get moving."

The forest pressed close around us, the damp air thick with the earthy scent of moss and rotting leaves. Each step sank slightly into the soft ground, our boots muffling what little noise we made. The sky above was still a murky gray, the sun not yet brave enough to show itself.

Peter muttered under his breath for the hundredth time. "Too early for this nonsense. We should've waited till proper daylight."
Svend, walking just behind him, rolled his eyes. "Relax, Peter. It's not like Cedric's men care what time it is."

Peter turned his scowl on Svend, his mouth twitched with a retort. "Easy for you to say, you don't have an old knee that locks up when it's damp."

"Maybe if you moved it more, it wouldn't," Svend quipped, smirking. Peter grumbled something about Svend being too young to know anything, his words half swallowed by the thick trees.

I stayed quiet, biting back my own irritation. Peter's voice was like a dull saw grating against the silence of the forest, and it was too early to deal with it.

Wulfric, ahead of us all, finally turned, his bald head glinting faintly as he leveled Peter with a stern look. "Settle your tongue before I settle it for you," he said, his voice low and sharp.

Peter huffed but kept his mouth shut after that. The quiet that followed was a relief, broken only by the rustle of leaves and the occasional snap of a twig underfoot.

Wulfric slowed his pace and fell back beside me. He clapped a heavy hand on my shoulder. "Tomi, scout ahead," he said, his tone easy but firm. "Make sure there's no one watching or waiting for us."

I hesitated, glancing at the thick trees ahead. "Why me?"

"You're a hunter, aren't you?" Wulfric asked, grinning faintly. "Only scout we've got, other than Blae. And even she's new at it. Besides, you've got young eyes. Use them."

I couldn't argue with that. The prospect of some quiet time away from Peter's grumbling was enough to sway me. I nodded, slipping the bow off my shoulder. "All right. I'll call out if I see anything."

"Don't call," Wulfric said with a chuckle. "Come back and tell us. Quietly."

I gave him a half-smile and nodded, stepping ahead of the group. The forest opened up a little as I moved further away, the stillness wrapping around me like a heavy cloak. For the first time since we'd set off, I felt my shoulders ease.

The forest opened up before me, damp and alive with the early morning. My boots made no sound against the leaf-strewn ground as I moved at my own pace—a faster, quieter pace than the Forsworn warriors behind me. They lumbered through the woods like oxen not as bad compared to the mad scramble of our retreat days ago. It felt good to be free of their noise, free of their heavy steps and grumbled complaints.

I breathed in deeply, the crisp scent of moss and bark filling my lungs. The bow rested lightly in my hand, and with each step, I felt more like myself. I wasn't sure when that had started slipping away, but it had. Maybe back in the gaol. Maybe before.

Crosse's words gnawed at me, still sharp in my mind: *You're not one of us.* He hadn't meant it unkindly. It was just a fact. The Forsworn were a battered tribe of survivors bound by shared loss and purpose. I was only passing through, a shadow trailing behind them. When it was over—when Wulfric found Jory and the others—I'd leave. I had a plan, didn't I?

Elkswood. I'd sneak in if I had to. Find Anni. Get my father's book back. Finally read it.

I paused, crouching to study a faint impression in the dirt—a deer's track, but hours old. My fingers brushed the ground as I stood. The plan seemed so clear in my head, but after? What then?

A sharp crack split the air, dragging me back to the moment. My pulse spiked as I froze, crouching low and slipping an arrow onto the bowstring in one fluid motion. I scanned the brush ahead, straining to listen. Foolish. I'd been so lost in my thoughts I hadn't sensed it.

The underbrush rustled, and my breath caught as a shape

emerged—a creature, low to the ground, its fur catching the faint morning light. A fox. It stopped, tilting its head toward me, its amber eyes glinting with mischief. For a moment, it seemed to mock me, its body quivering as if suppressing a laugh before it darted off into the woods.

I let out a breath, my arms lowering as the tension melted away. My heart still pounded, but I shook my head at myself. Reckless. I couldn't afford that. Not when we weren't sure if Cedric's men were out there.

Closing my eyes, I reached out with my pathos. The others were behind me, lumbering and slow, but steady. The forest came alive in my mind—the skitter of squirrels, the rustle of birds overhead, the quiet hum of insects. Further out, I stretched my senses. I could feel the faint tug of life back at the village, distant and warm. No other people nearby, though. Not yet.

I stood, tightening my grip on the bow, and pushed forward toward the river, this time keeping my focus sharp. The plan could wait. Right then finding Jory and the others came first.

Finally, the river came into view through the trees, its steady rush filling the silence as I stepped into the clearing. The bridge—or what was left of it—hung in tatters. Ropes dangled uselessly into the churning water below, and planks bobbed against the rocks like driftwood. I scanned the area, crouching low near the bank.

No one was there. My pathos stretched outward, feeling only the echo of animals moving along the forest's edge. No human presence lingered, but signs of a fight remained. Blood streaked the dirt in dark stains, the kind that didn't wash away with the first rain. Scattered boot prints marred the earth where the skirmish had taken place. Whoever Cedric had sent, had moved on—quickly, it seemed. There were no bodies, which was a relief, but the sharp tang of iron in the air made my stomach tighten.

I crouched closer, my fingers brushing the dried blood. The memory of the fight felt sharp, like a blade still humming from the strike. My chest tightened at the thought of the Forsworn who hadn't made it across. Shaking it off, I stood and turned back the way I'd come.

The others were a ways back, Wulfric's broad silhouette leading the slower forms of Peter and Svend. As I approached, Wulfric's eyes narrowed in question.

"No one's there," I said, keeping my voice low. "But the place is a mess. Blood everywhere. No bodies, though."

"Good," Wulfric grunted. "Means they moved on."

"Or they're just ahead, waiting to pick us off," Peter muttered, kicking a loose rock with his boot.

"Relax, Peter," Svend said with a lazy grin, his steps light despite the weight of his pack. "If anyone's out there, the boy would've sniffed them out. He's got the nose of a bloodhound."

"Better than your nose for trouble," Wulfric said, smirking. Peter shot them both a glare but said nothing.

I nodded toward the river. "The bridge is gone. We'll need to follow the bank south."

"Lead on, scout," Wulfric said, his tone easy but firm. "We'll keep up."

The journey south along the river's edge was slow. The current roared beside us, its voice a constant reminder of how far we'd come—and how far we still had to go. I stepped out ahead, moving lightly over the uneven ground, pausing every so often to listen or stretch my senses outward.

Peter grumbled behind me, his voice cutting through the quiet like a dull blade. "Feels like we're walking into a trap. Just wandering along the river like this, begging to get spotted."

"Then why don't you wander a bit faster?" Svend shot back, the grin still on his face. "Maybe they'll shoot at you first."

Peter muttered something under his breath, and Wulfric let out a low chuckle. "If the lad can keep quiet and do his job, so can you. Settle your tongue, Peter, before I do it for you."

I couldn't help but smile faintly at that, though I kept my eyes on the path ahead. The forest thickened as we moved further south, the trees leaning closer to the water as if watching our progress. Every now and then, I stopped, crouching low to study a bend in the river or a trail of disturbed leaves. Each time, I returned to find Peter grumbling and Svend teasing him, their bickering filling the air like a half-hearted song.

It wasn't much, but it kept the quiet from settling too heavily. And right then, that was enough.

The ford was exactly as Blae had described, though the reality of it felt heavier, older, as if the place itself held its breath. The river widened there, the banks carved deep by time and water. Mist clung low to the ground, swirling around the remnants of an ancient rope bridge. It sagged in the middle, its planks blackened with age and spotted with moss. Some were missing entirely, leaving gaping holes that revealed the rushing water far below.

I crouched on a rock near the edge, scanning the area. My pathos reached out, brushing the edges of the world around me. No sign of life, not even the faint stir of creatures. Just the endless flow of water and the mournful creak of the bridge swaying gently in the wind.

Wulfric's broad frame was the first to appear through the trees. Svend followed close behind, his face flushed but grinning, while Peter stumbled out last, muttering under his breath.

When Peter caught sight of the bridge, his muttering turned into a full-blown curse. "Spirits' teeth, this thing looks ready to collapse!"

"It's held this long," Wulfric said, his voice steady. "It'll hold a little longer."

"Let's hope it doesn't have a taste for fools," Svend added with a smirk.

My stomach churned. I didn't answer, my eyes glued to the water below. The river surged, dark and cold, its currents twisting like unseen hands. The thought of being pulled under, of sinking into that suffocating depth, clenched around my chest.

Wulfric stepped up beside me, his hand heavy but steady on my shoulder. "Stay sharp, lad," he said, his voice calm, grounding. He took Halder's reins and moved toward the bridge, leaving me rooted to the spot.

The first plank groaned as Wulfric stepped on, the ropes creaking like an old ship in a storm. Halder balked, his hooves scraping against the wood, ears flicking nervously. Wulfric tugged firmly, his voice low and steady, coaxing the horse forward. They moved slowly, each step an argument with the bridge's protests.

Peter pushed past me with a sharp shove, muttering, "I'm not waiting for that beast to take us all down." He stepped onto the swaying planks with a sneer, ignoring the way the ropes trembled under his weight.
Svend gave me a look, half amused, half concerned. "You coming?" he asked, but his tone lacked the usual bite. He followed Peter onto the bridge, leaving me standing alone at the edge.

I took a shaky breath, my legs leaden. The river below roared in my ears, louder than it should have been, louder than anything else. The memory of Riverhalv clawed at me—icy water, strong hands shoving me in, the panic, the helplessness. My fingers curled around the bow at my side, knuckles whitening.

The bridge swayed, and I swallowed hard. "You've got this," I muttered under my breath, trying to convince myself. The first step was the hardest.

The crossing was slow. Each step felt like a gamble, the planks shifting slightly underfoot. Ahead, Halder snorted, his hooves clicking nervously against the wood. Then it happened—Peter's boot hit a plank, and it snapped with a loud crack. He stumbled, one leg plunging through the gap. Svend lunged, grabbing his arm and yanking him upright.

"Watch your damn step!" Svend barked.

Peter scowled but didn't answer, his knuckles white as he gripped the ropes on either side.

Then as if from nowhere at all and everywhere at once, came the song.

It was faint at first, a sweet, lilting melody that seemed to drift on the mist. My breath caught, and I turned my head, trying to pinpoint the source. The sound wasn't coming from the forest or the river. It was everywhere.

"What in my mother's bosom is that?" Peter's voice rose in panic.

The singing grew louder, curling through the air like water slipping over smooth rocks—sweet, alluring, but edged with a dangerous undercurrent. Halder froze, his ears swiveling back, his muscles trembling as he let out a sharp, nervous whinny. Wulfric cursed, yanking at the reins with a growl.

"Keep moving!" he barked.

But Peter froze, his knuckles white as he clutched the ropes, his wide eyes fixed on the water below. His panic seeped into the air like poison, and I felt it double, both his and my own. Our combined fear only spooked Halder further. The horse reared slightly, his hooves scraping against the unstable planks. The entire bridge rocked beneath us, sending a fresh wave of terror clawing up my throat.

I couldn't breathe. My own grip tightened on the ropes, my palms slick with sweat. The rushing river below seemed louder, closer, pulling at me with invisible hands. My chest heaved as the memory of icy water and choking panic gripped me. My legs trembled, refusing to move. I felt like a child again, flailing in a river I couldn't escape.

Svend lunged forward, grabbing Peter's shoulder and shoving him ahead, snapping me back to the moment. "Move man!!" Wulfric roared, his voice cutting through the haunting song.

The dirt bank was so close, just a few more steps away. But the bridge swayed violently, the ropes creaking like they might snap. Halder let out a piercing neigh, his hooves stomping in fear. My heart hammered against my ribs, every part of me screaming to freeze, to stop.

I forced my legs to move, one step, then another, my fingers gripping the ropes so tightly it felt like they might break. The cold air stung my face, but all I could hear was the rush of the water below and the pounding of my own pulse. Just a few more steps. Just a few more.

Then it stopped. The singing, the swaying—everything went still.

We stood frozen for a moment, the silence heavier than the song had been. Wulfric glanced back, his face pale and grim. Peter leaned against the ropes, gasping for breath, while Svend muttered curses under his breath.

I let out a shaky exhale, loosening my grip on the ropes. That's when the plank beneath me gave way. Feeling the world drop out from under me, my body plunging through the gap. My hands shot out, grabbing wildly for the ropes. But all I caught was air.

And then, I was falling.

The cold hit me like a fist. The water swallowed me whole, an unforgiving torrent that ripped the breath from my lungs before I could even scream.

The current dragged me under, spinning me like a leaf caught in a storm. My limbs flailed, desperate to find something solid, something to hold on to, but the river was all motion, all power. It tugged and pulled, the currents like hands clawing at me, dragging me deeper.

I broke the surface, gasping, only for the river to slam into me again. Water filled my mouth, bitter and icy, and I coughed, choking as it rushed in. My arms thrashed, searching for the sky above, but it was lost behind the dark waves and the spray that stung my eyes.

Somewhere above the roar of the river, I could hear shouts. Wulfric's voice, deep and booming, called my name, but it was faint, muffled by the crashing water. I tried to answer, tried to yell back, but the river forced me under again, its weight pressing on my chest like a stone.

For a moment, a flash of memory broke through the chaos. The siege of Riverhalv. Bryn shoving me into the icy waters of the moat, laughing as he dared me to swim. I hadn't been able to then, either. I'd flailed and sputtered, and my father had pulled me out, shaking his head but smiling as he told me, "The water's no place for a hunter."

The river spun me again, snapping me back to the present. My lungs burned, my chest tightening with every second I spent beneath the surface. I kicked, clawed, anything to break free, but the current was relentless. My head broke the surface for the briefest of moments, enough to hear Wulfric's voice again, shouting something I couldn't make out.

Then the river dragged me down once more. The cold was sharper now, biting into my skin, into my bones. My arms grew heavy, my legs weaker with each frantic kick. The current tugged me further, faster, its icy grip unyielding.

I couldn't breathe. Couldn't fight. My vision blurred, the world turning to shadows and dim light. The river roared around me, a deafening sound that swallowed everything else, even the sound of my own thoughts.

And then, there was nothing. Just the black.

Chapter 8 - Nixie

The current cradled me, a strange, weightless pull that felt almost gentle at first. My arms floated at my sides, my legs limp as the water carried me. I couldn't tell if my eyes were open or closed—everything was dim, the light above rippling like a distant, unreachable surface.

Fish darted past me, silver and sleek, their movements quick as whispers. I tried to lift a hand, to reach for something, anything, but my body wouldn't obey. Reeds swayed in the unseen rhythm of the current, their tips brushed my skin like cold fingers. Algae floated in tangled clumps, swirling around me, catching on my arms and legs as if trying to pull me deeper.

Shapes emerged from the gloom—shadowy silhouettes drifting just beyond reach. They moved with eerie grace, their edges indistinct, as if they were part of the water itself. I couldn't tell if they were watching or ignoring me entirely, but they circled closer, their presence suffocating. Lights flickered around me, tiny pinpricks that flared and dimmed like fireflies trapped beneath the surface.

The water grew cold, biting at my skin, the chill burrowing deep into my bones. The light above dimmed further, swallowed by the depths. The current became stronger, no longer cradling but pulling, dragging me down into the freezing dark. My chest burned, my breath caught somewhere between my ribs. I tried to scream, but the sound was swallowed by the water.

The world shifted, a jarring blur of cold and dark, until it spat me out into silence.

I woke to the sound of dripping water, the faint echo of each drop bounced off the hard walls around me. My body ached, every muscle trembling as I tried to sit up. The air was freezing, sharp as a blade against my skin. I wrapped my arms around myself, shivering so hard my teeth clattered.

The ground beneath me was slick and cold, a jagged surface that bit into my palms as I steadied myself. The cave was dark, but not entirely. A soft, eerie glow emanated from moss clinging to the walls, a pale green-blue light that pulsed faintly, almost alive. Shadows flickered across the stone, thrown by the water nearby—a pool so still it looked like glass. The reflections danced on the ceiling, rippling with every drop that fell from somewhere above.

I swallowed, my throat raw, my chest rising and falling in shallow, ragged breaths. A single drop of water slipped from my hair and landed on my bare chest. My stomach twisted. I was naked, stark and bare, the cold seeping into every part of me. I instinctively reached for my neck, my fingers brushing over the damp skin.

The necklace wasn't there.

My hand froze, the absence a sharp, cutting weight. My mother's necklace—the stone, smooth and cool, threaded onto its simple cord—it was gone. I felt the ache settle in my chest, a hollow space that had nothing to do with the chill.

I clenched my fists, my nails biting into my palms as I scanned the cave. The moss continued its faint glow, the pool its quiet, unnerving stillness. I was alone. At least I thought I was.

A sound reached me, faint and elusive, like the murmur of a distant stream, but threaded with something sweeter, a melody rising and falling as if it were breathing. It brushed against my ears, alive and delicate, sending a shiver down my spine. I froze, my breath catching in my throat as my gaze locked on the shadows dancing on the far wall.

They didn't just flicker—they undulated, moving like smoke caught in a slow current. For a heartbeat, they seemed to take shape, a figure, more fluid than solid, limbs stretching languidly as if carved from water. It became clearer, the outline surprisingly feminine, impossibly smooth, her form both alien and familiar. Her hair swayed like tendrils in the deep, and her body glistened with an otherworldly sheen, reflections rippling across her skin like light on the riverbed.

She turned, the movement impossibly graceful, the curve of her back flowing into a long, sinuous tail. Not human—not entirely. The sight was intimate, haunting, a vision of something meant to exist beyond reach, beyond comprehension. Just as quickly, the shape dissolved back into the shadows, leaving me gripping the icy stone wall, my breath shaking as a sweet hum reverberated off of the stone.

My teeth chattered as I tried to force the word out. "H-hello?"

The cave swallowed my voice, warped it. The echo came back twisted, wrong, like something that had been dragged through the water and reshaped. It made my skin crawl. I couldn't feel anyone—not with my pathos, not with my senses. But there was something. A movement, a fluid presence, like rippling water pressing against my chest.

The Forsworn flashed through my mind. Wulfric. Halder. The river. My pulse raced as fragments of memory clawed their way back. The bridge tilting. The fall. The water closing over my head. I gritted my teeth and wrapped my arms tighter around myself. *Where was I?*

The hum grew softer, as if teasing me to follow. I forced my shaking legs to move, the cold biting into me with every step. The jagged floor was slick under my bare feet, the stone rough and unforgiving. The light from the moss dimmed further down the cave, the walls closing in, slick with dampness. I had no idea where I was going—only that standing still felt worse.

I moved toward the sound, each step echoing faintly.

The bend opened into a small chamber where a shallow pool of water shimmered with a faint, unearthly glow. The light from the moss on the walls cast a gentle radiance over the surface, shifting like liquid moonlight. At the pool's center, resting just beneath the surface, lay my mother's necklace. The smooth, green-blue stone caught the soft illumination, its reflection rippling and shifting with every step I took closer. My breath hitched as I reached the edge.

The water was impossibly still until, without warning, ripples spread out in concentric circles, distorting the image. There was no sound of a stone dropping, no movement in the air—just the ripples, alive and purposeful.

I crouched, my knees pressing into the cold, damp stone. My fingers trembled as I reached out, the tips hovering just above the surface. The water was so clear I could see every detail of the necklace, the faint thread that once rested against my neck. But as my fingers brushed the surface, the image wavered, bending and warping before disappearing entirely.

I froze, blinking at the empty pool, my hand still dripping. A soft glimmer caught my eye, and I turned sharply. Across the chamber, another pool shimmered faintly. The necklace was there now, resting at its center like an offering.

"Spirits," I muttered, my voice swallowed by the damp air. I rose and moved toward it, careful with my steps. My chest tightened, each breath growing heavier.

When I reached the second pool, the same thing happened. My hand stretched toward the necklace, and the moment my fingers brushed the water, it vanished. My pulse quickened as it reappeared in a deeper pool further ahead, the faint glow leading me into the labyrinthine cave.

A giggle broke the silence, faint and childlike. The sound sent a jolt through me, my skin prickling as it echoed off the walls. It didn't seem to come from one place—it surrounded me, layered and distant, as if the cave itself were laughing.

I swallowed hard, the sound of my breath loud in my ears as I moved toward the next pool. My steps faltered, the water's glow pulling me deeper, the echoing giggle still lingering at the edges of my mind.

The cave widened into a chamber dominated by a darker, deeper pool. Soft glows from the moss that clung to the walls painted the space with an otherworldly sheen, their faint light just strong enough to caress the water's surface. The pool reflected the surrounding shadows like polished obsidian. At the center, faintly glimmering beneath the surface, was the necklace. The sight of it filled my chest with equal parts relief and dread.

The water was still, unnervingly so, as though it waited for me to act. My stomach twisted. I didn't know how to swim—hadn't even before what had happened in Riverhalv. The memory clawed its way back: Bryn's laugh as his hand shoved me, the icy water closing over my head, my panicked kicks that only dragged me deeper. Even now, the thought makes my chest tighten.

I hesitated at the edge of the pool, my toes curling against the slick stone. The necklace shimmered faintly, as if daring me. My hands clenched and unclenched at my sides. "It's just water," I whispered to myself, the words brittle. "Waist-high. You've done harder things."

The first step was the worst. The cold bit into my legs like sharp teeth, the weight of the water pressing against my skin as I waded in. My breath came in shallow bursts, each step slower than the last. The pool wasn't deep, but the shadows it cast seemed endless.

When I was close enough to reach, I crouched, my reflection staring back at me. But it wasn't just my image. The water rippled unnaturally, the image distorting as though something darted just beneath the surface. A faint, shimmering figure flickered in the doppelganger—a flash of movement so quick it made my heart leap.

"Who's there?" My voice cracked, swallowed by the cave. Only the faint hum of the song responded, weaving through the air like a guide.

I reached for the necklace, my fingers brushing the surface. The water stirred gently, shifting the necklace just out of reach. My hand stopped mid-motion, my brow furrowing. It wasn't random. The shift felt deliberate, teasing—like it was daring me to try harder.

The hum of the song grew louder as I adjusted my stance, moving closer to the necklace. When I leaned the wrong way, the melody faded, subtle but clear. It was a game. Or a challenge.

"Alright," I murmured, steeling myself. "Let's play."

The words barely left my lips before I moved, each step careful, deliberate. The rhythm of the song swirled around me, its melody like a thread pulling me forward. I let it guide me, testing its cadence, feeling for its subtle cues. The necklace floated tantalizingly close, only to drift further with every misstep, teasing my resolve. My pulse quickened as frustration turned into determination, each failure sharpening my focus.

The cold water lapped higher, numbing my skin, but it wasn't just the temperature that sent a shiver through me. Movement flickered at the edge of my vision. I stopped, breath catching as my eyes locked on a ripple—no, a shape beneath the surface. It shifted, delicate and almost human. A graceful curve of waist and hip emerged, then the soft suggestion of a chest, slender arms trailing like ribbons in the water. My heart pounded, the moment intimate and surreal.

When I turned to see it clearly, the vision dissolved into the dark, undulating depths, leaving only ripples and silence. My breath hitched, and the chill creeping along my spine felt like a warning, as much from the water as from the game I'd begun to play.

The water grew colder as I waded in deeper, each step stealing the warmth from my skin until it felt like the river itself was leeching my strength. My teeth chattered, but I pushed forward, driven by a pull I didn't understand. My feet slid on the slippery stones beneath me until there was no more ground, just emptiness. I paddled awkwardly, my movements jerky and frantic as my legs kicked beneath me. The water churned, stinging my face. I wasn't drowning, but the fear bit at me all the same. My pulse roared in my ears, but I forced myself to keep going.

Patience. That was what it demanded. The cold, the stillness, the unspoken rules of this game—it wasn't something I could win by force. I slowed my movements, letting the water cradle me. My arms swept out carefully, my breaths steadied, and I let myself float just enough to stay above the surface.

The necklace gleamed ahead, a quiet beacon resting in a calm pocket of the pool. Its glow didn't shift, didn't dance, but seemed to wait, daring me to try again. I reached out, inching closer with deliberate care. The air and water both trembled as though holding their breath. I followed their lead, moving silently until my fingers brushed the cool surface of the stone.

Just as I closed my hand around it, another hand appeared beside mine. Faint and shimmering, its fingers brushed my own, then pulled away with a ripple that disturbed the entire pool. My heart slammed against my ribs as the water swirled. I clenched the necklace in my fist, gasping, as the presence vanished into the shadows once more.

The water surged around me, a sudden rush pulling me off balance. It rose in a swell, engulfing me completely. My arms flailed, but the current wrapped me like a fist, dragging me deeper. The humming, sweet and sharp, swelled to a crescendo, vibrating through my skull as the cave dissolved into darkness. I twisted in the torrent, my lungs burning, my chest tight. Then—light.

I broke the surface with a gasp, the air cold and thin. Water stung my eyes as I blinked against the moonlight reflecting off the river, the world spinning in fragments of silver and black. My arms thrashed, searching for purchase, but the current carried me relentlessly, the riverbanks a blur of dark shapes.

I kicked, forcing myself to stay afloat, drawing on what I'd just learned—or had I? My mind spun, fragments of the cave and the melody slipping through my thoughts like water through my fingers. Was it a dream? No, it was night, the moon high above, silver light glinting off the waves. How long had I been out? We'd left in the morning. It didn't feel that long. My movements felt heavier now, the weight of damp clothes pulling at me. I hadn't been wearing them in the cave. When had they returned? The thought only added to the disorientation, the gaps in my memory widening with every passing moment.

My hands skimmed the surface, slow and deliberate, pushing the water away in steady strokes. Each movement felt measured, careful, like I had done it a hundred times before. I paddled toward the faint shadow of the shore, inching closer with every agonizing pull. My arms screamed, my breath burned in my chest, but I refused to stop. The necklace. My fingers tightened around it, the stone cool and solid in my palm, the only anchor in the chaos.

The river finally spat me out, and I collapsed onto the bank, coughing and heaving as mud and grit scraped against my hands. I lay there, drenched and shaking, the cold seeping into my bones. The forest around me shimmered faintly under the moonlight, broken beams cutting through the canopy, painting the ground in fractured silver.

I sat up slowly, dragging my knees to my chest. My clothes clung to me, heavy and soaked through. My bow lay beside me, the string limp and useless for now, my axe still strapped to my belt. My fingers uncurled, and there it was—the necklace.

It was the same, but it wasn't. The green-blue stone glimmered faintly, the light catching a sheen that hadn't been there before—or was it a flaw, a crack too fine to feel? I ran my thumb over it, the surface smooth but different, almost alive. The melody, faint now, still echoed in the back of my mind, distant but persistent, like a whisper I couldn't quite shake.

I let my head fall back, staring at the sky. My chest rose and fell in slow, deliberate breaths as I sat on the bank, dripping and exhausted. The forest was quiet, save for the steady rhythm of the river behind me. Right then, it was just me, the night, and whatever had left me there.

Chapter 9 - Riding

The cold clung to me, seeping into my skin and settling in my chest like a stone. My clothes hung heavy and wet, clinging to me with every step as I tried to steady my breath. The necklace lay cool against my palm, its cord tangled in my fingers. I shoved it back around my neck, the familiar weight somehow comforting despite everything.

I couldn't stay there. The moon hung high above the trees, casting pale light through the swaying branches. I needed to find Wulfric, Peter, and Svend. If they'd crossed, they were ahead of me now, somewhere in the forest. I forced my legs to move, each step sluggish and uneven as I trudged toward what I thought was the direction of the bridge.

It took me longer than I'd expected. The forest stretched on, shadows twisting and blurring with the moonlight. My teeth chattered as I stumbled over roots and through tangles of brush. The air smelled damp and earthy, the lingering scent of moss clinging to the back of my throat. Finally, I saw it: the bridge, or what was left of it.

The ropes still swayed slightly, creaking faintly in the breeze. The missing planks gaped like broken teeth, the one Peter had cracked and the one I'd fallen through glaring reminders. My stomach twisted, a sour knot of unease.

I stepped closer, my boots sinking into the soft dirt of the bank. The bridge loomed above the river, the water below black and roiling in the moonlight. My reflection stared back at me in shards, rippled and unsteady, and I looked away.

Their trail wasn't hard to find. The churned-up earth where

Halder's hooves had stamped a path was impossible to miss, even in the dim light. Peter's boots had left deep prints beside it, his uneven strides breaking twigs and crushing leaves. Svend's steps were lighter but deliberate, his pace steady. Wulfric's were broad and sure, the weight of his stride pressed firmly into the forest floor.

I followed the path, the faint rustle of leaves and distant chirping of night insects keeping me company. The trail wound through the trees, twisting and looping like a thread unraveling. My fingers brushed the rough bark of a tree as I steadied myself, the damp moss cold against my skin.

The forest pressed closer around me, the moonlight breaking through in patches, guiding my way. Clenching my fists, focusing on the tracks ahead. My body was aching, my lungs heavy, but I kept moving. I didn't know how far they'd gone, but I wouldn't stop until I found them.

By the time I stumbled into their camp, my legs felt like stone, stiff and unyielding. Every step was a battle, my teeth chattering so hard I thought they'd crack. The firelight flickered through the trees, the faint warmth drawing me like a moth. My breath came in harsh gasps, visible in the frigid night air.

The brush crackled underfoot as I pushed through, and the reaction was immediate. Halder reared slightly, his ears pinned back as he let out a sharp whinny. Peter shot to his feet, his hand on the hilt of his blade. "Spirits' teeth, what the—" His words were drowned out by the scrape of steel as he drew his weapon.

Svend followed suit, fumbling with his belt as he yanked out a dagger. "A nix," he hissed, his eyes wide and wild. "Come to drag us under."

"Stop being fools!" Wulfric's bark cut through the chaos like a blade. He stepped forward, raising a hand to calm Halder, his eyes fixed on me. "Tomi?"

I swayed on my feet, barely able to lift my arms in surrender. My voice cracked, weak and hoarse. "It's me."

Peter didn't lower his blade. His face was pale, his lips pressed into a thin line. "You were dead, boy. Dragged down. We saw it."

"Doesn't look dead to me," Wulfric said sharply. He stepped between Peter and me, one hand on Peter's arm. "Put the damned blade away before you hurt yourself."

Peter hesitated, his eyes narrowing as he looked at me. "If you're not a nix, what in the spirits are you then?"

"Cold," I managed, my voice shaking as much as the rest of me. "And tired."

That seemed to be enough for Wulfric. He clapped Peter on the shoulder hard enough to make him wince, forcing him to sheath his weapon. "Go on, sit down. You're embarrassing yourself."

Peter muttered a curse under his breath but obeyed, slumping back onto his log. Svend stayed where he was, still clutching his dagger, his knuckles white.

Wulfric turned back to me, his brows furrowed. "What happened, lad? We looked for you all day. Thought you were gone."

I shook my head, my fingers clumsily unfastening the soaked cord of my cloak. "I fell in. Lost consciousness. Woke up downriver." My words came haltingly, my throat dry and raw. "I followed your trail."

Wulfric studied me for a long moment, his eyes sharp. "And that's it?"

I nodded, though the memory of the dream—if it was a dream—and the figure in the water flickered in my mind like an unspoken question. "That's it."

"Spirits' breath," Peter muttered, throwing up his hands. "He's a damn wraith, that's what he is."

"Enough," Wulfric snapped, his tone leaving no room for

argument. "Get him a blanket, Svend. And stew. He's earned that much."

Svend moved reluctantly, handing me a coarse wool blanket before ladling a steaming bowl of stew into a wooden bowl. I took it with trembling hands, the heat radiating through my palms.

I sank down near the fire, the blanket wrapped tightly around me. The warmth of the stew and the flames seeped into me slowly, chasing away the chill that had taken root in my bones. The broth was salty and thick, tasting of root vegetables and meat, and I ate it as if I hadn't eaten in days.

Peter scowled from across the fire, muttering to himself. "I'll tell you one thing, nix or not, he's lucky we didn't leave him behind."

"Shut your mouth and go to sleep," Wulfric growled, settling himself near Halder. The horse was calmer now, his dark eyes watching me as if still unsure.

The camp quieted. The fire crackled softly, the only sound in the still night. I leaned back against the rough bark of a tree, my body heavy with exhaustion. The necklace lay cool against my chest, its weight grounding me as I finally closed my eyes.

By morning, the fire had done its job. My clothes were stiff but dry, the warmth of the flames lingering in my bones. The soreness in my limbs from the river's grip remained, but I didn't complain. It was better than being cold and wet.

The next few days passed in a steady rhythm. Wulfric and Svend carried on as they always did—Wulfric with his gruff steadiness and Svend with his easy-going humor. Peter, on the other hand, couldn't seem to shake his suspicion. He kept stealing glances at me, his lips pressed into a thin line, muttering to himself whenever I got too close.

I spent most of the time scouting ahead. It gave me space and kept me from having to meet Peter's glare. I'd range through the undergrowth, listening for signs of movement or studying the faint paths of game trails, and when I returned, I'd take Halder's reins from Wulfric for a time. The horse snorted at me occasionally but seemed to tolerate my company well enough.

One afternoon, as the sun broke through the forest canopy in long, golden beams, Wulfric tugged Halder to a stop and turned to me. "You keep walking beside him like that, lad," he said, "you'll wear out your legs before we're halfway there."

I frowned, unsure what he was getting at. "What else am I supposed to do?"

Wulfric raised an eyebrow. "Ride him. You've got the look of someone who could use a rest."

Peter let out a dry laugh from behind us. "That'll be a sight."

"Quiet, you," Wulfric barked, his voice sharp. "Tomi's more use than you on most days." He turned back to me, his tone softer. "It's time you learned proper. Get up."

It wasn't a request. Wulfric showed me how to place my foot in the stirrup and swing my leg over Halder's broad back. My first attempt was clumsy, nearly earning me a faceful of dirt when the horse shifted beneath me, but Wulfric's steady hand on the reins kept Halder calm.

"You've got to sit straight," he said, his voice carrying the authority of someone who'd done this a thousand times. "Keep your back straight, legs steady, but don't grip too tight. You'll wear yourself out."

I adjusted as best I could, though the horse's movements felt foreign under me. "Like this?"

"Close enough," Wulfric said with a chuckle. "Now hold the reins—not too tight, you're guiding him, not strangling him."

The first few hours were a struggle. Halder seemed to sense my inexperience, testing me with subtle shifts and stops. Peter's occasional snickers from behind didn't help. But Wulfric was patient, barking corrections when I leaned too far forward or let the reins go slack. "It's not a fight, lad," he'd say. "It's a conversation. You ask; he listens."

By the second day, I found my rhythm. The sway of Halder's gait became familiar, less like being tossed on a restless sea and more like moving with the tide. On open stretches where the trees thinned, Wulfric urged me to try a faster pace. Halder's hooves thundered against the ground, the wind whipping past my face as I clung to the reins. It was exhilarating, even when I almost lost my balance more than once.

By the end of the third day, I could guide Halder without constant correction from Wulfric. The horse responded to subtle pulls on the reins and gentle shifts in my weight. When I dismounted that evening, my legs ached in a way they never had from walking, but there was a sense of pride in it. I could feel Halder's warmth through the fabric of my trousers, the steady rise and fall of his breathing. I ran a hand down his neck, murmuring thanks as he nickered softly in response.

Wulfric clapped me on the back, his grin broad. "Not bad for a first-timer. Told you he'd be a good teacher."

Halder snorted as if agreeing, and I couldn't help but laugh.

The days blurred together as we pressed on, the forest stretching endlessly ahead. As we walked, the stone around my neck felt heavier than it should, its smooth surface cold against my chest. I couldn't stop fiddling with it, my fingers brushing over its faint sheen as if trying to make sense of the unfamiliar weight. My pathos, usually quiet unless I reached for it, seemed to hum faintly whenever I touched the stone. It wasn't a voice exactly, more like a ripple in still water, something just out of reach.

Peter's grumbles filled the silence more often than I liked. "Nice for some, getting to ride the beast every other stretch," he muttered, his eyes flicking toward Halder as I guided him through the trees.

"Maybe if you stopped whining, he'd like you better," Wulfric said, his tone light but laced with warning.

I smirked but kept my focus ahead. Halder's emotions came through clearer now—impatience when the terrain slowed him, contentment when we found a smooth trail, irritation whenever Peter got too close. It was strange but comforting, as though the horse and I had reached some quiet understanding.

When I wasn't riding, I'd walk beside him, my hand resting lightly on his flank. I could feel his steady pulse, his warmth bleeding into my palm like the reassuring presence of an old friend. It made Peter's sharp looks easier to ignore.

Our pace was quicker than the Forsworn's had been during their frantic escape. Without the burden of fifty exhausted bodies, we moved like breeze through the leaves, the days slipping by faster than I'd expected. It wasn't long before the familiar signs of Elkswood began to appear—the dense undergrowth, the sharp tang of pine in the air, the faint rustle of life all around.

The closer we got, the more restless I became. I found myself scouting ahead more often, not just to escape Peter's pointed silences but because I needed the space to think. My pathos prickled constantly, the faint hum of the stone mingling with the emotions of the men behind me and the life around us. When I stretched it out further, the forest responded in whispers—birds startled into flight, a hare darting through the brush, the faint trail of something larger moving in the distance.

Near the road, that hum shifted. It was louder, sharper, pressing against my senses like a rising tide. I crouched low, focusing, and felt it—a mass of emotions, a crowd gathered too close for comfort. My stomach tightened.

I moved closer, my steps careful and deliberate, until the shapes came into view. Dozens of people, maybe more, clustered near a bend in the road. Most were on foot, a few on horseback. Their faces were indistinct at this distance, but their movements were purposeful, their energy humming with tension.

I crept back, my heart pounding. Wulfric needed to see it. Whatever they were, whoever they were, it wasn't good to stumble on them blind. Halder flicked his ears at me as I approached, sensing my unease. I placed a hand on his neck to calm us both, then turned to Wulfric and the others.

"There's something ahead," I said, my voice low. "A lot of people. You'll want to see for yourself."

We crept through the underbrush, the sounds of shouting and steel clashing growing louder as we approached the road. The sharp tang of iron filled the air, mingling with the acrid scent of smoke. I crouched low beside Wulfric, Halder's reins clutched tightly in my hand. Through the breaks in the trees, the scene unfolded like a living nightmare.

Men in Prince Harlan's colors—red banners with a heart pierced by a sword—fought fiercely against Erik's soldiers, marked by the raven emblem stitched onto their tabards. The battle was chaos, raw and unrelenting, bodies colliding in a frenzied storm of blades and shouts. Blood spattered the dirt, staining the road dark, while the wounded staggered or fell without a sound.

Svend let out a low whistle. "Didn't think the princes would go at it this soon. The frost isn't even on the ground yet."

Wulfric's expression was grim, his jaw tight. "This won't be the first skirmish. They'll want their men's blood boiling before winter sets in. Easier to get them to march when they're already angry and hungry for more."

Svend shifted uneasily, his eyes on the melee. "A lot of bodies out there for a warm-up."

"More to come," Wulfric said. "Harlan and Erik won't stop until one's dead or they're too broken to fight anymore."

Peter snorted softly. "That's the problem with royalty—they never seem to know when to stay in their own bloody keeps."

The words hit harder than I expected. My mind flicked to Sanne, her steady gaze hiding years of being locked away, her voice tinged with bitterness every time she spoke of her uncle. And Niklas—her brother, trapped even now in Erik's grasp, groomed to become another pawn in a game neither of them had chosen to play. I could still hear Sanne's words: *I'll never be free, Tomi. Not truly.*

I stared at the chaos before us, wondering if this was what freedom meant for princes and kings—war, blood, and the bodies of men who'd never even met them.

The sound of splintering wood drew our attention as a wagon overturned near the edge of the fray, spilling supplies and bodies into the dirt. A horse screamed, its rider dragged down into the crush of men. My stomach twisted at the sight, the sheer brutality of it. I turned my gaze to the forest floor, gripping Halder's reins tighter.

"We'll want to avoid the roads, then," Peter said, his voice tight.

"No question there," Wulfric replied, his eyes never leaving the battle. "We'll swing wide, stay in the trees."

We veered away from the road, cutting through the forest to avoid the chaos of the battle and the unpredictable dangers of travelers desperate or bold enough to use the paths. The air was cooler under the trees, the canopy thick with late-summer green, but the tension in our group hadn't eased. Each snap of a branch, each distant birdcall, had us glancing over our shoulders.

The forest gave way to a clearing, and the ruins of the old fort came into view. It had never been much—just a broken shell of stone and timber—but now it looked worse. Walls that once held back the forest had crumbled into heaps of rubble. The gate hung loose, splintered and half-embedded in the dirt. The scent of damp wood and earth lingered, thick in the still air.

I walked beside Wulfric, Peter and Svend trailing a few paces behind. Halder snorted softly at my side, his breath misting in the cool air. My eyes swept the scene, taking in the remnants of what had been the Forsworn's refuge. It wasn't just abandoned—it had been left in a hurry.

Wulfric stopped just inside what had once been the courtyard, his boots grinding against scattered stones. "Looks like they took your warning, lad," he said quietly, his voice a low rumble. His hand rested on the hilt of his axe as he surveyed the wreckage.

Peter kicked at a loose plank with the tip of his boot, the wood cracking under the pressure. "No one sticks around when there's trouble breathing down their necks," he muttered. His gaze flicked to me, suspicious and sharp. "What about you? Can you track where they went?"

I hesitated, crouching to inspect the ground. The dirt was churned up, boots and wagon wheels etched faintly into the earth, but the signs were old. Rains had washed away most of the detail, leaving only fragmented impressions. Two distinct paths veered away from the fort—one leading toward the road, the other deeper into the forest.

"I can try," I said finally, brushing my fingers over a faint mark in the dirt. "But it's been too long. The rains didn't help, and there were too many people. Two groups, large enough to blur everything together."

Wulfric grunted, his eyes narrowing as he followed the direction of the tracks. "Two groups splitting up means they were planning for trouble. Smart."

"Smart doesn't mean safe," Peter added, his voice tight. His hand drifted to the sword at his side, his gaze lingering on me. "We'd better stay sharp."

Wulfric turned toward him, his expression unreadable. "Aye, Peter. We're staying sharp."

The unease settled over us like a damp fog as we moved deeper into the ruins, each of us scanning the shadows for signs of life—or worse.

The air around the ruins felt too still, too quiet. My pathos prickled faintly, and I stopped short, straining to make sense of the feeling. It wasn't an animal. My senses stretched further, latching onto something sharp, raw—someone was near. I turned my head slightly toward Wulfric and whispered, "I hear something."

His brow furrowed, and he leaned closer, keeping his voice low. "Young ears too," he muttered, then gestured for us to follow.

We moved slowly, the forest swallowing our footsteps as we followed the faint trail. It twisted through the underbrush, leading us toward a clearing where a crude makeshift camp came into view. Bottles of wine lay scattered like forgotten relics among crumpled bedding and scraps of food. The smell hit me first—a sour tang of old drink and something worse.

Peter wrinkled his nose, waving a hand in front of his face. "Smells like piss."

Before anyone could respond, a man stumbled out from behind a bush, fumbling with his hose. His face was ruddy, his hair sticking to his forehead with sweat. He froze, eyes wide, as Wulfric stepped forward.

"Dugal," Wulfric said, his tone sharp and cold.
Dugal's head snapped up, his panic plain. He tried to run, yanking up his hose as he scrambled backward. His foot caught on a root, and he went down hard, landing in a sprawl with his pants around his knees.
Svend crossed his arms, smirking faintly. "Drunk."
Peter snorted. "Pissed as an old man's fart."

Wulfric closed the gap, reaching down and hauling Dugal to his feet. The man swayed, blinking blearily as his gaze tried to focus. "W-Wulfric?" he stammered, recognition dawning slowly.
Wulfric's grip tightened on his arm. "What happened here? Where is everyone?"
Dugal's face crumpled, his body going slack. "Cedric's men," he mumbled, his voice thick. "They came, and the others... they were taken. I—I couldn't—" He broke off, shaking his head violently.
"You were meant to protect them!" Wulfric's voice was like a growl, his hand shaking Dugal hard enough that his head snapped back and forth. "You were supposed to be there for them!"
Dugal let out a strangled sob, his knees buckling as he clutched at Wulfric's arm. "Donn," he whispered, the name tumbling out like a broken prayer. "Donn, Donn. He was like a brother to me. More."

The mention of Donn's name hit Wulfric like a blow, and his grip loosened slightly. Donn had died in a raid the year before, his loss leaving a deep scar on all of them—but none more than Dugal.

Svend stepped forward, placing a steadying hand on Wulfric's shoulder. "Easy," he said, his voice soft but firm. "Let him talk."

Wulfric exhaled sharply, shoving Dugal back onto a fallen log. Svend crouched down, his tone turning friendlier. "Dugal, listen. Where did they take them? The women, the children, Jory—where are they?"

Dugal sniffed hard, wiping his face with a dirty sleeve. "Whitestone," he said finally, his voice trembling. "They took them to Whitestone."

Chapter 10 - Time to Scout

Whitestone sat perched on the cliffside, its pale walls rising like sentinels carved from the same stark stone that lined the riverbanks below. The fortress wasn't massive, but it didn't need to be. Its presence alone commanded the landscape, a barrier of white against the dark, churning river that reflected fragments of gray sky and jagged rock. The road sloped gently downward, curving along the water's edge, offering glimpses of the fort through the trees—a stark reminder of its dominance over this stretch of land.

The fort's position was deliberate—a natural stronghold perched high above the water, with a narrow bridge connecting it to the main road. From that vantage, its defenders could spot anyone approaching from miles away. The white stone seemed to glow, even under the muted light, its surface weathered but imposing, as if carved from the bones of the earth itself.

Banners fluttered in the breeze, bearing the crest of Cedric's forces—a green field with a red dragon rearing above it. Men milled about the outer walls, their armor catching stray rays of light as they moved with purpose. A group of soldiers stood clustered near the gate, their conversation punctuated by sharp laughter. Others walked along the road, some leading horses laden with supplies, others in pairs or groups, their swords and spears glinting.

On the far side, below the fortress, barges floated lazily along the river, tied up to wooden posts driven into the rocky bank. I could see a small dock built into the cliffside, soldiers hauling crates and barrels onto the shore. The movement was constant, an efficient rhythm of loading and unloading.

A pair of guards on the road passed close enough that I could hear snippets of their conversation—a shared joke, followed by a gruff laugh. Their expressions were weary but alert, eyes scanning the treeline. One adjusted the strap of his shield while the other rested his hand casually on the hilt of his sword.

The fortress didn't look impenetrable, but it felt untouchable. Every path to it was watched, every corner reinforced by stone and vigilance. It was a cage, cleanly carved, and the thought of what lay inside—Jory, and the others—sent a sharp twist through my stomach.

It had taken us days to reach Whitestone, days filled with contemplation broken only by the sound of footsteps and Halder's steady breathing. During that time, Wulfric had gotten the full story out of Dugal. The man was still pale, jittery, as if each word he spoke was pulling teeth.

Wulfric crouched by the fire, poking the embers with a stick. "Alright, Dugal," he said, his voice low but insistent. "From the start."

Dugal ran a hand through his hair, the greasy strands sticking up at odd angles. "Jory came back quick after we got the boy's warning," he began, not meeting anyone's eyes. "He knew we couldn't outrun Cedric's men, not with the injured and the little ones slowing us down."

My chest tightened. I could see Jory's face in my mind—friendly but cautious, always looking for a way out.

"He split us up," Dugal continued. "Women, children, and the hurt, he sent them to a village with burnt out fields… Lon… Lin… Linden. Figured it was far enough out of the way to keep them safe."

The name hit me like a blow. "Linden?" I said, my voice barely a whisper. "That's where I'm from."

Wulfric glanced at me, his face softening. "Sorry, lad."

I nodded, swallowing the lump rising in my throat. My mother. My father. All the things we'd lost there, burned with the fields. I didn't need to see it again to know what dark spirits waited in that place.

Dugal rubbed the back of his neck. "The rest of us—those who could hold a blade—we went to meet Cedric's forces. A dozen against fifty. We knew it was a death sentence, but Jory didn't want them to follow the others."

Wulfric's hand stilled over the fire. "And?"

Dugal's gaze dropped to the ground. "We fought. Some of us died quick. Some... not so quick. Jory and a few others were taken. Five, I think, maybe six." He took a shaky breath. "I got knocked out. Woke up a day later, half-buried under the brush. The rest were gone."

Wulfric's expression darkened, his shoulders taut. "You were supposed to protect them," he growled. "Be there for them."

Dugal flinched, shrinking under Wulfric's glare. "I tried! Donn..." His voice cracked, his eyes welling up. "Donn was like a brother to me. More than a brother. I couldn't... I couldn't leave him."

The name lingered in the air, jagged and unhealed, like an old wound torn open anew. Donn had been dead for over a year, though Dugal spoke of him as if the loss were fresh. His fractured mind bore the weight of grief that felt to me like shards of shattered glass, each thought sharp and painful, scattered too widely to piece back together. Wulfric drew a deep breath, his anger simmering to embers, though his voice still carried the precision of a blade slicing clean through. "You should've stayed with the living."

I clenched my fists, the firelight casting flickering shadows across my face. "We have to get them back."

Wulfric shook his head, his voice weary. "Hold on, lad. We don't know the situation. We don't know what condition they're in—"

"We'll find out," I snapped, my voice rising.

Wulfric started to reply, but Svend cut him off. "The boy's right," he said, leaning forward, his gaze steady. "We can't just leave them there."

To my surprise, Peter—always the first to complain—nodded. "They're our men. It's as simple as that."

Wulfric sighed, rubbing a hand over his face. "You lot will be the death of me," he muttered. Then he straightened, his eyes hardening. "Fine. But this isn't some reckless charge. We will check out the situation first, scout. We plan. We move smart. Understood?"

We all nodded, determination hardening in the space between us. The fire crackled, its embers drifting into the dark, and in that moment, Whitestone wasn't just a fortress. It was a promise.

Now, that promise stood before us, carved into the cliffside like a pale scar. The fortress loomed in the distance, its stark stone walls cutting against the gray sky. From the cover of the tree line, I could make out figures on the battlements, their movements sharp and deliberate. A pair of banners flapped lazily in the breeze—one bearing the dragon crest of Cedric, the other unmarked, likely that of a local lord.

Peter crouched beside me, his expression sour. "There's too many. Couple dozen at least. What's he got so many here for? Expecting an army?"

Svend shifted, his hand resting lightly on the hilt of his blade. "It's not just us. They're on edge because of the war. Bound to be more patrols, more eyes. They're ready for trouble."

Dugal, slumped against a tree trunk, squinted at him. "War? Since when is there a war?"

Wulfric shot him a look sharp enough to cut. "While you were busy drinking yourself stupid in the woods, the princes decided to start their little dance again."

Dugal blinked, his face slack with disbelief. "What do you mean? How? We—"

"We helped," Wulfric growled, cutting him off. "Now shut your mouth before someone hears us."

I pressed my back against the bark of a tree, frustration burning in my chest. I wasn't there for the politics. I was there for Jory and the others. My fingers tightened around the string of my bow, the damp wood creaking faintly.

Wulfric's gaze swept over the fort again, his lips pressed into a grim line. "Right now, with just us and what little we've got in our packs, there's no way in hell we're getting in there. Not with them armed to the teeth."

"What do you mean, no way?" I hissed, my frustration spilling over. "We can't just leave Jory and the others there!"

Wulfric turned to me, his voice low but hard. "And what happens when we get caught, Tomi? What happens when we're chained up next to them—or worse?"

Peter's face darkened, and he jabbed a finger in Wulfric's direction. "He's right, Wulfric. They're our men. You expect us to turn around and pretend like they're already dead?"

Svend nodded, his usually calm demeanor edged with tension. "We've made it this far. We know where they are. If we go back now, what's to stop them from being moved—or worse?"

Wulfric sighed heavily, rubbing his shoulder where the arrow had struck him during their raid a year ago. When Dugal had lost Donn. The movement seemed almost unconscious, as though the ache was a weight on more than just his body. "You think I don't want to get them out? I do. But what do we have, really? Four of us and a horse? What do we do when we're surrounded?"

I clenched my fists, the string of my bow biting into my palm. "We've come this far. We owe it to them to try."

Dugal, leaning against the tree, muttered, "He's not wrong, Wulfric. If it were you in there, we wouldn't think twice."

Peter's sour tone sharpened. "So what's it going to be? We sneak in, get Jory and the others, and get out. We've done worse with less."

"That's madness," Wulfric said, his voice rising slightly. "We don't even know what condition they're in. They could be chained, under constant watch, or half-dead. We walk into that, we might not walk out."

"Then we scout," Svend countered. "We don't charge the gate like fools. We figure out the layout, see where the weak spots are. But if we leave them here, we might not get another chance."

Wulfric shifted uncomfortably, his fingers pressing harder against his shoulder. "And when Cedric sends more men here, knowing they've got prisoners worth holding? You don't think they'll fortify this place even more?"

Peter let out a harsh laugh. "You're just making excuses. We've faced worse odds before."

I looked at Wulfric, my chest tight with anger and desperation. "If you want to turn back, fine. But I'm going in. I've been locked up before, and I wouldn't wish it on anyone—not even the people who hate me."

Wulfric's jaw tightened, his gaze flicking between each of us. For a moment, he didn't speak. The tension in the air was thick, the forest around us eerily silent except for the distant sound of the river. He rubbed his shoulder again, his hand pausing there as if weighing the ache against the risk.

Finally, he let out a long breath. "Alright. We scout. We take a closer look, find out what we're dealing with. But I'm telling you now—one misstep, and we're finished. We move quiet, and we don't act without a plan. Clear?"

Peter nodded, his scowl softening slightly. "Clear."

Svend clapped Wulfric on the back, a rare smile breaking through. "That's the Wulfric I know."

I met Wulfric's gaze, my resolve hardening. "We'll make it work."

His shoulders relaxed, just slightly, as he glanced toward the fort. "Let's hope so, lad. Let's hope so."

We moved quietly through the dense forest, each step deliberate, the fortress fading behind layers of shadow and bark. The trees closed in around us, their trunks standing like silent sentinels. Halder's steady breathing and the occasional rustle of leaves were the only sounds that broke the uneasy silence. When we finally stopped, it was in a hollow tucked deep within the woods, where brambles and underbrush wove a natural wall around us.

Wulfric crouched, drawing a rough map into the dirt with the tip of his knife. "Here's how it's going to go," he said, his voice low but firm. "Tomi, Svend, you're taking the perimeter. Split up once you're close. Svend, head toward the river, see if there's anything along the banks worth noting—weak points, patrols, anything. Tomi, stick to the walls. Keep your eyes open."

Svend nodded, the glint of determination in his eyes. I swallowed hard, my pulse quickening. Wulfric's gaze landed on Peter. "You take the road. Watch for anyone moving in or out. No heroics—just eyes and ears. If you see anything, don't engage. Pull back."

Peter muttered under his breath but gave a sharp nod. "Yeah, yeah. Watch the road, don't get caught. Simple enough."

Wulfric straightened, his hand resting on the hilt of his blade as he turned toward Dugal. Dugal, who had been silent until now, glanced up, his brow furrowed. "What about me? What am I supposed to do?"

Wulfric's jaw tightened. "You're staying here."

Dugal bristled, his face flushing. "Why? I can—"

"You can stay put," Wulfric cut him off, his voice like the crack of a whip. "Right now, I can't trust you to keep your head. And if something happens to Halder because you're off chasing spirits or drowning yourself in the river, we're done."

Dugal flinched as though struck, his mouth opening and closing before he looked down. "Fine," he muttered, his voice raw. "I'll stay."

Wulfric's eyes lingered on him for a moment, then shifted back to the rest of us. "You've got until sundown. If you're not back by then, we're moving without you."

I tightened the strap on my bow and stood, my legs tense with readiness. Svend cracked his neck and adjusted the belt that held his blade. Peter let out a low grumble, hoisting his pack over one shoulder. Halder raised his head, watching us as we moved.

Wulfric's voice cut through the quiet as we prepared to leave. "Stay low, stay quiet, and for the love of the spirits, don't get seen. One slip, and the whole thing's over. Understood?"

We nodded, the weight of his words settling like a stone in my chest. Wulfric gave a sharp motion with his hand, sending us off into the forest. The shadows deepened as I moved, my steps quiet but deliberate. Behind me, I could feel the weight of Dugal's silence and Wulfric's watchful gaze.

Svend and I moved through the forest, our pace measured and deliberate. The woods felt different there—heavier somehow, as if the trees themselves knew we were drawing closer to something dangerous. The usual symphony of birdsong and rustling leaves was muted, replaced by the crunch of our boots against the damp ground and the occasional creak of a distant branch. We didn't speak much, but when we reached a point where the underbrush grew thinner, Svend stopped and turned to me.

"Good luck, Tomi," he said, his voice low but steady.

I nodded, gripping my bow a little tighter. "You too."

We exchanged a brief glance before splitting off, him veering left along the fort's edge while I pressed forward toward the river.

The forest was quieter near the fort, the natural sounds of birdsong and rustling leaves muted under the weight of something heavier. Each step I took was deliberate, my boots pressing into the damp earth with a whisper of sound. The trees thinned as I got closer, the pale stone of Whitestone fortress rising in stark contrast against the gray sky. I paused, crouching low behind a cluster of shrubs, and peered through the gaps in the foliage.

Whitestone's walls loomed, white and imposing, with banners of Cedric's red dragon fluttering lazily in the breeze. Men patrolled the ramparts, their movements precise but not hurried. Even from the distance, I could feel their tension. My pathos stirred, the faint pulse of unease bleeding through the air. These men weren't relaxed; they were restless. Their emotions flickered in overlapping waves—agitation, worry, and the sharp edge of fear.

I crept closer, weaving between the trees, careful not to snap a branch or disturb the undergrowth. A low murmur of voices reached me, carried on the wind. I pressed myself against the trunk of an old oak and peered out. Two soldiers stood by a cluster of rocks near the wall, their swords resting loosely at their sides. They weren't talking loudly, but their words carried the weight of worry.

"...can't believe it's already started," one muttered, his voice rough.

"The princes have been spoiling for it for years," the other replied. "This was bound to happen. We're lucky it's not our blood they're spilling yet."

"Yet," the first repeated, a bitter edge to the word. "Just give it time. We'll be the ones on the front lines soon enough."

I didn't wait to hear more. My heart thudded in my chest as I slipped further along the edge of the trees, my senses stretching. The emotions around me blurred together—uncertainty and vigilance, the nervous anticipation of men who knew something was coming but didn't know when.

A sudden rustle of leaves snapped me back to the present. I froze, pressing myself into the shadows as a patrol emerged from a gap in the trees. Three men, their boots crunching against the gravelly earth, walked in a loose formation. One carried a spear, the other two swords. They didn't speak, their faces grim. I held my breath as they passed within feet of me, their gazes sweeping the forest but not lingering. My fingers itched toward the hilt of my axe, but I stayed still. They didn't see me.

When they were out of sight, I exhaled slowly, the tension in my chest easing just enough to let me move again. I kept low, skirting the edge of the trees, until I found a spot where I could see the fortress more clearly. My pathos pulsed again, reaching for something—anything—that could give me a better sense of what lay within.

The emotions came in layers, an overwhelming tide. It was too much at first, too many people, too many feelings crashing into one another. I closed my eyes, forcing myself to focus, to sift through the chaos. Then I felt it—a thread of despair, sharp and cold, cutting through the noise. It was distant, but unmistakable. Sadness, frustration, anger. The same feelings that had twisted in my chest during my time in the gaol. Yet there was something else there, thrumming with more than the negative—a well of emotions I couldn't quite pinpoint.

I opened my eyes, my gaze falling toward the lower levels of the fortress, closer to the docks. I couldn't see them from this angle, but the despair was stronger there. It lingered like a bruise, deep and throbbing. That's where they were. I was certain of it.

But there was no way in. Not from here. The walls were unbroken, the guards watchful. My fingers tightened into fists as I pulled back from the edge of the treeline. The frustration gnawed at me, but I couldn't linger. Wulfric had said not to be seen, and every moment I stayed risked breaking that.

The journey back to camp was slower, every snap of a twig or rustle of leaves setting my nerves on edge. My mind was already working through what I'd tell Wulfric and the others, but the heavy weight of despair lingered in my chest, refusing to let go.

I stepped into the hollow where we'd set up camp, my boots scraping against a root as I ducked under the low-hanging branches. The others were clustered near Halder, Wulfric standing with arms crossed, his broad frame casting a shadow over the makeshift map etched in the dirt. His head lifted as I approached, his sharp eyes locking onto mine.

"Well?" he asked, his tone rough but not unkind.

I exhaled, crouching beside him. "I found their trail," I said, my voice steady. "Guards were moving supplies toward the docks. Looked like they were keeping something—or someone—down there. Probably prisoners."

Wulfric's brow furrowed, his hand brushing over his beard. "And the way in?"

I shook my head. "Didn't see one. The place is tight, Wulfric. Guards at every angle, no gaps."

He grunted, a low sound of frustration, and leaned back against a tree. His gaze drifted toward the direction of the fort, sharp with thought.

Svend and Peter returned together, their steps heavier and their faces grim. Peter flopped down with a groan, tugging off a piece of burr stuck to his trousers. "The roads are crawling with patrols," he said, his voice edged with annoyance. "In and out, constant movement. You'd have to be invisible to cross without getting caught."

Wulfric sighed, the sound weighted like a stone dropping into still water. "Not what I wanted to hear," he muttered, rubbing the back of his neck. His eyes slid to Svend. "You got anything better?"

Svend nodded, crouching down and tracing a rough line in the dirt near the river's edge on the map. "I got close enough to see the docks," he began. "The fort gets its supplies from barges running up and down the river. If we head upriver, we could slip onto one of the barges, ride it down, and get inside through the docks."

Peter scoffed, sitting up straighter. "And what if they spot us? Toss us in the drink before we even get near?"

Svend shrugged, his expression calm but resolute. "That's a risk. But it's a better one than trying to walk through their front gate."

Wulfric's face shifted, the faintest smile tugging at the corner of his mouth. He slapped a hand against Svend's shoulder, the gesture both approving and heavy. "You've got the right of it. Once we're in, it's just a matter of finding our men. And thanks to Tomi here, we've got that part figured out."

The weight of his words pressed against my chest, but I nodded, keeping my face steady. The plan wasn't perfect—it was dangerous, and it would require more than a little luck—but it was something.

Wulfric straightened, his eyes glinting with a spark of

determination. "Get some rest. Tomorrow, we move upriver. If this works, we'll be inside those walls by nightfall."

The faint sound of the river drifted through the forest as we settled down for the night. My hand drifted to the necklace at my throat, the cool stone grounding me as I stared into the darkness.

Chapter 11 - Whitestone

The hike took us a day, each step pulling us further from the fortress and closer to the narrowing river. The air changed as we climbed higher, cooler and sharper, carrying the scent of damp earth and pine. By the time we reached the spot where the river spilled from the lake and cut into rapids, the water's roar had swallowed all other sound. The forest there was denser, shadows pooling between the trees, but the river itself was exposed, twisting white and wild as it forced its way downstream.

I perched on a thick branch of a tree leaning over the water, its bark rough beneath my hands. The leaves above filtered the light into dappled patches, casting shifting patterns over the surface of the river. Through the gaps in the greenery, I watched the barge emerge from the lake.

It was flat, its hull low and wide, built for heavy loads rather than speed. The edges were reinforced with dark wood, worn smooth from years of use. A waxed cloth tarp stretched over the center, covering crates and barrels stacked tightly beneath. At the front, two men stood armed with spears, their stances tense despite the gentle rocking of the barge. The steersmen at the back fought the current with long poles, pushing against the river's pull as it quickened into the rapids.

The barge swayed, the guards shifting their weight to stay upright. Their armor caught the pale light filtering through the trees, dull but serviceable. One of them barked an order to the steersmen, his voice barely audible over the rush of water. The other scanned the banks, his eyes darting over the trees, never lingering long enough to catch me.

I drew a deep breath, holding it for a moment before releasing it slowly through my nose. My fingers flexed around the bow resting in my lap, the string taut beneath my thumb. My heart thudded in my chest, steady but hard. As the barge drew closer, I felt every nerve sharpen, every sense tune itself to the moment.

The river was no friend here. The current tore at the edges of the barge, dragging it forward, giving the steersmen less and less control. Svend had been right. They'd be too busy wrestling the water to notice us. That didn't make it any easier to watch them approach.

I focused on the movement of the guards, on the way their boots shifted and their spears angled toward the unknown. The leaves above me rustled softly in the breeze, blending with the river's relentless roar. I gripped the branch beneath me, steadying myself as the barge slid closer, the men aboard oblivious to the ambush waiting in the trees.

The river rushed below me, its surface fractured into foaming streaks of white where it met the jagged rocks. It churned violently, as if daring anything to try and master it. I should've been terrified—spirits, a part of me was—but instead, my thoughts settled on the cool weight of my mother's necklace against my skin. Its smooth surface rested lightly above my chest, a quiet, steadying anchor.

The barge drew closer, its flat hull cutting through the water. The guards at the bow shifted uneasily, their boots scuffing against the wooden planks. The steersman at the back fought with their poles, bracing against the rapid current that dragged the vessel forward. The tarp-covered cargo swayed slightly with the barge's movements, its edges flapping weakly in the breeze.

I clenched the branch beneath me, muscles coiled. A breath in. A heartbeat. The barge passed directly below. I let go.

The impact jarred through my legs as I landed squarely on the tarp, the wood beneath the fabric groaning under my weight. My arms shot out to balance myself, the shifting surface threatening to send me tumbling. The guards spun around at the noise, shouts ripping from their throats. My heart raced, but I forced my body to move.

In one motion, I slung my bow off my shoulder, notched an arrow, and leveled it at the steersman. The string hummed against my fingers, the point of the arrow aimed dead at his chest.

The man froze mid-motion, his pole dipping into the water. His face paled, his eyes darting between the arrow and my face. He was older, with streaks of gray in his hair, but his fear made him look young. His lips parted, trembling, as if searching for words that wouldn't come.

"Don't," I said, my voice low but steady.

Behind me, boots thudded against the deck. The guards were moving closer, their shouts sharper now, their weapons scraping against their belts as they drew them. I kept my arrow trained on the steersman, my body tensed like a bowstring. His knuckles whitened on the pole, his breaths coming fast and shallow.

"Stay where you are," I growled at the guards without turning. The steersman's eyes widened further, sweat beading along his temple. The current tugged at the barge, a deep rumble beneath the chaos, as the moment stretched, thin and taut like the string in my hand.

The barge jolted beneath me, the uneven motion sending a fresh rush of adrenaline through my veins. Behind me, the sharp thuds of boots on wood cut through the river's roar, followed by the heavy sound of bodies colliding. I stole a glance over my shoulder.

Wulfric was a blur of motion, his thick arm swinging down to catch one of the guards square across the back of the head. The man dropped like a sack of grain, his weapon clattering to the deck. Svend wasn't so lucky. His target, broader and quicker, dodged the first blow and turned on him with a snarl. Svend ducked under the swing of a blade and lunged forward, wrapping his arms around the man's neck in a headlock.

"Little help here?" Svend grunted, struggling as the guard twisted and kicked against him.

Meanwhile, Peter was in a comical battle of his own. Half his body was sprawled on the barge, the other dangling precariously over the rushing water. His fingers scrabbled for purchase on the slick wood. "For the love of—someone pull me up!" he shouted, voice tight with panic.

"Well, that went smooth," Svend managed between heavy breaths, still wrestling his opponent, whose weight pressed him into the deck.

Wulfric grunted, striding toward Peter. With one hand, he grabbed the man by the back of his tunic and hauled him fully onto the barge. "Keep your legs inside next time," Wulfric muttered. Then he turned to the steersman, who was frozen in place, his hands trembling on the pole. "You. Keep steering."

The steersman gave a quick, jerky nod, his wide eyes flicking between Wulfric and the unconscious guard sprawled on the deck.

The barge tilted slightly as it glided toward the shallows, the river's pull weakening. Wulfric barked orders, his voice steady and commanding. "Strip them down. Tie them up. We'll leave them with the steersman."

Svend and I worked quickly, fingers fumbling with the knots as we secured the guards and the steersman to the base of a tree. The steersman, pale and shaking, glanced between us, his voice wavering. "What... what's going to happen to us?"

Svend straightened, brushing his hands on his trousers. "If you're clever, you'll wriggle out in a day or two," he said, his tone light, almost casual. Then he added with a wry grin, "Just watch your toes until then—boars'll have them right off if you're not careful."

The steersman's face turned an even lighter shade, his mouth opening and closing like he wanted to argue but couldn't find the words. The absurdity of Svend's comment tugged a chuckle from me, cutting through the lingering tension.

One of the guards groaned, his eyes fluttering open. He struggled against the ropes, his voice rising in anger. "You won't get away with this! Lord Cedric will—"

Wulfric cut him off with a swift motion, shoving a wad of cloth into the man's mouth. "Hush now. You're giving me a headache."

The guard's muffled protests faded into low, frustrated grumbles. Wulfric straightened, brushing his hands off on his trousers. His gaze swept over the group, his expression as calm as ever, though there was a sharpness in his eyes. "Let's move. This is only the start."

The barge bobbed gently as I climbed back on, the chill of the river still clinging to me. Peter had taken over at the rudder, his face set in a grimace as he tested the creaking wheel.

Wulfric and Svend moved quickly, stripping the guards' clothes and armor. Svend managed to fasten the mismatched pieces without much trouble, but Wulfric's broad shoulders strained against the leather straps and buckles.

I couldn't help myself. "Armor might be a little small for you," I said, a hint of a grin tugging at the corners of my mouth.

Wulfric chuckled, adjusting the chest plate with a shrug. "It'll do. Better than showing up bare-chested, eh?"

He turned his attention to the tarp, lifting a corner to inspect the cargo beneath. Wooden crates were stacked tightly, some with wax seals on the lids, others bound with thick rope. He rifled through one, pulling out a jar of honey and holding it up to the light. "Honey, dried fish, wheat… Looks like they're keeping the soldiers well-fed."

Svend grunted, adjusting his helmet. "Wish we'd taken this one upstream instead of down."

Wulfric replaced the jar and turned to us, his face serious now. "Here's the plan. Svend and I will go in wearing these," he said, gesturing to the ill-fitting armor. "Tomi, you'll stay hidden in the cargo. Peter, you stay with the boat."

Peter's eyebrows shot up. "Stay with the boat? What if you don't come back, eh? I'll be stuck here playing ferryman for nobody."

"You'll be stuck here alive," Wulfric growled, his tone leaving no room for argument. "We'll find Jory and the others, bring them to the barge, and sail downriver to Dugal and Halder. That's the plan. Clear?"

Peter muttered something under his breath, but nodded, his grip tightening on the rudder. "Fine. Just don't take all day."

Wulfric turned his gaze to me, his voice softening a fraction. "Tomi, you'll need to hide under the tarp. If they're expecting three men, they can't see three men and a…" He paused, the correction coming almost reluctantly. "A young man. Position yourself so you can watch what's happening, but keep low. Got it?"

I nodded, swallowing against the sudden dryness in my throat. I moved toward the cargo and slid between the crates, wedging myself against a pallet. The waxed tarp overhead smelled faintly of fish and mildew, its edges stiff and unforgiving. I shifted, finding a spot where a small tear in the fabric gave me a sliver of a view.

The river stretched ahead, the pale walls of Whitestone loomed in the distance. Wulfric adjusted his helmet, his jaw set with determination. "Alright," he said, his voice low and firm. "Let's get ready."

The barge drifted forward, the faint creak of the rudder and the gentle slap of water against wood the only sounds as we moved closer to the fortress proper. Through the hole in the tarp, I watched the fortress grow larger, its walls rising like silent sentinels, the weight of what lay ahead pressing against my chest.

The barge drifted closer to Whitestone, the pale stone walls looming higher with each passing moment. Peter grumbled at the rudder, his inexperience showing in the jerky movements of the boat as it veered slightly off course before he corrected it. "Could've been a bloody miller's son," he muttered. "But no, I get stuck steering a cursed barge."

Wulfric shot him a glare but said nothing, his focus pinned on the docks ahead. Svend adjusted the straps of his borrowed armor, the faint creak of leather and clink of metal breaking the tense silence. I stayed hidden beneath the tarp, every muscle tight, my hand resting on my bowstring. The river lapped at the sides of the boat, a gentle sound that belied the storm building inside me. I could feel the others' nerves radiating like heat, their apprehension feeding into my own.

I closed my eyes, trying to steady my breath. Instead, I reached out with my senses, letting the pulse of my pathos stretch beyond the thin fabric covering me. It hit me like a wave—emotions churning together, a chaotic blend of anger, fear, and despair. The despair felt heavy, sticky, like wet cloth against my skin, pulling me down. But there was something else, too, something strange and tangled, a mix of emotions that felt almost like colors bleeding together, strong and foreign. Like when mother's dyes ran together they either made purple or they made white.

The boat thudded softly against the dock, jolting me back to the present. "Steady," Wulfric said under his breath. Peter cursed as he wrestled the rudder into place.

A soldier stepped forward on the dock, his boots clapping against the wooden planks. His armor gleamed, his tabard displaying Cedric's rearing dragon. He approached the barge with an air of practiced disinterest, his hand rested lazily on the hilt of his sword.

"What've you got?" the guard asked, his voice rough but bored.
"Supplies," Wulfric said, his tone steady but tight. "Honey, dried fish, some barrels of wheat. From upriver."
The guard glanced at the barge, his gaze lingered briefly on the cargo beneath the tarp. "Haul it onto the lift," he said, jerking his thumb toward something out of my view. "They'll take it from there."
"Yes, sir," Wulfric replied, the words catching slightly in his throat. The guard turned without a second glance, moving toward a cluster of soldiers loitering near the edge of the dock.

The pallet shifted suddenly beneath me, the wood creaking as it was lifted. My heart raced as I realized Svend had taken the front while Wulfric carried the back, the tarp rustling faintly with their movements. The world tilted as they began walking, and I braced myself against the wooden edges, the cool stone of my mother's necklace pressing against my chest.

Wulfric's voice was barely audible, a whisper slipping through the fabric. "Tomi, listen. There's a new plan."

My breath caught. "What?" I whispered back, my voice a harsh rasp.

"You're going in," he said, his tone clipped. "Find Jory and the others. Get them out. We'll stall the guards and wait for you."

"What?" I hissed, my pulse pounding. "Wait—"

"No time," Wulfric cut me off. "Keep quiet. Do what you have to do."

The pallet hit the ground with a dull thud, rattling the wood beneath me. I bit down on a gasp, the tarp brushing against my cheek as I pressed myself lower. Sweat beaded on my forehead, the stale, musty air under the tarp growing thicker with every second. My pulse pounded loud enough that I was sure someone outside would hear it.

Voices drifted through the fabric, muffled but close. Wulfric's low, steady tone mingled with the sharper, nasal timbre of a guard. "Supplies like these showing up like it's the spirits whim," the guard said, his words clipped. "Good thing, too. We've been burning through stock fast."

"You planning to fight the war on honey and fish?" Wulfric replied, the faint edge in his voice hidden under a veneer of gruff humor.

A chuckle answered, accompanied by the faint scrape of boots on stone. "No, but keeps the men from gnawing their own hands off between battles. And with Harlan's forces stirring, we'll need all we can get."

My breath caught as the conversation continued, blending into the background like a low hum. My fingers tightened around my bow. I wasn't sure what I was expecting—a sudden shout, the tarp ripped away—but the waiting was worse. Every second stretched into an eternity.

Then, motion.

The pallet lurched beneath me, my stomach flipping with the sudden lift. It felt like being caught in the rapids again, weightless and disoriented, my body left behind as the world shifted. I clung to the edges, the tarp brushing against my knuckles. The voices grew fainter, replaced by the groaning of ropes and the rhythmic creak of wood.

Light seeped through the seams of the tarp, fractured and dim. I watched the faint lines waver and then fade entirely, swallowed by darkness. The pallet slowed, the jerking motion evening out as a faint chill crept in, the stone walls radiating cold.

Minutes passed, though it felt longer. Finally, with a metallic click and a jarring stop, the motion ceased. My breath came out in a shaky exhale, the sound of my own heartbeat deafening in the stillness.

The silence pressed in, heavy and still. I waited, straining to hear past the pounding in my ears. Nothing. No voices, no footsteps. Just the faint scurry of rats clawing at wood. I took a shaky breath, inching toward the edge of the pallet. My fingers curled around the tarp's edge, and I slipped out into the cold air, landing softly on the stone floor.

The room was dimly lit, torches set into brackets along the walls casting flickering shadows over crates and barrels stacked high. Supplies—flour, dried meat, bundles of kindling. The faint, earthy scent of grain mingled with the tang of wax from the torches. My feet moved soundlessly over the worn stone, my breath a shallow whisper in the cavernous space.

Closing my eyes, I stretched my senses, reaching outward, seeking something beyond the thrum of the rats and the stillness of the supplies. The hum of the fort came to me in fragments—voices muffled by walls, boots echoing in distant halls. Too much, too scattered. I gritted my teeth, focusing harder.

There. Faint and buried beneath layers of stone and sound. A pulse of despair. It was sharp, jagged, and unrelenting, the kind of weight I knew too well. My chest tightened, and I opened my eyes, turning toward it.

I moved quickly but carefully, sticking close to the edges of the room. A heavy wooden door stood at the far side, iron hinges gleaming faintly. I pressed my ear to it, listening. Still nothing. I eased it open, the hinges creaking softly, and slipped into the narrow hall beyond.

The stone walls loomed close, the air cooler there. I kept my steps light, my boots grazing the floor just enough to keep balance. The hall split ahead, and I paused, glancing both ways before tilting my head, searching for that feeling. The despair was faint but unwavering, pulling me like a thread tugged from the dark.

Voices rose faintly to my left, and I froze, ducking into a shadowed alcove. A patrol passed, their conversation clipped and matter-of-fact. I held my breath, pressing my back against the cold stone as their footsteps faded. My hands trembled, and I squeezed them into fists, moving again once the silence returned.

The corridors twisted, unfamiliar and disorienting. I tried to keep my path straight, but the fort's layout was like a maze. I stumbled through another door, certain I'd find the way, only to hit a dead end or an empty room. Frustration burned at the edges of my focus, but that pulse of despair kept me steady, guiding me like a faint light in the dark.

I stopped at a heavy wooden door with iron rivets, the feeling stronger, humming beneath my skin. My hand hovered over the latch, the sound of my own breath loud in the stillness. I pushed it open. The room was cold, the kind of cold that clung to your skin and seeped into your bones. The door creaked as I opened it just wide enough to peer inside. The gaol stretched out in front of me, a long corridor lined with barred cells. A torch burned dimly on the far wall, throwing flickering shadows across the stone. The air smelled of damp straw and sweat, laced with something sour.

At a desk near the center of the corridor, a gaoler sat slumped in a chair, his head bobbing as he drifted in and out of sleep. His arms rested on the wooden surface, a set of keys gleaming faintly by his elbow. I drew back quickly, letting the door hang open just enough to keep watch. My breath hitched, heart pounding as I tried to decide.

Rush him? Sneak past? Wait? Wulfric and the others were counting on me. I didn't have time to wait for him to drift off completely. My fingers tightened around the doorframe, my mind racing.

Then I thought of the scout back in the forest. The sensation I'd sent him—the pull of uncertainty, the feeling of direction—had worked. What if I could do it again? I closed my eyes, letting the faint hum of the gaol settle around me, and focused on the gaoler.

Sleep. I let the thought swell, bringing with it every image and sensation I could summon. The heaviness of closed eyelids. The warmth of a blanket. The way exhaustion pressed down like a weight, pulling everything into stillness. I directed it toward him, willing it to take hold.

Seconds stretched into minutes. The gaoler's head lolled forward, his breathing slowing. Then, a faint snore broke the silence, steady and rhythmic. I stared at him, my chest tight with disbelief. It worked. It actually worked.

I didn't have time to question it. My legs moved before my thoughts caught up, carrying me silently across the stone floor. The keys jingled faintly as I lifted them from the desk, my eyes darting back to the gaoler as his snores deepened. I slipped past him, the cells looming on either side.

The first cell was cloaked in shadow, the figure inside little more than a huddled shape on the floor. "Jory?" I whispered, my voice barely audible. No answer. I crouched closer, gripping the bars. "Jory?"

The figure muttered something unintelligible, shifting slightly but not looking up. The air around them was heavy, thick with despair. It radiated off them like heat, curling around my senses and pulling me into its weight. I shivered, swallowing hard.

A voice came from behind me, soft but familiar. "Tomi?"
I froze, my hand tightening on the keys. The sound cut through the dark, threading through the tension like a lifeline.
Jory's voice was hoarse but unmistakable. "Tomi!"

I spun, my heart skipping as my eyes found him in the larger cell. Even in the dim light, I could make out his sandy hair sticking up at odd angles, his face pale and drawn, and his eyes—older, heavier than they should have been, but wide with disbelief.

"Shh," I hissed, pressing a finger to my lips. He nodded quickly, his shoulders hunching as if he could shrink the sound. I fumbled with the keys, finally finding the right one, and the door creaked open. Jory stepped out, and we clasped each other tightly, the kind of embrace that felt like anchoring yourself to solid ground.

"How are you here?" he whispered, his voice cracking.
"No time," I murmured, pulling back. "Where are the others?"
Jory gestured to the cells further down. "Three left. Barely."

We moved quickly, unlocking the cells one by one. The men inside were gaunt and battered, their eyes dull with exhaustion. One of them was badly injured, his leg splinted roughly and wrapped with dirty cloth. The other two looped their arms around him, half-carrying, half-dragging as we made our way to the door.

"We need to go," I said, my voice urgent but low. I pointed toward the door I'd entered through. "There are stairs that way."

The men began shuffling toward the exit, Jory at their side, his hand gripping the injured man's shoulder. I turned to follow but froze. That feeling from before, the confusing flood of emotions—despair, happiness, anger, love, suspicion—it was stronger now, clawing at the edge of my mind. It came from the cell I'd checked earlier, the one with the huddled figure.

"Tomi, come on," Jory hissed from the corridor. "We have to move."
"One second," I said, my voice tight.

I turned back to the cell and unlocked it. The blanket shifted as I stepped inside. My hand reached out, and I yanked the fabric back in one motion.

What I found made me step back. A man lay beneath the blanket, stark white hair falling in wild tangles around his face and shoulders. It glowed faintly in the torchlight, as if catching the flames in a way that seemed unnatural. His lean frame unfolded with a suddenness that made me take another step back, rising taller than any man I'd ever seen.

He loomed over me, his eyes wide and bright with an intensity that made my skin crawl. Then his head smacked against the low ceiling with a loud crack, and he reeled back, clutching it.

"Blast it to the void!" he snarled, hopping in place as he clutched his head. His voice carried a peculiar rhythm, half anger, half bafflement. "Who decides the sky should crouch in a place meant for thinking men? Walls pressing, ceilings shrinking—it's a prison within a prison, I tell you!" He spun, gesturing wildly at the low stone. "Is this what the world's come to? A cage, not just for the body, but for the spirit of upright posture?!"

I stared, stunned, as he banged into the wall, muttering curses. The sound echoed off the stone, and my stomach sank as I heard the gaoler stir, his chair creaking.
"Tomi!" Jory's voice was a harsh whisper, sharp with panic. "The gaoler's waking up!"
I turned, but the white-haired man was still cursing, oblivious. The gaoler groaned, and I heard the scrape of wood against stone as his chair shifted.

The gaoler stirred, his eyes fluttering open, then widening as he took in the open cells and the towering figure behind me. His mouth opened in a cry of alarm.

"Esc—"

The white-haired man moved faster than I thought possible, a blur of pale and wild motion. Before I could even process it, he rushed past me, slamming into the gaoler with an open-palmed shove. The gaoler's head hit the edge of the desk with a sickening crack, and he slumped back, unconscious. The white-haired man didn't pause. He darted out of the cell block like a spirit let loose, his long legs carrying him down the corridor before I could react.

"What just—" I muttered, my body moving on instinct as I followed. My feet pounded the stone floor, Jory and the others pressing themselves against the walls as the white-haired man's chaotic energy swept past them.

"Who was that?" Jory asked, his voice sharp with alarm.

"I don't know," I said, my breath ragged. "But we have to move—now."

Shouts echoed down the corridors, growing louder, closer. I led the group forward, my pulse thundered in my ears. My hands were clammy, gripping the keys I still had like a lifeline. We took turn after turn, the fortress an unending maze of stone and shadow, every corner a risk.

As we neared a bend, I felt it before I saw it—a bearing, steady and familiar, like a beacon through the chaos. My pulse quickened, and I glanced over my shoulder at the others. Then, rounding the corner ahead, came Wulfric.

"Wulfric!" I breathed, relief flooding my chest.

He froze for a moment, his eyes scanning our group and lingering on Jory before a grin broke across his face. "Tomi! You bloody did it." His gaze turned serious again as he waved us forward. "Come on, lads. We need to go."

We fell in behind him, Jory helping the injured man hobble along as we navigated the fortress. The shouts were still behind us, a constant threat growing louder with every step.

At a cross-section in the corridor, I felt it again—another presence. This time, it came fast, like a storm crashing into a calm. I threw out an arm, stopping Wulfric in his tracks. He gave me a look but didn't question it, following my gaze as the white-haired man tore through the adjacent corridor, his movements wild and frantic. Behind him came soldiers, three of them, marching with weapons drawn, their voices calling orders.

Wulfric let out a low sigh. "What in all the spirits was that?" "Doesn't matter," I said quickly. "We need to—"

A fourth soldier emerged from a side door just as we turned, his eyes landing on us. He opened his mouth to shout, but Wulfric was already moving. He closed the distance in two strides, his fist connecting with the man's gut, knocking the wind out of him. The soldier staggered, swinging wildly with his blade, but Wulfric sidestepped it, grabbing the man's wrist and slamming him into the wall.

The clash was brief, violent, and tense. My heart raced as I stood frozen, Jory whispering harshly for me to move. Wulfric brought his elbow down on the back of the soldier's neck, and the man crumpled to the ground.

"Quiet now," Wulfric said, his voice rough as he adjusted his grip on his blade. "Let's keep it that way."

Shouts in the distance swelled again, closer. Wulfric motioned for us to follow, his movements quick and deliberate. I took one last look at the fallen soldier, my stomach twisting, then forced my legs to move.

The tension clung to the air like smoke as we moved through the corridor, the echoes of footsteps and raised voices chasing us. Every shadow seemed alive, every turn tighter than the last. Then came the clash of steel—a sound sharper than any alarm, cutting through the stone walls like a blade.

Light filtering from the stairwell seemed brighter than it should have been, but it wasn't the sunlight that caught my attention—it was the sound. Steel meeting steel, grunts, and shouted curses echoed up the stone steps. My pulse quickened as I glanced at Wulfric. His jaw clenched, and without a word, he charged forward.

I followed, my breath catching as the scene below unfolded. Svend and Peter were on the barge, fighting off four soldiers. Peter's blade clashed with one of the guards, his movements jerky but determined. Svend, always more agile, dodged another's swing and countered with a heavy blow that sent his opponent stumbling. The soldiers were pressing hard, their numbers giving them the upper hand.

Wulfric was on them in a heartbeat. He didn't hesitate. With a roar that seemed to shake the docks themselves, he swung his axe in a wide arc. The nearest soldier turned too late, his blade clattering to the wooden planks as he stumbled back toward the river's edge.

I glanced at Jory and the others behind me. "Get to the barge!" I hissed. They moved quickly, the injured man leaning heavily on two others. I drew my bow, nocking an arrow, and aimed at one of the soldiers lunging for Peter. The arrow thudded into the man's thigh, dropping him with a cry. Peter swung his blade down, finishing him.

Another soldier charged Wulfric, sword raised high. Wulfric caught the blow with the haft of his axe, shoving the man backward with sheer brute force. The soldier stumbled, his boots skidding on the wet wood, before Svend shoved him hard in the chest. He toppled into the river, flailing, his armor dragging him under.

Svend's victory was short-lived. Another guard swung low,

catching him off balance. He yelped as he tumbled into the water, the river swallowing him in an instant. My heart leapt into my throat, but Wulfric reached down, his massive hand plunging into the water. He hauled Svend out in one smooth motion, the younger man coughing and sputtering, but alive.

Peter cried out, his sword falling from his grip as a blade slashed across his arm. Blood stained his tunic, but he didn't back down. Gritting his teeth, he barreled into his attacker, driving the man toward the edge of the dock.

My fingers trembled as I nocked another arrow, aiming for the soldier looming over Peter. I released the string, but the arrow sailed wide, clattering against the wood.

Still, the distraction was enough—the man staggered, his balance faltering. With a gasp, he toppled backward, splashing into the river below, next to his companion.

"Get on!" Wulfric barked, his voice hoarse with exertion. I helped Jory and the others onto the barge, stepping over the bodies of fallen soldiers. Svend clambered aboard, his clothes dripping, while Wulfric shoved the last of the cargo free from the dock.

A shout rang out behind us. I turned, my heart sinking as more men poured from the stairs. Arrows whistled through the air, one thudding into the wooden side of the barge as Peter ducked behind the rudder, his injured arm cradled against his chest.

The barge drifted free, carried by the river's current. Wulfric grabbed an oar, steering us out of reach as another arrow splashed harmlessly into the water. I crouched low, my breath coming in short, panicked gasps as the fortress walls loomed behind us.

The sounds of pursuit faded as the river carried us farther

downstream. The men aboard were silent, their breathing heavy, their faces pale and drawn. Peter winced as he pressed a rag to his bleeding arm, while Svend wrung out his sodden shirt, muttering curses under his breath. Wulfric stood at the bow, his shoulders rising and falling with each deep breath.

The river rushed below us, its current strong and fast, carrying the barge farther from Whitestone's towering walls. I couldn't stop glancing back, the fortress still looming in the distance, its pale stone catching the dim light. My breath was ragged, my hands gripping the wooden edge of the barge as though letting go would send me tumbling into the water.

Then I felt it again—that chaos of emotions stirring in the back of my mind. The mix was almost overwhelming now, like colors bleeding together in water, smearing into something incomprehensible. It made me look up instinctively, my chest tightening.

There he was. The white-haired man, standing in the window of the fort high above us. His lean frame was silhouetted against the gray sky, his hair wild, like some storm-tossed banner. He leaned out, teetering on the edge, and then he jumped.

It wasn't a fall—it was a leap, reckless and deliberate, arms spread wide as if he meant to embrace the river itself. The wind carried his scream, high and sharp, but it wasn't terror that fueled it. It was laughter, loud and unrestrained, echoing down to us as he plummeted. He hit the water like a stone, disappearing into the churning current.

I froze, my pulse pounding in my ears. On a balcony above, the soldiers chasing him skidded to a halt, staring at the spot where he'd gone under. None of them moved to follow, their hesitation clear in the way their swords hung slack at their sides.

"Spirits' breath," Wulfric muttered beside me, his tone caught between awe and irritation. "Is he mad or just too bloody stupid to care?"

"Maybe both," Svend said, shaking his head. "Either way, not our problem."

I glanced at them, their expressions a mix of disbelief and grudging admiration. The freed Forsworn sat in silence, their eyes fixed on the ripples where the man had vanished. The river's current carried us farther, the fortress shrinking behind us, and no one spoke for a long while.

I leaned back, my fingers brushing the necklace beneath my shirt, the stone cool against my skin. The man's laughter still echoed faintly in my ears, a wild and untamed sound. The river surged on, pulling us into the unknown, and I couldn't shake the feeling that we'd just witnessed something important, even if I didn't yet know what it meant.

Chapter 12 - Fire's Hymn

We were pulled downstream, the river—swift and relentless, a force no army on foot or horseback could hope to match. The fortress and its shouts faded into the distance, the current carrying us further into the safety of the forested banks. I felt the tension ease from my shoulders, though the unease about the white-haired man lingered. He'd jumped into the river, wild and free, but he was alone now. He wasn't our problem. Or so I told myself.

The boat rocked gently as it drifted. The urgency of our escape gave way to silence, broken only by the occasional splash of water against the hull. Wulfric sat near the bow, his axe resting across his lap. His face was stern, but his voice softened when he looked at Jory. "We've got time now. Tell me what happened."

Jory sighed, his sandy hair falling into his tired eyes. "After we left the fort, we did everything we could to buy time for the others to get away. It worked, for a while." His voice cracked, and he rubbed his hands over his face, his words spilling out like they'd been waiting too long to be spoken. "Cedric's men caught up. Took us to Whitestone in chains. One of us... Ulrik... didn't make it there."

The name hit like a stone sinking into the current. Wulfric's face hardened, his knuckles whitening around the haft of his axe. "Ulrik was a good man."

Jory nodded, his voice hollow. "The road wasn't the worst of it. At Whitestone, they interrogated us. They wanted names. Places. Anything." He looked down at his hands, flexing them like he could still feel the binds. "Colvin didn't make it through that. Being locked up, it was hard, harder than anything."

My stomach churned, and I moved closer to Jory, placing a hand on his shoulder. "I know what that's like," I said quietly. "To be there, to feel that... to lose yourself."

He looked up at me, his eyes searching mine for something—recognition, understanding, maybe just proof that he wasn't alone. He nodded, his voice low. "I thought I'd lost everything."

Wulfric leaned forward, his voice steady but firm. "You didn't lose everything, lad. You bought the others time. The women, the children—they're safe because of you."

Jory's face softened, though the guilt didn't leave his eyes. "They're safe?"

"They're safe," Wulfric repeated. "We'll pick them up next."

The river carried us on, but the weight of Jory's words and the memories they stirred stayed with me. I sat back against the wooden hull, my gaze on the rippling water, and let the silence settle between us. The night felt darker, heavier, but at least we were alive. At least we were still moving.

The river stretched endlessly, the steady rush of the current filling the silence between us. Peter sat near the stern, his arm stiff and awkward, blood seeping through the rough bandage he'd tied on earlier. I moved toward him, pulling a strip of cloth from what was left of the boat's cargo.

"Let me see," I said, nodding toward his arm.

Peter grumbled something under his breath but extended it, the cut angry and red. "Not like I'm gonna argue. Hurts like a bastard."

I worked quietly, unraveling the makeshift bandage and wrapping the new cloth tightly enough to stop the bleeding. The smell of iron and sweat clung to the air. "Hold still," I muttered, pulling the knot secure.

Jory, watching from the other side of the boat, cocked his head. "You're good at that, Tomi."

I shrugged, tying off the bandage. "Learned from Lyse. The same woman who patched up Wulfric's shoulder after Cedric's lot got him." I paused, my hands stilling for a moment. "Don't mean I trust healers, though."

Wulfric chuckled from his place near the bow. "Careful, lad. Do this good a job, you might end up one of them."

"Spirits forbid," I muttered, earning a laugh from Jory.

By the time the sun began its descent, painting the river in shades of gold and crimson, we found a quiet spot along the bank to make landfall. The barge bumped against the muddy shore, and we stepped off one by one, leaving it to drift aimlessly downstream. Wulfric pushed it off with his boot, the wood creaking as it floated away.

"If they're following, that'll keep them guessing," he said.

The forest stretched before us, dark and quiet except for the occasional call of a distant bird. The smell of smoke drew us forward, and soon enough, we found Dugal. He sat beside a small fire, Haldor grazing nearby. A pot of stew simmered over the flames, its aroma cutting through the damp chill.

Jory stepped forward, his sandy hair catching the firelight. Dugal froze, his eyes wide as they locked onto Jory's. "I…" he stammered, standing awkwardly. "I'm sorry, Jory. I let you down. Should've done more. Should've stayed."

Jory smiled faintly, shaking his head. "You did what you could, Dugal. None of us asked to be fighters, but you did well."

Dugal's shoulders sagged, relief softening his face. "Thanks, lad. That… means more than you know."

We settled around the fire, passing bowls of stew between us. The warmth seeped into my bones, driving away the chill of the river. Jory and Dugal spoke in low voices, catching up in bits and pieces, their words weaving through the crackle of the flames.

The fire crackled softly, the only sound breaking the heavy silence that had settled over us. Each of us sat lost in our own thoughts, the weight of the day settling over us like a heavy cloak we couldn't shake off. Dugal stirred the stew pot absently, his gaze distant, while Jory leaned against a tree, his eyes half-closed. Peter stretched out on the ground, muttering curses under his breath every time his injured arm shifted wrong. Even Wulfric, usually unshakable, stared into the flames with an uncharacteristic stillness.

Then, from nowhere, Svend's voice broke through the quiet, low and soft, carrying a tune that felt as old as the woods around us.

"Fire dances in the night, burning bright with endless fight. Flames that kiss, flames that bind, yearning for the spark they'll find."

His voice wove through the air, warm and smooth, like the fire itself. Peter let out a grunt, but it wasn't annoyed. Jory sat up straighter, a faint smile tugging at his lips.

"Fire burns with lustful glee, for the heart of the trembling tree," Svend continued, his tone playful now, drawing out the words. "It whispers, it begs, it longs for more, until all is ash on the forest floor."

A chuckle escaped from Peter. "You making this up as you go, or did some bard pay you for that nonsense?"

Svend grinned, his teeth catching the firelight. "It's tradition. You'd know if you had a lick of culture in you."

Before Peter could retort, Jory joined in, his voice thinner but carrying the same rhythm. "The spirit of fire, wild and bold, taking the warm and leaving the cold."

Dugal laughed then, surprising all of us, and clapped his hands in time. Even Wulfric cracked a smile, though it vanished quickly when Svend launched into another verse, louder this time.

"Flames that hunger, flames that cry, kissing the night, reaching the sky!"

"Keep it down," Wulfric growled, though his tone lacked real anger. "Unless you want Cedric's men singing along as they cut our throats."

Laughter rippled through the camp, soft but genuine. For a moment, it felt like the shadows eased back, the tension loosening around us.

"All right, all right," Svend said, raising his hands in mock surrender. "But don't blame me if the spirits take offense to cutting their hymn short."

"Let 'em," Peter muttered. "Long as they leave me be."

One by one, we settled into sleep, the remnants of laughter fading into the crackle of the fire. The world felt just a little less heavy as I pulled my cloak tight around me, the warmth of the moment lingering like embers against the night.

Morning light filtered through the trees, casting long, golden rays across the clearing. Wulfric's voice, low and rough from sleep, broke the quiet. "Tomi," he said, motioning me over as he cinched Halder's saddle. "You're from Linden. Think you can lead us there?"

The question landed like a stone in my stomach. My fingers tightened around the strap of my pack as memories surfaced unbidden—burnt fields, quiet streets, and the aching loss of home. "I… yeah," I said finally, my voice quieter than I intended. "I can do it."

Wulfric nodded, studying me with a sharpness that softened slightly when I held his gaze. "Good. We need you on this one, lad."

I swallowed the lump in my throat and turned to Halder, gripping the reins as Wulfric helped the injured man onto the horse's back. His face was pale, drawn tight with pain, but he managed a grateful nod as I adjusted the reins.

The path to Linden was one I knew well, but the familiarity made it worse. Each bend and break in the forest whispered reminders of what had been lost. I focused on the rhythm of the horse's steps, the reins firm in my grip, as the others walked in a loose formation around me.

Jory fell into step beside me, his sandy hair sticking up at odd angles, his eyes tired but alight with curiosity. "How're you holding up?" he asked, his voice quiet enough that the others wouldn't hear.

I glanced at him, my grip tightening. "Better now that you're out," I said. The truth felt heavier than I expected. "Cedric's lot locked me up, too. Two seasons in a cell."

Jory's brow furrowed, his expression darkening. "Two seasons?" He shook his head, disbelief mixing with anger. "We were in that pit for weeks, and it felt like a lifetime. I can't imagine."

"Don't," I said, forcing a bitter smile. "You don't want to."

He nodded, and the silence between us stretched, the sounds of the forest filling the gap. After a moment, I glanced his way again. "How're your snares coming along?"

The change in subject lit up his face, the weight of the previous conversation lifting slightly. "Better than ever," he said, grinning. "I've been trying new things—spring-loaded triggers, hidden pits. Had a few set up at the old fort before, well…" His voice trailed off, and his grin faltered.

I hesitated, not sure what to say. "You'll make new ones," I offered finally. "Better ones."

His smile returned, smaller but genuine. "Yeah. I will."

Halder snorted softly, his ears flicking back as we crested a small rise. The road ahead opened up into a familiar stretch of trail, and my chest tightened at the sight. I kept my eyes forward, the reins steady in my hands, as the weight of our destination settled over me.

The forest stretched endlessly around us, the dense canopy filtering the sunlight into soft patches of gold on the forest floor. The air carried a cool dampness, the scent of moss and soil sharp and clean. We moved slowly, keeping off the roads, the injured man swaying on Halder's back. The days blurred together, each step taking us closer to Linden but wearing us down.

Rations ran out on the fourth day, and it fell to me to fill the gap. It wasn't hard. The woods teemed with life if you knew where to look, and I did. Each hunt felt like slipping into a rhythm, an unspoken understanding between me and the creatures of the forest. The bow felt steady in my hands, the fletching of each arrow familiar against my fingers. The world quieted when I hunted, my senses sharpening until the rest of the group faded into the background.

By the river, crouched over a smooth stone, I gutted a rabbit I'd taken down that morning. The fresh smell of blood mixed with the clean scent of the water as the entrails slipped free. My hands moved automatically, but my thoughts wandered.

"You're good at that," Wulfric's voice came from behind me, rough and low.
I looked up, startled, to find him leaning against a tree, his axe hanging from his belt. He watched me with an expression I couldn't quite place—something between curiosity and calculation.
"Used to do it with my father," I said, turning back to my work. The words came easily, but the memory that followed didn't.

Wulfric stepped closer, crouching down beside me. "It's more than that," he said, his tone even but probing. "You've got a knack for it—hunting, finding things before anyone else does." He paused. "I thought maybe it was just sharp eyes and young ears, but it's more than that, isn't it?"

My hand stilled over the rabbit, the blade hovering just above the flesh. A knot tightened in my chest. My father's voice came back to me, a warning wrapped in affection. ***People might not understand. They fear what they don't know.***

"It's nothing," I said quickly, resuming my work.

Wulfric didn't budge, his gaze heavy on me. "Don't play me, lad. I've seen it too many times to ignore. You sense things, don't you?"

The words hung in the air, as sharp and cold as the blade in my hand. I hesitated, my pulse quickening, then nodded, just slightly. "I can... feel things. Living things. Creatures, people. I don't know how to explain it."

Wulfric sat back on his heels, his expression unreadable. For a moment, he said nothing, and I regretted every word.

"North of the mountains," he said finally, his voice softer than I expected, "there are people. Nomads, they're called. They follow the Path, or so they say. They listen to emotions like they're songs carried on the wind. Maybe you've got a bit of them in you."

The thought hit me strangely, like a truth I wasn't sure I wanted to believe. "I've never heard of them."

Wulfric shrugged, standing again and dusting off his hands. "Not many have. Doesn't matter either way. What matters is you're here, and you're damn good to have around." He glanced at me, a faint smile tugging at his mouth. "Are you sure you don't want to join us?"

I hesitated, my fingers tightening around the rabbit's leg. "Can I think on it?"

"Of course," Wulfric said. He clapped me lightly on the shoulder, his hand warm and heavy. "You're one of us, whether you realize it or not."

I watched him walk away, his broad frame disappearing into the trees, and I couldn't help but wonder if he was right. We continued on, the rhythm of our steps carrying us forward, though my mind lingered behind.

The trees thinned as we crested a small rise, the air shifting with the faint scent of smoke and damp earth. In the distance, nestled against the horizon, was the outline of a village. My chest tightened as the name formed in my mind before I could stop it.

Linden.

Chapter 13 - No Longer Home

Linden was not how I remembered it. The circle of buildings around the central well still stood, but their roofs sagged, and their walls bore the mottled stains of time and fire. Beyond the village center, the buildings grew sparse, scattered like forgotten stones. The fields stretched out beyond them, a patchwork of green and brown. Where once there had been a sea of golden wheat, now there were only scattered islands, the scars of the fire etched into the earth like a wound that never fully healed.

The sight of it stopped me cold. The air felt thinner there, heavy with memories. I stood at the edge of the treeline, my fingers brushing against the strap of my bow. For a moment, I debated turning back, leaving the Forsworn to gather their people without me. This place wasn't mine anymore, not after everything. I didn't even know what I was expecting to find.

"Tomi?" Jory's voice cut through the haze of my thoughts. He was ahead, his sandy hair catching the pale sunlight. He'd stopped in the middle of the path, glancing back at me with that steady gaze of his. "You coming?"

I swallowed hard, forcing my feet to move. My boots felt heavy against the dirt path, as if the weight of the past clung to them. I blinked, the word stuck in my throat, and followed.

Jory glanced at me, his voice low. "So, this is your home, is it?"

I nodded, my throat tight. "It was... before the war." My words hung heavy in the air, unfinished. There wasn't much else to say.

Jory didn't press. Instead, he placed a hand on my shoulder, the gesture grounding. I drew in a breath, steadying myself as we approached the center of the village.

The first faces emerged from doorways, cautious and slow. Older men, their backs hunched, trailed by two younger figures, nearly identical. My breath caught when I recognized them—Erland and Egon, the twins. They were taller than I remembered, broader, their faces sharper with age, but the same determination burned in their eyes. Each carried a scythe, the blades chipped and flecked with rust, but the way they held them said they meant business.

Behind them, others filtered out—women and men with weathered faces, their hands clutching whatever they could find. A wooden pole. A hatchet. A jagged shard of metal that looked like it had been snapped from the remains of a plow. Their gazes flicked over us, wary and hard.

The twins stepped forward, Erland leading with his scythe raised. "That's close enough," he said, his voice steady but sharp. "We don't want soldiers here. Or highwaymen. We've got nothing to give and less to take, so you'd best be on your way."

Peter's fingers twitched toward the hilt of his blade despite his injured arm, but Wulfric raised a hand, stepping forward calmly. "We're not here for trouble," he said, his voice low and even. "We're here for our people."

Erland narrowed his eyes, his grip tightening on the scythe. "Your people?" His tone carried suspicion and a thinly veiled threat. "I've heard that before. It doesn't end well."

"Listen to me, Lad." Wulfric said, his tone firm but steady. "We're not here to rob you. We're not soldiers. We're Forsworn."

The air felt heavier, the tension stretching taut. Erland glanced back at Egon, then at the others behind him. "Forsworn?" he echoed, his scythe lifting a fraction higher. "You expect us to believe that?"

Before Wulfric could answer, I stepped forward, the ground beneath my feet feeling unsteady but my voice firm. "Erland," I said, meeting his gaze. "It's true. We're here for the Forsworn."

His mouth fell open, his scythe lowering as recognition dawned. "Tomi?"

Egon stepped forward, his scythe lowering slightly as his eyes widened. "Tomi? Is that really you?" His voice carried an edge of disbelief, the same tone I'd heard in his voice a thousand times when we were boys, daring each other into mischief.

I managed a small smile. "Hello, Egon. It's me."

Erland's expression hardened beside him, his grip on his scythe tightening. "You're Forsworn now?" His voice was sharp, cutting through the air like the rusty blade he held.

The accusation in his tone knocked the breath out of me. "What? No—I mean, yes—no," I stammered, stepping back slightly. "We're just here for them."

Egon ignored his brother, stepping closer. "Tomi," he said again, his eyes searching mine. "What happened to you? Where have you been?"

The words stuck in my throat. What could I say that wouldn't sound like a lifetime crammed into a sentence? "It's… a lot," I said, my voice barely above a whisper.

Erland spat on the ground, his scowl deepening. Whatever I'd been through, he didn't seem interested in hearing it.

Before I could say more, a woman's voice rang out from behind them. "Wulfric?"

Wulfric's head turned sharply, a grin breaking across his weathered face. "Lyse? Is that you?"

The makeshift line of men and farmers parted as a woman stepped forward, her gray hair tied back in a loose braid, her posture steady despite the years etched into her face. She moved with quiet authority, a handful of other women trailing behind her, their wary eyes darting between us.

"It is you," she said, her voice softening. "These are our people. There's no need to fear them."

Erland hesitated, his scythe wavering in his hands. A glance from Lyse was all it took for him to lower it. Egon followed suit, his movements slower, his eyes never leaving mine. Around them, the others lowered their weapons, the tension draining from their stances like water from a broken dam.

Lyse stepped closer to Wulfric, her expression a mixture of relief and weariness. "What happened? Where did you go?"

Wulfric ran a hand through his beard, his smile fading. "It's a long story," he said, his voice carrying a weight that made it clear he wasn't ready to tell it yet. "We were ambushed. But we've found somewhere safe—a place to regroup. We've come for you, all of you."

Lyse's eyes narrowed slightly, skepticism flashing across her face. "Safe? These days, there's no such thing."

"Not yet," Wulfric admitted, his voice steady, "but we're working on it."

Lyse studied him for a moment longer before nodding. "We'd best get off the road before a patrol comes through," she said, her tone brisk. She turned to Erland, her gaze sharp. "Bring them in."

Erland hesitated, the conflict clear in his eyes, but eventually, he gave a curt nod. "Fine. Come on, then." Egon shot me a tentative smile, and the group began to move, the tension still lingering in the air like a distant storm.

The village center was alive with murmurs and shifting eyes as we made our way in. The weight of Halder's reins in my hands gave me something to focus on, something solid amidst the swirl of faces and memories. Then a sharp cry broke the uneasy quiet.

"Svend!"

A woman's voice, bright and clear, rang out. She darted through the crowd, her braid swinging behind her as she ran toward him. Svend's face lit up, and he dropped his weapon, stepping forward just as she leapt into his arms. He caught her effortlessly, spinning her once before setting her down. Their embrace lingered, her head buried against his chest.

Peter scoffed, loud enough for half the village to hear. "Well, look at that. Some of us are loved."

The gathered villagers chuckled nervously, but the tension began to ease. Other Forsworn appeared from the scattered homes, their faces lighting up as they spotted the women and children among the group. Quiet greetings turned to relieved embraces, the weight of separation lifting in bits and pieces.

I stayed back, tightening my grip on Halder's reins. The horse's warm breath steamed in the cool air as he nuzzled at my hand. I didn't belong in the cluster of reunions. I focused on Halder, brushing the length of his neck as his ears flicked lazily.

Erland's gaze burned a hole in my back. I could feel it without looking. The memory of his betrayal stirred in me—him running to

Captain Varek, pointing the way to the cabin, sealing our fate. I couldn't stop asking myself the same question I'd asked a hundred times since: why?

I kept my distance, hoping to blend into the background, but the sound of giggles pulled me from my thoughts. Three children darted toward Halder, their small hands reaching up to stroke his coat. The tallest, a boy with a shock of wild hair, marveled at the horse's sheer size.

"Look at his feet!" he exclaimed, pointing to Halder's thick, mud-caked hooves.

"Do you ride him?" asked a younger girl, her eyes wide with wonder as she smoothed her hand over Halder's flank.

The third child, a shy boy, stood back, his fingers twitching at his side before tentatively reaching to touch Halder's mane. I crouched down, murmuring something to soothe the horse as the children buzzed around him. Then I saw her.

Standing just behind the children, her arms folded, was a face I hadn't seen in years but would never forget. Her blonde curls were gone, now tamed into a braid that fell over one shoulder. She looked older—taller, her expression more guarded—but the freckles scattered across her nose hadn't changed. Neither had her eyes, sharp and curious, that now locked onto mine.

Freja.

The children continued to swarm around Halder as I took in my childhood friend, their wide eyes darting over his muscular frame and dappled coat. Their hands reached out tentatively, stroking his flank, brushing his mane, and marveling at the sheer size of him. Halder stood still, his ears flicking forward and back, his dark eyes glancing at the smallest of them, as if gauging their intentions. A little boy giggled when Halder huffed, blowing warm air into his face.

"You've always had a way with animals," a voice said, soft but unmistakable.

I turned, my chest tightening. Freja. She wasn't the child I remembered, running barefoot through the fields or hiding in the loft during storms. She stood taller now, her loose braid framing a face that still carried the freckles I remembered but with sharper angles. Her figure had filled out, her posture more assured. The curls were tamed, but her piercing blue eyes still carried that spark of curiosity, now tempered by something heavier. She had grown into someone I didn't quite recognize but still knew.

Her lips tilted into a faint smile. "The horse is calm. Must trust you."

I cleared my throat, smoothing Halder's reins in my hands. "He's better company than most."

Freja laughed, low and short. "Good to see you, Tomi. You've grown."

"So have you," I said, my voice careful. "You look… different. So does the village."

Her smile faded just slightly, replaced by something harder. "War does that to a place, doesn't it?" Her tone carried an edge. "Even after the men came back, nothing was ever the same."

The weight of her words hung between us. Guilt clawed at me, cold and sharp. She didn't need to say it outright—my father and I had left, and I'd always known what that meant for the village we abandoned. For the people we left behind.

"How's your family?" I asked, needing to shift the weight off my chest.

"Getting by," she said with a shrug, though her eyes softened. "Father still gets around, though he can't work the fields anymore. Took up mending tools instead. Something he can do sitting down.

Mother... well, she's getting older. Stays busy, but you can see it in her."

I nodded, unsure how to respond. The children were still tugging at Halder's mane, one daring to touch his tail before I warned them off with a sharp, "Don't pull that, or you'll regret it." Their giggles broke the tension briefly, but it settled again when Freja stepped closer, her voice quieter.

"And you, Tomi? How are you?"
I hesitated, gripping the reins tighter. "Surviving," I said finally. "A lot's happened."
Freja tilted her head, studying me, but whatever she wanted to say next was cut off by a voice calling her name.
"Freja!" It was Igna, her mother, standing near one of the larger houses in the village. She waved Freja over, her expression expectant.
Freja sighed and glanced back at me. "You should come," she said, her voice softer again. "See everyone."
I looked past her at the village, its worn and broken pieces pieced together like a patchwork quilt, its people carrying scars both visible and hidden. My chest tightened again, but I nodded, letting out a slow breath. "Alright."

Freja turned and started walking, and I followed, Halder's reins still clutched tightly in my hands. The children ran ahead, their laughter echoing faintly as we made our way toward the heart of Linden.

The Forsworn blended easily with the crowd, their worn faces softened by the presence of family and the tentative safety of the village. Women embraced their partners, children darted between them, their small hands clutching at hems or tugging on arms. The injured sat in the shade, their wounds hastily dressed but their expressions lighter than I'd seen in weeks. Svend stood with the young woman who had run to him earlier, their foreheads pressed together as if they were the only ones in the world. Dugal leaned against a post, a grin on his face and a jug of wine in his hand that I couldn't imagine he'd acquired fairly. Peter, meanwhile, was enduring the sharp tongue of an older village woman, his sheepish look making it clear he was losing the battle.

Wulfric was off to the side with Lyse, their voices low but familiar. The sight of it all hit me harder than I expected, the sounds of relief and faint laughter pressing against my chest.

As I walked further into the village, a familiar face turned toward me. Elsie. Her transformation was startling—her hair neatly tied back, her eyes brighter than I remembered, though a shadow still lingered there. She had lost her husband during the war, and yet there she stood, steadier somehow. Beside her was Ole Erik, her father, looking just as ancient and unsteady as always, leaning heavily on his cane. At her side, a small boy no older than five clung to her skirt, his face smeared with dirt but glowing with curiosity.

Freja grabbed my arm and pulled me forward, her braid swaying as she led me to Elsie and the others gathered there. Mrs. Ingrid, Rolf, Elin, and Maris stood in a loose cluster, their faces weathered but still carrying some spark of warmth. Igna smiled as we approached, her hand resting lightly on her hip.

"Tomi?" Elsie said, her voice soft with disbelief. "Is that really you? Look at you—you've grown."

I nodded, unsure how to respond as she stepped closer, her hand brushing my arm. "It's me."

"And your Ma and Pa?" Elsie's question was hesitant, her smile faltering.

The words stuck in my throat, and for a moment, I could only look at her. "They... they didn't make it. The war took them both."

Elsie's hand rose to her mouth, her eyes glistening. "Oh, Tomi. Your Ma… she was my dearest friend."

The others murmured their condolences, their voices heavy with the shared grief that seemed to hang over Linden like a shadow. "The war took so much from all of us," Maris said, her gaze distant.

Igna reached out and squeezed my shoulder, her grip surprisingly firm. "We've had to rebuild from ash before. We'll do it again."

Before I could reply, Igna raised her voice, calling across the square. "Lyse! Over here!"

Lyse broke away from her conversation with Wulfric, her gray hair catching the fading light like threads of silver. She moved with the steady purpose of someone who had seen too much but carried it well. The circle shifted to let her through, and Wulfric followed, his broad frame a silent shadow behind her.

"Lyse," Igna said, nodding toward me. "Are you taking care of our Tomi? He's one of yours now, isn't he?"

Lyse's sharp eyes landed on me, a flicker of recognition softening her expression. "Tomi has been helpful," she said, her voice calm and matter-of-fact. "He hunted for us, found food for us when we were hungry and aided in taking the arrow out of a big brute's shoulder" She tilted her head, her gaze steady. "But you've got a knack for finding trouble, don't you?"

I shifted under her scrutiny but managed a small grin. "I've been told."

Her lips quirked upward, just slightly. "Well, let's hope you continue to be good at getting out of it too."

Wulfric wandered over next, glanced at me, then back to Lyse. "Igna's offered us a place for the night," he said. "But we'll leave at dawn. Don't want to overstay our welcome."

"Or risk being here when a patrol passes," Igna added. Her tone was casual, but I caught the flicker of unease in her eyes.

Lyse hesitated, her hand brushing her chin. There was something unsaid between her and Igna, something I could feel without understanding. Wulfric seemed to sense it too but didn't press.

"Dawn it is," Wulfric said, his voice gruff but certain.

That night brought a chill that settled over the village, but the bonfire in the square crackled defiantly against it. Flames reached up to the dark sky, throwing light on faces old and new. Villagers had gathered on one side, Forsworn on the other, the divide unspoken but tangible. The air was heavy with tension, though laughter occasionally broke through, weaving awkwardly between the two groups.

I sat beside Jory near the edge of the firelight, where the shadows crept close. Across the flames, Egon and Erland flanked their mother, Elin. Freja sat beside Erland, her hands resting lightly on his arm. It wasn't the same Freja I remembered—the girl who used to trail after me and her the others, fearless and curious. This version of her, older and composed, leaning into Erland, was unfamiliar. Unexpected.

Jory nudged me, his voice low. "The one glaring at you like he wants to knock your teeth out—friend of yours?"

I followed his gaze to Erland, whose sharp stare hadn't wavered all evening. "Old friend," I said flatly, the words dry in my mouth. Jory raised a brow but didn't press.

Nearby, Svend was leaning back, gesturing animatedly as he regaled a small group of villagers and Forsworn with a story. "And so there I was, knee-deep in snow, just me, my spear, and the biggest damn boar you've ever seen. Its tusks could have gutted me in two—"

Peter interrupted with a scoff. "I thought you said the snow was up to your neck last time you told this tale."

"It grows with every retelling," Svend shot back with a grin. "Like the boar."

Peter shook his head, muttering, "Only thing bigger than that boar... is your mouth."

The girl next to Svend leaned closer, her eyes sparkling with mischief. "I'm more interested in the size of your spear," she said, her voice sweet but laced with cheek.

Svend paused mid-gesture, his grin broadening. "Well," he said, puffing out his chest, "it does tend to leave an impression."

Peter groaned, shaking his head. "Spirits help us all."

The exchange drew a chuckle from some of the villagers, though Elin's expression remained stony. Across the fire, Lyse leaned toward Wulfric, her voice softer. "How's the shoulder?"

Wulfric rolled it experimentally, his face betraying no discomfort. "Heals slower than it used to, but it'll hold."

Lyse gave him a pointed look. "You'll come to me if it starts acting up. No waiting until it's infected and half-rotted like last time."

Wulfric grunted, his lips twitching with the faintest hint of amusement. "Aye, healer. No rotting this time."

Her eyes softened briefly before shifting to the children clustered near the fire. "They've done well, considering. It hasn't been easy, but they're resilient."

"They always are," Wulfric said, his gaze flicking over the villagers. "But that doesn't mean they should have to be."

I let their words fade into the background. The fire's warmth brushed my face, but I felt cold, detached. I couldn't bring myself to sit with the villagers, not with Erland watching me like that. And I didn't belong with the Forsworn, not really.

Standing, I muttered to Jory, "I'll be back."

He gave me a curious glance but didn't ask. I slipped into the shadows, skirting the firelight as I moved toward the outskirts of the village. My feet carried me almost on instinct, past the familiar curve of the well, the crooked fence around the old pasture. The air was heavy with memory, pulling me toward the cabin at the edge of the field.

The cabin looked smaller than I remembered, its roof now patched with mismatched shingles, the once-cracked windows replaced. The door hung slightly straighter, its frame reinforced with new wood, but the familiarity still clawed at my chest. Light flickered within, spilling golden warmth onto the worn path outside. Laughter filtered through the thin walls, soft but unmistakable, accompanied by the faint clatter of dishes and the savory scent of something cooking.

It wasn't ours anymore.

Someone lived there. Someone had taken my home, scrubbed away the soot and grief, and filled it with their lives. Of course, they had. It had been years. The village had to rebuild, to move on. But seeing it like this—whole, alive—felt like a knife twisting in my gut. Like they'd trampled over something sacred. Something that wasn't theirs. My memories. My family.

My breath hitched, and I took a step back, my hand brushing the rough bark of a tree behind me. A sound broke the silence—a sharp crack, like a snapped twig. I spun, my heart leaping into my throat.

Egon and Erland stood a few paces away, shadows in the moonlight. Egon's hand was on Erland's shoulder, holding him back. "Tomi," Egon said, his voice soft, almost apologetic. "We didn't mean to startle you."

I frowned, my fists clenching. "What do you want?"

Egon's grip on his brother tightened as Erland leaned forward, eyes blazing. "I told you, Egon. He doesn't belong here."

"Erland," Egon warned, his tone firm but patient. He turned back to me, his face lined with something between guilt and relief. "It's just... strange, seeing you here again. After all this time."

"Strange?" I echoed, my voice flat. "Is that what we're calling it?"

"You're Forsworn now," Erland spat, his voice sharp. "What are you doing back here, Tomi? Stirring up trouble? Haven't you done enough?"

The words hit like a slap, but confusion quickly turned to anger. "What are you talking about?"

Egon shifted uncomfortably, but Erland shoved his brother's hand away and took a step closer, his scythe clutched tightly in one hand. "You don't get it, do you? You and your father—"

"What about us?" I snapped, my fists curling tighter. "What did we do that was so wrong, Erland?"

Erland's face twisted, his voice rising. "You're the reason they came! You and your family. You're the reason the fields burned, the reason—"

My voice cut through his like a blade. "We had to run because of you! Because you told them where we were. You betrayed us, Erland. My father—" My voice cracked, but I forced myself to continue. "We trusted you."

"You think I wanted this?" Erland shouted, his face red with fury. "You think I wanted any of this? It's your fault!"

His scythe clattered to the ground as he swung at me, his fist coming hard and fast. The blow landed on my cheek with a sharp crack, and I stumbled back, the sting of it exploding through my face.

Erland's fist came at me again, but this time I ducked, feeling the air ripple just over my head. His movements were broad, heavy, each swing carrying the weight of his frustration and anger, but they were slow. Predictable. We were no longer children playing with wooden swords and I had experience, real experience from very real fights. I stepped back, twisting away as his scythe handle scraped the mud where my feet had just been.

He had the advantage of reach, his arms longer and his frame broader from years of toil on the farm. But reach meant little when every swing left him exposed. I darted in, a quick jab to his ribs before retreating just out of range. The strike wasn't powerful, but it was enough to make him hesitate. His breaths came harder, each one dragging through clenched teeth, and the strain showed in the way his shoulders sagged, his movements losing their precision.

"You always think you're better!" he shouted, lunging forward. His fist clipped my jaw, sending a burst of heat across my face. I stumbled but caught myself, raising my arms in defense.

"You're wrong," I growled, sidestepping another swing. His boot slid in the mud, throwing him off balance. I took the opening, slamming my shoulder into his chest which sent him sprawling.

Erland hit the ground with a wet thud, panting heavily, the fight drained from him. He didn't get up right away. Instead, he stared at the dark sky, his face twisted in anger and something deeper. His voice was raw when he spoke. "It was you. You and your father. It's your fault the fields burned. Everything... everything was your fault."

My chest heaved, the ache in my cheek forgotten as his words sank in. "How, Erland? Tell me how this is my fault."

He turned his head to me, his eyes glistening. "When you and your father came back," he said, his voice cracking, "the soldiers saw you. They came into the village. They took Freja." His fists clenched in the mud. "They said they'd hurt her unless we told them where you were."

The words hit me harder than any punch. I stepped back, staring down at him.

Erland's voice rose, shaky and defiant. "I had to, Tomi! I had to save her. You don't understand. I loved her. Even then."

"Erland…" Egon stepped forward, his face stricken, and reached down to his brother. "Enough. Come on."

Erland slapped Egon's hand away, his frustration boiling over. "No! You don't get it, Egon. None of you do. I didn't know what would happen. I didn't know they'd—" His voice broke, and he crumpled further into the mud, his shoulders shaking. "I didn't know they'd burn everything. I didn't know."

The weight of his words pressed into me like a stone. For a moment, I didn't know what to say, didn't know what I felt. Then, slowly, I stepped forward, reaching out my hand. "It's okay, Erland," I said, my voice steady despite the storm in my chest. "We all did things during the war. Things we didn't want to do. Things we had to do. It wasn't right, but it wasn't your fault. I forgive you."

He looked up at me, tears streaking the mud on his face, his expression torn between disbelief and something softer. After a long moment, his hand met mine. I gripped it firmly and pulled him to his feet.

We stood there, face to face, the tension that had hung between us for so many years dissolving into the night. Then, without a word, Erland stepped forward, his arms wrapping around me in a fierce, desperate embrace. I returned it, feeling the weight of the past finally start to lift.

"Are you two okay?" Freja's voice cut through the quiet, soft and concerned.

We broke apart, turning to see her standing there, her braid catching the moonlight. Her eyes flicked between us, searching for answers. When no one spoke, Freja's lips pressed into a faint smile, soft but knowing.

As the night stretched on, we found ourselves under the old oak, as if drawn there by some shared instinct. It was a place that had always been ours, even before the war had taken everything else. The old oak tree hadn't changed. Its massive trunk stood firm, its sprawling branches stretching high into the dark, freckled sky. The moonlight filtered through its leaves, casting shifting patterns across the ground. I leaned back against the bark, its rough surface pressing into my shoulder blades, while Egon sat cross-legged nearby, absentmindedly carving something with a small knife. Freja rested on a low root, her hands folded neatly in her lap, while Erland stood a little apart, staring out into the night like he was still holding onto some of his earlier frustration.

"It's been years since I came here," I said, breaking the quiet. "Feels… smaller somehow."

"That's because you're bigger," Egon replied, glancing up with a faint smirk. "I still remember you trying to climb it and getting stuck halfway."

"That was you," I shot back, smirking despite myself. "I had to pull you down."

"Only because you dared me," he retorted, shaking his head before returning to his carving. "You were always good at dragging us into trouble."

Freja laughed softly, a sound I hadn't heard in years. "Nothing's changed, then."

Erland turned back, arms folded. "Some things have," he said, his voice quieter than before. "Egon's taken up helping the blacksmith—making new tools for the fields. Someone has to keep the farms running."

"And you're doing the work of three men," Egon said, tilting his head toward his brother. "Head of the house now. Keeps him busy."

"Busy enough." Erland's eyes flicked toward Freja, lingering for a moment before he added, "Not alone, though. Freja's been keeping the little ones in line. She's better at it than I'd ever be."

Freja gave him a sidelong glance but didn't argue. "Someone has to. They're going to inherit this place one day. If they're not ready…" She trailed off, her expression hardening briefly before softening again. "It's good work."

I nodded, looking down at the ground. "Sounds like you've all found your places."

Egon's knife stilled as he tilted his head toward me. "What about you, Tomi? What have you been doing all this time?"

I hesitated, unsure where to begin. "After we left the village, my father and I just kept moving. We stayed in the woods, living off the land. We avoided people when we could, but we had to trade sometimes. Then, we… we crossed paths with royalty."

That got their attention. Egon straightened, Freja leaned in slightly, and even Erland's stern demeanor cracked with curiosity.

"Royalty?" Freja asked. "You mean actual princes and princesses?"

I nodded. "Prince Niklas and Princess Sanne." I explained the story that took my father and I into the mountains to hunt down royalty.

"What were they like?" Egon asked, his tone incredulous.

"Rich, I bet," Erland muttered. "Bet they've never had to plant a seed or swing a scythe in their lives."

"They've had it harder than most," I said firmly. Erland frowned, but I kept going. "They're not free, not really. They're pawns, being used by people more powerful than them. Cedric. Erik. Harlan. All of them."

Freja's brow furrowed. "Used? How?"

"Leverage. Symbols to rally armies, promises to keep others in line. They don't get a say in it," I explained, my voice quieter. "They've lost more than you'd think."

Erland didn't reply, though he still looked unconvinced. Egon broke the silence with a low whistle. "And you've been living in their world? Meeting kings and soldiers and all that?"

"Not really," I said, shaking my head. "Just the children of princes, and even then, not by choice. The war doesn't let anyone sit still for long."

The conversation shifted after that. We talked about the war, the village, the lives we'd lived since the old days. Erland shared stories of long nights in the fields, battling weeds and storms. Egon talked about his work with the blacksmith, Rolf, the burns and blisters a constant reminder of what the village needed to survive. Freja's voice softened as she described the children she cared for, their laughter keeping her grounded even when things felt impossible.

I shared what I could about my journey with the Forsworn, about Cedric's prison and the fight at the bridge. Their questions came fast, some curious, some skeptical, but none unkind. We talked long into the night, the memories of our childhood mingling with the weight of everything we'd endured since. For the first time in what felt like forever, the war felt distant, like something happening in another world.

The next morning, the air was thick with the smells of damp earth and the faint tang of smoke from the village fires. Wulfric stood with Lyse and the Forsworn, the villagers gathered around them in loose clusters. It wasn't the same as the chaotic goodbyes of battle or retreat; this was quieter, heavier, like a thread being frayed at the edges.

Lyse's voice was calm but firm as she addressed Wulfric. "Half of them have decided to stay," she said. Her gaze swept over the villagers who stood with her. "The children, the injured, the ones who've had enough of running. There's space here, and they need a real home."

Wulfric's jaw tightened, his hand gripping the axe at his belt. "And you?" His voice was rougher than usual.

"I'll stay and lead them," Lyse replied. "The Forsworn deserve more than the road. They deserve something lasting."

Wulfric's silence was louder than any words. Finally, he nodded, his jaw tight. "We'll make do without a healer. We'll survive," he said, though the weight in his voice made the words feel brittle.

Lyse's gray eyes softened. "You always do, Wulfric," she said quietly. She stepped forward, placing a hand on his arm, and after a beat of hesitation, they embraced. It wasn't just a goodbye—it was something heavier, full of unspoken understanding and the burden of shared battles.

I looked away, the moment too intimate to witness, and turned toward Egon, Erland, and Freja. Egon shifted awkwardly, his hands shoved into his pockets. "You should stay, Tomi," he said, his voice low but earnest.

I glanced back at the cabin, the place that had once been home. A flicker of laughter echoed from its walls, a life that wasn't mine anymore. "It's not my home," I said after a moment, my voice barely audible.

Freja stepped closer, her brow furrowed. "Then where will you go?" she asked, her tone tinged with something I couldn't quite place—curiosity, maybe, or something heavier.

I shrugged. "I don't know yet."

For a moment, none of us said anything. Then Egon reached out and gripped my shoulder. "Wherever you go," he said, "don't forget us."

I nodded, swallowing hard. "I won't."

Freja smiled faintly, but it didn't reach her eyes. "Safe travels, Tomi."

Erland stood back, his arms crossed, his gaze avoiding mine at first. But then, with a hesitant shrug, he muttered, "Try not to get yourself killed out there. Wouldn't feel right if I didn't get another crack at you someday."

A wry smile tugged at my lips. "I'll keep that in mind."

Erland smirked faintly, though it didn't quite hide the weight behind his words. Egon glanced at him, then back at me, his expression softening further. "Take care of yourself, Tomi."

We exchanged our goodbyes, and I turned to join the Forsworn who were already gathering at the edge of the village. As we moved out, the villagers standing with the Forsworn that remained, Lyse included, raised their hands in a quiet wave, and I found myself glancing back one last time. The old oak tree stood tall, its branches framing the fading view of Linden.

Halder's reins felt solid in my hands, a grounding weight. Wulfric fell into step beside me, his sharp gaze flicking my way. "How are you doing?" he asked.

"I'm fine," I replied, though the word felt hollow.

"Why didn't you stay?" he pressed, his tone gentler than usual.

I glanced at the horizon ahead of us. "It's not home anymore."

Wulfric considered that for a moment before asking, "Then where is?"

I didn't answer. I wasn't sure I could.

After a pause, Wulfric spoke again. "Lad, are you coming back with us?"

I hesitated, my grip on Halder's reins tightening. "Yes," I said finally, making the decision. "But I have to do something first."

Wulfric's brow arched, a small smile tugging at the corner of his mouth. "Oh?"

Chapter 14 - Break In the Wind

The path out of Linden was narrow, winding through the fields and thinning into a dirt trail lined with grass bent by the wind. I walked with Wulfric, Jory, and the Forsworn, their steps heavy but steady, a quiet resolve settling over the group. When we reached the main road, I felt it in my chest before my legs stopped moving—my path wasn't with them. Not yet.

Wulfric held Halder's reins loosely in one hand, the other resting on the horse's neck. The big animal shifted, ears flicking as the Forsworn milled about behind us. I stared down the road, my boots scuffing the dirt as I worked up the words.

"This is it," I said quietly.

Wulfric turned, studying me for a moment before nodding slowly. "So, you're off to do what you need to do?" His voice had that low, rough edge it always carried, but there was something softer beneath it. "And then you'll come back to us?"

I shifted, glancing toward Linden one last time. "Yeah. I need to get my father's book. See some people. After that…" My eyes flicked to him, and I tried for a small smile. "I'll come back. I can't keep wandering forever."

Wulfric's hand ran down Halder's neck, a faint smile pulling at the corner of his mouth. "Good. Wandering suits some, but not all." He paused, studying me again. "Just make sure you come back in one piece, lad."

Jory stepped forward, his brow furrowed, his voice quieter. "So, are you really going to join us?"

The weight of his question pressed against me. I hesitated, the answer stirring uneasily in my chest. "Maybe," I said finally, the word slipping out slow. "I'm thinking about it."

Jory's face broke into a grin, wide and boyish despite the exhaustion etched into him. "That's close enough to a yes," he said, clapping me on the shoulder with enough force to nearly knock me off balance. "We'll take it."

"Careful, Jory," Wulfric grunted, though his tone was light. "Don't knock the lad over before he's even set out."

Halder snorted softly, and Wulfric gave the reins a small tug, leading the horse a step closer.

Svend and Peter wandered over, their curiosity drawn by the conversation. Jory tugged the cloak off his shoulders, the fabric still fresh and uncreased from its time in Linden. He handed it to me, the weight of it familiar and comforting. "Here. It'll help keep you hidden."

I took it, running my fingers over the coarse weave. "Thanks, Jory."

Svend reached into his belt pouch, pulling out a few silver coins and pressing them into my hand. "Don't go spending it all on booze," he said with a smirk.

Peter stepped up next, thrusting a bundle of rations at me. "Not much, but it'll keep you from starving."

"Thanks," I said again, my voice low, as the three of them stepped back. Wulfric remained beside Halder, his hand resting on the horse's broad neck. The beast shifted, snorting softly, as if sensing something.

Wulfric ran his hand down Halder's neck, his expression softer than I was used to. He nodded, almost to himself, then held out the reins. "It'll be a hard trek, lad. Not sure if Crosse has that bridge fixed yet. Halder wouldn't handle a crossing like that too well anyway." He paused, his voice low and steady. "For now, why don't you take him?"

I froze, staring at the reins dangling from his hand. "Take Halder?" The words tumbled out awkwardly. "I… I don't—" My eyes flicked to the horse, then back to Wulfric. "I don't know how to care for a horse. Or ride one, really."

Wulfric chuckled softly, the sound carrying a hint of something fatherly. "Lad, what do you think I've been teaching you this whole time? You'll manage. Halder's smart enough to make up for what you don't know."

The horse snorted, as if agreeing, and I couldn't help but huff a weak laugh.

"And," Wulfric added, his grin faint but genuine, "if you're riding, people are less likely to ask questions. Makes you look like you belong."

Svend's voice cut in from behind. "Depends on the people, doesn't it? Some might think he's some fancy runaway lord."

Peter groaned. "Svend, shut up."

Wulfric didn't break his smile as he glanced back at the others. "Enough, you two." He turned back to me, pressing the reins into my hands. "You've earned him, Tomi. And besides…" His tone dipped slightly, gentler. "Everyone needs someone by their side, even if it's just a horse."

I stood there, the leather warm in my hands, Halder's dark eyes watching me as if he understood. My throat felt tight, but I managed a quiet, "Thank you."

Wulfric clapped my shoulder, the weight of it grounding. "Take care of him, and yourself. We'll be waiting."

I stood there, gripping the reins tighter, the weight of their trust settling on my shoulders like a cloak I wasn't sure I'd earned. Halder stood steady beside me, his dark eyes calm, intelligent, watching me as if he already understood more than I did.

Wulfric lingered for a moment, his gaze meeting mine. He gave a nod, slow and deliberate, then turned to join the others. Jory followed, his steps lighter than they'd been in days, but he glanced back once, offering a grin that didn't quite hide the tired lines on his face.

Peter adjusted the strap of his pack, muttering something to Svend, who laughed and shook his head. The two of them exchanged a few more words, their voices fading as they fell in with the others.

The group moved slowly, warriors and injured men walking alongside women and children, their shapes blending into the horizon as they began their march toward a new home. A faint breeze stirred, carrying the muffled sound of their footsteps and a snatch of conversation. It was an ending and a beginning, and I stood rooted in place, watching until they disappeared around the bend.

Halder nudged me gently, his warm breath brushing against my arm. It was enough to pull me back, out of my thoughts and into the present. I turned to him, resting a hand on his neck. "Alright, boy," I murmured, my voice quieter than I meant it to be. "Let's go."

He snorted, as if agreeing, and I gave him a soft pat before turning toward the road. My legs felt heavy as I took the first steps, the village of Linden fading behind me. Halder followed easily, his steady presence beside me grounding in a way I hadn't expected.

I glanced over my shoulder one last time, but the Forsworn were gone. With a deep breath, I faced forward again, my fingers brushing the reins as I walked. "Come on, boy," I said softly. "We've got a ways to go."

The road stretched ahead, winding lazily through the trees, dappled with shifting patches of sunlight. Elkswood wasn't far—not on horseback. But I wasn't in a hurry. For the first time in seasons, I felt no urgency to run, no need to press forward like something was chasing me.

Halder moved at his own pace, his steps steady, his ears flicking back to catch the sounds of the forest. Sometimes, when the roads were empty, I gave him his rein. His head would lift, nostrils flaring as if testing the wind, and then he'd pick up speed, his gait smoothing into a rhythmic trot that felt like water flowing beneath me. I closed my eyes once, just for a moment, and I could almost feel his satisfaction. It wasn't just the wind brushing against my face, but a current of simple joy coursing through him, something I sensed more deeply than words could describe.

We stayed off the main roads unless we had no choice. When we did take them, they were eerily quiet, the aftermath of war leaving stretches of forgotten paths. Farmers were in their fields at the edges of villages, tending crops that had finally started to grow back after the raids and fires. But for the most part, the roads were empty, save for the occasional traveler, who gave me and Halder a wide berth. I didn't blame them. A lone rider could mean anything—a messenger, a bandit, or worse.

When the woods swallowed us again, I let out a breath I hadn't realized I was holding. I liked the Forsworn well enough, but traveling with other people—always hearing their voices, their footsteps, the subtle weight of their emotions—had worn me down in ways I couldn't explain. Now it was just me and Halder, the trees a quiet audience, the undergrowth brushing against his legs as we wandered through paths that weren't marked on any map.

At night, we camped in the forest. I'd find a clearing near a stream or a meadow, somewhere Halder could graze while I built a small fire, careful to keep it low so it wouldn't catch attention. He'd wander off a little, his tail swishing, and I'd sit by the fire, patching up my clothes or working on an arrow shaft, my hands busy while my mind wandered. The quiet didn't feel like an absence anymore. It was a presence in itself, something that filled the air and let me think without crowding me.

Sometimes, when I hunted, I felt Halder watching me from the shadows of the trees. His dark eyes followed every step I took, ears flicking with curiosity as if he were learning the process alongside me. The woods would grow quieter as I moved, my breath slowing to match the rhythm of the forest. My bow rested comfortably in my grip, the string taut under my fingers as I scanned the underbrush for signs of life.

I loved this part—the stillness before the strike. The way the world seemed to hold its breath. A snapped twig, the soft rustle of leaves, the faintest flicker of movement in the brush, and there it was: a rabbit. It crouched low, its fur blending with the shadows, its nose twitching as it tested the air.

I crouched too, my knees brushing the damp earth, my hand steady as I raised the bow. Drawing the string back, I felt the tension humming in my chest, a thread of anticipation that tightened with each heartbeat. I exhaled slowly, letting the breath guide my aim. The arrow flew true, slicing through the air with a faint whistle before hitting its mark.

The rabbit didn't make a sound, just crumpled where it stood. I let the bow fall back to my side and crossed the clearing to pick it up. The weight of it was light in my hands, but I treated it with care, whispering a small thanks to the spirits under my breath. My father had taught me that, long ago—acknowledge the life you take. Don't waste it.

The sun filtered through the trees as I worked, the light catching the blade of my knife as I gutted the rabbit over a flat rock. The task was methodical, almost meditative. The slick feel of the hide under my hands, the faint metallic scent of blood, the soft squish of the entrails as I set them aside—it was messy work, but it felt honest.

Halder wandered closer, his hooves crunching softly against the leaves. He lowered his head, sniffing at the air with mild interest. "It's not for you," I said, glancing at him with a small smile. He snorted, as if in response, and went back to nibbling at the grass nearby.

This was fulfillment. Not the kill, but the quiet moments after—the satisfaction of knowing I'd provided for myself, the rhythm of working with my hands. I sat back once I was done, my knife cleaned and sheathed, the rabbit ready to be cooked later. The forest felt alive around me, the soft hum of insects, the distant chatter of birds. It was a world I could lose myself in, one that didn't demand answers or force me to be anything but what I was.

Halder's gaze met mine, calm and steady, like he understood. He flicked his ears, nudged at the grass, and I laughed softly. "Alright, boy. Let's move." I stood, shouldered the rabbit, and whistled. Halder followed without hesitation, his steps falling into rhythm with mine. Together, we disappeared into the trees, the forest closing behind us like a curtain.

During the day, I let him drink his fill from streams and graze in the meadows we passed. He liked that—his head would lower, his teeth tearing at the grass, his tail swishing contentedly. I could feel it in the way he moved afterward, his steps lighter, his neck arched like he'd forgotten the weight of the saddle. Through my pathos, I could sense the simple joy in him, and it was infectious. He was happy, and that made me happy in turn.

At night, when the fire was just embers and the forest was alive with the hum of crickets and the distant hoot of an owl, I'd lie back and stare at the stars. Halder would settle nearby, his breathing deep and steady, the sound a comfort in the stillness. I wasn't alone. Not really.

The days blurred together, a rhythm I hadn't realized I'd missed. Hunting, patching, riding. Stopping to watch a squirrel dart up a tree or to let Halder splash his hooves in a shallow stream. It was simple. It was quiet. It felt like freedom, and I wasn't ready to give that up just yet.

On one of those days, as the sun hung low in the sky and the trees whispered of autumn, I found the stream. I hadn't even realized it was late in the season. Since my imprisonment, time had blurred, the seasons slipping past unnoticed. Now, they revealed themselves to me again—the crispness in the air, the soft decay of fallen leaves, the muted golden light filtering through thinning branches. It was like waking up to something I'd forgotten was there.

The stream widened into a small pond, encircled by smooth, moss-covered rocks. The water shimmered, its surface rippling as Halder lowered his head to drink. He snorted softly, the sound breaking the stillness as I scanned the clearing. The scene was quiet, untouched, the kind of place that felt like it had existed forever. Despite the chill, the pond called to me, promising a kind of purity I hadn't felt in what seemed like years.

I stripped down, folding my clothes neatly and placing them on a nearby rock. The necklace my mother had given me stayed against my skin, cool and steady. Wading into the water, I felt its bite immediately—a sharp, bracing cold that made me suck in a breath—but I kept going. The pond was shallow at first, but as I moved further, the water lapped at my chest, and its chill became something I could bear. For some reason, the old fear didn't grip me anymore. Maybe it was everything I'd been through. Or maybe it was the steady weight of the necklace, like an anchor holding me to the present.

I let myself float on my back, the water lapping at my sides, my limbs loose and weightless. Above me, the sky stretched endlessly, a patchwork of blue and white. Clouds drifted lazily, their edges glowing with sunlight. A red kite soared high above, its wings cutting gracefully through the air, a speck of russet against the heavens.

Curious, I reached out with my pathos, tentatively brushing against the kite's awareness. What I felt made me gasp, almost losing my balance in the water. The bird sent me flashes—images of endless skies, of the sun warming its feathers, of wind rushing against its body as it dove and rose again. The sensation was intoxicating. For a moment, I wasn't Tomi anymore. I was soaring, weightless, untethered, riding the currents like I was born to them. Freedom. Real freedom. My chest ached with the sweetness of it, the want to hold onto that feeling forever.

A sound broke the spell. A broken twig. The connection snapped, leaving me breathless as I turned sharply in the water. My eyes landed on a figure at the edge of the pond, crouched over my bags.

It was a man—tall, lean, with a mane of bright white hair that seemed to catch the light like snow under the sun. His clothes were ragged, hanging off him like they'd been through years of wear, and his movements were quick, almost frantic, as he rifled through my things. His features were strange, caught somewhere between youth and age, his expression a wild mix of focus and distraction.
"Hey!" I shouted, my voice echoing off the water and trees.

The stranger froze, his hand halfway through my bag. His stark white hair glinted in the sunlight, wild and untamed, and his lean frame was tense, like a rabbit poised to bolt. His head turned slowly toward me, pale eyes wide with startled innocence. For a moment, I thought he might say something, but then he clutched my clothes tighter and bolted into the forest.

"Damn it!" I splashed out of the pond, water cascading down my bare skin as I stumbled onto the mossy bank. Cold air bit at me as I grabbed the nearest branch for balance and started after him. My wet feet slipped on the damp earth, but I didn't stop. My chest burned with the effort as I crashed into the underbrush, twigs scratching at my skin.

The man was fast, faster than I'd expected, darting through the trees with a fluidity that seemed almost inhuman. His ragged clothes flapped as he moved, his bare feet barely making a sound on the forest floor. I reached out with my pathos, trying to feel his presence, to track the emotions that should have radiated from him. Instead, I was overwhelmed. It was like the entire forest was alive with him, his emotions diffused through every leaf and shadow. I felt everything—mischief, exhilaration, fear—and nothing distinct. He was everywhere and nowhere at once.

Branches slapped against my face as I pushed forward, my breath coming in ragged gasps. The forest blurred around me, the sharp scent of pine mingling with the earthy dampness of rotting leaves. I focused on the flashes of white ahead, his hair like a beacon weaving through the trees. The distance between us grew, and I snarled under my breath, forcing my legs to move faster.

The underbrush thinned suddenly, and I burst onto the main road. The sunlight blinded me for a heartbeat, and I stumbled to a halt, my bare feet skidding on the gravel. A gasp sounded nearby, followed by a muffled scream.

Standing a few paces away was a merchant family—a man in a wide-brimmed hat, two young women holding baskets, and a boy clutching a stick. They stared at me, their expressions a mixture of shock and horror. The father stepped forward, shielding the women with his arm. One of the girls dropped her basket, apples spilling onto the road.

My face burned hotter than the sun overhead. "Uh…" I stammered, glancing around wildly. "It's not what it looks like."

The younger woman's eyes darted toward the forest, and I followed her gaze. There—just beyond the tree line—the white-haired man hesitated for a split second before turning and vanishing back into the woods.

"Sorry!" I blurted, my voice cracking. Without waiting for their response, I bolted after him, ignoring the father's angry shouts. The forest swallowed me again, the scent of pine and damp earth closing around me. I pushed forward, my chest heaving, determined not to lose him.

The forest felt endless, every shadow and rustling leaf mocking me as I ran. My breath burned in my chest, and my legs ached with every step. I didn't know how long I'd been chasing him—moments, a span, the whole damn morning? It felt like I'd been running naked after that maddening flash of white hair forever.

Finally, I stopped. My knees buckled as I leaned against a tree, my heart pounding like it might break free of my ribs. My pathos, stretched thin from effort, only told me what I already knew: he was gone, slipping through the forest like some spirit. "Fine," I muttered, raking a hand through my wet hair. "Keep the damn clothes, you bastard."

A wry smile tugged at my lips despite my frustration. Maybe the spirits were paying me back for that time I'd stolen the gate guard's uniform. Turnabout was fair play, I supposed—though I would've appreciated it if the spirits had left me a shred of dignity.

The walk back to the pond was slower, my shoulders slumping with each step. Halder greeted me with a soft snort, his tail flicking as if to say, "About time." I stopped short when I saw my clothes draped neatly across his saddle, every piece folded like some kind of mockery. My mouth twisted in frustration, but I didn't say a word. I yanked the shirt off the saddle and slipped it on, the damp fabric clinging to my skin.

I was pulling on my trousers when I heard it—a soft crunch, the unmistakable sound of teeth biting into an apple. My head shot up, and there he was.

The white-haired man sat across the pond, his bare feet dangling in the water. His ragged clothes hung loose on his lean frame, and his stark hair glinted in the sunlight, almost blinding against the autumn hues. He chewed leisurely, his pale eyes watching me like I was some amusing curiosity.

"You run well," he said finally, his voice lilting, almost musical. He took another bite of the apple, juice dripping down his chin. "But not as well as me."

I stared at him, dumbfounded and still breathless from the chase. "You—what in the spirits was that?" My voice cracked, raw from yelling.

He smiled, wide and mischievous, as though I'd just asked him the most ridiculous question in the world. "That was breakfast," he said, holding up the half-eaten apple. "Care to join me, or are you hoping to air out the family jewels for the entire forest to see a bit longer?"

Chapter 15 - A Lesson

"You're the man from Whitestone," I said, my voice steady, though I still felt the weight of everything—the morning, the chase, him. "The one from the cell."

The white-haired man didn't answer. He tapped the rock beside him with two fingers, a soft, rhythmic sound. An invitation.

I narrowed my eyes. "Who are you?"

Tap. Tap. He gestured again, his pale, sharp features tilted toward me with faint amusement. I let out a breath, my shoulders sagging, and walked over. Halder snorted behind me, clearly unimpressed with the situation. I lowered myself onto the rock, the smooth stone cold against my skin. The man cleared his throat, staring down at his feet still submerged in the water. His toes wiggled, sending ripples through the pond's surface.

I sighed and began rolling up my hose. "Just so you know," I muttered, "I already had a bath."

The corner of his mouth twitched. "And yet your feet are dirty."

"So?" I shot back, dipping my toes into the water. The chill bit at my skin. "Who are you? Why were you in Whitestone? Was it for stealing?" I glanced at him sideways. "Like how you stole my clothes?"

He chuckled—a low, light sound that somehow filled the quiet space between us. Shaking his head, he said, "No. I stole your garments because you stole that bird's flight and nearly its life."

I blinked at him, a frown pulling at my mouth. "What?"

His pale eyes turned to me, clear as ice and just as unsettling. "Who taught you?"

"Taught me?"

"To sense motion. Commotion. Emotion," he said, his voice

lilting like a breeze. "To feel life itself?" He lifted his hand and tapped two fingers against his chest, as though mimicking a heartbeat. "Who taught you that, boy?"

My breath caught. My fingers curled over the edge of the rock, steadying me. I stared at him, the world suddenly too still, too bright. "What... what are you talking about?" I managed to ask.

He tilted his head, considering me, the faintest glimmer of a smile on his lips. "Ah," he murmured, as though he'd just uncovered something valuable. "You don't even know, do you?"

My eyes went wide.

"You mean pathos?" I said, the word hesitant on my tongue. My father had warned me—always warned me—about telling people. My gaze darted to the man's pale eyes, searching for something I couldn't name. "My father... he had it too. At least a little. Do you have it? pathos?"

The white-haired man's smile deepened, slow and deliberate, as if savoring a secret. "So that's what you call it here."

"What exactly are you?" I asked, the question slipping out before I could stop it.

He tilted his head, strands of his wild hair catching the dappled sunlight that fell through the canopy. "A traveler," he said. "A wanderer. A nomad."

"But do you have it?" I pressed.

For a moment, he didn't answer. Then, he lifted his hand into the air, fingers outstretched. From somewhere high above, the red kite descended, spiraling through shafts of sunlight that cut golden through the branches. The bird's wings caught the light in flashes of deep crimson and shadowed brown. It landed softly on the man's arm, talons curling with a delicate certainty. My breath caught as he held it there, the bird utterly calm, its head turning to look at me.

"I do not call it that," he said.

The red kite's sharp gaze lingered, unnervingly intelligent, before it turned back to the man.

"What do you call it?" I asked, my voice quiet.

"The Path," he replied, his voice lilting like a melody. I nodded slowly. "My father called it that once. Wulfric, too." The man raised a brow, his pale eyes glinting with curiosity. "Wulfric?"

"No, Wulfric doesn't have it," I added quickly.

"Everyone has it," the man said softly. "To some extent. Not everyone learns to do what we do, though. What you nearly did."

I frowned. "What did I nearly do?"

The man's gaze drifted upward as the kite stretched its wings briefly before folding them again. The sunlight caught in the feathers, glinting like fire. "You nearly took a life—either yours, or…" He raised his hand slightly, the bird shifting on his arm. "Hers."

I stared at the bird, my skin prickling. "How?"

"You nearly passed your mind into hers. Bodies are only meant for one spirit," he said, the words slow and deliberate, like he was measuring each one. "When a second intrudes, strange things happen."

"Is that what I did?" I whispered. My voice felt small, childlike. My chest tightened with the memory of the wind, of the sky opening wide above me. "I felt free. Like I could fly."

"You did," he said, his lips curling faintly. "But in doing so, you nearly took that freedom from her. You must be careful. You can share, exchange feelings, glimpses—images—but do not go too deep. A soul does not welcome company."

The red kite let out a soft cry, a sound like the wind sweeping through dry leaves.

"How do you know all of this?" I asked, my voice steadier now.

The man looked down at me, and for the first time, the

playfulness in his face faded into something heavier. "I have spent my life following the Path," he said.

The words settled between us, quiet and unshakable, like stones dropped into still water. I stared at him, my heart thudding against my ribs.

"Can you teach me?" I asked.

The man's expression shifted, the mischief dulling into something unreadable. Without a word, he raised his arm. The red kite lifted off, wings snapping open as it climbed, spiraling back into the sky until it was a speck of crimson against the clouds.

The man slid his feet from the water, droplets trailing off his pale skin as he stood. He looked taller somehow, straighter, as though some unseen weight had fallen from his shoulders. "I cannot teach you," he said plainly. "I came here today to return a debt."

I frowned, pulling my feet from the water, the cold biting at my skin as I stood. "A debt?"

He nodded, brushing his hands together as though wiping away dust. "You saved me from that cell. I have returned the favor by making sure you do not create a cell of your own. That clears the slate."

"Wait, what?" I took a step forward, the ground cool and soft beneath my bare feet. "That doesn't make sense—please, I need to know more."

The man ignored me, turning on his heel with an almost casual indifference and walking toward the forest. I felt something rising in my chest, a panic I hadn't expected, and I ran in front of him, blocking his path.

"Please!" I said, my voice sharper than I intended. "I need to know more. My father—he had this, but he never explained it. Not like you. He didn't… he couldn't do what you did. To tell animals what to do, to—"

"Control them?" The word came like a crack of thunder, the man's voice suddenly hard. His pale eyes flashed, and the smile was gone, replaced with something sharp and dangerous. "We do not control."

I froze, my pulse quickening.

The man's voice dropped, quieter but no less intense. "Never assume you *control* another, boy. We ask. We influence. We share. We…"

I turned, hearing the word echo behind me. "Divert."

The man stood there, feet planted where I'd been moments before. I spun back to face where he'd been just seconds ago—empty. My head snapped between the two spots, breath catching in my throat.

"How did you do that?" I asked, my voice cracking.

"Do what?" came his voice, this time from a different direction. I turned sharply, and the man stood several paces to my left, as though he'd always been there.

A strange dizziness swept over me. It was like watching something through glass warped by rain—he moved, I *knew* he moved, but my mind felt stretched, pulled, like something was forcing my senses to see something else entirely.

"You feel it, don't you?" His voice came again, quieter. "It's not pleasant, is it?"

The forest around me grew darker. Shadows thickened, the branches twisting together like claws. The air felt colder, heavier, pressing against my skin. My breaths came quicker. "What are you doing?" I whispered, my voice small. "Please. Stop."

The man didn't stop.

The shadows fell away, replaced by light so sharp it stung my eyes. The trees glowed brighter, the greens too green, the browns of the trunks rich and deep, the light almost golden. My heart hammered as something pressed against me—an emotion, powerful and consuming, too much for me to grasp.

"Stop!" I cried out, stumbling backward, nearly falling.

Suddenly, a hand gripped my shoulder. I spun, and there he was—behind me, close enough that I could see the faint lines on his face, the glint in his pale eyes.

"It's not nice when you influence others, is it?" he said softly, his voice carrying a quiet weight. "They notice. They always notice."

I stared at him, breathless, my skin clammy with sweat.

He let go of my shoulder, stepping back. "Every being manipulates others. It is how we communicate. How we live." He held up a finger as if counting. "A wolf bares its teeth, and the pack falls into line. A bird calls out, and its mate answers, guided by instinct. A mother scolds her child, and the child learns fear—and love. Every look, every word, every silence, it all carries influence."

He tilted his head, his expression shifting back into something softer, though still edged with mystery. "But you—*we*—have a choice. You must decide how you affect others. To guide, to soothe, to protect. Never to harm. Never to take what is not freely given. Do you understand me, boy?"

I swallowed hard, my throat dry, and nodded.

The man smiled faintly. "This is the only lesson I will teach you today."

The white-haired man vanished again. One blink and he was gone, as though the forest had swallowed him whole. I spun on my heels, the dizziness rushing back, my breath unsteady. "Wait—" My voice cracked in the empty stillness. "My name is Tomi!"

A pause.

Then, faint, a voice slipped through the trees, distant and close all at once. "My name is Felix."

I turned sharply, trying to pinpoint the sound, but it seemed to come from everywhere—above, behind, the shadows, the wind. My stomach twisted as I stretched out with my pathos, reaching for something—anything. Instead, the forest pulsed back at me, too much all at once. Emotions scattered in every direction: faint echoes of calm, mischief, stillness, freedom. Like sunlight breaking through clouds, only to vanish again.

The voice called again, soft but clear. "If you want to know more… go north. Find the Path. I'll be walking it."

And then silence.

The forest settled back into itself. The wind rustled through branches, the faint sounds of birds and distant water creeping back into my ears. I stood there, my chest rising and falling with uneven breaths, my feet growing colder in the damp earth. He was gone.

Felix. I rolled the name over in my mind, trying to anchor it. Nothing felt real anymore.

I walked back to the pond slowly, every step heavy with confusion, my thoughts a tangled mess. Halder raised his head as I approached, his ears flicking forward like he'd been waiting for me to reappear. He gave a soft snort as I dropped onto a flat rock beside him, the stone cool against my skin.

I dried my feet, rubbing warmth back into them, before sliding my boots on with stiff, cold fingers. The leather felt snug and familiar, grounding me. I pulled my cloak tight around my shoulders, the weight of the fabric comforting, then pushed my hood up to shield my face.

Halder watched me, his dark eyes calm as ever, a sharp contrast to the storm that still swirled in my mind.

"Time to go, boy," I said, my voice hoarse. I ran my hand along his neck, the soft, thick coat warm beneath my touch. "Let's get out of this forest. Back to Elkswood."

Halder flicked his tail, as if to say he agreed, and I took his reins. The forest loomed behind us, quiet and watchful, as we left the pond and headed toward the edge of the trees. My feet found the path easily enough, but my mind stayed tangled somewhere back in the shadows, where a white-haired stranger had disappeared and a voice had promised answers far to the north.

Chapter 16 - Inkling

The forest thinned as Halder and I moved on, the trees growing sparse and the underbrush giving way to packed dirt and stones. The soft thud of his hooves broke the quiet, the rhythm steady and patient. I didn't rush him. There was something about the forest that made time feel slower, less urgent. I let it stretch out.

But soon enough, the path turned toward the road, and the quiet faded. The sound of people reached me first—wheels creaking, horses clopping, voices rising and falling like the pull of the river. The main road snaked out of the trees, a long, worn ribbon of mud and trampled grass, crowded with travelers. Merchants with carts, farmers with sacks slung over shoulders, mothers dragging tired children, and old men leaning on sticks. Everyone moved with purpose, even if their pace was slow.

I guided Halder onto the road, shifting in the saddle as we slipped into the flow of bodies. I kept my hood low, the fabric shadowing my face. Halder seemed to sense the change. His ears twitched at every sound, but he didn't falter.

"Can't tell one soldier from the next these days," a man up ahead grumbled, his voice carrying. He had a cart full of firewood, and his words were sharp with frustration. "Harlan's men say one thing, Erik's men say another. They're all the same—taking what they want."

Another man, older, huffed beside him. "Aye, they're not after us. It's each other they're gutting."

"They'll come for us soon enough," the first said. "They always do."

I glanced to the side as a small group of soldiers passed by, their cloaks marked with green and gold. They looked weary, their faces lined and unsmiling, hands never far from their sword hilts. One of them gave me a glance as he rode past, his gaze lingering under the shadow of my hood. I kept my head down and my grip steady on Halder's reins, my heart ticking faster.

"Move aside," one of the soldiers barked to a merchant who wasn't moving quick enough. The man grumbled but pulled his cart to the side.

The soldiers rode on. No questions, no trouble. I let out a breath I hadn't realized I was holding.

The road grew busier the closer we got to Elkswood. I could see the roofs rising in the distance, the pale streak of smoke curling from chimneys. Halder's ears flicked back as I led him to the stables outside the main gates. It was crowded there, too—wagons pulling in, horses tied off, stable boys running back and forth.

I swung my leg over the saddle and dropped to the ground with a thud, my knees stiff from the ride. Halder snorted, flicking his tail against my shoulder as if to say I'd taken too long. I patted his side and led him toward a quieter corner of the stable.

A boy—probably eleven, maybe younger—straightened up from brushing a gray mare. I say boy but I myself was only fourteen or fifteen summers old. He wiped his hands on his trousers, eyeing Halder with an exaggerated squint like he was sizing up a king's warhorse. "That's a big beast you've got there," he said, dragging out the words. "Room, feed, and a fresh stall'll be five crowns for the night. Can't have him eating the walls, can we?"

"Five?" I asked, pulling up short. "You sure you're not feeding him gold?"

The boy grinned, a lopsided, gap-toothed thing. "Big horse, big price. He's worth it, though. Look at the shine on him."

Halder snorted again, probably agreeing. I sighed, reaching into my pocket and fishing out some of the coins Svend had given me.

"Fine," I muttered, handing them over.

The boy pocketed the crowns, bouncing them once in his hand before jerking his head toward an empty stall. "I'll take good care of him, don't worry."

"You better," I said, pointing a finger at him for emphasis. I turned to Halder, rubbing the broad patch of his nose. "You behave," I murmured under my breath. Leaving my bow and axe in his saddlebags.

Halder huffed, warm breath brushing my face as if to say he always did. I gave him one last pat, pulling my cloak tighter as I turned away. The boy led him off, whistling some out-of-tune song, and I watched Halder's dark form disappear into the stalls before turning toward the gates of Elkswood.

Elkswood hadn't changed much, but it felt different. The streets were busy, louder than I remembered, people moving in clusters as if drawn together by the weight of the war. I kept my hood pulled low, shadows spilling across my face as I slipped into the crowd. My boots scuffed against the dirt road, the sound swallowed by the noise of carts, chatter, and the occasional distant clang of a blacksmith's hammer.

The houses grew tighter as I moved further in, the sparse edge of town giving way to cobbled streets and crooked doorframes. I caught the faint scent of roasting meat, of ale, and something sour that clung to the wind. The Lame Mule came into view soon after—a squat, two-story building with warped shutters and a swinging sign painted with a lopsided mule. Its windows glowed faintly, and I could hear the muffled rise and fall of voices inside.

I slowed as I passed it, my feet dragging for just a moment. Viktor would be in there, no doubt swanning around behind the bar, a cloth in hand and a sly tilt to his chin, muttering to himself in that theatrical way of his—like every word deserved its own stage.

His sleeves would be rolled with perfect precision, his waistcoat unbuttoned just so, irritation etched onto his face in a way that looked almost deliberate, like he wore it as carefully as the rings on his fingers.

The hunters—Rolf, Brynja, Oliver—would be sitting around the tables, trading stories over mugs of ale. I could almost see them, Brynja's sharp laugh rising above the others, Oliver trying to outdo himself with tales of impossible shots he'd taken. For a heartbeat, I wanted to duck my head in, see their faces. Maybe they wouldn't notice me. Maybe they'd just smile, call me over like nothing had happened.

But I didn't move.

Would they call out my name? Would their eyes widen, and would Viktor send for the guards? Would I hear the iron clatter of chains, feel the bruising grip of a gaoler pulling me back to a cell?

The thought sent a shiver down my spine, spreading like frost through my chest. I forced my feet forward, my head down.

The tavern faded behind me, the noise softening into a distant murmur. I didn't look back.

Instead, I pressed deeper into the town, where the streets narrowed and the buildings crowded close like whispers leaning in.

The market buzzed with the hum of voices and the clatter of carts, the smell of roasting meat and fresh bread hanging thick in the air. I wove through the crowd, careful not to bump shoulders or draw too much attention. My hood stayed low, but I knew how easy it would be for the sunlight to catch a stray lock of red hair. A flicker of familiarity might mean the wrong pair of eyes on me, and I'd be back in the Gaol before I could so much as spit.

I stopped at a small stall where chestnuts sizzled in a battered iron pan, their shells crackling in the heat. The vendor, an older man with soot-blackened hands, grunted out a price without looking up. I handed over a coin and watched the chestnuts tumble into a scrap of cloth. They burned my fingertips, but I welcomed the heat as I made my way back through the press of people.

Soldiers lingered in loose clusters, swords at their hips, but there were fewer of them than before—no patrols clogging every corner, no captains barking orders. Most of them would be out, stationed in fortifications or fighting in the prince's war. I still kept my distance, moving through the crowd like smoke.

I avoided the streets I'd once walked as a hunter. No need to chance running into familiar faces: the butcher who'd haggled over a boar, the tanner with his sharp eye for pelt quality, or worse, Rolf and the others from the Lame Mule. My chest tightened at the thought of Brynja or Rolf catching a glimpse of me. What would they say? Would they turn me in? Or worse, pity me? I wasn't ready to find out.

Eventually, I spotted the shop. The Scribe's Place sat tucked between taller buildings, its faded sign creaking gently on rusted chains. It looked the same—narrow and unimposing, the scent of ink and parchment leaking out when someone opened the door. Anni would be there.

But I didn't go in. Not yet. I found a spot near the edge of the market where a sagging cart piled with burlap sacks offered some cover. Leaning against it, I peeled back the makeshift cloth of my chestnuts, steam curling into the cool air. One by one, I cracked the shells, the nutty warmth spreading over my tongue as I chewed slowly. I wasn't watching the shop—I couldn't be watching the shop—but my eyes kept darting back to the door.

People trickled in and out. A man with ink-stained fingers. A harried-looking woman with a ledger tucked under her arm. No one lingered long. The scribes ran a quiet trade, copying letters, handling official records—nothing flashy. Still, it was one of the busiest places in town for those who knew its worth.

I froze mid-bite when I saw him. A soldier, tall and broad-shouldered, his armor polished and well-kept—a man of rank, no doubt. He strode with purpose, a scrap of paper clutched in his gloved hand. I ducked my head, pulling my hood lower as he walked past me, the scrape of his boots on stone loud in my ears. He vanished inside the shop, the door clicking shut behind him.

I forced myself to breathe, slow and steady. The chestnuts in my hand were suddenly too hot, too much. My eyes stayed on the door, waiting, watching. A few minutes later, it creaked open again, and the soldier emerged. His face looked relieved, whatever burden he carried lightened by the task inside. He walked off down the street without a glance in my direction.

After that, fewer people went in. The sun dipped lower, brushing the rooftops with a golden haze. The market noise softened as the crowd began to thin, merchants packing up their wares, voices calling out last deals of the day. I tossed the last chestnut shell into the dirt, wiped my hands on my trousers, and fixed my gaze on the shop.

Not long now.

The door to the scribe's shop creaked open again, and this time, it wasn't a soldier or a merchant who stepped out. She appeared with a bucket in hand, its contents sloshing thick and heavy as she walked. Her wild red hair tumbled down her back, loose waves catching in the evening light. A few strands stuck to her face where sweat or ink smudged her cheek, but she didn't seem to care. A leather girdle cinched her tunic, small books and a penknife tucked snugly at her sides, swaying softly with her steps.

I straightened, my chest tightening. Anni.

She turned down the side of the building, her boots barely making a sound on the cobbled stones as she moved with a familiar, absentminded grace. I glanced around—no soldiers in sight—and pushed off the wall, trailing her at a distance. I kept quiet as I rounded the corner, stepping lightly on the stones.

She stood at the back of the shop, hefting the bucket and sending its contents splashing across the street. Water mixed with swirls of dark ink spread over the cobbles, shimmering like oil in the low light. The streaks spread unevenly, curling into abstract shapes, twisting until they almost formed letters or strange, unspoken symbols.

"Almost looks like a picture," I said, my voice soft. "A letter, maybe."

Anni froze mid-step, her shoulders stiffening. Slowly, she turned. Her eyes, wide behind the thin frames of her glasses, fixed on me. For a moment, she just stared, the ink-stained fingers of one hand still clutching the empty bucket.

"Tomi?" Her voice barely carried, soft as breath.

I hesitated, then reached up, pulling back my hood.

Her eyes widened further, a sharp inhale escaping her lips. "Tomi," she said again, louder this time. The bucket slipped from her hand, clattering to the stones, forgotten. She ran toward me, closing the distance before I could think to move.

Her arms wrapped around me, pulling me in tightly enough to drive the breath from my chest. I froze, my hands hovering awkwardly at my sides for half a heartbeat before I finally returned the embrace. Her hair smelled faintly of parchment and ink, her shoulders trembled ever so slightly beneath my palms.

The lump in my throat kept me silent.

Anni pulled back after what felt like an eternity, her hands still resting on my arms as she took a good look at me. Her gaze swept from my face to my boots and back, a mixture of relief, curiosity, and concern swirling in her ink-dark eyes. "Tomi," she said softly, "what happened to you?"

I glanced around, tugging my hood up again and lowering my voice. "Is there somewhere we can talk?"
She frowned for half a heartbeat before her expression shifted—sharp and decisive. "Hang on. Give me a moment."

Anni turned and bolted toward the front of the shop, her boots clattering against the cobbles. I watched as she ducked through the door, disappearing inside. Through the warped glass of one window, I could see her rushing from one corner of the shop to the other, her figure a blur as she locked the door, slid shutters closed, and snuffed out a few lamps. Finally, her freckled face appeared in the back window, framed in pale light. She waved a hand at me before disappearing again.

I made my way around the side of the building, where the back door was already open, Anni waiting with one hand on the frame. "Come on," she whispered urgently, jerking her head inside. I ducked through the doorway, and she shut it quietly behind us.

The room smelled of ink, old parchment, and faintly of smoke.

Shelves lined the walls, stacked with scrolls and ledgers. A small hearth crackled dimly in the corner, barely enough to cut through the chill.

Anni folded her arms, leaning her weight on one leg as she studied me again. "My father's out running missives for the Lord," she said, almost as if reading my mind.

"Cedric?" I asked, the name bitter on my tongue.

Anni shook her head, her mouth quirking into a smile. "No, the minor one. Another fief lord's son—he's been raised to look after the barracks here, though I don't know who thought that was a good idea. He's barely older than us."

I let out a breath I hadn't realized I was holding. "Cedric's not here, then?"

"No." Her smile faded slightly, as though weighing the memory. "He left when the war started. Off playing commander somewhere, I imagine."

"Good," I muttered, the relief settling like a weight off my chest. I looked up at her again. "And your mother? How is she?"

Anni's grin returned, bright as ever. "Travelling, of course. War or no war, she sings her songs, plays her music, and tells her tales to anyone who'll listen."

A small, unexpected smile tugged at my lips. "At least someone's out there nudging the world in the right direction," I said, the words slipping out before I could stop them. My mind drifted to Felix for a moment—his cryptic lessons, the strange weight of his words—and I wondered if that's what her mother had always been doing in her own quiet way. Influencing people for the better.

Anni studied my face, her brow furrowing as though she was piecing something together. There was something in her eyes—sharp, searching, like she was deciding what to say next. Finally, she spoke. "I was worried about you, you know. You just…

disappeared from your cell. At first, I thought they'd moved you or—" Her voice wavered slightly. "Or worse."

I glanced away, the memory of the Gaol pulling at me like a weight. "They didn't hang me," I said quietly. "Oliver told you I escaped?"

She nodded, the tension in her shoulders easing slightly. "He said you got out somehow, but not much more than that. Just that you'd vanished. We all figured you'd be halfway to the mountains or dead in a ditch."

"Almost was," I muttered. Anni raised an eyebrow, waiting, so I sighed and began. "There was an ambush. Forsworn—My friends. Cedric's lot were going to kill them. I got out to warn them." I hesitated, my thumb tracing the rim of the mug she'd set in front of me. "They chased us after that."

"Of course they did," she said softly, turning to the kettle hanging above the small iron stove. She worked quickly, her movements efficient as she measured out the leaves, poured hot water into the cups, and stirred. The room filled with the faint, earthy smell of steeping herbs.

I watched her quietly, the soft scrape of her spoon against the ceramic cups filling the silence. After a moment, she handed me one, the steam curling like ghostly threads into the air. "Drink," she said. "It'll help."

I took a cautious sip. The tea was strong, bitter at first, but there was something grounding about it—a hint of mint, a little sweetness that lingered at the back of my throat. "It's good," I said, surprised.

Anni smiled faintly, settling onto the bench opposite me with her own cup. "Benefits of working with ink. You learn the properties of each leaf. Not just for writing."

I raised an eyebrow. "You sure you're not a healer?"

She smirked, lifting her cup to her lips. "Don't insult me."

I huffed a quiet laugh, wrapping my hands around the warm

ceramic. The heat soaked into my palms, chasing the lingering chill from my skin. For a moment, neither of us said anything, the silence hanging between us, not heavy, but thoughtful. Anni's eyes flicked toward the window, as though she were seeing something far away. I looked down into my tea, watching the ripples settle, waiting for the words to come.

Anni's gaze lifted from her tea, fixing on me with that sharp, thoughtful look again. "You're here for your map, aren't you? And your father's book."

I nodded, fingers tightening around the mug. "Yeah." The word sat heavy in my throat, and I hesitated before saying more. "I… I still don't know if I can read all of it." My voice faltered, the rest of what I wanted to say getting stuck. I cleared my throat and tried again. "I might need to stay a little longer. To learn. If… if that's okay."

Anni's face softened, and her smile curved in that familiar way—gentle, patient, the way it always did when she explained letters to me for the hundredth time. "Of course it's okay," she said, a hint of pride slipping into her voice. "I'd be glad to keep teaching you. You've come a long way already, Tomi."

I exhaled a breath I hadn't realized I was holding, but before I could say anything else, her smile faltered. "But staying here…" She set her mug down, her fingers tapping absently against the wood. "It's dangerous, Tomi. They're still looking for you. If you're caught—"

The sound of the front door creaking open cut her off.

Anni's eyes widened, her face draining of color. My stomach twisted, the warmth from the tea turning to ice. The faint scuff of boots echoed through the shop, followed by the heavy clink of something—armor, perhaps—shifting.

I stared at her, barely breathing.

She mouthed one word: *Hide.*

Chapter 17 - Hide

Anni's eyes went wide, her lips parting in alarm. "Tomi—hide," she whispered sharply, already moving toward the front of the shop.

I spun in place, my heart hammering, eyes darting for somewhere—anywhere—to disappear. The room offered nothing. No cabinets big enough to squeeze into, no shadows deep enough to swallow me. My fists clenched at my sides, teeth gritted, and I backed toward the farthest corner, readying myself for the worst.

The front door creaked open.

"Da?" Anni's voice rang out, steady but tight. I heard the shuffle of boots across the wooden floor.
I braced myself, muscles coiled to fight or flee, and strained to listen.
"Oh," Anni said after a pause, her tone shifting. "It's you."
Her words barely registered before a shadow stretched across the doorway.

I surged forward instinctively, my hand twitching toward my belt for a weapon I didn't have. But then I stopped dead, my breath catching as the figure stepped into the light.

He was older than me by a year or two, his sandy-blonde hair tousled like he'd spent the morning in the wind. The first hints of stubble darkened his jaw, and a bow sat slung across his back, the string taut and well-used. His blue eyes darted around the room before landing on me.

"Oliver?" I said letting out a long breath, my hands falling to my sides as the tension bled away.
"Tomi, " Oliver said in return.

Anni appeared in the doorway, one hand on her hip, the other brushing stray curls from her face. "Thought I'd locked the door, but look who wandered in," she said, her voice dripping with dry amusement. "It's practically a gathering."

Oliver grinned, leaning casually against the frame. "Didn't mean to scare you." His eyes flicked to me. "Tomi." He straightened, his grin softening into something more sincere. "Good to see you made it."

"Oliver," I said, my voice steady but low. "Thank you. You helped me that night."

Oliver shrugged, looking away as if it meant nothing. "Wasn't much," he muttered. "But why'd you come back? You know they're looking for you, right?"

I glanced at the corner of the room where the book sat, its worn leather cover catching the dim light. "For this," I said, pointing to it. "My father's book."

Anni sighed, walking past Oliver to scoop up the book. "Tomi plans to stay for a while," she said, glancing between the two of us. "But you can't stay here. My father will be back soon, and if he finds you…"

Oliver nodded knowingly. "He's a good man, Anni, but he'll follow the law. He'd turn Tomi in whether he wanted to or not."

There was something in the way he said her name, familiar and easy, like they'd spent time together. Anni didn't rise to it, just rolled her eyes and muttered something under her breath before setting the book in my hands.

Oliver spoke up again, his tone more certain now. "I know a place," he said. "Just outside of town, in the forest. It's quiet, hidden. You can hide there for awhile. I'll bring Anni out to you tomorrow."

I looked at Anni, hesitating. She gave me a reassuring smile and adjusted her glasses. "I'll bring the map," she said softly. "And more tea if you're lucky."

Her words made me smile faintly, though it felt heavy. I stepped forward and hugged her, holding her tightly for just a moment before pulling back. "Thank you," I said, my voice barely above a whisper.

She handed me the book again, her fingers brushing mine. "Be careful, Tomi."

I nodded, slipping the book under my cloak. I pulled my hood up, letting the fabric shadow my face as I turned to Oliver. "Let's go."

Oliver held the door open, and I stepped out into the cooling air. The streets had grown quiet, shadows stretching long across the cobbles. I glanced back once, seeing Anni still standing there, silhouetted by the faint light inside. Then I turned forward, following Oliver into the growing dusk.

The market was quieter than when I'd come in, the day winding down as the last of the vendors packed up their wares. Lanterns swung lazily from posts, flickering with soft orange light. Oliver and I moved through the thinning crowd, and every now and then someone would nod his way—an older man carrying a bushel of onions, a woman in a patched shawl, a pair of boys kicking a rock down the street.

Oliver returned their gestures with just enough of a smile to seem polite, but no more.

"They still celebrate you here," I said, my voice low as we passed a vendor hauling sacks of grain onto a cart.

Oliver snorted softly. "Yeah, well. After killing that deviant of a boar, I suppose I've earned a nod or two." He shook his head like it didn't sit right with him. "It's not fair, though. Should've been both of us."

I smiled under my hood, though I kept my face turned down toward the cobbled stones. "It's alright," I said quietly. "I've had enough of people, anyway."

Oliver's lips twitched in a half-smile, but he didn't argue.

We left the market behind, the sounds of chatter and bartering fading as the streets widened and grew quieter. The buildings turned smaller there, shops giving way to homes and empty sheds. Oliver glanced back at me, his brow raised. "You on foot all this way?"

I shook my head. "I've got a horse. He's at the stables outside the gate."

Oliver nodded without missing a step. "Alright. Let's go get him."

He led the way without another word. Halder was still where I'd left him, his dark coat gleaming faintly in the evening light. The stable boy, the same scrawny thing from earlier, emerged from the shadows of the stall. He wiped his nose on his sleeve and squinted up at us. "Back already, then?"

"I'm here for my horse," I said, loosening the hood just enough so he could see my face.

The boy crossed his arms. "You paid for the whole day. If you're leaving early, that's on you."

"It was barely an eighth of a day," I countered, my voice sharper than I'd intended.

Oliver stepped forward, his presence seeming to fill the space. "Two copper crowns," he said, his tone easy but firm. "For a horse that stood here long enough to blink. You don't want to cheat me now, do you?"

The boy swallowed, his confidence faltering. "Well, no, but—"

"Then two copper crowns," Oliver repeated, still smiling faintly. "Seems fair, doesn't it?"

The boy muttered under his breath but finally ducked into a small chest by the wall. He returned with a few coins, dropping them into Oliver's waiting hand. "Fine. Two crowns."

Oliver handed the money to me, his grin turning smug as he stepped back. "See? That wasn't so hard."

I smirked, giving the boy a look as I took Halder's reins. "Thanks," I muttered, pulling the horse away from the stall.

The boy glared at the ground. "Next time, pay for what you use."

Oliver chuckled, clapping me lightly on the shoulder as we turned back toward the road. "People don't argue much with me," he said, still amused. "You're welcome, by the way."

I rolled my eyes, but I couldn't keep the small smile from my face. Halder snorted, his breath misting in the cooling air, and I led him away from the stables, following Oliver toward the forest beyond town.

The road stretched out ahead of us, pale and dusty, the edges eaten up by creeping weeds where the forest loomed closer. Halder's hooves clopped softly against the packed earth as I led him by the reins. Beside me, Oliver reached out, running his hand along the horse's neck.

"He's a good one," Oliver said, his voice light. "Where'd you pick up a beast like this?"

"The Forsworn," I replied, glancing up at Halder's dark coat. "Wulfric gave him to me. I've only just learned how to ride."

Oliver raised an eyebrow, grinning as he scratched under Halder's mane. "Wulfric, huh? You sure he didn't just saddle you with a walking bag of coin? This horse'd fetch a damn good price at market."

I shot him a look, biting back a laugh. "Not happening. You'd sell your boots before I'd sell Halder."

Oliver barked a laugh, the sound echoing through the quiet forest edge. "Fair enough," he said, grinning wider. "With my newfound reputation—I'd probably get more for the boots anyway. Unless you intend to piss in them again."

That set us off both chuckling.

We walked into the shade of the trees, the air cooling instantly as the canopy swallowed us. Sunlight scattered in thin beams, dappling the ground in shifting golds and greens. The forest had the same smell it always did—earthy and sharp, with hints of pine and damp leaves. Halder flicked his tail, swatting at a fly, and Oliver shoved his hands into his pockets.

"How have things been?" I asked, breaking the silence.

"Fine enough," Oliver replied, though there was a weight behind the words. "Cedric's been sniffing around, trying to recruit hunters for something. He came to me and Rolf a while back. We told him to shove his offer where the sun don't shine."

I turned my head sharply. "Really? You said that?"

Oliver smirked, eyes glinting. "In nicer words than that, obviously, but the message was the same."

I shook my head, surprised. "I thought for sure Cedric would have your bow by now."

"Nah," Oliver said, his tone quieter. "But Brynja took him up on it. Haven't seen her since."

That surprised me, the strong confident huntress who hated taxes, "Brynja?" I asked, almost to myself. I remembered her—her sharp tongue, her steady aim. She'd been the kind of person who didn't let much slip past her. "Why?"

Oliver shrugged, though his expression had tightened. "Guess she had her reasons. Not everyone has the luxury of saying no."

The forest felt different now, the quiet thicker somehow, as if the trees were holding their breath. Halder plodded calmly beside me, his reins slack in my hand, but the stillness wasn't the same—it felt emptier, like something had shifted.

Darkness crept through the forest like ink spilling over parchment. The last threads of daylight had long since vanished, leaving the world cold and shadowed. Oliver walked ahead, holding the torch high. The flame crackled, flickering against the trees as Halder's hooves thudded softly behind me. The only sounds were the occasional snap of a branch underfoot and the low murmur of leaves shifting in the wind.

Eventually, the trees thinned, and a small, squat shape appeared through the gloom. It was a hut—little more than four walls and a sloping roof, leaning slightly to one side as if it had grown tired of standing straight. The glow from the torch caught a neatly stacked pile of wood beside it, gray and dry with age.

"This is it," Oliver said, motioning to the post just off the path. "Tie him here. There's grain inside."

I glanced at the hitching post, surprised to see it in such a place. It didn't seem like the kind of spot anyone would keep a horse. I shrugged, tying Halder securely and giving him a pat on the neck. "Don't get too comfortable," I murmured, slipping him a handful of grain. He huffed softly, the warmth of his breath clouding in the night air.

"More of that inside," Oliver said, nodding to the door. He pushed it open and ducked in, the torchlight spilling inside like a wave.

I followed him in, stooping slightly as I stepped through the narrow door. The place was smaller than it looked—just one room, barely enough space for the two of us to stand without bumping into something. Dust clung to everything: the cot in the corner, the crates stacked against the wall, the rusted tools that lay scattered across a small table.

I took a step forward, and the floorboards groaned under my weight. My nose tickled, and before I could stop it, I sneezed.

Oliver smirked, jamming the torch into a holder on the wall. "Not used in a long time."

"You don't say," I muttered, rubbing at my nose. I glanced around again, taking in the place. The cot looked more like a suggestion of a bed than anything you'd actually want to sleep on. An old axe leaned against the crates, alongside a coil of rope and a crowbar with a handle splintered from use. "What is this place?" I asked.

Oliver moved toward the table, brushing dust off the edge with the back of his hand. "Used to belong to my parents," he said. "They don't use it anymore."

I raised an eyebrow at that, waiting for him to elaborate, but he didn't. The words hung there, heavy, like a door that wouldn't quite close.

Instead, Oliver turned back to me, his expression serious. "Make sure no one else finds out about this place. If they do…" He let the words trail off, but the warning was clear.

I nodded. "I won't."

"Good." He headed for the door, pausing with his hand on the frame. "I'll bring Anni out tomorrow. You two can talk then. For now, make yourself at home."

I stepped forward, and we clasped wrists briefly, his grip firm. Then he was gone, his silhouette swallowed by the darkness outside.

With a sigh I turned back to the room, shaking my head as I eyed the cot. It looked like a breeding ground for fleas. I grabbed the cloak Jory had given me, laying it out flat on the floorboards instead. Before settling down, I checked on Halder, running a hand over his flank and brushing a stray leaf from his mane. "You'll be fine on your own for tonight, I'm just inside," I said quietly. He snorted, his dark eyes blinking slowly in the torchlight.

Back inside, I pulled my shirt tighter, stretching out on the cloak. The dusty air itched at the back of my throat, but at least it was quiet—save for the occasional creak of the walls in the wind. I stared at the ceiling, the torchlight casting faint, flickering shadows across the beams.

It wasn't much, but it would do for the night.

The cold morning air stung my cheeks as I stepped out of the hut, pulling my cloak tight around my shoulders. Halder greeted me with a low snort, flicking his tail against the chill. I scratched behind his ears, his dark coat warm under my hand. "Morning, boy," I murmured. "Let's get you sorted."

I found a small, moss-lined well a short way from the hut, hidden just off the path. The water was clear and cold, and Halder drank greedily, his head bobbing with each pull. I poured the rest into my own cupped hands, splashing it on my face. It shocked the sleep right out of me.

Back at the hitching post, I pulled a sack of oats from the grain Oliver had left me. Halder snuffled eagerly as I poured a generous portion into a hollowed-out trough. "Eat up," I said, patting his flank. "You've earned it."

With Halder taken care of, I set to work on something for myself. The fire pit beside the hut was little more than a circle of charred stones, but it would do. I pulled some kindling from the pile of wood Oliver had stacked, arranging it carefully before striking a flint. It took a few tries, but soon enough, flames sputtered to life. I let the fire grow while gnawing on a bit of stale bread from my pack, staring into the flickering light as it licked at the wood.

My eyes drifted to the hut behind me. Dusty, sagging, and reeking of neglect. I sighed, brushing crumbs from my cloak. The least I could do was clean it up.

I wandered into the trees, searching for something I could use. Pine was easiest, its stiff needles perfect for sweeping. I hacked a small branch free with my axe and stripped it down, bundling the needles tight until I had something that would pass for a rough brush.

Inside, the air still held the stale bite of dust. I started with the cot, dragging the thin mattress outside and propping it against the wall. Gripping the pine brush tight, I beat it, hard and steady. Clouds of dust exploded into the air, swirling like smoke. I coughed, turning my head away until it settled. "Spirits above," I muttered, smacking it again for good measure. The old wood creaked beneath each strike, as though sharing its complaints.

The crates came next, stacked in a corner. I swept beneath them, pushing dust and leaves into the fire pit outside. My senses stayed stretched the whole time, listening for anything—voices, footsteps, the snap of a twig. Halder snorted from time to time, lifting his head to watch me work.

One crate caught my eye. I knelt beside it, brushing dust from the lid before prying it open with my knife. Inside was grain—still good, by the looks of it—along with horse tackle, leather straps neatly coiled and oiled, and a few tools for repair. I frowned, pulling one of the bridles out and turning it over in my hands. "Strange," I muttered, glancing toward Halder. "Never thought Oliver's parents were horse folk."

I packed everything back the way I found it, sliding the crate shut with a dull scrape. Just as I stood, a prickle ran up my spine. I froze, holding my breath as my pathos stretched outward. Halder stiffened too, his ears flicking toward the trees.

Two figures. Moving slowly, steadily, their footsteps just audible above the rustling leaves. I couldn't see them yet, but I could feel them—a faint hum, like ripples in still water. Halder snorted again, nostrils flaring, and I rested my hand on his neck to steady him.

I stayed still, eyes fixed on the treeline, waiting for the shapes to emerge.

The forest crackled with the sound of footsteps. I turned just as Oliver emerged from the trees, Anni trailing behind him, her arms full and her hair an untamed mess with twigs and leaves tangled through it. She huffed, brushing strands out of her face.

"This path of yours is awful," she muttered, pushing past a thorny bush. A stubborn twig stayed lodged in her hair, and I bit down a smirk. She caught the look. "Say one word, Tomi, and I'll dump this tea in the fire."

I held up my hands, grinning. "Didn't say anything."

Oliver rolled his eyes and strolled toward Halder, giving the horse a friendly pat. "He's been behaving, I see," he said, glancing my way.

"He's better company than most."

Anni stepped forward, holding out her hand toward Halder like a nervous offering. "Well, I'd better introduce myself properly," she said, her voice soft, careful. "Hello there—"

The words cut off as Halder stretched his neck, lips tugging at the greenery still tangled in her hair. Anni yelped, stumbling back, and Oliver barked out a laugh. "You've made a new friend, Anni."

"More like a thief!" she shot back, swatting at Halder's muzzle while the horse chewed happily. I shook my head, taking the pot and bundle of leaves she'd brought with her.

"Serves you right for showing up with half a tree in your hair," Oliver teased, leaning against the hitching post.

Anni glared at him, cheeks flushed. "You could've warned me the forest has no manners."

I let their banter play on as I crouched by the fire, pouring water into the pot and adding the leaves. The steam began to curl, faint and fragrant, as I hung it over the fire pit. "It's better than that bitter stuff you brewed yesterday," I muttered.

"I'd like to see you do better," Anni shot back, brushing Halder's slobber off her sleeve. She stomped over and sat by the fire, scowling at Oliver when he didn't stop laughing.

We settled down, the heat from the fire sinking into the cool morning air. I stirred the tea with a stick, the scent rising stronger now, while Halder munched contentedly nearby. Oliver stretched his legs, looking over at me. "Alright then, Tomi. Let's hear it again."

I gave him the short version—escaping Cedric's gaol, the Forsworn ambush, the chase, and everything since. Oliver stayed quiet, his expression serious, though his fingers tapped idly against his knee.

Anni listened too, her brow furrowed, but when I finished, she spoke up. "The letters we've been copying for the new Fief Lord and his soldiers," she said quietly, "they're all pointing to the same thing. This war isn't creeping like the last one—it's sprinting. If it weren't for winter rolling in, I think it would've erupted already."

Oliver grunted, scratching his chin. "Figures. They're always itching for something to fight over." He pushed himself to his feet, brushing the dirt from his trousers. "Well, I've got hunting to do.

Can't let Rolf beat me to all the game. You two behave yourselves." Anni shot him a look, her tone dry. "We'll try, but it'll be hard without your shining example to guide us."

Oliver barked a laugh, clapping a hand on my shoulder as he passed. "Keep an eye on her, Tomi. She's trouble."

"I heard that," Anni said, rolling her eyes.

With a grin, Oliver disappeared back into the trees, his bow slung lazily over his shoulder. The forest quieted again, save for the faint crackle of the fire. I glanced at Anni, who was still fussing with her hair. Halder snorted from his post, chewing on something leafy.

"Don't say it," she muttered, catching me watching.

"I wouldn't dream of it," I replied, smirking as I poured her a cup of tea.

A little later; Anni spread the map and her notes across the ground between us, smoothing the creases with the edge of her palm. The fire crackled quietly, smoke curling into the cool morning air, while Halder grazed just out of reach. I sat across from her, my back pressed against the base of a pine tree, knees bent and hands smudged with charcoal ink.

"Alright," she said, tapping a finger against the open page of one of her books. "You remember this one, right? Here." She held the quill out toward me, the faintest smile tugging at her lips. "Write it."

I hesitated, the quill hovering above the parchment. The letters swam for a moment before they settled, their shapes strange but familiar. I clenched my teeth, scratching them out one by one—awkward and crooked, but legible. My heart kicked up when I glanced up and saw her watching, her head tilted slightly, curls tumbling down her shoulder.

"Not bad, Tomi," she said softly, leaning over to inspect it.

"Better than the chicken scratches you left through the window."

I flushed, scowling down at the page. "You try learning with a rusty nail and a filthy wall for practice."

She laughed, a sound like stones skipping across water, then gently nudged my hand with hers. "You're doing fine now. See? It's just practice."

"Easy for you to say." I muttered it under my breath, but her smile stayed, sharp and teasing.

"Easy because I know what I'm doing." She reached for my hand then, guiding my fingers back to the quill. Her skin was cool and soft against mine, and I froze for a moment. My breath caught, but I focused on the parchment, the shapes of the letters she was coaxing me to write.

"You're too tense," she said, her tone matter-of-fact. "Loosen your grip. It's like holding a bow—you can't shoot straight if you're strangling it."

"I don't strangle my bow," I said, shifting my fingers where she held them.

Anni grinned, tilting her head. "You do. A little."

I rolled my eyes, the corner of my mouth twitching. "You've never even held one."

"Maybe, but I've watched you." She let go of my hand then, and it lingered for a second too long. My knuckles tingled where her fingers had been.

I turned back to the parchment to keep my face hidden, the letters coming more easily now, less jagged. Each time I scratched something out, Anni leaned closer, pointing, correcting, encouraging. Her voice filled the quiet space between us—steady, confident, not like the girl who had once whispered through a tiny window.

"See? This one—here," she said, brushing a loose strand of hair from her face. "It curves up at the end. Like this."

She demonstrated, her own hand fluid and precise. When she looked back at me, our eyes caught. I fumbled for the next word, my chest tight.

"What?" she asked, eyebrow arched.

"Nothing," I muttered, turning back to the page.

"You're blushing."

"I am not."

"You are." Her grin widened, and I couldn't help but huff out a quiet laugh.

We went back and forth like that for a while—her teasing, me grumbling, but neither of us pulling away. My writing improved, and she made me read aloud—halting, careful, but clearer than I remembered. The sun climbed higher as we worked, the fire burning down to embers.

Eventually, she leaned back, stretching her arms above her head. "Not bad," she said, eyeing my work with approval. "You're getting there."

I set the quill down, flexing my fingers. "Just a little more practice, I guess."

Anni's smile softened. She tilted her head, watching me carefully. "Do you think you'll be able to read your father's book now?"

I looked down at the parchment, the words and letters smudged but they were mine. My chest tightened as I thought of the book—the weight of it, the secrets locked within. "I don't know," I admitted. "But I'll try."

I stood, brushing the dirt from my hands and shaking the stiffness from my legs. "I'll give it a go tonight," I said, nodding toward the cabin. Anni pushed her glasses up her nose, watching me curiously as I crossed to the door. Halder flicked his tail nearby, uninterested in either of us.

Inside, I gestured to the bed where the book lay—still closed, its cracked leather cover catching the fading light. "It's just been sitting there, waiting for me," I admitted, my voice quieter. "Haven't brought myself to open it yet, but... tonight, maybe." I glanced back over my shoulder as Anni followed, her head ducking under the low doorframe.

The cabin suddenly felt much smaller with her inside it. We stood there, close enough that I could hear the faint catch of her breath, the rustle of her tunic as she adjusted her belt. My shoulders tensed, and I turned abruptly toward the crates I'd opened earlier. "Uh, I found these this morning." I crouched, pulling the lid off one of the wooden boxes and waving her over. "Grain, oats, tackle... stuff for horses. Strange to have it all out here."

Anni knelt beside me, peering into the crate. "Strange?" Her lips quirked into a smirk. "You're slow, Tomi. Oliver's a horse thief."

I blinked at her. "What?"

"Or at least he *was* one." She sat back on her heels, brushing her hands together. "This place hasn't been used in years. And yet there's enough here to keep a horse fed and ready to ride. What does that tell you?"

I rubbed the back of my neck, thinking about it. "Or maybe he just... liked horses?" I said, though the words sounded thin even to me.

Anni's brow lifted, her smile teasing. "Liked them enough to collect other people's?" She shook her head. "It's clever, really. If he had a place like this back when he was hunting for coin, it'd make sense."

"Or maybe he's just generous and didn't think to mention it," I muttered. "Doesn't matter now. The place is mine for a bit."

Anni laughed softly and stood. "Fair enough. Just don't let Halder wander too far, or someone might come looking."

I followed her out of the cabin, my brow furrowed as I tugged the door closed behind us. "You'll be alright heading back with Oliver, yeah?"

She waved me off, unbothered. "Of course. I can handle myself." Then her tone turned sly, her smile faint. "Besides, we've been talking while you were off playing hermit in the woods."

The comment hit like a stone in my gut. "Talking?" I said, trying to sound casual and failing. "What about?"

She shrugged. "This and that. Don't worry, he didn't say anything bad about you—well, not much." Her grin widened at my scowl. "Relax. I won't mention what we found to anyone. But you *will* tell him, right?"

"When the time's right," I mumbled. "It's… not easy."

Her teasing faded, and her expression softened. "I know. You'll figure it out."

The sun dipped lower as the day stretched on, shadows thickening under the trees. By the time Oliver showed up, a low torch flickering in his hand, the woods were already growing dark. Halder snorted as Oliver approached, his bow slung across his back.

"Everything alright?" Oliver asked, scanning the small clearing. He glanced at Anni, and a smile tugged at the corner of his mouth. "You ready?"

"Always," Anni said, slinging her bag over her shoulder. She turned back to me, her face half-lit by the torchlight. "Try not to set the place on fire, Tomi. I'll see you tomorrow."

"Yeah," I said, forcing a smile I didn't quite feel. "See you."

Oliver gave me a nod, lingering for a beat longer than I liked before he turned and led Anni back toward town. I watched them disappear between the trees, their voices carrying faintly before being swallowed by the night. Something uneasy settled in my chest, but I trusted them—trusted her. At least I thought I did.

I turned back to the cabin, the chill of the evening creeping in around me. Halder snorted softly as I passed him, as if sensing my thoughts. "Don't look at me like that," I muttered, patting his neck as I walked by. "They'll be fine."

Inside, the fire in the pit was little more than glowing coals. I lit the stub of a candle and sat cross-legged on the ground, pulling my father's book into my lap. I ran a hand across the worn leather cover, the edges rough beneath my fingers. The faint smell of ink and dust lingered in its pages, like it had been waiting for me.

"Alright," I said quietly, opening it. "Let's see what you've got to say."

Chapter 18 - Father's Book

The candle's flicker cast a wavering light across the pages, and the smell of wax mingled with the scent of old parchment. My fingers trembled as I turned the first page, the weight of the book somehow heavier than before. The letters stared back at me, unfamiliar shapes slowly becoming words as I read aloud under my breath, halting at first but gaining confidence with each phrase.

"Tomi, my biggest fear is that one day I will not be there for you."

I stopped, the words hitting me square in the chest. My father's voice seemed to rise from the page, quieter than I remembered, softer. I swallowed hard and kept reading.

"I know the day will come, whether it's a season away or many hunts from now, when I won't be there to answer your questions. I wish I could be the one to tell you everything in person, to share what you need to know man-to-man. But if that's not possible, then through these words, I'll do my best to give you what I can, even if I'm no longer there to say it myself."

The candlelight wavered, shadows dancing across the small shack. I could almost hear him, the way his words would've sounded if he'd said them by a campfire, practical yet laced with something he didn't often show.

"The first thing you should know is the most important: I love you, my son."

A dark blot formed on the page, just above the words *I love you*, another drop falling beside it, swelling the ink into a blurred edge. My heart skipped. I scrambled to wipe at the paper, my fingers fumbling as I reached for my sleeve.

"Spirits, no—" My voice broke as I dabbed at the wet spots, trying to keep the ink from smudging further, but the words still bled, softening into the fibers of the page. My chest tightened, my breaths hitching as I stared at the damage.

It wasn't until the tears stopped falling that I realized they were mine. I sat back, my sleeve damp, my pulse slowing. The book rested heavy in my lap, the candlelight flickering over the smudged ink like it was alive, the edges of the letters just barely holding their shape.

"I love you too, Papa," I whispered, the words slipping out before I could stop them. My voice trembled in the quiet room, fading into the corners of the shack. My hand lingered on the page, steadying myself. Then, with a deep breath, I turned to the next line.

"At the back of this... book, journal? I'm not sure what to call it. I've written down some simple rules—lessons I've already tried to teach you in bits and pieces—to help you live a good life. A life I stumbled into by chance, and one I hope will guide you to something better."

I paused, the words pulling at something deep in my chest, and then I read on.

"I did not come from this land, though I bear its people's likeness. I came from a place afflicted by a plague—not one that ravaged the body, but one that gnawed at the mind and spirit. Writing about it now feels too heavy, too soon. What I need you to know is this: coming here, meeting your mother, and having you—those were the best things that ever happened to me. You are my greatest gift, Tomi."

The candle flickered as I turned the page, the slight scrape of paper against my fingertips grounding me in the moment. The ink flowed steady, measured, like his words were chosen as carefully as a hunter setting a trap.

"I left my homeland on a ship, one of many, with nothing but the clothes on my back and the hope for something better. The voyage was long, and I was just a lone hunter, no one of importance. The sea punished me, twisting my stomach with every wave, but spirits, it was beautiful. The endless expanse of water, so wild and untamed, stretched farther than the eye could see. The storms weren't just weather—they were giants, roaring their defiance at the world, shaking the very air. I wish to show it to you one day, my boy. Let you see how vast it all is, how small it makes a man feel, and yet how boundless, how utterly free."

My throat tightened, the image of the sea forming in my mind. I could almost hear the crash of waves, the smell of salt and brine clinging to the wind.

"It was during that voyage that I learned to read and write. The seasickness had its grip on me, relentless, and no herb the ship's healer gave could chase it away. Instead, she offered me something better—distraction. With tablet and chalk in hand, she spent the long weeks at sea teaching me and a handful of others our letters, our words. It was humbling, realizing how little I knew. But spirits, it was also exhilarating—to feel my mind stretching, to see shapes and symbols turn into meaning. In those moments, the sickness faded, and the world opened just a little wider."

Letting the book rest in my lap for a moment, staring at the uneven flicker of the candle. My father's world felt so close now, as though the waves he spoke of were crashing just beyond the wooden walls of the shack. I wanted to see it—the sea, the storms. I wanted to feel it all.

I traced my fingers along the page, letting the grooves of the ink and the slight unevenness of the letters pull me further into my father's world. His handwriting wasn't beautiful, not like Anni's careful script, nor was it jagged and wild like my own. It was simple, deliberate. Honest. It was him.

I turned the page, the parchment crackling softly in the stillness.

"Words were the second greatest gift ever given to me, and through this book, I hope to pass that gift to you. Knowing you've sought someone to teach you fills me with pride more than I can put into words. Though, in truth, it should have been me to guide you. Did you know I taught your mother? She never told you, I'm sure. But it's true. That's how we met. How she—a sharp, beautiful lass from a warden's family—came to love a no-name hunter like me. She saw something in me I didn't even see in myself, and for that, I'll always be grateful."

I paused, smiling faintly at the thought of them together, my father awkwardly teaching my mother her letters, her likely correcting him in her own way.

"After I got off the ship and traveled inland…"

My vision blurred as my eyes drooped. I blinked hard, trying to force myself awake. The words swam before me, their weight holding me to the page. I wanted to keep reading, to hear his story, to see the world through his eyes. But the ache of hunger gnawed at my stomach, and a loud snort from outside reminded me that Halder would need tending.

I reluctantly closed the book, running my hand over its worn cover. My stomach rumbled as I set the book on the cot, standing and stretching. Outside, the forest had fallen into full dark, the chill creeping into the edges of the little shack.

Halder greeted me with a nudge as I stepped out, his breath misting in the cold air. I poured water into his trough, tossing in a handful of oats from the supply I'd found earlier. He ate contentedly, his big, calm presence steadied me.

After a quick meal of dried meat and stale bread, I forced myself to bed. The book sat just out of reach, tempting me, but I resisted. Sleep tugged at me hard, the images of my father's words blurring into dreams. The sea, vast and untamed, filled my mind as I drifted off. Waves crashed in my thoughts, an ocean I'd never seen but felt as though I had, its call distant and endless.

The next morning, light spilled through the cracks in the wooden walls, painting the small shack in strips of gold. My eyes blinked open, and I sat up, the sleep falling away as a thrill ran through me. The book. My father's words. I hadn't felt this kind of excitement in… I couldn't remember how long.

I scrambled out of the cot, my bare feet hitting the cold floor as I crossed to where the book sat on the makeshift table. My fingers brushed the leather cover, the memory of my father's handwriting fresh and vivid in my mind.

Halder snorted outside.

The sound jolted me, and I froze. My father's voice echoed in my head, the lessons he'd drilled into me again and again: *Take care of the things in your care, lad. Work before pleasure. Always.*

I sighed, closing the book gently. The sharp edge of guilt had taken the edge off my excitement. It could wait.

Outside, the crisp air greeted me, carrying the scent of damp earth and pine. I hauled a bucket of water up from the well, splashing it over my face until the chill shocked me fully awake. Halder stood nearby, stamping his hoof lightly as he waited. I ran a hand along his dark coat, his warmth bleeding into my fingers.

"All right, all right," I muttered, reaching for the oats. He ate eagerly, his ears flicking with satisfaction as I poured water into his trough. Afterward, I led him out for a short walk through the clearing, his steps steady and unhurried beside me.

When I finally returned to the shack, I felt settled, grounded. I brewed a small pot of tea, the aroma filling the air as I sipped slowly. But my thoughts were already back on the book.

Inside, I took my seat at the table. My hands hovered over the leather cover, anticipation thrumming through me as I opened it again. The pages smelled faintly of age and ink, and my father's familiar, simple script waited. I reached for the first line—

My head jerked up. Someone was coming.

The faint crunch of footsteps through the underbrush drifted to my ears. I stilled, reaching out with my senses. One presence, steady and familiar, moving with purpose.

Oliver. Alone.

The door creaked as I opened it, stepping out into the clearing to meet Oliver. He was waiting just beyond the tree line, leaning casually against a birch, his bow slung over one shoulder and a small satchel dangling from his hand. His sandy blonde hair caught the morning light, the first hints of stubble on his jaw more noticeable than before.

"Morning," he said, tossing the satchel to me. I caught it and opened the flap, finding dried meat, hard bread, and a small wedge of cheese.
"Thanks," I muttered, tucking the rations away.
"How'd you sleep?" Oliver asked, pushing off the tree and stepping closer.
"Well enough," I replied, shrugging. "Where's my little Anni?"

Oliver scratched the back of his neck, his expression shifting slightly. "She couldn't make it out today. She's got work to do at the shop—something she couldn't get away from. But tomorrow, she said."

I felt the weight of disappointment settle in my chest, but I forced myself to nod. "Right. Tomorrow."

Oliver gave me a knowing look. "She'll be here, Tomi. Don't worry about it."

Glancing back at the shack, at the table where my father's book waited. I could almost feel the weight of the leather cover calling me back. But then Oliver spoke again.

"I thought you might want to go hunting instead. Figured you could use some fresh air." His tone was light, but there was a challenge in his eyes, as though daring me to say no.

I hesitated, my gaze flicking between the shack and the forest. The book would still be there when I returned, and the thought of the forest—of tracking game, of the silence broken only by the soft crunch of leaves and the hum of the bowstring—made something in me stir. I needed the distraction.

"Yeah," I said finally. "Let's go."

Oliver grinned, pulling his bow from his shoulder and gesturing for me to follow. Together, we stepped into the woods, the air cool and sharp with the scent of pine and earth. The canopy above filtered the sunlight into soft, shifting patterns, and the only sound was the crunch of leaves beneath our boots as we disappeared deeper into the trees.

Oliver led us to a clearing not far from the edge of the camp, where a large oak stretched its gnarled roots like a web over the ground. He stopped suddenly, glancing back at me with a grin that seemed both sly and proud. "Wait here," he said, disappearing behind the tree.

I raised a brow, folding my arms as I leaned against a low-hanging branch. "What are you up to?"

"Patience, Tomi," Oliver called back, his voice muffled. "You're going to like this."

He emerged a moment later, carrying something that made my breath catch. A weathered pack and a bow—my father's bow. The one I'd carried down from the mountains, the one I thought I'd lost forever. My chest tightened as he held them out to me, the faint sunlight catching on the worn leather and polished wood.

"Where did you get this?" I asked, my voice low with disbelief as I stepped forward to take the bow. My fingers traced the familiar grain of the wood, the weight of it grounding me like an anchor.

Oliver shrugged, looking more than a little sheepish as he scratched the back of his neck. "Let's just say I may have... liberated it. After you ran off to warn your friends, I figured it was better in my hands than in Cedric's."

"You stole it?" I said, half-laughing as I slung the pack over my shoulder and gripped the bow tightly. My voice softened. "Oliver, thank you. You have no idea—"

"Yeah, yeah," he interrupted, waving me off with a grin. "I know what it means to you, Tomi. Figured you might want it back before we headed off. And hey, it's not stealing if you're just taking back what's yours."

I nodded, my throat tightening with gratitude as I glanced down at the bow and pack. "It means everything," I said quietly. "Truly, Oliver. Thank you."

He clapped me on the shoulder, his grin widening. "Well, don't get all weepy on me now. Let's see if that bow still knows how to sing."

I laughed, shaking my head as I slung the bow over my shoulder. The forest stretched ahead, alive and inviting, and for the first time in what felt like years, I felt whole.

The weight of the bow across my shoulder felt familiar and new all at once as we stepped deeper into the woods. Each step seemed to ground me, the sturdy wood of the bow a connection to everything I thought I'd lost. This was more than a weapon—it was a piece of my father, the man who had taught me to hunt, to survive, and to listen to the forest. Carrying it again made the ache of his absence sharper, but it also gave me something I hadn't felt in a long time: strength.

"There," Oliver whispered, stopping suddenly. He pointed through the trees where a small clearing opened. A pack of deer grazed, their heads down, ears twitching at the faintest sound.

We crouched low behind the underbrush. I nocked an arrow, my fingers finding their place on the string as though no time had passed. Drawing it back, I kept my breathing steady, letting the tension in the bow settle into my muscles. Oliver leaned closer, his voice barely audible. "How's the book coming?"

I hesitated, my eyes on the deer. "Good," I murmured. "It's… a lot to take in. He wrote more than I thought he would."

Oliver nodded, his gaze scanning the deer. "Seems like he wanted to leave you something real."

I glanced at him, his words landing heavier than they should have. "Yeah," I said, keeping my voice low. "I just wish I could've asked him about some of it. Makes me feel like I don't know him as well as I thought."

Oliver didn't respond immediately. He lifted his bow and took aim, his movements smooth and practiced. "You're lucky to have something at all. Some of us…" He let the sentence hang in the air, unfinished, before releasing his arrow.

The sharp twang of his bowstring broke the quiet, and the deer scattered. One stumbled, falling to the ground as my own arrow flew past its mark. Oliver grinned, giving me a quick nudge. "Keep practicing."

We moved toward the fallen deer, Oliver making quick work of the field dressing while I stood by, my fingers brushing against the fletching of my missed arrow. As he worked, I tried to fill the silence. "That shack," I said. "What was it really for?"

Oliver glanced at me but didn't pause in his task. "I told you. Just a place my parents used between towns."

I frowned. "And what did they do?"

He wiped his blade on the grass and stood, slinging the deer over his shoulders. "Traders," he said simply.

I stared at him, feeling the pull of a lie in the way his voice didn't quite match the confidence in his movements. But I let it go, for now.

The walk back was quiet, the weight of the deer shared between us as we took turns carrying the load. When we reached the clearing near the shack, Oliver handed me a smaller haunch of meat. "This'll keep you for a while," he said, adjusting his bow as he prepared to head back toward Elkswood.

I nodded, watching him disappear into the forest. The stillness settled around me once again, and for a moment, I just stood there, staring at the place where the trees swallowed him up.

Halder snorted, breaking my thoughts. I turned, carrying the meat to hang near the shack before stepping inside. The book waited on the table, its leather cover catching the light of the midday sun. I sat down, running my fingers over the worn edges, and let the quiet pull me back into my father's words.

Chapter 19 - Berries

"After I left the ship and traveled inland, I sought work the only way I knew how—selling my trade as a hunter. It didn't take long to make a name for myself, and soon enough, I found myself standing before the Warden, the keeper of spirits—your grandfather. A restless spirit had stirred the land, its presence making the animals wild, unpredictable. The Warden, as I still think of him even now, was working with a local lord and his men to restore balance. That's where I came in. And that's where I met your mother—the moment that changed everything."

My father's words were more than I'd ever expected—they weren't just answers but a piece of him. I let out a slow breath, my chest heavy but warm, and placed the book gently beside me. For the first time, I didn't feel the need to rush through it. I wanted to savor every word, to linger on every page. The night stretched long and quiet, and I let myself drift to sleep with thoughts of his voice carrying me.

Over the next few days, the season crept forward. The gold of autumn dulled, the forest slowly fading into the brittle grays and whites of approaching winter. My time was split between Anni and Oliver, both bringing a sense of normalcy I hadn't realized I craved.

With Anni, mornings turned to afternoons over sheets of parchment. She'd lean close, pointing out the finer strokes of letters or guiding my hand with hers as I practiced. Her laughter came easy when I stumbled, her teasing gentle but sharp enough to keep me trying. She showed me how to map out the land with precision, turning the forest paths into neat lines and curves on paper. When the ink ran dry, we'd sit by the fire, the crackle of the flames filling the quiet between words.

Sometimes, she'd share snippets of the missives she wrote or copied at the shop. "There was another big battle just before the cold set in," she said one afternoon, her tone more thoughtful than usual. "It sounds like both sides are regrouping now. Waiting for spring. It's like they're holding their breath, preparing for something bigger."

I frowned, the weight of her words settling uncomfortably in my chest. "Aren't you worried about sharing that with me?" I asked, my voice low. "What if someone found out?"

She tilted her head, the corner of her mouth quirking up in a wry smile. "The soldiers don't think much about the people writing their letters," she said, her tone light but edged with something sharper. "To them, I'm just a girl with ink-stained hands. As long as the words get where they need to go, no one asks questions."

It was said so simply, but there was a quiet defiance in her words that made me respect her more than I already did. The thought lingered as we turned back to the maps and letters, her world of ink and mine of forest paths merging in the glow of the fire.

With Oliver, the forest became our focus. We hunted together, moving in practiced rhythm through the underbrush, our footfalls soft against the leaves and frost-covered ground. Sometimes, we'd turn it into a game—who could spot the tracks first, who could take down the cleanest kill. His smirk when he bested me was infuriating in the best way, and I made sure to gloat just as much when the tables turned.

There was camaraderie between us now, a far cry from the harsh pranks and rivalries of the past. Where we once might have sabotaged each other for sport, now we worked together, sharing techniques and trading jabs with a warmth that felt earned. Oliver showed me tricks I hadn't known—how to judge an animal's age by its tracks, how to wait for the perfect shot instead of rushing it. In return, I shared what my father had taught me about the rhythm of the woods, about watching the wind and trusting your senses.

Our conversations rarely strayed from the hunts, even when I tried to pry. When I asked about his family, his answers came short and vague, his gaze fixed ahead as if tracking something invisible. But when he spoke of the other hunters, his tone softened, his words painting vivid pictures of Rolf's gruff humor or Brynja's sharp wit. "She was always the better archer," he admitted once, a hint of pride in his voice. "Shame she went off with Cedric, Could hit a sparrow mid-flight without breaking a sweat."

I didn't push him further, and he didn't ask about the book or my father. It was a quiet understanding, a space where words weren't needed, and for now, it was enough.

When the forest was quiet and my companions returned to their lives in Elkswood, I returned to my father's words. I'd sit by the fire, Halder's quiet huffs a steady rhythm in the background, and lose myself in the pages. The world outside faded as I walked in my father's footsteps, his voice guiding me with every line. Winter crept closer, but for the first time in what felt like forever, I didn't feel the cold.

On one of those mornings, frost clung to the edges of the grass, shimmering in the pale morning light. Halder's breath came out in soft clouds as he stood patiently beside Anni, who was wrapped in a thick winter cloak, her red hair spilled over her shoulders like embers against the cold. She held an apple in one gloved hand, her other stroking Halder's neck as she murmured to him.

"You know," she said, her tone conversational, "you're much

better company than some people. Always listen, never interrupt. Isn't that right, Halder?"

The horse nuzzled her hand, his lips brushing the apple with intent. Anni laughed softly, tilting her head to glance at me. "He's better at pretending to like me than you are, at least."

I rolled my eyes but couldn't help smiling. "He just wants the apple."

"Don't ruin my illusions," she teased, breaking off a piece of the fruit and offering it to him. "There you go, big guy. See? I'm the nice one."

We stood there for a while, the cold biting but not unbearable. Anni leaned her head against Halder's neck, her fingers tracing idle patterns on his coat. "My mother should be back soon," she said, her voice quieter now. "She mentioned it in her last letter. Maybe... maybe you could sneak into town to hear her play."

I hesitated, the idea tempting but dangerous. "Probably not the best idea."

Anni sighed, her breath misting the air. "No, probably not. Still... you know how she is. She has a way of making people feel like the world isn't quite so dark."

"Does she ride?" I asked, shifting the conversation.

She straightened, giving me a flat look. "Do you know how much a horse costs? No, she prefers her own two feet, thank you very much. This—" she gestured toward Halder, who was now sniffing her cloak "—is the closest I've ever been to one."

Halder nudged her gently, and she laughed again, her cheeks flush from more than just the cold. I watched her for a moment, then spoke before I could overthink it. "Do you want to learn?"

Her eyes went wide, catching the light like they were suddenly brighter. "Learn to ride?"

I nodded, grinning a little. "You taught me to read and write. Seems fair I teach you something in return."

Her mouth opened, then closed, a rare moment of

speechlessness from her. Finally, she smiled, a little shy but unmistakably excited. "I'd love to."

The forest opened up ahead of us, the trees thinning to reveal a clearing bathed in the pale light of the frost-heavy morning. Anni held Halder's reins, her gloved hands gripping them tightly, her knuckles pale against the dark leather. I'd handed them to her earlier, just as Wulfric had done for me when I was learning. There was something steadying about it—having that connection, feeling the rhythm of the horse through the reins. Her breath puffed in little clouds as she walked ahead, Halder trailing behind her with his usual calm, curious gaze, his large hooves crunching softly against the frost-kissed underbrush.

"This feels strange," she said, glancing over her shoulder at me. "It's like he's judging me."
I smirked, catching up to walk beside her. "He probably is. Wulfric said horses can tell if you're nervous."
"Oh, great," she muttered. "That's exactly what I needed to hear."
When we reached the clearing, I stopped, motioning for her to do the same. "Alright," I said, rubbing my hands together against the chill. "Time to get you in the saddle."
Anni's eyes narrowed suspiciously. "Me? Up there?" She pointed at Halder like he was some towering beast.
"Yes, you. You've been feeding him apples all morning. He practically loves you more than me at this point."
Halder snorted, as if in agreement. Anni took a hesitant step back, but I grabbed the reins from her hand and guided her toward the horse. "It's not that bad. Here, I'll show you."

I had her place her foot in the stirrup, explaining as I went. She managed to swing her leg over the saddle, though her face was a mix of triumph and terror as she settled into place.
"I feel ridiculous," she said, gripping the reins like they might

vanish.

"You look fine," I replied. "Now, hold onto those—"

"Are you crazy?" she interrupted, cutting me off with a sharp look. "I'm not doing this alone."

Before I could respond, she grabbed my arm, pulling me toward the horse. "Get up here."

I climbed up behind her, adjusting awkwardly to fit into the saddle. The proximity was… closer than I'd expected. Her back pressed against my chest, her hair, wild and red, carried the faint scent of ink and lavender.

"Alright," I said, clearing my throat. "Hold the reins steady, and when you want Halder to move, just nudge him with your heels. Gently."

She hesitated, then did as I said. Halder started forward with a lazy trot, his movements smooth under us. I placed my hands lightly over hers, guiding the reins when she wobbled.

"See?" I said, leaning close to her ear so she could hear me. "Not so bad."

She laughed, a nervous sound that turned genuine. "Okay, maybe it's not terrible."

We rode in slow circles around the clearing, her confidence growing with each pass. Halder seemed to sense her hesitance, keeping his pace steady. But then she nudged him a little harder than before, and Halder took off with more speed than either of us had anticipated.

"Wait—Tomi—!" Anni's voice pitched as the horse surged forward.

"I've got you!" I shouted, though my grip on the saddle was less than reassuring. Halder swerved, and in a moment of pure chaos, I lost my balance and tumbled backward into a bush.

The world tilted, then stopped, my back hitting the frozen ground with a thud. Above me, Anni was laughing so hard she nearly fell off the horse herself. Halder came to a halt a few paces away, his dark eyes watching me with what could only be described as mild amusement.

I groaned, pulling a branch from my hair. "You're welcome," I said flatly.

Anni slid off the saddle, clutching her sides as she came over. "That was amazing," she said between giggles. "You looked like a sack of potatoes."

I rolled my eyes, but her laughter was infectious. Even as I sat there in the frost-covered bushes, I couldn't help but grin.

Halder snorted softly as Anni slid down from the saddle, her boots crunching against the frost-crusted ground. She came toward me, her gloved hand extended, teasing grin already playing at her lips. "Need a hand?"

I clasped her hand, her fingers cool but steady, and she tugged. I let out a mock groan, leaning heavily to make it harder, her laugh rising like the frost-bitten morning air. In a flash of mischief, I pulled back. Her balance faltered, and before I could react, she toppled forward, her weight sending me sprawling back onto the cold earth beneath.

The world seemed to slow. Her hand landed square on my chest, her hair falling loose from her hood, framing her flushed face. Our eyes locked—mine wide with surprise, hers flickering with something I couldn't name. She hesitated, her breath a soft whisper against my cheek. Then, she kissed me.

It was slow, deliberate, a kind of stillness in the chaos of the moment. Her lips were warm, soft against mine, and for a heartbeat, everything else fell away. My senses sharpened, stretching out instinctively. I could feel the way her pulse raced, the faint tremor in her hands, the mix of curiosity and nervousness radiating from her like a fragile thread. I drew back sharply, guilt biting at the edges of the moment. *Stop*, I scolded myself, she's right here—*don't invade that.*

When the kiss ended, silence wrapped around us, heavy but not unwelcome. She didn't move, her hand still on my chest, her face just inches from mine. My fingers brushed something cool in the grass. I lifted it, twisting it between my fingers—a small, waxy berry.

"So," I murmured, breaking the stillness. "Juniper."

Her gaze followed mine to the berry in my hand. She blinked, the spell of the moment broken, and pulled herself to her feet, extending her hand to me once more. This time, I took it without hesitation, letting her help me up. Her cheeks were as red as mine felt.

"They were my mother's favorite," I said quickly, softly, the berry turning over and over in my fingers. "She used to gather them when they ripened, always said they reminded her of home."

Anni tilted her head, confused but with a small smile tugging at her lips. "Juniper berries are good for all kinds of things. Wards off pests, helps with digestion…" She trailed off, watching as I lifted the berry toward Halder's mouth. "Not for horses!" she said sharply, her hand darting out to snatch it back. "They're toxic."

The moment shifted, a soft laugh escaping her as I lowered my hand sheepishly. Halder nudged me with his nose, clearly unimpressed with the interruption. The warmth that had bloomed between us dimmed, replaced by something quieter, more familiar. Without saying much more, we turned Halder back toward the trail, the forest stretching ahead, quiet and unassuming.

The woods were still as we made our way back to the shack, the only sound the crunch of frost beneath our boots and Halder's steady plod behind us. The sun dipped low, casting long, golden shadows over the trees. I tied Halder to the post, brushing his neck as he snorted softly. Anni stood beside me, her arms crossed tightly against the chill.

"Oliver will be here soon," she said, her voice just loud enough to break the silence.

I nodded, unsure what to say. My hands found their way to my pack, fumbling for the piece of dried meat I'd tucked away earlier. When I pulled it out, I paused, realizing my dagger wasn't at my belt. I frowned, patting at my side again as if that might conjure it.

"Think you dropped it in the bush?" Anni asked, her voice lighter now, cautious.

I nodded, brushing my hands on my tunic. "Yeah. Need to get it before the sun sets." I turned toward the woods but hesitated. "Do you want to stay here and wait for Oliver?"

She raised an eyebrow, a wry smile tugging at her lips. "You think it's a good idea to leave a girl alone in the woods by herself?"

The tension cracked. I let out a laugh, the sound surprising me. "Fair point."

She held out her hand, palm open. I stared at it for a moment, caught off guard, before realizing what she meant. My fingers clasped hers, warm despite the chill.

"Let's go," she said, tugging me toward the trees.

Her grip was steady, and for a moment, so was everything else.

The forest felt different this time, quieter, softer somehow. Anni's hand was small in mine, her fingers light but steady. My palm was sweating, but I didn't dare let go. My heart thudded in my chest, a rhythm that didn't match the calm around us. Every step felt too loud, the crackle of frost beneath our boots too sharp.

This was new, all of it. My mind wrestled with the sensation of her hand in mine, her presence so close. I wanted to use my pathos, to reach out and feel what she felt. Did her pulse race like mine? Was her head swimming too? But Felix's words echoed in my mind. It wouldn't be right. This wasn't for me to take.

Anni stumbled on a root, the motion pulling her hand from mine. Before I could react, she pitched forward, and I caught her, my back hitting a tree with a solid thud. She braced herself against me, her palms flat on my chest. Her wide eyes searched mine, and for a heartbeat, we stood frozen in place, the space between us electric.

"Are you alright?" I asked, my voice low and unsteady.

She nodded, breathless, her cheeks flush from more than the cold. Her gaze dropped to my lips for just a moment, and before I could second-guess myself, I leaned in.

Our lips met, hesitant at first, but when she didn't pull away, I deepened the kiss. Her hands fisted lightly in my tunic, and I slid my palms to her waist, holding her close. The world around us faded, the trees, the cold, the weight of everything we carried—it all fell away.

When we broke apart, I kept my forehead against hers, my breath mingling with hers in the cold air. Her laugh was soft, almost breathless. "We should probably find that dagger."

I nodded, my words caught somewhere between my chest and my throat. We walked again, her hand slipping back into mine like it belonged there. When we reached the juniper bush, I knelt to retrieve the dagger, brushing away frost and dirt. I turned it over in my hand, its weight grounding me as I glanced at her.

Then the sharp, panicked squeal of Halder tore through the quiet. My head snapped up, and Anni froze.

Chapter 20 - Horse Thieves

The sharp sound of Halder's squeal pushed me into motion before I could think. My fingers tightened around Anni's hand, pulling her with me as I broke into a run. The forest blurred, the chill air biting at my face.

"What's happening?" Anni's voice was strained, her steps faltering as she tried to keep up.

I didn't answer right away, stretching my senses out like Felix had taught me, letting my pathos find the familiar pulse of life. Halder's presence flared—moving, pulling away. Not alone. Three others. My chest tightened. One of them was Oliver.

The realization hit me like a blow to the gut. Was Oliver… taking Halder? Betrayal tangled with disbelief in my stomach, but I swallowed it down. I couldn't tell Anni, not yet. "Something's happened to Halder," I said instead, my voice sharper than I intended. "We have to find him."

Anni's breath came hard and fast beside me, but she didn't protest. The forest thinned as we neared the shack, the clearing bathed in the dying light of the sun. Halder was gone. The hitching post stood empty, the ropes frayed and discarded in the dirt.

The tracks told a story, but I barely needed to look at them. Deep impressions in the dirt where Halder had been tied, the scrape of hooves digging into the earth, the erratic drag of human footprints. A struggle.

I knelt, running my fingers over the trampled ground. My senses reached out again, confirming what I already knew. Halder was farther now, moving in a straight line away from the shack. I closed my eyes, focusing on the others. One of them carried Oliver's familiar thread, tangled with something sharp and... desperate.

The tracks were erratic, but I followed them with practiced ease, pointing out the patterns for Anni as we crouched near the hitching post. "Look," I said, keeping my voice steady. "Halder was pulled hard. You can see it here, the way the dirt's scuffed. Someone forced him away." I gestured at the faint indentations leading into the forest. "They headed west."

Anni's face tightened. "What do we do?"

I straightened, glancing at her before looking toward the treeline. "You stay here. I'll—"

"Not happening." Her voice was firm, her hands on her hips. "What if they come back?"

She had a point, and it gnawed at me. I couldn't sense anyone else near the shack now, but that didn't mean they wouldn't circle back. Still, the idea of taking Anni into whatever this was churned uneasily in my gut.

I grabbed her shoulders, the weight of my hands steadying my words. "Anni, listen to me. Trust me. I need you to stay here. I can handle this, but I can't focus if I'm worrying about you."

"I can handle myself!" she shot back, defiance flaring in her eyes. But there was something underneath—fear she wouldn't admit to, not even to herself.

I shook my head. "You're a scribe, Anni. Brave as you are, I don't think a quill is going to scare whoever's out there."

Her cheeks flushed, a mix of anger and embarrassment. Before she could argue again, I softened my voice. "Please. I need to go see what's happening. I promise I'll come back."

Her eyes searched mine, hesitation giving way to reluctant trust. Finally, she nodded, stepping back toward the shack. "Fine," she muttered. "But you better keep that promise."

I held out a dagger, its hilt worn but sturdy. "Take this. Just in case."

She hesitated before accepting it, her fingers curling around the weapon. Then, before I could turn away, she leaned in, brushing a kiss against my cheek. "Stay safe."

I smiled faintly, gripping my bow and axe. "I'll try."

With a final glance over my shoulder, I stepped into the forest, the weight of her trust and that kiss lingering with me.

The forest stretched endlessly ahead, the trees cast long, jagged shadows as the sun dipped low in the sky. The dying light didn't matter; my senses were sharper than the fading day. I crouched low, brushing my fingers over a broken twig. Fresh. They weren't far, but Halder, Oliver, and whoever else was with them had kept a steady pace, pulling farther ahead.

I adjusted my grip on the bow slung over my shoulder, my axe tapping lightly against my side as I moved. The trail twisted and turned through the underbrush, but I didn't hesitate, my focus narrowed to the hoofprints and the faint sense of motion ahead. Each step was deliberate, soundless, my boots pressing into the soft earth as I closed the distance.

Branches clawed at my cloak, the forest's chill biting through the fabric. My breath came steady, controlled. I stretched my pathos further, feeling for Halder's steady presence. It flared faintly, then again, closer now. But there was something else—another thread pulling at my awareness.

A familiar presence. Moving, not far behind.

I stopped, spinning to glance over my shoulder. My pathos sharpened, narrowing on the faint ripple of movement in the forest. Anni. My jaw tightened as I let out a low curse. "Spirits, why can't she stay put?"

The trail before me demanded attention, but now my mind split in two, each step forward weighed down by the knowledge that she was following. I pushed ahead, frustration curling in my chest, hoping to close the gap before she caught up. The forest grew darker with each passing moment, the sun's last light scattering across the canopy like shattered glass. I kept going, until finally I found them.

The clearing was small, bordered by the jagged shadows of pines. A fire crackled at its center, sending thin tendrils of smoke curling into the twilight. I crouched low, moving carefully through the underbrush, the cold earth pressing against my palms. Halder was there, his reins tied haphazardly around a rock as he munched on a small pile of oats. It was almost laughable. Halder could snap the rope and leave whenever he wanted.

Two men stood around the fire. One, a wiry man with a bald head that gleamed in the flickering light, stirred a pot balanced over the flames. His movements were sharp and impatient, his skinny frame tense like a drawn bow. The other, larger and more imposing, sat on a log, his thick beard hiding most of his face but doing little to soften his presence. His hands rested on his knees, fingers drumming in a steady rhythm.

I shifted forward, careful to stay in the shadows. Across the clearing, Oliver sat slumped against a tree, his wrists bound in front of him. His face was set, his lips pressed into a thin line, but his eyes burned with defiance.

"Didn't think you'd go soft, boy," the bearded man said, his voice rough like gravel grinding underfoot. "Your ma and pa would be spinning to see you now. What's the game, huh? You think you're too good for us?"

Oliver straightened, his jaw tightening. "I'm not like you," he said, his voice sharp despite his position. "I never was."

The bald man let out a laugh, high and grating. "Not like us? That's rich. You were born into it, boy. Blood don't lie. Maybe you've been playing pretend, but we both know you're one of us."

"I'm nothing like you," Oliver snapped. His voice rose, breaking slightly. "I've got nothing to do with your schemes, your theft. Whatever you think I've done, you're wrong."

The bearded man leaned forward, the firelight catching the glint of something cruel in his eyes. "See, that's where you're mistaken. We followed you, boy. Right to that little stash of yours. Thought you were out of the game, but here you are. Back in it, clear as day."

Oliver shook his head, anger flashing across his face. "The horse isn't mine. You followed me for nothing."

"Don't lie, lad," the bald man said, setting the pot down with a clatter. "You've got your daddy's blood, and that means you've got the same itch. Don't matter if you want to admit it."

The larger man's voice dropped, quieter but no less threatening. "So, let's make this easy. Tell us where the rest is. The real haul. You've got something worth more than that beast, don't you?" His gaze flicked toward Halder. "A fine horse, but not enough to make it worth dragging your sorry hide out here."

Oliver didn't answer. His silence felt like a battle, heavy and tense.

I stayed low, gripping the handle of my axe. My mind raced, searching for a way to get him—and Halder—out of this. My heart pounded against my ribs, my pathos reaching out to the clearing, catching flashes of emotion: the bald man's erratic hunger, the bearded man's simmering control, and Oliver's desperate, defiant pulse. I tightened my grip, steadying myself.

The brush around me pressed tight, the low-hanging branches clawing at my hood as I crouched lower, trying to steady my breath. My bow lay useless across my lap—there wasn't enough room to raise it without snapping half the forest around me. My axe felt heavier than usual at my side, its weight a reminder of what I wasn't sure I could do. Two men, both armed. Oliver tied up and too close to the fire for a clean shot.

Could I wait? The thought churned uneasily in my mind. If I held off until they slept, maybe I'd stand a chance. But then I felt it—Anni, her presence stumbling closer through the forest like a spark flaring against my senses. My stomach dropped. Spirits, she was coming straight for us. I could double back, try to catch her before she reached the clearing, but what if I missed my chance? What if the men decided to move before then?

Halder's nervous energy pulled my focus. The horse's ears flicked, his tail swishing erratically as he shifted his weight from one hoof to the other. His muscles twitched, tense and uneasy. He knew something was wrong—of course he did. His nostrils flared as he let out a low, sharp snort, his unease clear even in the dim firelight.

"Stupid beast," the bald man muttered, glaring at Halder. "Why'd you bring a damned skittish thing like that anyway?"

Halder shifted again, his hooves scraping against the dirt. Then, as if on cue, he lifted his tail and let loose.

"Are you bloody kidding me?" the bald man hissed, stumbling back as the smell wafted toward him. "Disgusting!"

The bearded leader chuckled, low and gravelly. "Sort it out," he said, his tone bordering on a command.

"Sort it out?" the bald man shot back, his voice climbing. "How am I supposed to sort that out?"

I gritted my teeth, watching the exchange with my muscles

coiled tight. Halder's anxiety mirrored my own, sharp and restless, but there was something else there too—an edge of frustration.

Closing my eyes for a brief moment, stretching my pathos toward the horse. Images, feelings, nudged their way through the connection. A kick. That's all I needed. A solid, deliberate kick. Halder wanted it too; I could feel the urge bubbling beneath his tension. I sent a gentle push, a quiet agreement, feeding into the moment.

And then I waited.

The skinny man circled Halder warily, muttering curses under his breath. He crouched low, hands outstretched like he was taming a wild beast. "Easy, you stupid—"

Halder kicked.

The force sent the man sprawling backward, a startled yelp cut off by the sharp crunch of his body hitting the dirt. He groaned, clutching at his side, and stayed down.

"Rannik!" the bearded man barked, leaping to his feet. His chair clattered behind him as he drew a short sword from his belt. "You bloody nag, I'll—"

He didn't finish. I surged from the underbrush, my axe raised. He turned just in time, his blade flashing as it met mine with a jarring clang. The shock of the impact rattled my arms, but I held firm, teeth bared as I pushed forward.

The man was stronger, his weight driving me back a step, then another. I broke away, stumbling around the fire as he followed, the glow of the flames throwing wild shadows across his face. His short sword swung again, faster than I expected, and I barely got my axe up in time to block. The blade skidded off the handle, a hairsbreadth from my shoulder.

He grinned, baring crooked teeth. "Not bad, boy. But not good enough."

I tightened my grip, my breath pounding in my ears like war drums. Memories of Commander Crosse's drills surged forward, his voice sharp and unyielding. Use your footing. Find the gaps.

The man loomed over me, his sword flashing as the firelight caught the blade. I feinted left, a shallow move to draw his attention, then darted right, swinging my axe low. The blade clipped the edge of his boot, throwing him off balance. He snarled and lashed out wildly, the tip of his sword grazing my arm. Pain shot through me, hot and immediate, but I gritted my teeth and pressed forward.

He stepped back and the fire crackled between us, its light dancing across the clearing. I forced him back, step by step, through the blaze. His heavy boots kicked up dirt, his movements slowing as he realized his position. Halder's snorts came louder now, his hooves stamping nervously at the forest floor, a frantic rhythm that matched my own heartbeat.

The man hesitated, glancing at the flames. That was all I needed. I surged forward, leaping over the fire with a shout, the heat blistering against my legs. My axe came down hard, aiming for his weapon hand.

The blade bit deep. Bone cracked. Blood sprayed across the fire, sizzling where it struck the embers. His sword dropped to the ground with a dull clatter, his severed fingers following in its wake.

He howled, clutching the mangled remains of his hand, his face twisted in agony. He staggered back, nearly tripping over the firewood scattered behind him.

My chest heaved as I stood there, my axe still raised, the weight of it more than steel and wood. For a moment, I thought it was over. The man stumbled, his eyes dulling but still full of hate, and I wondered if he'd flee, if I'd won.

The moment froze as I saw movement out of the corner of my eye. The skinny, bald man stumbled forward, his arm hanging at a sick angle, his face twisted in pain—but not enough to stop him. His other hand held a dagger, its tip pressing against my ribs before I could raise my axe.

"Drop it," he hissed through clenched teeth. The blade nicked my skin, cold and sharp. "Now."

My grip on the axe faltered. The fight had drained from me, replaced by a knot of cold dread. I started to lower the weapon when the man's arm tensed, his intent clear. He was going to stab me whether I dropped the axe or not.

Before the blade could bite, a blur slammed into him from the side. The dagger fell to the ground as the skinny man tumbled sideways, Oliver on top of him. They hit the dirt hard, Oliver straddling him in an instant. His fists came down like hammer blows, one after the other, relentless.

The skinny man struggled at first, twisting and bucking, but Oliver didn't stop. Each punch landed with a sickening crunch until the man went slack, his head lolling to one side. Oliver sat there for a moment, his shoulders heaving as he caught his breath. Blood dripped from his knuckles.

I stared, the world spinning in the aftermath of the fight. My ribs ached where the blade had pressed. My mind reeled. "How—?" The question died on my lips as my eyes darted to the corner of the clearing.

Anni stood there, pale but steady, holding the dagger I'd given her. A few cut ropes lay discarded at her feet, frayed at the edges. She met my gaze, her lips pressed into a thin line, her hands trembling just enough for me to notice.

I swallowed hard, forcing myself to move. Together, we tied up the two men. The skinny one groaned faintly as we bound his wrists, but he didn't stir. The larger man was still out cold, his ruined hand cradled against his chest, his face pale from the blood loss.

The clearing fell silent except for the crackling fire. My chest heaved as I sat back on my heels, staring at the two unconscious men. The axe rested in the dirt beside me, streaked with blood and soot. Halder snorted nearby, his ears flicking nervously as the tension lingered.

I looked up at Oliver, who was wiping his bloodied hands on his trousers. He gave a sharp nod, his expression unreadable. Anni stepped closer, her eyes searching mine.

Oliver's voice was low, cold. "We should kill them."
Anni stiffened beside me. "No." Her tone cut through the quiet like a blade. I nodded, my jaw tight.
"Turn them in," I said. "Let the Fief Lord deal with them."
Oliver scoffed, shaking his head. "The Fief Lord doesn't care about a couple of horse thieves. They'll bribe their way out or run again. And what happens then? They come back. They find us. They find her." He nodded toward Anni, his face hard. "Their lives aren't worth the risk."
Anni's cheeks flushed as she stepped forward, her voice

trembling but sharp. "And who are you to decide that? Huh? Who gave you the right to weigh someone's life like it's nothing?"

Oliver glared at her but didn't answer. She didn't back down.

"Why are they here, Oliver?" she demanded. "Why follow you? What did you do to make them come after you?"

For a moment, he didn't speak. Then, with a sigh that seemed to deflate him, Oliver dropped his gaze to the fire. "They knew my parents," he said quietly. "We lived on the move, always running. My parents were horse thieves, like them. They were caught—hung—when I was barely old enough to remember. Left me alone." His voice wavered, but he pressed on. "I swore I'd never be like them. Built a life, honest work. But I guess… some people don't let you leave that behind."

The fire popped, filling the silence. I didn't know what to say. Anni looked at him, her anger softening but not fading. Before she could respond, distant voices drifted through the trees.

"Anni!" a man's voice called, strained but clear. Other calls followed.

My heart leapt into my throat. Anni turned toward the sound, her wide eyes meeting mine. Oliver was already moving, crouching low and reaching for his bow.

"Go," Oliver hissed, glancing at me. "Get out of here. Take Halder and get back to the shack."

"What about you?" I whispered, my grip tightening on Halder's reins.

"We'll handle this," he said. "They won't say anything about the shack. Even after this… they're not rats."

Anni stepped closer to me, her hand brushing my arm. Our eyes met, and for a moment, nothing else existed. I wanted to say something, anything, but the weight of the situation crushed the words before they could form.

Oliver nudged me with his shoulder. "Now, Tomi."

I nodded, swallowing hard. I turned and led Halder into the shadows of the forest, the voices fading behind me. As we moved through the trees, I glanced back once. Anni stood near the fire, her face unreadable, Oliver at her side.

Then I turned away, my thoughts heavy as I guided Halder back toward the shack.

Chapter 21 - Disguise

The shack felt smaller with each passing day. The walls seemed to close in, the air heavier despite the winter chill seeping through the cracks in the wood. I paced the narrow floor, my boots scuffing the dirt, Halder's occasional snort the only sound breaking the oppressive silence.

Neither Anni nor Oliver came. Not once. I told myself they were fine—that they could handle themselves. Anni was smart, Oliver capable. But the doubt gnawed at the edges of my thoughts like a rat in the dark.

What had happened to the horse thieves? Were they turned in, silenced, or something worse? Would the questions start—questions that led back here, to the shack?

I kept my senses stretched thin, searching the forest for any sign of life beyond the usual rustle of leaves and scurry of animals. Every snap of a branch made my muscles tighten, my hand brushing the hilt of my axe.

The hunts I allowed myself were quick and distracted. I'd leave Halder tethered close to the shack, never wandering too far. The thought of him alone, of missing Oliver or Anni's return, kept me tethered as tightly as the horse's reins.

Halder seemed to sense my unease, his dark eyes watching me as I moved about the clearing, his breath steaming in the morning air. I patted his neck absentmindedly, offering him grain, though my own appetite had all but vanished.

"They're fine," I muttered aloud, the sound strange in the empty space. "They're fine."

But the words didn't settle the tension coiled in my chest.

I sought distraction in my father's book, my fingers brushing the edge of the page as I turned it to where I had left off. His words rose from the parchment, steady and honest as though he were speaking them aloud.

"Our quest took us throughout the land, and eventually, we tracked and defeated the raging bear that the warden said the spirit had inhabited. It was no ordinary hunt, my son. That creature was fury given form, and it put my bow and every ounce of my courage to the test. Steen and the others—rough men at first glance, but loyal and steadfast—became my brothers during that hunt. By the time it was done, I was no longer a lone hunter but part of something greater. Fief Lord Aldwin rewarded me handsomely for my efforts, and from that day on, if he needed a scout or a hunter, I was his man."

"But despite the coin in my pocket and the stories I had to tell, I did not know where to go from there. It was the warden, your grandfather, who took me back to his home in Riverhalv. It was there that I met his daughters—Aunt Linette and your mother, Lotte."

The words blurred for a moment before I blinked them back into focus. Aunt Linette and my mother. I could almost hear his voice soften as he wrote those names.

I turned the page, the faint smell of old ink and parchment filling the quiet room.

"Your mother and I hit it off from the start, though I couldn't believe it at first. She was studying the spirits, following in her father's footsteps to become a warden herself. Her sister, Linette, was already spoken for by then—your Uncle Garret, a man who could charm the thorns off a bramble. But it was your mother who took my breath away.

She was knowledge itself, my boy. She knew the stories, the songs, the spirits as though they were old friends. I was a hunter, but she showed me the forest in a way I had never seen before. We spent days by the river, her laughter mingling with the rush of water. We picnicked in the fields when the flowers were in bloom, and we danced under the moonlight, the stars our only witnesses."

The page under my fingers trembled slightly. The warmth in his words, the vividness of his memories, made it easy to picture them—my father, quiet and practical, and my mother, bright and full of life. For a moment, the shack around me faded, and I was there with them, standing in a field bathed in moonlight, hearing the laughter my father tried so hard to capture on the page.

I closed the book carefully, letting my fingers linger on the leather cover for a moment longer than necessary. My legs were stiff from sitting too long, and Halder's snort reminded me I wasn't alone in the world, not entirely. Stretching, I stood and walked to him, running a hand along his neck, his coat warm beneath my palm. His ears flicked back at me, curious as ever.

"Good boy," I muttered, rubbing the spot between his ears. Halder leaned into the touch, his quiet companionship grounding me more than I cared to admit.

The forest called, and I found myself wandering into its quiet embrace. The crunch of frost beneath my boots and the faint rustling of leaves filled the air, but my thoughts were louder. My mother—knowledgeable about the spirits, my father had said. A warden's daughter. But I'd never met my grandfather. Not once. Why?

The wardens, keepers of balance and lore, were spoken of in stories and whispers. I'd imagined them as imposing figures, solemn and wise. But they were supposed to be part of my family.

Why had they never come to us? Why had my mother never spoken of them?

The questions swirled, heavy but strangely comforting in their mystery. They pushed aside the worries I'd carried about Oliver and Anni, about what had happened in the clearing. For once, my mind had space for something other than fear.

I paused, resting a hand against the rough bark of a tree. My senses stretched out instinctively, seeking without meaning to. A familiar thread tugged at the edge of my awareness, and my breath hitched. Oliver.

Instead of waiting, I stepped forward, following the pull like a thread winding through the trees. Each step felt deliberate, the cold air sharp against my cheeks. I didn't bother calling out. He'd know I was coming, just as I knew he was there.

The crunch of leaves beneath my boots must have been louder than I realized because when I stepped into the clearing, Oliver spun, his hand twitching toward the hunting knife at his belt.

"Spirits, Tomi!" he hissed, his shoulders relaxing as he recognized me. "You trying to get yourself shot?"

I raised a brow, suppressing a grin. "Didn't think you'd spook so easy."

Oliver muttered something under his breath and shook his head, clearly still on edge.

"How are you?" I asked, stepping closer. "What happened?"

He exhaled sharply, his hand raking through his hair. "I'm fine," he said, though his voice carried the weight of something unspoken. "The Lord wasn't as merciful as I expected. He hung the thieves in the town square. Didn't even give them a chance to talk."

Relief surged through me, the kind that came like a gasp of air after being underwater too long. They wouldn't be able to reveal anything about me, about where I'd been or what I carried. But it wasn't a clean feeling. The relief was knotted with unease, a sharp pang of guilt twisting in my chest. They'd stolen horses, yes, but that didn't mean they deserved the noose.

I nodded slowly. "That's... good," I managed, though the words felt heavy on my tongue. My eyes flicked to Oliver. He stood still, his shoulders squared, his face set in a careful mask. But beneath it, I could feel the faint ripple of guilt brushing against my senses. He wouldn't say it, wouldn't show it, but the weight of those men's deaths hung between us like smoke.

"Where have you been? How's Anni?" The questions spilled out of me before I could stop them, each one sharper than the last, a way to push the conversation forward and away from the unease pressing at my ribs.

Oliver's lips twitched, but it wasn't quite a smile. "Couldn't leave Elkswood too soon," he said. "Would've raised suspicion. As for Anni..." He trailed off, his face coloring slightly.

"What?" I pressed, narrowing my eyes.

Oliver cleared his throat, clearly uncomfortable. "It was her father in the forest that night. Him and some others." He hesitated before adding, "Anni and I had to... spin a tale."

"A tale?" I echoed, frowning.

He looked away, rubbing the back of his neck. "Told him we were... you know... lovers."

I blinked, trying to picture Halwin, the intelligent, round-faced scribe, angry at Oliver for such a claim. It was almost laughable, though Oliver's flushed expression kept the humor at bay.

"He didn't take it well," Oliver added quickly. "But it got us out of trouble. He's keeping a closer eye on her now, though. She can't leave town for the time being."

The news settled over me like a damp cloak. I nodded, my chest tightening. "At least her mother's back," I said after a moment, trying to focus on the one silver lining.

Oliver glanced at me, his expression softening slightly. "Yeah. Mirva's back. That should help."

I nodded again, my gaze falling to the ground. The forest felt heavier somehow, quieter. But at least Anni was safe. For now.

The forest's chill was creeping in when Oliver finally broke the silence. "Don't worry," he said, adjusting his bow across his back. "It'll sort itself out. Yule's not far off. You want to hunt?"

I glanced at Halder, his reins looped around my hand, then back to Oliver. "Already hunted today," I replied.

He nodded thoughtfully, his eyes scanning the clearing. "Spirit's Reckoning, then?"

I blinked, caught off guard. "The dice game?"

Oliver's grin tugged at one corner of his mouth. "Unless you're scared of losing."

The challenge was enough to shift my mood. I led Halder to a tree, tying his reins loosely, and joined Oliver on the ground near the campfire.

Oliver pulled a small leather pouch from his pocket, shaking it until three dice tumbled into his hand. The dice were etched with crude but distinct symbols: flames, waves, stars, and more.

We played three rounds, the dice clicking softly against the packed dirt.

In the first round, Oliver tossed the dice first, his roll showing two Fire Spirits and a Water Spirit. "Well, there's a disaster waiting to happen," he muttered, setting the Fire Spirits aside.

On my turn, I rolled two Earth Spirits and a Shadow Spirit. "Grounded," I said with a smirk, forgoing my next roll to force Oliver to skip his turn.

He grumbled, tossing the dice back at me. "Lucky start."

Onto the second, Oliver got his revenge quickly. His roll landed three Wind Spirits on the first throw. He leaned back with a triumphant grin. "And just like that, I win a point."

"Beginner's luck," I shot back, but there was an edge of respect in my tone.

The final round came down to precision. I rolled and re-rolled, holding back two Light Spirits while Oliver fumbled with mismatched symbols. His last roll left him with nothing but Fire Spirits.

"Three Light Spirits," I declared after my last roll, holding the dice out for him to see. "That's game."

Oliver snorted, leaning back against the tree. "Didn't take you for someone who liked dice."

I shrugged, stacking the dice back into their pouch. "I don't mind a bit of strategy."

Oliver smirked, shaking his head. "You're as smug as the spirits you rolled."

I grinned and reached for Halder's reins. "Maybe next time, you'll win."

Oliver dusted his hands off and rose from his seat by the fire. "I'll try to come back soon," he said, adjusting the quiver on his back. His tone was casual, but there was a flicker of something behind his eyes—concern, maybe, or something close to it.

I nodded, keeping my gaze on the flickering flames. "Safe travels."

He gave Halder a pat on the neck, nodded once more, and slipped into the forest. The quiet that followed was different from before, heavier somehow.

The days passed in a rhythm I couldn't quite settle into. Mornings started with feeding Halder and stretching my legs on rides through the woods. My grip on the reins grew more confident, my balance steadier. Hunting filled the afternoons—sometimes with Oliver, more often alone. The forest became my companion, its sounds familiar, its paths less wild.

When I wasn't riding or hunting, I buried myself in my father's book. His words painted stories of a life I could barely imagine, of battles and rivers and a love that seemed too big to fit between the pages. I clung to every word, turning them over in my mind like stones in a riverbed.

Still, the restlessness gnawed at me. It wasn't just the quiet or the solitude—it was her. Anni. Ever since that kiss, I couldn't stop thinking about her. I wanted to see her, to hear her laugh, to feel the warmth of her hand in mine. The space between us felt unbearable, and the uncertainty even worse.

One morning, as the sun hung low in the pale winter sky, I stood by the shack's window, staring out at the forest. The air smelled sharp and cold, the promise of snow lingering. My cloak hung on its peg by the door, the fabric heavy with the weight of unspoken decisions.

I grabbed it, the movement sharp, decisive. Swinging it around my shoulders, I fastened the clasp and pulled the hood over my head.
"Come on, Halder," I muttered, leading him toward the forest path. My pulse quickened, the quiet resolve in my chest growing louder with each step.

The forest thinned as I neared Elkswood, the afternoon sun casting long shadows over the dirt road. The faint hum of voices and laughter reached me before I saw the town, growing louder with each step. By the time I reached the stables, the noise was a steady rhythm, broken by bursts of music and cheers.

Halder snorted, pawing the ground as I dismounted. "Easy, boy," I murmured, guiding him into an open stall. The stable boy looked up, his face red from the cold, but I handed over a few coins before he could ask questions.

"Take care of him," I said, running a hand over Halder's mane. The horse nudged me in response, his dark eyes steady.

The streets were busier than I'd expected. Families bustled past, children darting between stalls, and vendors called out their wares. I pulled my hood tighter, keeping my head low as I slipped into the crowd. That's when it hit me.

Yule.

Simple garlands of pine and dried berries draped over doorways, their red and green muted against the weathered wood. Candles flickered in windows, casting warm light into the crisp winter air. Someone had hung a star made of straw above the market square, its points slightly uneven but charming all the same.

I let myself weave through the crowd, my steps slow as I took in the scene. The air smelled of roasted nuts and spiced cider, and somewhere nearby, a fiddle played a lively tune. For a moment, the weight I'd been carrying lifted, replaced by something quieter, softer.

Outside the Lame Mule, Viktor stood with his arms crossed, his grin wide as he called out to passersby. "Don't be shy, folks! Warm drinks and warmer company inside!" His voice carried over the din, and despite myself, I smiled.

For the briefest second, his gaze flicked my way, and I froze. Did he see me? But his attention moved on, and I exhaled, telling myself it was nothing. Just a trick of the light.

I turned toward the market square, the noise drawing me closer. A small stage had been set up, and a group of performers held the crowd's attention. A man in bright, patched clothes juggled flaming torches, the fire reflecting in the wide eyes of the children watching.

I lingered at the edge of the crowd, the festive energy pulling at something deep in my chest. Not for the first time, I felt like an outsider looking in.

The crowd pressed closer to the stage, their faces lit with the flickering glow of nearby torches. On another, larger, makeshift platform, a bard stood tall, her voice rising clear above the murmur of the market. A plume of blue feathers crowned her wide-brimmed hat, and her winter garb shimmered faintly under the firelight. She held a lute in her hands, the strings humming with each practiced stroke.

Her voice carried like a winter wind, strong and haunting:

"To the northern woods, where the frost spirits sing,
The nomads bring gifts for the Yule-tide ring.
By star and flame, through snow they roam,
To share with the lost and those without home.

A wind-spun cloak for the weary and worn,
A song for the heart that is tattered and torn.
The spirits' touch in every thread,
A warmth for the living, a grace for the dead."

The children near the front swayed with the rhythm, their faces bright with wonder. The bard's fingers danced over the strings, her notes rising and falling like whispers through the trees.

"From the mountains high to the rivers low,
The gifts of the spirits in hands they sow.
Through hearth and hall, through quiet despair,
The nomads bring light to the Yule-tide air."

I recognized her instantly. Mirva. The first time I'd met her, I'd been fumbling for an escape, caught in the act of stealing clothes I desperately needed. She'd smiled like she'd known a secret and hid me from view from the others as I ran. The second time, she'd been standing in the glow of a fire, watching as I disappeared into the night with the Forsworn.

Now, she sang with the same quiet power, her voice cutting through the cold like a blade. And standing at the edge of the stage was Anni.

Her father, Halwin, stood beside her, his broad frame bundled against the chill. But it was Anni who caught my attention. She wore a thick blue dress, the fabric hugging her form as she watched her mother, her hands stuck in each of her armpits for warmth. Her red hair spilled loose over her shoulders, vivid and bright like the embers of a dying fire, defying the frost that painted the edges of the square.

An idea sparked in my mind, unbidden but impossible to ignore. My breath caught, the flicker of it warming something restless in my chest.

The stall smelled of wool and cedar, the scent rising from the neatly folded cloaks stacked on a makeshift table. My fingers brushed over the coarse fabric until I found one that caught my eye—a deep green with subtle embroidery at the edges, like trailing vines. The woman tending the stall, her gray hair twisted into a braid, glanced at me with a raised brow.

"There's nothing wrong with the cloak you're wearing," she

said, her voice dry but not unkind.

"It's a gift," I replied, slipping a few crowns from my pouch. Her lips curved into a knowing smile as she took the coins, her hand lingering for a moment. "A fine choice, then. She'll like it."

I nodded, tucking the folded cloak under my arm as I stepped away. The square had thinned slightly, the crowd drifting toward stalls and fires as Mirva finished her songs. Anni stood at a table near the edge of the market, her gloved fingers brushing over trinkets and baubles. Her father, Halwin, had moved toward Mirva, his broad back disappearing into the shifting crowd. They were such an odd pair—a scribe and a traveling bard—but together they worked, in a way that felt both foreign and familiar.

I waited until the moment was right, scanning the square to ensure no one's eyes lingered on me. When the coast was clear, I walked toward Anni, the cloak held at the ready. I draped it gently over her head, the fabric settling like a whisper against her shoulders. Leaning close, I murmured, "For the cold, my lady."

She froze for a heartbeat, then turned, her eyes bright beneath the hood as a slow smile spread across her face. "My lady?" she said, her tone dripping with mock offense. "Is that supposed to charm me, Tomi?"

I smirked, shrugging. "Worth a try."

"What are you doing here?" Her voice dipped low, her smile softening. "What if you get caught?"

"That's what the cloaks are for." I tugged the hood up a little higher, letting it shadow her face.

She laughed quietly, the sound light and quick. "Clever," she said, her own words turning mischievous. Her hand slid out from under the cloak, and she held it toward me.

For a moment, I stared, then reached out, my fingers curling around hers.

The market square had transformed, the air thick with the scent of roasted chestnuts, mulled cider, and pine. Lanterns dangled between stalls, their soft glow bathing the crowd in warm, flickering light. Music drifted from a corner, a lively tune played on a fiddle, and laughter echoed like bells in the cold evening air.

Anni tugged at my sleeve, her gloved fingers slipping under the edge of my cloak. "Look," she whispered, her breath misting in the cold as she pointed toward a stall lined with steaming pastries. "Mead cakes. Have you ever tried one?"

I shook my head. "No, but they smell good."

"Then we're getting one," she said, already pulling me toward the stall. The cloak I'd given her earlier shadowed her face, but I could still catch the gleam of excitement in her eyes.

The baker handed her a cake wrapped in brown parchment, the honeyed scent making my stomach growl. She broke off a piece and held it out to me. "Here. Try it."

I hesitated. "Aren't you supposed to eat first?"

Her grin turned sly. "Don't worry, I won't poison you. Probably."

I snorted, taking the piece and popping it into my mouth. The cake was warm, sticky, and sweet enough to make my teeth ache. Anni watched me with raised brows, waiting for my reaction.

"Alright, it's good," I admitted, licking the honey from my thumb.

"See?" She broke off another piece and took a bite herself, her eyes closing briefly in contentment. "Told you."

We wandered from stall to stall, blending easily into the crowd. The cloaks helped, but mostly, no one paid us any mind. Anni would dart ahead, her curiosity pulling her from one thing to the next—a bundle of carved wooden animals, a set of dyed scarves, a young boy tossing flaming batons in the air.

At one point, I caught her hand, lacing her fingers through mine. She glanced back, startled at first, then smiled, her cheeks flushed either from the cold or something else.

We stopped near a fire pit where a group of children were singing a Yule carol, their high, clear voices carrying over the hum of the square. Anni leaned into me, her shoulder brushing mine. "This is nice," she murmured.
"Yeah," I said, my voice quiet.

Her gaze flicked up to meet mine, and the warmth of her expression made something in my chest ache, like it was too much and not enough all at once.

"Do you think they know?" she asked suddenly, her tone light but teasing.
"Know what?"
"That we're rebels cloaked in the guise of festivity."
I laughed, shaking my head. "Rebels? You're the one buying pastries and scarves. Hardly subversive."
She feigned offense, gasping and placing a hand over her heart. "I'll have you know I'm a master of disguise."
"Oh, is that what this is?"
"Absolutely." She twirled in her cloak, the fabric billowing slightly. "No one suspects a thing."
"No one suspects a thing," I echoed, my tone dry but affectionate.
We stayed like that for hours, weaving through the crowd, stealing moments where the world felt smaller—just the two of us.

Eventually our wanderings brought us back to the scribe's shop. It was dimly lit, the lantern Anni lit casting flickers of gold across the shelves lined with ink pots, parchment, and stacks of books. We slipped inside like thieves, our laughter soft and breathless from the cold air outside. Anni turned, her cloak hood slipping back, and her hair caught the lantern light—a cascade of copper flames, wild and untamed.

I stepped closer, pulling my own hood down. "This is reckless," I murmured, though the words held no weight.

Her grin was mischievous, her breath clouding the space between us. "You started it."

Before I could reply, she closed the distance, her lips brushing mine, tentative and warm. The kiss deepened, her hands reaching for the edges of my cloak to pull me closer. I stumbled against the edge of the counter, my hands finding her waist. We moved together, awkward but eager, her back pressing into a shelf as books wobbled dangerously above us.

Her laughter broke between kisses. "Careful," she whispered, her lips brushing mine. "If you knock something over, my father will know."

"Your father…" I started, but she silenced me with another kiss, her fingers tangling in the fabric of my cloak.

We turned, bumping into a stool that scraped loudly against the floor. I froze, my heart pounding, but Anni only giggled, her face flushed. She guided me backward, her hands on my chest until my back hit the opposite wall. Her hair was a riot of red against her pale skin, her eyes bright and filled with something that made my knees weak.

Then the bell over the shop door jangled.

Voices followed—low and familiar. My blood ran cold.

"Quick," Anni hissed, grabbing my hand. She pulled me toward the storage closet, and we slipped inside, the door shutting with a soft click. The space was tight, her body pressed against mine, her warmth seeping through my tunic as I tried not to breathe too loudly.

Through the slats of the wooden door, I saw her parents. Halwin's round frame loomed, his boots heavy against the floorboards. His face was drawn tight with worry as he scanned the room. "Where's Anni?" he asked, his voice gruff.

Mirva stood by the counter, idly tracing a finger along a stack of books, her expression calm, almost amused. "I think she's with her boyfriend," she said lightly, glancing toward the shop door.

Inside the closet, I felt Anni stiffen against me, her breath catching. Her wide eyes darted to mine, a flush rising in her cheeks.

Halwin's voice sharpened, his posture rigid. "Her what?"

"Don't start," Mirva said, her tone breezy as ever. "I saw them together, hiding in their cloaks like little spirits. It's Yule, Halwin. Let her enjoy herself."

"She's my daughter," Halwin growled, his hands balling into fists at his sides. "She's too young to be running around with some boy."

Mirva stepped closer, placing a hand on his arm. "And you're too old to remember what it's like to be young. They're only young once," she said softly, a knowing smile playing on her lips. "Besides, it's sweet. He looked... attentive."

Halwin's frown deepened, but his shoulders sagged slightly under Mirva's touch. "If he hurts her—"

"He won't," Mirva interrupted. "Now come upstairs. The fire's warm, and I've got something to show you." She said with a playful smile her finger pulling at Halwin's shirt.

"Something to show me?" Halwin repeated, his tone skeptical but curious.

"Come on," Mirva urged, tugging at his sleeve. She shot a glance at the closet door, then led him upstairs, the creak of their footsteps fading as they ascended.

Inside the closet, Anni exhaled a shaky breath, her forehead dropping briefly to my shoulder before she looked up at me, her cheeks still red. "Boyfriend?" she mouthed silently, her lips quirking into a smirk despite the tension.

I grinned, leaning in just close enough to whisper, "Should I be flattered or terrified?"

She rolled her eyes, but her smile lingered as we waited for the last of her parents' footsteps to fade.

Silence.

I exhaled, realizing how tightly I'd been holding my breath. Anni shifted against me, her face barely an inch from mine, her cheeks flushed and her lips parted. I could feel her heartbeat, rapid and strong, as her hand brushed mine.

"This is…" I started, my voice low.

"Ridiculous," she finished, her lips quirking into a smile.

We stumbled out of the closet, her hair catching the faint light and looking as wild as the moment itself. She laughed softly, brushing a hand over her dress. I couldn't help but grin, though my chest ached with the knowledge that I had to leave.

"I should go," I said, though I didn't move.

"Not yet," she whispered, stepping closer. She pulled me down, her fingers curling into my tunic, and kissed me deeply. Her hair brushed against my face, her warmth chasing away the cold from outside.

When we finally broke apart, her hand lingered on my chest. "Stay safe," she murmured, her voice soft.

"You too," I said, brushing a strand of fiery hair away from her face before slipping out into the night.

Days blurred, each one marked by the crisp bite of winter air and the quiet rhythm of a life that, for the first time in years, felt like it was my own. These were the days of my youth, and spirits knew I had earned them.

It wasn't the last time I crept into Elkswood. Over the next few weeks, I found myself slipping through the forest and weaving through the crowds under the cover of my cloak. Sometimes, I managed to meet with Anni, sharing stolen moments in shadowed corners or beneath the stars. Other times, I lingered in her shop, pretending to browse books and quills while Halwin muttered about the soldiers and the lord's missives under his breath.

Once, he caught me. I froze, certain he would recognize me. Instead, his face softened, and he clapped a heavy hand on my shoulder. "Oliver," he said, shaking his head. "Keep an eye on her, will you?"

I nodded mutely, biting back a laugh as Anni ducked behind the counter to hide her expression. It was risky, these little games, but the thrill of it made each success sweeter.

Back at the shack, the days passed in quiet contentment. I hunted, the forest my sanctuary. I rode Halder, feeling more at ease in the saddle with each passing day. And when I wasn't reading my father's words or sketching paths on my map, I thought of Anni. Her laughter, her wit, the way her hand fit in mine.

Winter moved swiftly, the frost giving way to whispers of spring. For once, I didn't rush to meet the future. I held it, steady and sure, like her hand in mine.

Chapter 22 - Spring Soldiers

Spring unfolded in vivid greens and bursts of color, the forest trading its frost for blossoms and the air filling with the chatter of birds. Those days, though far from carefree, felt closer to the best I'd ever known. Hidden though I had to be, I found moments of joy—time spent with Anni and Oliver, laughter that rang out like music between the trees and in the quiet corners of Elkswood. Despite my promise to return to the Forsworn I found myself lingering, enjoying the time with my friends.

One of those days found us in the scribe's shop. Halwin and Mirva had gone out together, Mirva savoring a rare pause before taking to the road again. The shop was ours for the afternoon, its shelves of parchment and ink standing witness to our mischief.

Anni sat cross-legged on the counter, a loose strand of red hair tucked behind her ear. She was sketching something in the corner of a page, her tongue poking out slightly in concentration. "What do you think?" she asked, holding up the paper to reveal a crude stick figure perched atop a horse.

"That's supposed to be me?" I asked, leaning closer. "My legs are that short?"

"They are compared to Halder's," she shot back, grinning. Her blue eyes sparkled with mischief, and I couldn't help but laugh.

Oliver groaned from where he leaned against the shelves. "Spirits save me. Can you two go ten minutes without flirting? Some of us don't want to die from secondhand embarrassment."

Anni tossed a wadded-up scrap of paper at him. "You're just jealous no one's sketching your stubby legs."

"They're not stubby," Oliver muttered, swatting the paper away.

He grabbed a quill and dipped it into ink, scrawling something haphazardly across a scrap of parchment before holding it up. It was a stick figure with wild hair and exaggerated hands. "See? Perfect likeness."

"That's supposed to be me?" Anni said, mock-outraged. She lunged forward, snatching at the paper, but Oliver held it high above her reach. I couldn't help but laugh as she turned to me. "Tomi! Help me!"

I shrugged, though I couldn't hide my grin. "You called me short. This seems fair."

"Oh, so that's how it is?" she said, her voice playful but with a glint of challenge. She leaped off the counter and lunged at Oliver, who yelped and stumbled back into the shelves. Ink bottles wobbled precariously, one tumbling to the floor and rolling under the desk.

"Spirits, Anni, careful!" Oliver said, barely dodging her grab. "If you break something, your father's going to make me scrub this place with a toothpick."

"Well, then stop being a pain," she retorted, finally wresting the paper from his hand. She smoothed it out, her cheeks pink from the effort. "There. That's better."

I leaned back in my chair, watching them with a smile. The room smelled of parchment and ink, sunlight streaming through the small window. For a moment, I let myself savor it—the warmth of the space, the easy banter, the rare quiet in a life so often defined by running and hiding. These were my friends, my family in all but name, and for the first time in a long while, I felt like I belonged.

But belonging didn't erase the outside world and the war that plagued it. My hand drifted back to the missive on the table, its sharp edges a stark contrast to the comfort around me. I traced the bold ink with my thumb before scanning the lines again, the coded words pulling me back to a harsher reality. The missive was written in the formal, clipped hand of someone used to issuing orders, its meaning hidden behind layers of vague language. It spoke of "valuable cargo" being moved down from Sjoheim, soldiers required to secure its passage, and preparations for what was ominously referred to as "what happens after the battle."

"What do you think the cargo is?" I asked, my brow furrowed.

Oliver leaned back against the shelf, arms crossed. "Could be anything—arms, gold, prisoners." His eyes darkened. "None of it's good. And it means there'll be more soldiers about. Explains why I saw so many earlier. You're lucky you weren't caught sneaking in, Tomi."

I grinned, leaning back in my chair. "I'm good at sneaking around now. Practically a shadow."

Oliver rolled his eyes, but before he could reply, Anni stepped into the room carrying a tray. The scent of tea drifted through the air, mingling with the ever-present ink and parchment. She set the tray down and handed us each a cup. "That's not a skill you should boast about," she said, arching an eyebrow at me.

I caught the faint blush that crept across her cheeks and grinned. "You enjoy it too," I said, keeping my voice light. Her blush deepened, and she busied herself with adjusting the tray, but I didn't miss the small smile tugging at her lips.

Oliver groaned softly. "Spirits save me from the two of you." He took a long sip of his tea, his gaze flicking toward the missive still in my hand. "Do you think it'll come to a head, then?"

I looked down at the paper, the weight of its implications settling in my chest. "I'm not sure," I said honestly. I raised the cup to my lips and took a sip, the warmth of the tea doing little to ease the tension that had begun to creep into my thoughts.

Through the window, I watched as soldiers marched in formation down the street. Their polished boots struck the cobblestones with precision, their faces hard and unreadable.

Whatever this "cargo" was, it felt like a storm was gathering, and we were all standing in its path.

Anni leaned against the doorway, folding her arms. "You two should stay in here until they're gone. No sense in tempting fate."
Oliver raised an eyebrow, looking up from his tea. "Why me?"
She tilted her head, a sly smile spreading across her face. "Because you've got a reputation."
"A good one," Oliver shot back, his tone defensive.
"Sure," Anni said, dragging out the word just enough to make Oliver frown.

I couldn't help but grin, watching their back-and-forth. But my eyes drifted back to the window, to the soldiers filling the streets. Their armor gleamed in the sunlight, their movements too orderly for casual patrols. "What if your parents come back?" I asked, trying to keep my voice light, though the sight outside made my stomach twist.

"We'll hide you," Anni said breezily, then turned her grin on me. "And they think Oliver is my beau anyway."
Oliver nearly choked on his tea. "Spirits, don't say that."
Anni laughed, mock slapping his arm just enough to make him spill tea down his sleeve. "Oh, hush. You should be so lucky."

I barely heard them, my focus still on the window. There were so many soldiers—more than I'd seen in months. "That must be the cargo," Oliver said, his voice dropping into something quieter, more serious. "The one the letter mentioned. Probably coming in from the Whitestone river dock."

I nodded, leaning closer to the glass, my breath fogging the pane. "Yeah. Just look at how many there are. If I'd known, I wouldn't have come today." I turned back toward Anni, catching her eye. My lips tugged into a small smile. "Worth it, though."

Her cheeks flushed, the color rising against her pale skin and her fiery hair. "You're lucky you're charming," she said, shaking her head as she moved toward the kettle. Her teasing tone stayed light, but her eyes lingered on me just a second longer than usual.

I was about to take another sip of tea when I saw it. The soldiers' movements blurred as my eyes caught on something—someone. A carriage rolled through their ranks, flanked by mounted guards. Inside, seated with his usual air of smug authority, was a figure I knew too well.

Cedric.

My tea slipped from my hand, sloshing across the table and dripping onto the floor. My heart pounded against my ribs, so loud I thought everyone in the room could hear it. I stumbled back from the window, gripping the edge of the chair for balance.
"Tomi?" Anni's voice was sharp, cutting through the fog of panic. "What's wrong?"
"Lord Cedric," I managed to choke out. My throat felt tight, and my breath came too fast. "He's here."

She darted to the window, her eyes wide as she scanned the street. "It's probably nothing," she said quickly, though her voice trembled at the edges. "He's likely just passing through. For the battle at Riverhalv. He's not here for you."
Oliver joined her, his expression grim but steady. "She's right," he said. "But… who's that sitting opposite him?"

I swallowed hard, forcing my feet to move. My legs felt like lead as I crossed back to the window, the fear gnawing at my gut warring with the need to see for myself. I peered out, my fingers clutching the windowsill until they turned white.

The figure across from Cedric sat with an unease that didn't match the heavy finery he wore, his pale blond hair catching the sunlight like winter straw. He wasn't the little boy I remembered, but neither was he yet a man. Innocence lingered in the slope of his face, but there was something else too—a hardness edging through, like a blade just starting to take shape.

"Niklas," I whispered, the name tasting strange on my tongue after all these years. "Prince Niklas."

The weight of what I'd just seen hung heavy as Oliver broke the silence. "What's the prince doing here?" His voice was low, taut with confusion. "I thought he was locked up in Sjoheim with his sister."

I dragged my hand down my face, my mind racing. "His sister isn't there. She's with the Forsworn. It's what started this whole war."

"So why bring him out now?" Oliver asked, his brow furrowing as he glanced between me and Anni.

Anni straightened, her lips pressing together in thought. "The missives," she said suddenly. "The ones the Fief Lord had me copy. If there's a reason, it might be in those."

I blinked, surprised at her quick deduction. "You still have them?"

She nodded, already moving toward the back of the shop. "Give me a moment," she said over her shoulder, her dress swishing as she disappeared into the shadows of the shelves.

Oliver shot me a baffled look. "What's she doing?"

"We're just seeing if anything stands out," I said, moving away from the window and steadying my breath. My heart still raced, but I pushed the fear aside. "Something that might explain why Niklas is here."

Oliver leaned against the counter, arms crossed. "You really think a stack of letters is going to tell you that? Cedric's out there parading a prince around, not writing love notes."

"Maybe," I muttered, glancing toward the back where Anni was still rummaging. "But it doesn't hurt to check."

Oliver shook his head, his smirk faint. "You two and your paper chasing." But for once, he left it at that.

Anni returned with a stack of parchment bundled in twine, setting it on the floor and spreading them out with care. I knelt beside her, the smell of ink and parchment filling the air as I began scanning the lines. Anni's hand brushed against mine as she reached for a missive, her brow furrowed in concentration.

Most of the letters were mundane: lists of grain shipments, troop movements scrawled in dry precision, and one awkwardly written love letter that made us both pause. Anni read it aloud, her voice light with amusement, while I tried not to laugh at the fumbled metaphors comparing the recipient's eyes to twin suns. We exchanged a small smile, a rare moment of levity breaking through the tension.

But then, halfway through the pile, we found it. The parchment was finer, the ink darker and more deliberate. The handwriting was Cedric's—bold strokes that carried a weight the others lacked. The words were guarded, the tone too cryptic to brush off. Anni's brow furrowed as she read it silently, her finger trailing along the lines.

"This one," she murmured, her voice low and cautious, like speaking too loudly might make the words vanish. I leaned closer, the air between us heavy with anticipation as we scanned the missive together.

"'The pieces fall into place as winter wanes,'" Anni read aloud, her voice quiet but firm. "'The cargo is the key to the crown, and all who bear its burden will see the truth.'"

"What does that mean?" Oliver asked, squatting beside us and craning his neck to see the parchment.

Anni didn't answer right away, her sharp mind picking apart the words. Her lips pressed into a line before she spoke, her tone clipped. "It's not about cargo. It's about the prince. Cedric's got plans for him, something big—something that'll give him power."

"Plans like what?" I pressed, my stomach twisting.

She glanced up, her eyes meeting mine. "Think about it, Tomi. If Niklas dies—if all the royals die—who's left to rule?"

Oliver's voice cut through the room like a blade. "They're going to kill the monarchy. Erik, Harlan, Niklas—all of them."

The realization hit me like a blow. I looked back at the missive, the coded words taking on a sinister edge. Cedric wasn't just playing politics. He was playing for keeps.

The room felt tighter with every step I took. My boots scuffed the floorboards, the rhythm sharp against the silence that had fallen. Anni's eyes tracked me, her expression soft with concern but lined with something harder—knowing. Oliver leaned against the counter, arms crossed, his face a mixture of irritation and restraint.

"Calm down," Oliver said, his voice even. "Wait until the soldiers leave. Maybe send a missive to your Forsworn friends. Let them deal with it."

"Deal with what?" I snapped, rounding on him. "If Cedric's planning this—whatever this is—it's not just Niklas. What about Sanne? Would they need to kill her too?"

Oliver's brow furrowed, his jaw tightening, but it was Anni who broke the silence. "Tomi..." Her tone was careful, but I could feel the weight behind it.

I looked at her, my chest tightening. "It's my fault," I said, my voice quieter now but no less raw. "Niklas, Sanne—all of it. I saved them from Varek, but I handed them to Cedric. I put them on this path."

Oliver pushed off the counter. "That wasn't—"

"It was," I cut him off. "And now, Cedric's got them both in his grip. Do you really think he'll just let them live if it gets in the way of his plans?"

Anni stood, crossing the room to place a hand on my arm. "I know that look," she said softly, her green eyes sharp. "What are you thinking?"

I swallowed hard, glancing between her and Oliver. The tightness in my chest didn't ease, but it steadied into something else. Something clearer.

"I'm thinking," I said, meeting Anni's gaze, "that I am a hunter."

I stepped away, grabbing my cloak from where it hung on a peg. The weight of it settled across my shoulders like an old promise.

"And I need to go on a hunt."

Chapter 23 - Replacements

Anni's voice was steady, her words cut through the silence like the snap of a bowstring. "I'm going with you."

I turned, caught off guard by the conviction in her tone. For a moment, I couldn't find words. She stood there, framed by the dim light filtering through the shop window, her red hair like an autumn blaze against the soft blue of her dress. Her face—so beautiful, so earnest—made something in my chest tighten. I couldn't take her with me. Not this time.

"You can't," I said, my voice firmer than I intended. "It'll be dangerous."

She tilted her head, her lips pressing into a line. "Dangerous? Tomi, everything we've done since meeting has been dangerous. And I'm not just going to sit here while you—"

I raised a hand, cutting her off. "Anni." My voice softened, but I held her gaze. "I'm not charging into battle. I'm just going to see what's happening. I need to stay hidden. Like on a hunt."

Her expression didn't change, but I could see the wheels turning in her mind. "You don't think I can stay hidden?" she said, arching an eyebrow.

"I think you're incredible at a lot of things," I replied, a smile tugging at the corner of my mouth despite the tension. "You can read, scribe, even make paper from practically nothing. You've got more wit than anyone I've ever met." My gaze lingered on her, softening. "But you can't stalk, Anni. You'd trip over a twig and apologize to it."

She opened her mouth to argue again but stopped. Her shoulders slumped, and she let out a sigh. "Fine," she said, crossing her arms. "But you'd better come back."

"I will," I promised.

I moved to the window, pulling the curtain back just enough to see the soldiers still filing through the streets. The line was thinning, the last ranks nearing the edge of town. The carriages had already passed, the clatter of wheels fading into the distance.

Oliver joined me, his presence a steady weight at my side. "We need a plan," he said, his tone low but resolute.

"We?" I glanced at him, raising an eyebrow.

"You can't chase me off, Tomi," Oliver said, smirking faintly. "I can trail and stay hidden as well as you. Better, even."

I sighed, knowing there was no use arguing. "Fine," I said, my voice resigned. "We wait for them to leave the town. Give them a span, then follow."

Anni stepped closer, her expression tinged with worry. "Are you taking Halder? Does Oliver even have a horse?"

I shook my head. "Halder's fast, but he's too loud. We'd never stay hidden. We'll be on foot, and we can keep up with the army that way." I turned to her, the concern in her eyes twisting something in my chest. "Will you take care of him? Make sure he's fed, watered?"

Her lips curved into a small, reluctant smile. "Of course I will."

I nodded, letting my fingers brush hers briefly before pulling away. "Thank you."

She hesitated, her eyes searching mine as though she wanted to say more. Instead, she stepped back, giving me room to prepare. Oliver clapped me on the shoulder, his smirk fading into something more serious.

"Let's hope you're as good a hunter as you think you are," Oliver said quietly.

The rumble of boots and hooves faded into the distance, leaving the town in a lull that felt unnervingly quiet. Oliver and I crouched near the edge of the shop's back door, our packs slung over our shoulders. From the shadows, Anni emerged, a bag cradled in her arms.

"I packed what I could," she said, handing it to me. Her hands lingered on the strap as I took it. "Fruit, bread, dried meat. It's not much, but it'll keep you fed. Don't worry about my parents. My mother would understand, and my father... well, he'll grumble, but he always does."

"Thanks, Anni." I pulled her into an embrace, her warmth grounding me for a moment. She pulled back just enough to look up at me, her hands still clutching my arms.

"Be safe," she said, her voice steady but her eyes betraying her worry. "Nothing dangerous, okay? And come back. We still have a map to finish."

A soft smile tugged at my lips. "Wouldn't dream of leaving it incomplete. Besides," I added, a teasing edge in my tone, "you'd probably draw something ridiculous on it without me."

Her laugh was soft, a sound I wanted to hold onto. "I might add a dragon or two. But you'll never know if you don't come back."

I nodded, brushing a strand of her fiery hair from her face. "I'll come back. That's a promise."

Oliver cleared his throat behind us, a pointed reminder that it was time. Anni stepped back, her fingers trailing down my arm before letting go.

Oliver and I slipped through the alleyways as the crowd that had gathered for the passing army began to thin. People trickled away in twos and threes, chatting about the soldiers, the carriages, and the prince. Their voices faded into the general hum of the town, a perfect cover for us to blend in. We moved quickly, darting between buildings until we reached the edge of Elkswood.

As we passed the stables, I paused, stretching my senses toward Halder. I sent him an image of calm, of open fields and warm sunlight. In my mind, the horse's presence stirred faintly, like a soft snort of acknowledgment though he wasn't happy with just waiting. I swore he could feel the distance growing, but I let him know I'd be back. I would always come back—to him, to Anni.

Oliver glanced over his shoulder, his brow furrowed. "You ready?"

I nodded, stepping past the last building. "Let's go."

The woods stretched around us in every direction, the underbrush dense and alive with the rustle of creatures. The trees were just beginning to bloom, their canopies tinged with the soft greens of early spring. The air smelled of damp earth, and the occasional snap of a twig beneath our boots was the only sound breaking the quiet.

Oliver moved ahead, his steps steady and purposeful. I stayed close behind, my eyes darting to every rise in the terrain. We climbed small knolls and hills, pausing at the crests to catch glimpses of the army's procession through the forest edge. The line of soldiers stretched long and unbroken, their metallic glint visible even at a distance.

"You going to tell me what the plan is?" Oliver's voice was low, almost casual, but the edge to it was unmistakable.

I pulled myself up onto a rocky ledge, scanning the horizon before answering. "First, we see where they're headed. If it's Riverhalv, we follow them there."

"And then?" Oliver leaned against a nearby tree, his bow slung over his shoulder.

"Then we figure out what's happening with Niklas. If they're moving him toward something... if Cedric has plans for him..." My jaw tightened, but I forced myself to focus. "The closer we get to Riverhalv, the closer we are to the Forsworn camp there. If we see something, I'll go to them. Let them decide what to do."

Oliver's brow rose. "So, no trouble? No fighting?"

"No fighting," I repeated firmly. "Just scouting."

He let out a long breath, nodding. "Alright. But if you go charging into something, don't say I didn't warn you."
I smirked faintly. "Noted."

We moved on, our pace steady but cautious. Every so often, we veered closer to the road, finding vantage points that let us keep track of the army's progress. The soldiers marched in tight formation, the carriages rolling steadily behind them. I could just make out the one that carried Niklas, a dark box amongst the other carts laden with supplies.

The more we saw, the heavier my gut felt. The Prince and Cedric weren't simply moving troops; this was calculated, methodical. Whatever was coming, it wasn't small.
Oliver caught my glance and clapped a hand lightly on my shoulder. "Come on. Let's keep moving."
I nodded, pushing the thoughts aside. The road stretched ahead, and so did our hunt.

The army moved like a sluggish beast, its long columns of soldiers and wagons snaking down the dirt road at a crawl. It was nothing like the Forsworn raids—swift, lean, and quiet. This was loud and deliberate, a lumbering show of force weighed down by its own mass. Supply wagons creaked under their loads, horses snorted and stamped, and the clink of armor echoed through the forest like distant thunder.

Oliver and I stayed well off the road, shadowing them from the tree line. The underbrush scratched at my legs, and the weight of the supplies in my pack dug into my shoulders, but I kept going. Each night, when the army halted, so did we. Our camp was nothing more than a patch of ground concealed by the trees. No fire, no hunting. We lived off the nuts and berries we foraged and the dwindling rations Anni had packed. Among them, to my surprise, was my map—folded neatly and tucked into a corner of the bag. It brought a fleeting smile to my face each time I saw it.

Each night followed the same routine, a pattern etched into the quiet darkness. By the fourth night, it had become almost ritualistic. From the edge of the forest, Oliver and I crouched low, peering out at the sprawling camp below. The glow of fires lit the sea of tents, their silhouettes casting flickering shapes against the trees. Soldiers moved like ants, their chatter carrying faintly on the wind. At the center, larger tents stood out, more ornate, undoubtedly belonging to Cedric and his officers. Niklas would be there too.

Oliver nudged me, his voice low. "There. Near the eastern edge. Same pattern."

I followed his gaze. The guards patrolled in pairs, their paths overlapping just enough to leave a small window—a brief break where no one was watching. It was the same every night, a rhythm that made them predictable.

"That's the gap," I whispered. "Right there."
Oliver shook his head. "It's a gap, sure. But not one you can sneak through. They're still close enough to catch you if you're not fast enough."
I ignored his warning, my eyes fixed on the eastern tents. "That one," I said, nodding toward a tent pitched as the army settled earlier in the evening. "We saw him go in. Niklas is there."
Oliver followed my gaze, his frown deepening. "Heavy guard, though. Same pattern as last night."
"I know," I said, my jaw tightening. "But it's him. It has to be."
Oliver exhaled sharply through his nose. "You've thought this through. That's not making me feel better."

I didn't answer. My mind was already racing ahead, tracing paths through the camp, mapping out the soldiers' movements.

The guards were lazy—too secure in their numbers. That break was all I needed.

Oliver's hand clamped on my arm, dragging me out of my thoughts. "Tomi. Don't."

I looked at him, his expression hard but laced with something close to worry.

"I have to," I said, my voice steady. "I've got to try. If I can talk to Niklas—"

"Or get caught. Or killed."

"Then I'll make sure I don't."

His jaw tightened, but he didn't say anything more. I glanced back at the camp, the fires now little more than glowing embers in the distance. I adjusted the axe strapped to my hip, my fingers brushing the rough leather of the hilt for reassurance.

"I'm going in," I said, and before he could argue again, I was gone.

The drop from the rise wasn't far, but the ground jarred my knees when I landed. The underbrush clawed at my cloak as I crouched low and started forward, weaving through the shadows of the trees. Behind me, Oliver hissed, his footsteps crunching faintly as he followed.

"Tomi, stop," he whispered sharply. "Think about this. You can't just sneak into a camp like that."

I didn't answer, my heart hammering against my ribs. I didn't know what it was driving me forward—something sharp and raw. It tightened my chest and burned in my gut, pushing me past reason. I turned my head just enough to murmur, "I'll be careful."

He swore under his breath, but when I crossed the tree line, he stayed behind. I risked one last glance over my shoulder. Oliver stood in the shadows, his expression furious. I gave him an apologetic look, pulling my hood up as I turned back to the encampment.

The first thing that hit me was the sound—a low murmur of voices rising and falling, the occasional burst of laughter, the metallic clang of pots and weapons. The fires were small, their light flickering across rows of tents and soldiers scattered in loose groups. Some sat hunched over their meals, others leaned back with mugs in hand, singing raucously.

I kept low, my steps slow and deliberate. Every placement of my foot was chosen with care, avoiding loose rocks and dry twigs. The hunter in me knew how to move unnoticed, how to read the terrain and let it guide me. The soldiers didn't bother to look past their own circles, the glow of the firelight creating a wall between them and the dark beyond.

The air was thick with the smell of roasted meat and unwashed bodies, mingling with the acrid tang of smoke. I breathed through my nose, keeping my senses sharp. This side of the camp was quieter, rows of pitched tents standing like sentinels. A few men sat on bedrolls nearby, their heads bowed as they muttered over a game of dice.

I slipped past them, my pulse quickening as the large eastern tent came into view. The one where we'd seen Niklas. It loomed ahead, its shadow stretched long against the canvas of others. My hands itched, tightening into fists at my sides. I wasn't experienced at this, not like some outlaw or thief, but I knew how to tread carefully, how to watch for breaks in the rhythm of my surroundings.

As I crept closer, the noise of the camp faded into a dull hum, and all I could hear was my own breathing.

The tent loomed ahead, its flaps faintly glowing with the light of a candle inside. I crouched low, my heart hammering as I watched the two guards stationed at the entrance. They shifted, their armor clinking softly, murmuring something to each other before one clapped the other on the shoulder and strode away into the night.

That was my chance.

I darted forward, sticking close to the shadows. The remaining guard yawned, stretching his arms wide as he leaned against the tent pole. My pulse raced as I slipped behind him, sliding into the narrow gap between the tent flaps. The canvas whispered faintly against my cloak, and then I was inside.

It was warmer than I'd expected, the air thick with the faint scent of wax and old paper. Inside, the tent felt worlds apart from the crude bedrolls scattered outside. Carpets softened the ground, their colors rich even in the dim candlelight. A proper bed stood in one corner, draped with thick blankets far removed from the spartan army cots I'd seen. A desk occupied the center of the space, cluttered with papers, an inkwell, and a quill. Yet, for all its comforts, the tent was still a gilded cage—luxurious, perhaps, but a prison all the same.

Niklas sat there, bent over a piece of parchment, his pale hair catching the flicker of the candle. He was dressed plainly but finely, his back straight as he wrote with measured precision. For a moment, I just stared. He looked older, his features sharper, his movements deliberate. But there was still a boy there, somewhere beneath it all.

I shifted my weight, and my boot brushed against a stray piece of carpet. The faint noise was enough. Niklas froze, his head snapped toward me. His hand clenched the quill, and I saw his mouth open, ready to shout.

But then he stopped, his face softening into something else—something like resignation. "It's time then?" His voice was quiet, brittle. He straightened in his chair, looking me over with a strange detachment. "This is how they plan to kill me?"

I blinked, stepping forward without thinking, pulling my hood down. My heart was in my throat as his eyes locked onto mine. The sharp tension in his face faltered, replaced by something closer to shock.

"Tomi?" His voice was a whisper now, the quill slipping from his fingers.

I smiled, faint and uncertain. "Hello, Niklas. I'm surprised you recognise me."

Niklas stared at me, the candle causing light to dance upon his features. His voice was sharp and low, tinged with that upper-crust crispness I'd almost forgotten. "Of course, I recognize you. How could I not? We were just children in the mountains, but... that day is burned into my memory." He glanced over his shoulder, nerves breaking through his otherwise composed demeanor. "How did you get in here? Are you working for Prince Erik? Harlan? Or one of the Fief Lords?"

I shook my head. "No. I'm just a hunter now."

"Then why are you here?" His words were edged, wary.

I met his gaze, steady. "I saw you in Elkswood and followed. I wanted to see if you were alright."

His eyes narrowed, his suspicion not yet gone. "I thought you were here to kill me. An assassin sent to finish me off."

"By who?" I asked, leaning closer.

Niklas's laugh was quiet and bitter, his fingers brushing over the edge of the desk. "By anyone. Everyone. I'm only here as a pawn for Erik anyway."

"Sanne said as much," I said, keeping my voice calm.

His head snapped up, his pale blue eyes sharp and bright. "You've seen my sister? Is she here?"

"No." I raised a hand as his panic rose. "She's safe, Niklas. I was with the Forsworn for a time. They rescued her. She was being transported as... valuable cargo. They didn't know it was her."

His face paled, his breath catching. "Spirits. She's with the Forsworn?"

I nodded. "She's safe. I swear it."

Niklas sagged back into his chair, the faint creak of the wood breaking the heavy silence. His hands curled into fists, knuckles pale as they pressed into his lap. "Good," he muttered, barely more than a breath. "I knew they'd taken her. She was meant for Harlan, and I..." His voice faltered, then steadied, sharper now. "I was meant for Erik. That was the plan."

"The plan?" I asked, leaning closer, trying to piece it together.

Niklas nodded, his gaze drifting somewhere far away, the weight of memory pulling at his features. "To marry us off," he said softly. "To secure the lines of power between Sjoheim and the Crown. That's all Sanne and I were ever meant to be—a safeguard. A contingency." He paused, his hands tightening on the arms of his chair. "Erik and Harlan, barren as their fields. They needed heirs. And if, by some miracle, their wives bore them children, we'd still be there. Insurance."

I felt a chill creep up my spine. "So, you and Sanne were... replacements."

"Replacements," Niklas repeated, his tone flat but edged with something sharper. "Pawns. Pieces to keep the game going, no matter how it played out. And then the war began." His voice dropped further, heavy with exhaustion. "It didn't make sense. Why Erik would risk it all. Why he'd abandon his own plan. None of it made sense."

My stomach churned, the familiar bitterness rising in my throat.

"Cedric." His name came out like a snarl, my fists clenching at my sides.

Niklas's head snapped up, his eyes narrowing. "Cedric," he repeated, tasting the name like a curse. "You think this is his doing?"

I nodded, the memory of Cedric's cold gaze cutting through me like a blade. "I know it is. He orchestrated this. Just like he planned your death in the mountains three years ago."

Niklas flinched, his jaw tightening. "Cedric..." He said the name again, slower this time, like it was a puzzle he hadn't yet solved. "Now that you say that... He's always been in my uncle's ear. I saw it even then, how Erik hung on his every word."

"He's manipulating him," I said, the words spilling out. "Just like he manipulates everyone. He thrives on chaos, and the prince's ambition is the perfect tool."

Niklas's lips pressed into a thin line, his gaze fixed on the desk as though he could burn through the wood with his anger alone. "I tried to talk to my uncle," he said finally, his voice low and tight. "To make him see reason. But he wouldn't hear it. He sees nothing but red now. All he wants is the kingdom—no matter the cost."

"And Cedric's there, feeding the fire," I added bitterly, "pushing him further. Whispering in his ear. This battle, this war—it's all him."

Niklas exhaled slowly, his hands loosening in his lap as his shoulders slumped. "I should have seen it," he said quietly. "But Cedric's always been good at hiding his moves until it's too late."

"He's not hiding anymore," I said, my jaw tightening. "He's setting the trap, driving us all toward it like a hunter closing in on his prey."

Niklas looked up at me then, his pale blue eyes shadowed with resignation. "And we're all just the prey, running right into his trap."

"Let's get you out—" The words were barely out of my mouth before the tent flap rustled. My breath hitched, and Niklas's eyes widened. He moved faster than I thought possible, nodding toward the bed. I dove underneath it, the thick carpet muffling my movements, and pressed myself flat against the floorboards.

The flap swung open, and a guard stomped in. His boots were heavy, his voice gruff. "Oi, who were you talking to?"

Niklas didn't miss a beat. "Talking to myself, of course. Penning a letter." He gestured casually to the desk, where the candlelight glinted off a half-finished sheet of parchment. "Sometimes it helps to read aloud. Would you like to hear it?"

The guard grunted, his suspicion palpable. "No."

Niklas cleared his throat theatrically. "Dearest Lord Torrence, I write to you with inquiries about the coastline under your watch. Is it the abundance of fish that inspires the sudden increase in shipbuilding? Or perhaps something more lucrative? I must confess my curiosity..."

The guard interrupted with a groan. "Spirits' sake, enough. Keep your prattling to yourself."

But he didn't leave. My stomach tightened as the boots shifted, pacing closer. I held my breath, my fingers gripped the edge of the carpet. He was going to search. He had to.

The sound of Niklas rising from his chair cut through the tense air. "You know," he said brightly, "I've been told my penmanship has improved. Look at this—"

The guard turned, his attention reluctantly snagged by the letter. Niklas held it up, stepping close enough that the man couldn't see much else. "What do you think? The curves on the 'R,' quite elegant, don't you think?"

The guard leaned in, his back now to me. "I don't give a—"

Niklas shot me a pointed look and mouthed, *Go.*

I didn't need to be told twice. I eased out from under the bed, my movements deliberate, my breath shallow. The guard's voice droned on, his annoyance clear, but his attention never wavered from Niklas.

I mouthed back, *I'll come for you.* Niklas gave the barest nod.

The moment I slipped out of the tent, the cold night air slapped my face. I ducked low, weaving between shadows as the guard's voice drifted out behind me. "Just keep it down, all right? My lord," he added with a sneer.

The pounding in my chest felt like it might give me away. My heart was a drumbeat, my breath shallow, every muscle taut as I crept through the camp. Sweat slicked the back of my neck, dampened my palms. This had been a mistake—a stupid, reckless move—but there was no taking it back now. At least I had something to show for it. Information. Just not enough to know what to do next.

I moved slower, each step deliberate, feeling the tension around me. It hung thick in the air, masked poorly by the raucous laughter, the clinking of tankards, and the occasional burst of song. But beneath the noise, anxiety simmered. They were scared, every single one of them. Of the battle to come. Of what waited beyond it.

Rounding a corner between tents, the faint crackle of a fire reached me, followed by voices. One of them snagged my attention, its tone familiar yet distant, as if dredged from a memory I'd left behind. I edged closer, careful not to rustle the loose fabric of the tents.

Around the fire sat four figures, the flames casting flickering shadows across their faces. One of them—I froze. Lars. My cousin.

He wasn't the boy I remembered, scrawny and eager. He'd grown into a soldier, his face leaner, his expression harder. His dark hair was cropped short, and in the firelight, he looked almost like his father, Garret. The resemblance hit me like a blow, the only thing missing was the beard.

Beside him were Bryn, Colm, and Dael, the trio always by his side in Riverhalv, back when they'd played at being watchmen. But this was no game now. The laughter didn't reach their eyes. The camaraderie was a fragile shield against the looming fight ahead.

I wanted to call out. To step into the firelight and tell Lars to run. To convince him that this wasn't his battle, that he shouldn't die for these people, these ambitions that didn't belong to him.

But then the twig snapped under my foot, sharp as a crack of thunder. All four heads whipped toward the sound. My breath caught, and the blood roared in my ears.

Spirits help me. I thought.

The voice cut through the night like a blade. "Who's out there?" Bryn called, sharp and wary. His silhouette stood against the firelight, head turning toward the darkness where I crouched.
My throat tightened, panic locking me in place. The sound of my breath felt impossibly loud, and I willed my body to disappear into the shadows. *What now? Run? Stay? Reveal myself?*
Before I could decide, another voice broke through, gruff and casual. "Just me," Oliver said from behind, his tone carrying the perfect edge of irritation. "Going for a piss. Leave me be."
Bryn's shoulders relaxed a fraction, though his eyes stayed fixed on the dark. Lars, seated beside him, leaned forward, his voice steady but edged with warning. "Best head back to your own fire when you're done."
Colm piped up, his laugh low and easy. "And don't piss on my

bedroll this time."

Laughter rippled through the group, the tension diffusing in an instant. I swallowed hard, my heart pounding in my ears as I felt Oliver's hand clamp down on my arm.

"Let's go," he murmured, the words low and deliberate. He didn't wait for me to answer, pulling me away from the clearing. I stole one last glance over my shoulder as Lars leaned back, the firelight flickering across his face. He looked so much like Garret it made my chest ache.

The campfire shrank behind us as we slipped through the edge of the camp and into the cover of the trees. My muscles burned, my breath unsteady, but Oliver kept us moving until the lights of the soldiers were just a distant glow. Only then did he let go of my arm, his expression unreadable in the moonlight.

Chapter 24 - Marching On

The army's march carved its presence into the forest, every sound from the rhythmic tramp of boots to the creak of wagon wheels blended into a steady pulse that drowned out the wilderness. Leaves clung to the damp air, the faint smell of overturned earth mixing with the distant tang of campfires. I kept my steps light, the uneven ground muffled beneath me. Hunger gnawed at me, a dull ache in my belly that Anni's long-gone supplies had done little to ease.

We crouched behind a fallen log, its mossy surface pressing against my palms. Oliver shifted beside me, his face grim as he stared toward the campfires that dotted the dark expanse ahead. "You were lucky to get out the first time," he muttered, his voice a low growl. "Don't push it."

I leaned back, letting the rough bark of the log press against my shoulders. My arms folded across my chest, and I looked at him. "Niklas is important, Oliver. If Cedric's planning to kill him, we can't just leave him there."

Oliver let out a derisive snort, turning to face me fully. "We? Who's this 'we' you keep talking about? Because I sure as hell didn't sign up for a one-way trip to a pike."

I stiffened at his words but met his glare. "You heard what I told you. He's a pawn. Cedric's going to use him and then toss him away when he's done."

His laugh was bitter, devoid of humor. "And you think we can stop that? Two of us against an entire army?" He jabbed a finger toward the distant lights. "You think they're just going to let us waltz in and out with a prince like it's market day?"

His words hit harder than I wanted to admit. I turned my gaze back toward the camp, the flickering fires lighting up silhouettes of wagons, guards, and shadows I could only guess at. "I'm not giving up on him," I said finally, my voice quieter but firm.

Oliver rubbed his face with both hands, his frustration clear. "You're a stubborn ass, you know that? I don't know what's worse—the fact that you're serious or that I'm too stupid to leave you to it."

"You don't have to come," I said, even though the idea of being alone in this made my chest tighten.

He scoffed, leaning back against the log beside me. "Oh no, you'd probably get yourself killed in an hour without me. Somebody has to keep you from doing something idiotic."

I smirked despite myself. "You just said it's idiotic to even try."

He didn't answer right away, staring into the distance. Finally, he let out a long sigh, his breath curling into the cool night air. "Yeah, but if I don't try to stop you, I'd never hear the end of it. Either from you, Anni, or my own damn conscience."

The weight of his words settled between us, heavy and unspoken. For a moment, the forest seemed quieter, the din of the army muffled by the distance and the enormity of what we were contemplating.

My thoughts drifted, unbidden, to Lars and his friends, sitting by their campfire. They'd looked so different from the boys I remembered—faces harder, voices louder, as if they were trying to convince themselves they belonged among those soldiers. Lars had always been a follower, even as a kid. He, Dael and Colm had followed Bryn everywhere back then, and it seemed they still did. Maybe even into the war.

I wanted to do something, say something to pull them out of this mess. But what could I do? They'd made their choice. They'd put on the uniforms, sworn the oaths. It wasn't for me to decide their path. Still, the thought of them marching into a battle they didn't understand, dying for someone else's ambition, left a bitter taste in my mouth.

Pushing the thought aside, I focused on the task ahead. Whatever guilt lingered over Lars and his friends would have to wait. Right now, there were more pressing concerns. We had to be smart, had to bide our time.

That time came sooner than expected. The lack of food became a bigger problem two days later. Anni's supplies were long gone, and the forest offered little more than a few bitter greens and handfuls of berries. My stomach twisted in protest as we crouched at the edge of the army's encampment, the scent of roasted meat wafting through the air like a cruel taunt.

Oliver shifted beside me, his voice low and sharp. "Are you sure about this?"

I didn't look at him, my eyes locked on the supply wagons parked just beyond the tree line. "The rations aren't as guarded as Niklas. We just grab what we can and get out."

He muttered something I didn't catch but stayed close as I slipped through the underbrush. The camp was just waking up—soldiers yawning, stretching, and grumbling as they stirred from their bedrolls. The faint glow of rekindled campfires cast flickering shadows, and we used every movement to keep ourselves hidden.

The wagons loomed ahead, their contents spilling out in barrels and sacks. My stomach clenched harder at the sight of them, the promise of food close enough to touch.

I moved first, my steps deliberate as I crept up to the nearest wagon. My fingers trembled as I untied a sack of dried fruit, the sweet scent making my mouth water. I stuffed as much as I could into my pack, my movements quick but clumsy. Oliver worked beside me, his actions smoother, practiced.

"That's Enough," he hissed, his voice cutting through the quiet. "Let's go."

I nodded, slinging my pack over my shoulder. But as I turned, a sharp voice rang out behind us. "Hey! Stop!"

Time froze for a heartbeat before adrenaline surged through me. "Run!" I barked, bolting for the trees.

The sound of pursuit crashed behind us—boots pounding the dirt, shouts splitting the air. My heart hammered in my chest as I sprinted through the undergrowth, branches clawing at my clothes. Oliver stayed close, his breaths harsh and quick beside me.

The forest seemed endless, the noise of the camp fading but never disappearing completely. My lungs burned, my legs ached, but I didn't stop until the shouts were swallowed by the distance.

We collapsed against a tree, gasping for air. My pack slid from my shoulder, hitting the ground with a muffled thud. Oliver's glare cut through the lingering dark, his voice dripping with anger.

"That," he panted, "was stupid."

I shot him a look, my pulse still pounding in my ears. "We got food, didn't we?" I held up the pack, shaking it for emphasis.

"Barely." He leaned back against the tree, his frustration bleeding through his words. "And now they'll double their guards. If you think sneaking in to see Niklas was hard before, it's impossible now."

I didn't answer right away. He was right, of course. But the thought of leaving Niklas behind, trapped in that tent, gnawed at me more than the hunger ever had. I looked away, my jaw tightening as I stared into the darkness that had just started to fade with the sunrise.

"We'll figure it out," I said finally, though the weight of doubt sat heavy in my chest.

The days passed with no breakthroughs. Each day, Oliver and I scouted the army's camp, but the doubled guard made it nearly impossible to get close. The soldiers were more alert, eyes scanning the woods, and the army had sent out scouts of its own. We kept our distance, careful to avoid any close encounters. Thankfully, the soldiers seemed to think they were chasing thieves, not enemies. That was something, at least.

Soon enough, the wooden walls of Riverhalv loomed on the horizon, the city stretched across the Halv River like a sentinel. Its jagged silhouette broke through the morning mist, a reminder of how little time we had left. The army slowed its march as it approached the city, its lines stretching further back along the road.

Oliver and I made our way back to our camp, slipping through the forest like shadows. Oliver glanced at me as we moved. "We've done enough," he said, his voice low but firm. "We should find these Forsworn of yours. Let them deal with this."

I chewed on the inside of my cheek, reluctant to agree but knowing he was right. "Once we grab our packs," I said finally, my voice tight. "We'll head downriver. It's a few days' hike to their camp."

Oliver nodded, satisfied, but something pulled at me before we could move further. A flicker in my senses. Two things, distinct and clear. The first was distant, running wild, sending flashes of longing and the feel of the wind. Halder? My heart skipped, but I couldn't focus on him now. The second was closer. Much closer. A presence ahead, where no one should have been.

I stopped short and grabbed Oliver's arm, my voice sharp. "There's someone up ahead."

Oliver froze, his eyes narrowing as he crouched low. His bow came off his shoulder in a practiced motion, and he strung it in silence. "I don't see anyone," he murmured, scanning the trees. "How do you know?"

I didn't answer, my senses tightening around the presence like a snare. "Trust me," I whispered.

We moved slowly, careful not to snap a twig or disturb a single branch as we neared our makeshift camp. The fire pit was cold and the clearing quiet—except for the figure crouched over our packs, rummaging through them like they had all the time in the world.

I gestured to Oliver, and we split up, circling wide through the underbrush. The figure didn't seem to notice, too focused on whatever they were searching for. My heart pounded in my ears as I drew closer, my fingers tightening around my father's bow. A quick glance across the clearing told me Oliver was in position, his bow raised, the string drawn tight.

We leapt out of the brush at the same time, bows trained on the intruder. They jerked back, startled, their hand flying to their belt—but we had them dead to rights.

"Don't move," I said, my voice low and steady, the arrow aimed for their chest.

The figure twitched.

"He said, don't move," Oliver growled, his bowstring taut. The figure froze, their fingers twitching toward a dagger strapped to their belt. I caught the sharp glint in their green eyes, defiant and unyielding, and then recognition slammed into me.

"Blae?" I said, my voice cracking in disbelief.

Her eyes flicked toward me, narrowing before softening with surprise. "Tomi?" She straightened slightly, though her fingers still hovered near her weapon. "I thought it might be you."

I lowered my bow immediately, relief washing over me like a

tide. "It's me."

Oliver glanced between us, his grip still tight on the bow. "You know her?"

"She's Forsworn," I explained, my tone easing. "A scout. Blae's one of ours."

Oliver hesitated for a heartbeat longer, his gaze hard as he studied her. Finally, he lowered his bow, though his hand didn't leave the string. "One of yours, huh?"

Blae's sharp features pulled into a smirk as she straightened fully. "Good to see you've still got a knack for making friends, Tomi." Her short-cropped hair stuck out at odd angles, and her wiry frame seemed coiled for movement, even at rest.

I stepped closer, gesturing between them. "Oliver, this is Blae. Blae, Oliver. What are you doing here?" I asked her, a knot of curiosity forming in my chest. "Shouldn't you be back in Kyrne with the others? I was about to go find them."

Blae rolled her eyes, the smirk lingering on her lips. "Well, I'll make it easy for you, then. They're here. Just a few clicks downriver. Want me to take you to them?"

Relief and anticipation bloomed in equal measure, my smile breaking through without thought. "Yes," I said, the word firm and certain. "Take us to them."

Her grin widened, sharp as her blade. "Follow me."

The forest grew denser as we trailed behind Blae, the underbrush crunching softly underfoot. She moved with an effortless grace, her wiry frame weaving through the trees like she was born to them. I clutched my pack tightly, the familiar weight of it a strange comfort. Oliver, silent but ever-watchful, followed just behind me.

"We've made a home in Kyrne," Blae said, her voice low but carrying easily through the quiet forest. "Wulfric, Svend, Peter, and Dugal all made it back with the others. Everyone's found new homes there."

The tension I'd been carrying for days eased slightly at her words. "It's good to know what we did mattered," I said softly. "That they're safe."

Blae cast a glance over her shoulder, the sharpness in her green eyes softening for a moment. "It did. But safe's a relative term these days."

I stepped over a root, adjusting the bow slung across my back. "Then why are you out here?"

She gave a low chuckle, brushing a stray branch aside. "The princess hasn't left Commander Crosse alone. Stubborn as a mule, that one. Once we got word that Erik and Harlan were dragging their armies this way, she convinced him to bring our forces here too."

My chest tightened at the mention of Sanne. I hadn't seen her in months, but I could picture her clearly—her fierce determination, the fire in her eyes. "Do they know Niklas is here?"

"Of course," Blae said, her tone matter-of-fact. "That's the whole reason we came."

The forest began to thin, and she led us up a gradual incline. The air grew cooler as we climbed, the trees giving way to rocky outcrops and patches of grass. The scent of the river reached me before I saw it, crisp and clear. Blae stopped at the top of the rise, gesturing for us to join her.

I stepped forward, my breath catching as I took in the scene below. The wide expanse of the River Halv cut through the land like a glistening blade, its waters reflecting the pale light of the sky. On either side of the river, two armies sprawled across the open fields, their tents and banners spreading like stains on the earth. The air seemed taut, heavy with anticipation, as if the land itself was holding its breath.

In the center, perched atop the river like a sentinel, stood the town of Riverhalv. Its wooden walls rose stark and dark against the horizon, but the town within them was eerily still. No smoke curled from chimneys, no figures moved along the ramparts. It was as though the town had been drained of life, its people fled or hidden, leaving it behind as a husk waiting for the storm to break.

The fields surrounding the town bore the marks of preparation. Trenches carved into the earth, hastily erected barricades, and churned mud where soldiers had passed. The encampments were alive with movement—soldiers sharpening weapons, voices carrying over the distance, the faint clatter of armor—but Riverhalv itself stood silent, abandoned, a ghost in the shadow of the two looming armies.

As Blae led us over the crest of the hill the Forsworn camp came into view. It was a small hollow tucked neatly into the rise, the kind of place a hunter might choose—hidden, but with a clear vantage of the land below. The tents were scattered in an informal circle, blending with the brush and trees around them. At the center, a low fire flickered, the flames kept deliberately small, more for warmth than light.

The ground bore the marks of recent activity—bootprints packed into the dirt, a few makeshift stools arranged haphazardly near the fire. The smell of worn leather and faint traces of smoked meat lingered in the air. They'd been there at least a day, maybe longer. Even with their small numbers—twenty-five at most—there was a sense of purpose to the way the camp was arranged. Guards stood at the edges, their eyes constantly scanning the shadows, bows and blades within easy reach. No mistakes, no room for surprises.

Blae turned back to us, "not much, but it gets the job done. Come on."

Near the fire, three familiar figures stood out—Commander Crosse, Wulfric, and Lenna. As Blae led us down the slope, they noticed us immediately, standing and watching as we approached. Crosse moved first, his stride steady and purposeful, while Wulfric trailed behind with that familiar grin already forming on his face.

"Well, look what the cat dragged in," Wulfric said, his voice as loud as ever, though there was warmth to it.

Blae, walking just ahead of me, rolled her eyes and crossed her arms. "What did you just call me?" she shot back, her tone biting but light enough to let him know she wasn't really offended.

I felt a flicker of a smile but kept my focus on Crosse as he stopped in front of me. He offered out his hand, his expression unreadable but his voice steady. "Good to see you again, lad."

I shook his hand, his grip firm and sure. "You have my thanks for what you did at Whitestone. I've heard all about it."

I swallowed hard, unsure how to respond. "I'm just... glad you're all safe."

"Where's my Halder, then?" Wulfric interrupted, stepping closer with an exaggerated look of concern.

I rubbed the back of my neck, sheepish. "I left him in Elkswood. We couldn't bring him with us while trailing the army. Too risky." I hesitated, glancing at Wulfric. "But... I think he got loose. Wouldn't be surprised if he's on his way here."

Wulfric laughed, loud and full of life, slapping a hand against his thigh. "That wouldn't surprise me at all. Spirited one, that horse. More sense than most men."

Crosse's sharp gaze lingered on me, his tone leveling out. "And what exactly are you doing here, Tomi?"

I gestured to Oliver beside me, the shadows of the firelight dancing across his face. "We saw Niklas at Elkswood. We followed the army here to see if we could... do anything." I nodded toward

Oliver. "This is Oliver. He's a friend."

"Brave, that," Wulfric said, though there was a hint of caution in his voice. "Tailing an army isn't a small thing."

Before I could reply, a voice from the shadows cut through the camp, laced with urgency. "You saw him? You saw Niklas?"

I turned toward the sound, my heart twisting at the sight of her. Princess Sanne stood just beyond the nearest tent, her face pale in the firelight, her eyes wide and sharp.

Sanne's eyes locked on mine, sharp and expectant and reiterated. "You saw Niklas?"

I nodded, swallowing hard. "Yes. He was in a carriage with Cedric—that's what brought me out here. I… managed to sneak into the camp and speak to him."

Commander Crosse's head snapped toward me, his brow furrowing. "You what?" The disbelief in his tone was as heavy as the air between us.

"What did he say?" Sanne pressed, stepping closer. Her pale blue eyes burned with a mix of hope and dread.

I took a breath, trying to find the words. "He's… He's scared, but he knows Cedric's up to something. He said this whole war doesn't make sense—that he and you were set up to be pawns, heirs for barren princes. But Cedric's twisting everything, pushing Erik into madness and using the war to secure his own power."

Sanne's jaw tightened, her expression hardening into something fierce. "I knew it. I knew Cedric was behind this. It doesn't make sense otherwise." She turned sharply to Commander Crosse, pointing at him with a trembling hand. "See? I told you they were up to something."

Crosse sighed, pinching the bridge of his nose as though he'd heard this before. "Yes, Princess, I know." He straightened, his sharp gaze settling on me. "And since you're here, lad, I suppose it's time to fill you in."

I exchanged a glance with Oliver, then nodded. "Go on."

Crosse folded his arms, his tone as steady as a marching drum. "We got wind of the battle near Riverhalv. Then we heard Niklas would be there, in Cedric's care. That's when the Princess"—he gave Sanne a pointed look—"managed to convince me to bring our forces out here on this… quest."

Sanne didn't flinch under his gaze, her chin lifting defiantly. "It's not a quest. It's justice."

Crosse sighed again but pressed on. "The plan is to liberate Niklas during the chaos of the battle. With both him and the Princess in hand, we intend to form a third faction—a true one. One that stands for the rightful heirs of the kingdom."

The words hit like a blow to the chest. I stared at him, my mind spinning. "A third faction?" My voice sounded distant, even to me.

Oliver let out a low, incredulous laugh, breaking the silence. "That's your plan? In the middle of a battle? Sounds like a fool's errand to me."

Sanne's head snapped toward him, her eyes narrowing. "What would you know about it?"

Oliver arched a brow, his smirk sharp as a blade. "I know a suicide mission when I hear one, Princess."

The title landed with a weight that made Oliver freeze for a moment, realization dawning too late. "Wait—Princess?" His gaze darted between her and Crosse, his usual confidence faltering. "You mean she's…"

Sanne crossed her arms, her voice colder than the River Halv's current. "Yes. I'm the Princess. Sanne of the House Vognsen. And if you're done with your commentary, we have real work to do."

Oliver blinked, then shook his head, muttering something under his breath. "Spirits save us."

"You'll need saving," Sanne bit back, "if you can't think beyond your next sarcastic quip."

"Enough," Crosse said, his voice cutting through the tension like a blade. "This isn't a tavern spat. We all have a part to play, whether it's foolhardy or not."

I stayed silent, my thoughts racing as I processed the enormity of what lay ahead. A third faction. A battle. Liberation. This was more than I'd ever bargained for—but it wasn't just about Niklas anymore. It never had been.

The fire crackled softly between us, its embers casting faint shadows over Commander Crosse's weathered face. He leaned forward, his eyes sharp beneath a furrowed brow. "I know it's a lot to take in, lad," he said, his voice steady but heavy with meaning. "But now that you're here, we could use your bow. It'll be risky, dangerous—but this is a way forward. A chance to set the kingdom to rights. We may have accidentally lit the spark for this war, but perhaps we can help snuff it out before it consumes everything."

Oliver crossed his arms, his expression skeptical. "Or just fan the flames higher by throwing in a third faction. That's what you're really doing, isn't it?"

Blae shifted her weight, arms resting loosely at her sides. "He's got a point," she said, her tone cautious but firm. "Another faction could make things worse. More splinters. More blood."

Princess Sanne, standing taller than she had moments ago, looked directly at Oliver. "We hope people will see the truth," she said, her voice laced with conviction. "We hope they'll do what's right. But that only happens if we give them something worth following."

"And what about Cedric?" I asked, my voice cutting through the tension like the twang of a drawn bowstring. "He's the one pulling Erik's strings. He's not just going to let this happen."

Crosse nodded slowly, the lines on his face deepening. "Once we have Sanne and Niklas, Cedric loses his leverage. With both of them alive and on our side, Erik may finally see through the man's lies and manipulation."

I stared at the fire, the warmth of it doing little to cut through the chill in my chest. It was a lot to process. The weight of it all—the risks, the stakes—pressed heavy on my mind. My fingers traced the edge of my father's bow, the worn wood grounding me in the moment.

Crosse leaned closer, his gaze pinning me in place. "So, have you decided?"

I swallowed hard, looking between the faces around me. Blae's quiet steadiness. Sanne's unwavering determination. Oliver's reluctant loyalty. Then Wulfric, who gave me a small, almost imperceptible nod.

"I'll join the Forsworn," I said, the words coming out firmer than I'd expected.

Wulfric let out a bark of laughter, clapping me on the shoulder. "Spirits, finally!" he said, grinning. "Thought we'd have to drag you into it."

The others exchanged looks—some relieved, some cautious. But for the first time, I felt like I was stepping into something bigger than myself. Something that mattered.

Later that night, the firelight flickered across the faces gathered around it, dancing in their eyes and softening the rough edges carved by time, war, and weariness. Peter and Svend greeted me with warm grins as I found a spot near the edge of the circle, their hands briefly clasping mine in welcome.

"Good to see you back, lad," Svend said, his voice like gravel but carrying an undeniable warmth. "Still skinny as ever, though."

"Skinnier," Peter added with a grin, tossing me a strip of dried meat. "Better eat up. You'll need your strength soon enough."

I caught it and smirked. "I've been keeping busy."
Oliver leaned back on his elbows beside me, glancing at the flames. "Doesn't this seem a bit... bold? Having a fire out here?"

Blae, sitting cross-legged across from him, smirked. "A few hours from Riverhalv, and all they'd risk sending after us are farmers with pitchforks. We're merchants, remember? Or perhaps humble hunters out here to find game." She raised a brow at Oliver. "Try to act the part."

Wulfric chuckled, taking a swig from his flask before passing it to Blae. "Aye, just a pack of merchants and farmers," he said, the sarcasm thick. "Don't let the weapons fool you."

The group chuckled, the tension easing for a moment. The fire crackled softly, casting long shadows that stretched into the forest around us. Commander Crosse sat silent, sharpening a knife against a whetstone, his eyes distant but not unkind. Princess Sanne, her chin resting in her palm, stared into the flames, the lines of her face softened by the flickering light.

I shifted on my makeshift seat, the curiosity gnawing at me. "What about Jory?" I asked, glancing at Blae. "Is he here?"

Blae smirked, shaking her head. "Jory? Nah. He's back at the village."

Peter chimed in from across the fire, his grin wide. "Leader of the non-combatants now. He's got them setting up new hunting traps, reorganizing the whole supply line. If I know him, he's probably giving some poor soul a lecture about the 'perfect snare' as we speak."

Wulfric chuckled, leaning back on his hands. "That sounds like Jory. Can't keep the man idle for long, not unless you tie him down."

"Or give him something to plan," Svend added, his tone light but fond.

I couldn't help but smile. It was good to know Jory was still around, still himself in all the ways that mattered. The fire crackled again, filling the brief silence that followed, and for a moment, the camp felt almost peaceful. Almost.

"Got a song for us, Wulfric?" Peter asked, his tone teasing but hopeful.

Wulfric groaned theatrically, shaking his head. "Not unless you want the spirits to scatter and leave us to fend for ourselves."

"I think we'll manage without a song," Blae said, her grin sharp. "Unless Peter's offering."

Peter held up his hands. "Not unless you want to clear the forest."

Laughter rippled through the group, the kind that felt rare and precious. Even Oliver cracked a smile, nudging me with his elbow. I let myself relax, just for a moment, leaning into the warmth of the fire and the company around it.

Commander Crosse spoke up, his voice firm. "There'll be plenty of time for noise later. Best we save our voices—and our strength."

The group quieted, the air growing heavier but not oppressive. I glanced around at the faces illuminated by the firelight, each carrying their own weight, their own stories. And yet, for this moment, we were just people, sharing the same warmth and the same hope, the flames reflecting in our eyes.

I leaned forward, the heat of the fire on my face. It was calm now, the kind of calm that always came before the storm.

Chapter 25 - Battle Begins

The dawn broke in a slow, relentless sweep across the horizon, the kind of light that didn't just touch the world but claimed it. The forest around me began to stir, the shadows of the night stretching thin as the golden hues of morning spilled over the land. Riverhalv stood silent in the distance, the wooden walls dark against the pale streaks of sky. Beyond it, the River Halv gleamed like molten silver, cutting through the heart of the battlefield.

The armies were already moving. Dark ranks formed on the fields surrounding the town, their banners snapping in the breeze. Horses pawed at the earth, the sound of their restlessness faint but carrying through the stillness. I watched as men broke from tents and fell into formation, the sharp glint of their weapons catching the first rays of sunlight. Smoke curled from dying campfires, mingling with the mist that clung to the ground like a shroud.

Footsteps behind me drew my attention. Wulfric joined me first, his heavy frame moving with an ease that belied the tension in his posture. He let out a low whistle as he took in the scene. "It's always strange, isn't it? The way a battlefield looks calm, almost peaceful, until it's not."

I nodded but didn't speak. Words felt thin against the weight of what lay ahead.

Oliver appeared next, his bow slung over his shoulder. He stayed quiet, his eyes fixed on the distant armies, his usual smirk replaced with something harder, sharper.

Commander Crosse was last, stepping up beside me with the quiet authority he always carried. He crossed his arms, his gaze sweeping the valley below. "They're moving," he said, his voice a low rumble. "It'll begin soon."

Behind us, the others gathered one by one. Blae leaned against a tree, her sharp green eyes narrowing as she tracked the distant movements. Svend and Peter stood close, murmuring to each other in hushed tones. Sanne lingered at the edge of the group, her arms crossed, her face unreadable as she stared toward the river.

The armies began to advance. Across the fields, banners rose like dark spines against the morning light. The wooden walls of Riverhalv seemed to brace themselves as soldiers on both sides pressed closer to the town. A stillness hung in the air, a collective breath held by the world as it waited for the inevitable clash.

None of us spoke. We watched as the pieces moved, as lines of men and steel shifted and merged, the distance between them shrinking with every moment. The rising sun bathed it all in light, a stark contrast to the shadows that loomed over what was to come.

The clamor of the armies below grew louder, a distant cacophony of metal on metal, shouts, and the uneasy snorts of horses. I stood with the others at the edge of the rise, watching as the battle unfolded, the sheer scale of it sending a chill through my chest.

Wulfric's voice broke the tension, his gruff tone cutting through the air like a blade. "This is like no battle I've ever seen. Looks more like a damned festival if you ask me—one where they're handing out death instead of ale."

I glanced at him, his scarred face set in a grim expression, there was no humor in his words.

Commander Crosse stood with his arms folded, his sharp eyes fixed on the chaos below. "This isn't a battle," he said, his voice low but firm. "It's a contest. A game between two princes—Erik and Harlan."

"Why here?" I asked, my voice barely above a whisper. "Why the town? Wouldn't it make more sense for one of them to take it and the other to siege?"

Crosse didn't answer, but it was Sanne who spoke next. Her voice was steady, but there was a tightness to it, a restrained edge of frustration. "Riverhalv was chosen as neutral ground. A place where neither side holds an advantage. It makes sense, for them at least, to use it as their final battleground."

"An arena," Oliver said, his tone tinged with disbelief. "They've turned the town into a stage for their fight."

Sanne nodded, her gaze locked on the scene below. "That's exactly it."

Blae leaned against a tree, her sharp eyes scanning the battlefield. "It'll be hard to find Prince Niklas in all that. If he's even in there."

Crosse's jaw tightened, and he turned to me. "His tent, Tomi. Where did you see it?"

I pointed toward the encampment, where the gray fabric of Niklas's tent still stood, tucked near the edge of the field. Each time they took it down and put it back up in the same pattern. The sight of it sent a chill down my spine. "There," I said, my voice steadier than I felt.

Crosse followed my gaze and nodded. "Good. Then we plan from there."

He turned and motioned for us to follow. We gathered around a makeshift table where a map of the town and surrounding fields was spread out, held in place by smooth river stones. The firelight flickered over the parchment, illuminating the careful lines and markings that showed the streets, the river, and the armies that now encircled Riverhalv.

Commander Crosse leaned over the map, his fingers tracing a jagged path through the narrow streets of Riverhalv. The firelight played across his face, highlighting the deep lines of concentration etched into his features. His voice was calm, steady, and impossible to argue with.

"We split into two groups," he said, his tone as sharp as the blade strapped to his side. "A wedge of warriors to drive through the chaos, pushing them toward Prince Erik's camp. The tip of that wedge will break off and head toward Niklas's tent."

Sanne didn't wait for him to finish. "I'm coming," she said, her voice cutting through the air like an arrow. She stood with her arms crossed, her defiance clear in every inch of her stance.

Crosse didn't even look up from the map. "Absolutely not," he replied, the words clipped and final. "You're staying here. That's not up for debate."

Her chin lifted, the glare she aimed at him sharp enough to draw blood. Before she could speak, Blae laid a hand on her arm. Sanne's lips pressed into a tight line, but she stayed silent, though the tension radiating from her was almost palpable.

Oliver shifted beside me, clearing his throat. "I'll stay behind too," he said, his voice measured. "Someone's got to protect her highness."

I glanced at him, nodding. I understood, it wasn't his fight. Still, a part of me wished he'd be coming along. Oliver had a way of grounding me when things went south, and things always seemed to go south.

Crosse straightened, looking up from the map to sweep his gaze over all of us. "Once we have Niklas, we withdraw. No heroics, no improvisation. Wulfric, you'll lead the tip of the wedge with Tomi and a handful of others. I'll take the larger group and handle the main push."

Oliver frowned, his voice low but firm. "Why does Tomi have to go?"

Crosse's eyes locked onto him, his expression unreadable. "Because he's seen the prince. Niklas knows him. That familiarity could save precious moments. And..." He looked at me then, his voice softening just slightly. "The kid's got a nose for these kinds of situations."

The words caught me off guard, and I felt a flicker of pride warming my chest. I tried to keep my face neutral, but I couldn't help the faint smile tugging at the corner of my mouth. Oliver met my gaze and gave me a grudging nod, the tension between us easing just a bit.

Crosse folded the map and tucked it into his belt. "Everyone clear on the plan?"

There were murmurs of agreement, heads nodding all around. I added my own voice to the mix, even though my mind was already racing ahead, thinking through the steps.

"Good," Crosse said. He gave us a nod and then gestured toward the rise overlooking the town. "Let's go watch the fight. We move as soon as the action's centered in Riverhalv."

The group began to disperse, their footsteps crunching softly in the frost-laden grass. I lingered, my gaze drifting to the town in the distance. The rising sun cast long shadows over the river, its surface a shifting blend of gold and red. My heart thudded in my chest, heavy with anticipation and dread. I clenched my fists, the weight of what lay ahead settling over me like a shroud.

From the rise, the battle unfolded like a grim dance, the armies moving like two storm fronts colliding. The fields surrounding Riverhalv became a sea of shifting metal and motion, the glint of sunlight off steel flashing like lightning. From that distance, the sound was muted—dull thuds of impact, the clash of weapons, and the occasional ragged cry carried on the wind.

The town itself stood as a jagged silhouette against the morning sky, the river curling around its wooden walls. The armies had spread across the fields, their formations like ripples in the grass, slowly pressing inward. Smoke began to curl from the outskirts of Riverhalv, dark and oily, marking the first fires of the battle. Soldiers surged through the gates, their lines breaking into chaos as the fighting spilled into the narrow streets.

Wulfric muttered something under his breath, his voice low and gravelly. "This is no battle. It's a butcher's field."

I nodded, my jaw tight as I scanned the chaos below. Even in the distance, I could see the lines break, soldiers falling in waves. The ground seemed to swallow them whole, mud slicked with blood.

Commander Crosse's voice cut through, sharp as the edge of his blade. "This isn't like the last war. That dragged on for years, drained the kingdom dry. No, this time they're in a hurry. Erik and Harlan don't want strategy—they want it over, and they don't care how many bodies it takes to get there."

Sanne stood behind him, arms crossed, her face a mask of control. But her eyes stayed fixed on the carnage below, her stillness heavy with something darker. "Riverhalv was meant to be neutral ground," she said quietly, her tone bitter. "Instead, they've turned it into their stage. The perfect arena for their final act."

"Perfect," Oliver echoed, his tone laced with sarcasm. "Right. Perfect for turning into rubble."

The town seemed to cave inward as the armies pushed through its gates. Smoke thickened, the dark plumes rising into the sky as fires spread. The fighting moved deeper, into the narrow alleys and wooden bridges that crisscrossed the river itself. It was chaos—a controlled chaos maybe, but chaos all the same.

Crosse watched the scene for a few more moments before

stepping back. "That's our cue," he said, his voice cutting through the tension. "Let's move."

The group stirred into motion, checking weapons and adjusting packs. As I turned to follow, Sanne stepped forward, her gaze fixed on me. Her blue eyes were intense, unwavering.

"Tomi," she said, her voice quieter now, almost gentle. "Promise me you'll bring him back."

I hesitated, her words heavy with meaning. I thought of Niklas—his pale eyes, the resignation in his voice when he'd asked if it was time. I nodded, meeting Sanne's gaze. "I will. I promise."

Oliver stepped in beside me, his hand resting briefly on my shoulder. "And I'll make sure there's something left to come back to," he said with a smirk, trying to lighten the weight that hung over us.

Sanne's lips curved into a faint, fleeting smile. Then, with a nod, she stepped back, her posture straight and regal even as her worry lingered.

The group moved out, twenty in all. We descended the hill, the trees thinning as we reached the forest's edge. The air was cool and carried the faint smell of smoke from the distant battle. Our steps were careful, quiet, the crunch of leaves underfoot barely audible as we kept low and out of sight.

As we crossed into the fields, the expanse of open land stretched ahead of us, dotted with wildflowers and scattered rocks. The golden stalks of grass swayed gently in the breeze, their movement at odds with the violence that loomed ahead.

Crosse led the way, his stride purposeful, the rest of us following in tight formation. My father's bow was slung across my back, my axe at my side. I felt the weight of both, familiar and grounding, as we made our way toward the encampment, our target clear in the smoke-choked distance.

The closer we drew, the more the world closed in around me. The din of battle grew louder, a cacophony of screams, clashing steel, and the dull, rhythmic thud of boots and hooves pounding the ground. My head swam as my senses stretched and twisted, catching fragments of emotion—panic, rage, pain, desperation. I gripped my father's bow tightly, the wood solid and familiar beneath my fingers, grounding me against the storm raging within.

The smell of smoke and blood hit us before we reached the outskirts of the encampment. The fields had become a mire of trampled earth, littered with abandoned supplies and the bodies of the fallen. Soldiers moved in chaotic clusters, their focus on the battlefield beyond, where the gates of Riverhalv stood shrouded in haze.

We weren't challenged at first. Crosse led us through the fringes of the camp, his steps deliberate, his eyes scanning for threats. The rest of us followed, weapons at the ready. Wulfric, his axe already in hand, moved just behind me, his breath steady and even like a predator waiting to strike.

It wasn't long before the shouts came. "Who are they?" a soldier barked from somewhere to our left. Another voice followed, harsher, closer. "Stop them!"

Steel hissed as swords left scabbards. The first clash came as one of Crosse's men deflected a wild swing, his own blade biting into the attacker's shoulder. The soldier crumpled with a scream, but more were already closing in.

"Form up!" Crosse's voice cut through the chaos like a blade itself. The wedge took shape around him, shields locking together as they drove forward with practiced precision. Wulfric, Svend,

Peter, and I broke to the right, taking the opening Crosse created for us.

A soldier lunged at me, his blade catching the light as it arced toward my chest. I twisted, my instincts honed from years of hunting, and brought the bow up to deflect the strike. The steel scraped against the wood, chipping but not breaking, sending a jarring vibration through my arms. I stepped back, drawing my axe and swinging low. The blade caught his leg, and he collapsed with a guttural cry.

Beside me, Wulfric moved like a whirlwind, his axe carving a brutal path through the melee. Blood sprayed as he cleaved through an opponent's shield, the man stumbling backward into another's sword. Svend and Peter covered our flanks, their blades flashing in tight, precise arcs that kept the soldiers at bay.

"Tomi, move!" Wulfric's voice snapped me out of the chaos. I turned to see him barreling forward, using his bulk to shove two soldiers aside and create an opening. The rest of us followed, breaking free of the skirmish and darting into the camp's interior.

The tents were closer together there, their dark canvas walls towering over us like silent witnesses. Fires crackled in makeshift pits, and the air was thick with smoke and the metallic tang of blood. We moved quickly, keeping low, our weapons ready as we approached the heart of the camp.

Crosse's wedge still held behind us, the sounds of their battle fading as we pressed on. My pulse hammered in my ears, but my steps were sure. The Prince's tent was ahead, its edges illuminated by the eerie glow of the flames surrounding us. Wulfric led the way, his axe at the ready, as we closed in on our target.

The path to the Prince's tent was a blur of chaos. Soldiers came at us in twos and threes, faces grim under the dull light of the flames. Wulfric barked orders, his voice cutting through the din, keeping us moving forward. Each skirmish ended quickly—brutally.

My bow hummed in my hands as I loosed an arrow into a man's leg, the impact spinning him to the ground with a scream. Another soldier lunged, and Peter's blade stopped him short, the sound of steel biting flesh making my stomach twist. I forced it down, notching another arrow.

"Keep moving!" Wulfric growled, shoving a body aside. His axe gleamed darkly as he surged forward, Svend close behind, their movements practiced and deadly. I glanced at the fallen soldier at my feet. His groan of pain echoed in my ears, but I turned and followed.

The Prince's tent loomed ahead, its sides rippling in the smoky breeze. Two guards stood at the entrance, their hands gripping spears as they shouted at us. Wulfric didn't slow. His axe came down with a wet crunch, and one of the men crumpled before he could raise his weapon. Svend took the other, his blade driving into the man's gut with terrifying precision.

Inside, the tent was a wreck. The desk stood askew, ink pooled and splattered across its surface. Papers littered the floor, many smeared with boot prints. A chair lay on its side, one leg broken. The fine carpets were rumpled, one corner pulled up to reveal the dirt beneath. My breath caught as I took it all in.

"Spirits," Peter muttered, his eyes scanning the room.
"Empty," Wulfric growled, his gaze narrowing. "He's gone."
I stepped closer to the desk, my hand brushing against a scrap of paper. The ink was still tacky under my fingers. Recent. There had been a struggle here, and not long ago.

"We fall back," Wulfric said, turning toward the entrance. "Now."

I didn't move. My fingers tightened on my father's bow as I reached out with my pathos, letting the emotions around me flood in. The cacophony of fear and anger hit me like a wave—soldiers fighting for their lives, for their Princes, for survival. Somewhere in the sea of feelings, I tried to find him.

Niklas. I didn't know him well, had only spoken to him a handful of times, but I remembered the boy he had been. Innocent. Nervous. Proud. I latched onto that memory, imagining how he must feel now—terrified, trapped, dragged into something far beyond his control.

"Tomi," Wulfric said sharply. "We need to move."

I ignored him, my eyes scanning the camp as I stretched my senses further. There—a thread, faint but distinct, tinged with panic and desperation. My heart raced as I turned, following the pull westward, toward the gates of Riverhalv.

"There," I said, my voice tight.

Wulfric stepped up beside me, his expression darkening as he followed my gaze. "Spirits help us," he muttered. Cedric and his men were dragging Niklas, their path lit by the faint glow of the distant fires. They moved with purpose, heading straight for the gates of the town.

My fingers clenched around the bow as I took a step forward.

Wulfric grabbed my arm, his grip iron-strong, his voice low but heavy with urgency. "Lad, we can't. There's too many. Hundreds, maybe thousands. We're too few, and you know it."

I shook my head, pulling my arm free. My heart thundered in my chest, each beat louder than the last. "I promised her," I said, my voice cracking despite my best effort to keep it steady. "I promised Princess Sanne I'd bring her brother back."

Wulfric's gaze bore into mine, hard and unyielding. "And you will. Just not today."

The words hit like a blow, but they didn't settle. Not in my chest. Not in my gut. I tore my eyes away from him, back to the west, where Cedric's shadowed figures dragged Niklas closer to the gates. Closer to the chaos. The screams and clangs of battle from the town echoed over the fields, an unrelenting reminder of what was at stake.

Wulfric's hand hovered near my shoulder, a silent command to move, to follow as the group began their retreat. My feet followed at first, step by step, but my gaze lingered on the distance. The glow of firelight. The faint outline of Niklas struggling.

I stopped. My throat tightened, the promise I'd made to Sanne ringing louder than the din of war. My fists clenched at my sides, nails digging into my palms. The pull in my chest was too strong, the knowledge that he wouldn't make it without me too sharp.

I turned. Wulfric saw the shift, his face darkening as he realized what I was about to do. "Tomi—"

"I can't," I said, the words tumbling out. "I can't just leave him."

Before he could stop me, I ran.

The wind tore at my hood, the ground uneven beneath my boots as I sprinted back toward the battle. Toward the gates. Toward Niklas. Toward the chaos I knew I might not survive.

Chapter 26 - Prince's Duel

The camp stretched wide, a maze of tents and makeshift barricades, the din of the battle a constant roar in my ears. My chest heaved as I sprinted through, heart pounding a rhythm that matched the clash of steel in the distance. I yanked my cloak free, its familiar weight pulling at my shoulders as I discarded it. Jory's colours hit the mud, forgotten, as I snatched a tattered green-and-red cloak hanging from a supply rack. The emblem of Cedric's house, a red dragon on a Greenfield, stood out stark against the grime.

Pulling the new cloak around me, I tucked my head low, my pulse a drumbeat of panic and determination. Soldiers passed by—some laughing nervously, others silent, faces carved from stone. They were the reserves, loitering at the edges of the camp, waiting for the call to move into the fight. Their gazes lingered on me, suspicion flickering in their eyes.

"Oi, you!" a voice barked. My feet faltered, but I forced them still, turning slowly toward the man. He was older, grizzled, with a jagged scar cutting across his cheek. His hand rested on the hilt of his sword. "Where d'you think you're going?"

My mouth dried, my thoughts racing. What would Oliver do? He'd bluff, easy as breathing, his grin disarming. Anni? She'd spin a tale so convincing even she might believe it. But they wouldn't be here, wouldn't have run into this mess to begin with.

"Messenger," I blurted, the word scraping from my throat. My voice wavered, but I straightened my back, forcing myself to meet his gaze.

The man narrowed his eyes, scrutinizing me for a heartbeat that stretched too long. Then he waved a hand dismissively. "Then get on with it. And stay clear of the burning buildings—unless you fancy being roasted."

I nodded sharply, my throat too tight for words, and turned away. My legs moved before my mind caught up, carrying me through the gates and deeper into the chaos. The man's warning hung in the air behind me, but it was the distant screams and the acrid tang of smoke that kept my focus ahead.

The chaos of Riverhalv wrapped around me like a storm, each step forward pulling me deeper into its heart. My breath came in sharp bursts, and I fought to keep my head down, to project the thought: just a messenger, only a messenger. Whether it was my pathos or the madness of battle that shielded me, I couldn't say. Soldiers brushed past, their gazes sliding over me without stopping, too consumed by the violence to question the lone figure weaving through the carnage.

The further I went, the fiercer the fighting became. Blades clashed, the metallic scream of steel cutting through the air, mingling with guttural cries of pain and fear. Smoke billowed from burning homes, stinging my eyes and filling my lungs. I ducked as a flash of movement caught my eye—a blade sweeping in my direction. I stumbled, falling into the dirt as the soldier was knocked aside, replaced by another man, his armor bearing the colors of Prince Erik. His hand extended, hauling me to my feet before he turned back to face the enemy.

He didn't last long.

The spear came from nowhere, skewering him clean through the chest. His mouth opened, but no sound escaped as he collapsed, the light in his eyes fading to nothing. I staggered back, my hands trembling as I clutched the edge of my borrowed cloak, my stomach churning.

Battle was chaos. Pure, unrelenting chaos. Blood ran in rivers across the cobblestones, pooling in cracks and crevices. The screams weren't just noise—they were a chorus of raw emotion, pain, anger, fear, despair. It hit me like a wave, dragging me under. My head spun, and for a moment, it felt as if the blood had drained from my body, leaving me cold and hollow.

I forced myself to breathe, to focus. Niklas. Cedric. That's where I needed to be. Clinging to that thought I pushed through the icy fog threatening to swallow me whole.

And then, just at the edge of my awareness, something else. A presence, distant but closing in. Running, charging forward with purpose. It wasn't a soldier, wasn't a threat, but it was driven by something fierce, something that mirrored my own desperation. A friend.

I shook my head, shoving the thought aside. I didn't have time to wonder what it was. My path was clear, the noise of battle narrowing to a single point. Niklas was close.

The closer I got, the thicker the chaos pressed in, like a living thing trying to smother me. The fighting had no order—no lines, no formations, just men locked in brutal combat. Steel sang and screamed, blood sprayed, and bodies littered the streets like broken dolls. Smoke and ash swirled in the air, mingling with the metallic tang of blood, and I had to force each breath through the suffocating stench.

I ducked low, weaving through the carnage. A blade swept too close, nicking the edge of my borrowed cloak, but I didn't stop. My eyes locked on Cedric ahead, his crimson-plumed helmet cutting through the madness like a beacon. Niklas was with him, his slight frame dragged along by Cedric's men, their armor a grim wall around the Fief Lord. They were heading toward the center, drawn deeper into the storm.

Buildings burned, flames licked at the sky as rubble spilled into the streets. Shouts and cries echoed off the remains of stone walls, and still, Cedric moved with purpose, his men carving a path through the chaos. I followed, my heart hammering against my ribs.

A sudden clash of bodies and blades stopped me short—a wall of men locked in furious combat. There was no going around, no way to wait it out. I took a deep breath and plunged forward, shoving past the chaos. A blade came from nowhere, its edge cutting a hot line across my upper arm. Pain flared, sharp and immediate, but I didn't stop. I pushed through, half-blinded by smoke and noise, until the street opened up before me.

Riverhalv's market square unfolded like the eye of a storm, an eerie calm at its center while chaos raged around its edges. The stone underfoot was slick with blood, the fountains cracked and dry, and the stalls that once bustled with trade were reduced to smoldering husks.

And there, in the center, were the two princes. Unmistakable, even to me.

Prince Erik stood tall, his gold-etched armor catching the light of the surrounding fires, his blade resting lightly at his side. Across from him, Prince Harlan, broader, his darker armor battered but formidable, his greatsword resting tip-down on the ground. Their gazes locked, their guards holding back, a circle forming around them as if the chaos itself had paused to witness what came next.

The two princes stood mere strides apart, their faces etched with sweat and blood, shadows flickering across them from the surrounding fires. They looked like reflections distorted by the choices they had made. Harlan, the elder, was stocky and broad-shouldered, his face calmer, his jaw set with a grim determination. His honey blonde hair clung to his forehead, streaked with ash. Erik, leaner with sharper features, had eyes like daggers, their edges honed by ambition and rage. Where Harlan seemed to carry the weight of a mountain, Erik looked like the storm threatening to tear it down.

"You never understood, brother," Erik said, his voice tight, loud enough to carry above the din. "The kingdom needs more than your stagnant peace. It needs strength. It needs fire."

Harlan exhaled slowly, shaking his head, his greatsword shifting slightly in his grip. "What the kingdom needs, Erik, is stability. What it doesn't need is your lust for conquest. You'd burn it to ashes and call the cinders a crown."

Erik's jaw clenched, his fingers tightening around the hilt of his sword. "And you would let it rot, let our enemies encroach from every side while you sit fat and content, hiding behind your walls."

Harlan stepped forward, his heavy boots splashing in the blood-soaked ground. "You're blind, Erik. Blinded by your own greed. You've always wanted more than your share, and now you'd drag the whole kingdom into chaos for it."

Erik's sneer deepened, his voice cutting sharp and cold. "Greed? You call it greed to take what's needed to secure the kingdom's future? Eldric's bloodline was weak. His heirs are nothing but pawns waiting to be seized."

Harlan's jaw tightened, the muscles working under his beard. "And so you seized them—your own niece and nephew. Stolen like spoils of war to twist into your plans."

"Our plans, Harlan—our plans. Lest you forget. You know that they were unfit to rule," Erik spat back, his eyes blazing. "Now suddenly you have a conscience? You think Eldric's feeble brood could hold this kingdom together after his death? They're a legacy of weakness, Harlan, a crumbling branch that needed to be cut before it broke under its own weight."

"They are children!" Harlan roared, his voice carrying over the battle's chaos. "He was our brother, Erik. You talk of strength and strategy, but you stole them from their family. You turned this kingdom into a battleground for your ambitions, and you dare call it securing the future?"

The argument grew louder, the weight of their words vibrating through the square as the tension coiled tighter. Around them, the circle of onlookers had grown—Fief Lords and generals, their expressions ranging from grim interest to cold calculation. At the edge of the group, Cedric stood out, his crimson like hair catching the firelight, his hand gripping Niklas's shoulder. The young prince stood stiff, his pale blond hair tousled and his face unreadable as Cedric whispered something to him.

"Enough," Harlan said, his voice cutting through the air like his blade soon would. He raised his greatsword, the heavy steel catching the light of the flames. But he didn't aim it at Erik. He pointed it straight at Niklas, standing captive beside Cedric.

My stomach tightened as I followed the line of Harlan's blade. Niklas, pale and wide-eyed, stood frozen, Cedric's grip firm on his shoulder. The tension in the air thickened, oppressive, as if the world itself was holding its breath.

Behind them, the crumbling spire of Riverhalv's chapel loomed, a stark silhouette against the burning horizon. The flames cast jagged shadows that danced across the rubble, and the sight made something cold settle in my chest. Whatever fueled this battle, it ran far deeper than what could be mended with words. This would not end here—not with words, and not without blood.

Cedric's eyes flicked between Harlan and Erik, a flicker of something smug curling his lips. His grip on Niklas tightened, his fingers dug into the young prince's shoulder as if he'd caught a prize he'd never let go. The firelight played across his face, painting every sharp line with cruelty.

The fight erupted with a sudden ferocity. Erik whipped forward, his sword cutting a gleaming arc through the smoke-filled air, the tip aimed straight for Harlan's chest. Harlan moved with practiced precision, bringing his greatsword up just in time to block the strike, the clash of steel rang out across the square. Sparks flew, and Erik pivoted, twisting to launch another attack, his movements sharp and fast, like a blade itself.

The ring of metal echoed, sharp and unrelenting, as the two princes circled each other in the center of the chaos. Erik lunged again, his blade slicing narrowly past Harlan's shoulder, missing by inches. Harlan countered with a heavy, calculated swing of his greatsword, the sheer force of the blow driving Erik staggering back a step, his boots slipping on the blood-slick cobblestones.

I weaved through the rubble and ash, my heart pounding in my chest. Each clash of the princes' blades seemed to reverberate through the market square, a raw, angry rhythm that made the air feel heavier. Erik was quick, striking with precision and speed, his sharp features twisted in fury. Harlan, stockier and solid, absorbed the blows with calm determination before delivering powerful retaliations, each swing of his sword driving Erik closer to the edge.

Ahead, Cedric stood firm with Niklas, his stance casual but his eyes calculating. I moved toward them, clutching my bow, but before I could get close, a hand clamped down on my shoulder.

I froze, my body going rigid as I turned to look up at the man who'd stopped me. He was tall, noble in bearing, with cropped white hair that gave him the air of experience rather than age. His cloak bore an emblem of a snowflake encircled by a wreath of pine, and his sharp eyes locked onto mine with unsettling precision.

"What are you doing here, boy?" His voice was low, calm, and carried a weight that made my skin prickle.

"I'm a messenger," I said quickly, my voice steady but my heart racing. "With a message for Cedric."

The man's hand didn't loosen. His gaze dropped to my chest, then down to my belt. "Where's your message, then? Your satchel?"

The fight below continued, the sound of boots scraping against stone and metal on metal growing louder. I could see Harlan feinting left before delivering a brutal kick to Erik's stomach, sending him to his knees. But Erik wasn't done. He rolled, swinging his sword upward in a wild arc that caught Harlan's side, blood blooming dark against the prince's already stained tunic.

"I said," the man repeated, his grip tightening, "where is it?"

I swallowed hard, the weight of his scrutiny pressing down on me. There was no way out of this—not without using it. Felix's warnings echoed in my mind, but I pushed them aside, reaching deep for my pathos. I let the man feel it: the urgency, the fear, the desperate need to be believed. I projected images—Cedric's emblem, a satchel, a hurried errand—layering them over the storm of emotions I sent his way.

His grip faltered, his sharp eyes blinking as if he was trying to clear a haze. His expression shifted, confusion edging into frustration, as though his vision blurred and his thoughts jumbled. "You're just... a messenger?"

"Just a messenger," I whispered, my voice almost drowned out by the furious battle below.

His grip on my shoulder tightened, his sharp eyes narrowing. "No," he said, his voice cold and deliberate. "You're no messenger." His face darkened, anger seeping into every line. "Liar," he spat, his grip like iron. His other hand moved toward the hilt of a dagger at his side.

The clash of swords peaked, and I turned my gaze back to the square just in time to see Harlan and Erik collide in a final, ferocious exchange. Harlan's greatsword cleaved downward as Erik's blade thrust upward. Both princes froze, their weapons finding their marks—Erik's sword buried deep in Harlan's abdomen, Harlan's greatsword carving into Erik's chest.

For a heartbeat, they stood locked together, blood dripping from their wounds and mixing with the mud and ash beneath their feet. Then, as if the strings holding them upright had been cut, they collapsed in unison, their bodies hitting the ground with a sickening thud.

The man's hand slipped from my shoulder, his sharp gaze snapping to the fallen princes. His breath hitched, his shock cutting through the chaos. The way was open, but the weight of what I'd just witnessed kept me rooted for a moment longer. Then I turned, slipping free, and moved toward Cedric and Niklas.

The air was a storm of shouting voices and clashing steel as I darted forward, slipping past the white-haired lord while his attention was drawn to the fallen princes. The gathering of Fief Lords surged toward their lifeless bodies, the chaos thickening around the square. Ahead, I spotted Cedric, his red hair pulled into a knot, his sharp, angular eyes cutting through the smoke as he hauled Niklas forward.

Even from this distance, I could feel it—Cedric's confidence radiating like heat, his arrogance curling at the edges of his posture. He was about to make a move, to seize control of the moment. My heart hammered as I slid my father's bow off my back and nocked an arrow, raising it toward the Fief Lord.

"Cedric!" I shouted, my voice ragged but steady. "Let go of Niklas!"

The disbelief on Cedric's face shifted to anger as his sharp eyes locked on me, recognition flickering there for just a heartbeat before he masked it. His grip on Niklas tightened, the boy stumbling as Cedric yanked him forward. Below us, a woman's voice cut through the din like a blade. "The princes are dead!"

Cedric's expression shifted, his focus narrowing. He pulled Niklas closer, the boy stumbling as he yanked his arm. "I don't have time for this nonsense," Cedric snapped. His gaze flicked to the soldier at his side. "Kill him."

The soldier lunged without hesitation, his heavy boots pounding against the stone as he charged me. I loosed my arrow, the string snapping against my fingers as the shaft flew. It struck true, burying itself in the man's shoulder with a sickening thunk. He staggered, crying out in pain as he fell backward, clutching at the shaft.

My hand trembled as I nocked another arrow, my eyes never leaving Cedric. The Fief Lord sneered, his face a mask of rage and disdain as he jerked Niklas forward again.

Cedric turned toward me, his sharp, angular eyes fixed in that predatory way of his, dragging Niklas along as he changed direction. But this time, he pushed the boy ahead of him, his hand gripping the prince's shoulder like a vice. The move wasn't subtle. Niklas was a shield, one Cedric wielded with no remorse.

"I have no time for foolish games," Cedric said, his voice cold and clipped as the chaos around us swirled. "With the princes gone, the kingdom needs a leader."

"And that'll be you?" I kept my father's bow raised, the string tight against my fingers, my breath steady despite the pounding of my heart.

Cedric smiled faintly, the kind of smile that cut. "Of course not. I am merely a steward, a servant of the realm. For the boy." His fingers dug into Niklas's arm, and he leaned closer, his voice dripping with mockery. "Isn't that right, Prince Niklas?"

Niklas didn't answer at first, his face pale, his jaw tight. Cedric's grip shifted, his knuckles whitening as he wrenched Niklas's arm back. The boy's gasp of pain cut through the air. "Yes, my lord," Niklas said, his voice strained and bitter.

But then Niklas did something I didn't expect. With a sudden twist, he drove his elbow into Cedric's ribs. The move was clumsy but effective; Cedric staggered, his grip faltering just long enough for Niklas to break free. The boy stumbled forward, wide-eyed, his breath ragged.

I didn't hesitate. My hands steadied the bow, pulling the arrow back until the string stretched taut. Every muscle in my body coiled, the air itself feeling tight around me.

And then...

Snap.

The world seemed to slow as the bow snapped in my hands. A sharp crack rang out, cutting through the noise of battle like a whip. The string recoiled violently, lashing across my face from my left temple to just under my right chin. The pain was immediate and blinding, a searing line of fire that left my vision swimming.

Splinters erupted from the fractured wood, sharp shards glinting in the firelight. One struck me high on the cheek, another grazing my lips, and a third caught me square in the eye. A burst of white-hot agony shot through my skull as my hand flew to my face instinctively.

I screamed. It wasn't just the pain—it was everything. The frustration, the fear, the sheer, gut-wrenching realization that my father's bow, the one thing I had left of him, was gone. The sound tore from my throat, raw and broken, as blood began to seep from the gash across my face, painting the world in a red haze.

Through that crimson veil, I saw Cedric step forward, his face a mask of cold disdain. His boot connected with my chest before I could react, a brutal, calculated kick that sent me sprawling backward. The air rushed from my lungs, and the earth hit me like a hammer, the back of my head bouncing against the dirt.

Pain was everywhere. It wasn't just the burning slash across my face or the sharp, stabbing ache in my eye. It was in the ground beneath me, in the air thick with the cries of the dying. It radiated from the men and women fighting for reasons that felt more hollow with every second. The princes were dead. Soon, new leaders would rise, and the bloodshed would begin all over again.

Voices rose around me, sharp and frantic, cutting through the din of steel on steel. It wasn't just the soldiers now—the Fief Lords were shouting too, their commands and curses mixing with the chaos. I tried to move, to push myself up, but the pain in my chest made every breath a struggle.

Through the haze of red and shadow, Cedric came into focus. He stood above me, sword in hand, the blade catching the glow of the fires around us. His angular features were sharp with fury, his red hair tied back tightly, making the venom in his eyes all the more striking.

"I'll end it now," he said, his voice calm in a way that made it worse. His gaze bore into me, cold and final. "You should have died with your father on that mountain."

I blinked up at him, the blood seeping into my good eye making it hard to see. Cedric raised his sword, the motion slow and deliberate, as though savoring the moment.

And then, a sound cut through the cacophony. A high, piercing whinny that seemed to echo from all around. My heart clenched at the sound, a flicker of recognition breaking through the fog of pain.

The sword hesitated, Cedric's head snapping to the side, his sharp gaze narrowing toward the source of the cry.

Chapter 27 - Royal Ride

Cedric's eyes widened, the arrogance draining from his face. He stumbled back, his sword faltering as he tripped over the uneven ground. His sharp shout of surprise was drowned out by the thunder of hooves.

I blinked up, my vision still blurred with blood and pain, and there he was—Halder. His dark eyes locked onto mine, fierce and steady, his coat slicked with sweat and dirt from a hard ride. He reared back, his hooves slamming into the ground as he snorted and neighed, the sound cutting through the chaos like a clarion call.

"You... you came for me?" The words choked out of my throat, hoarse and disbelieving. I didn't need an answer. I could feel it, an overwhelming wave of determination and connection flowing from the horse like a current. My chest tightened with something close to relief, and despite the searing pain, I smiled. "Thank you."

Halder dipped his head, a snort like an affirmation, and I reached for the saddle, hauling myself up with every ounce of strength I had left. Pain flared in my side, my chest, my face, but I swung my leg over and grabbed the reins.

Cedric scrambled to his feet, his angular features twisting with rage, but he wasn't fast enough. With a sharp kick, Halder lunged forward, his powerful body slamming into Cedric, sending him sprawling into the dirt. I didn't look back. My eyes were on Niklas, standing frozen amidst the chaos, his pale blond hair catching the flickering light.

"Get on!" I shouted, extending a hand as Halder skidded to a stop beside him. For a moment, Niklas hesitated, his eyes wide with disbelief, but then he grabbed my hand and swung himself up behind me, his grip tight around my waist.

"They've taken the prince!" Cedric's voice rose above the din, sharp and furious. "Get them!"

Halder snorted, his ears flicking back at the sound of shouts and the scrape of steel. "Go!" I barked, digging my heels into his sides. He didn't need much urging. Halder surged forward, his muscles coiled and powerful as he leaped over the scattered debris of the battlefield. Behind us, the commotion grew, the fief lords' soldiers scrambling to follow.

Halder twisted through the chaos with instinctive grace, dodging past fallen bodies and lunging blades. I gripped the reins tightly, the wind whipping at my face as Niklas clung to me. "Hold on!" I called back, my voice barely audible over the storm of noise.

Ahead, the battlefield stretched on, a churning sea of blood and fire. Behind, the cries of pursuit grew louder. There was no time to think, only to ride.

Halder thundered forward, his hooves pounding against the blood-soaked ground, the echoes swallowed by the chaos all around us. The air was thick with the metallic tang of blood and the acrid stench of burning wood. Soldiers swarmed through the ruins of Riverhalv, their shouts blending into a deafening cacophony of clashing steel and dying screams. It was a maze of death, and we were right in the middle of it.

A blade flashed from the left. Halder veered sharply, his flank brushing against the splintered remains of a wagon. The soldier lunged again, but Halder darted past, the man's sword catching only air. I clung to the reins, my fingers white-knuckled as I leaned into the horse's movements. Riding wasn't instinct yet, and I could feel every misstep in my balance.

A wave of desperation rippled through me. I reached for it, focusing my pathos like a lifeline, sending Halder everything I could—images of open paths, the urgency to move, to survive. His ears flicked back, catching the unspoken command, and he pressed onward, weaving through the chaos with a grace that wasn't mine.

Behind us, Cedric's furious voice cut through the din. "Don't let them escape! After them!"

I risked a glance over my shoulder. Cedric was there, his face twisted with rage, red hair wild, and his soldiers close behind him. Even in pursuit, he carried himself with that infuriating confidence, barking orders as if the chaos obeyed him. Beside him, other fief lords with their own men ran after us in a loose formation, their banners tattered but still visible through the haze.

"Tomi!" Niklas's voice trembled behind me, his grip like iron around my waist. "What do we do now?"

I grit my teeth, my mind racing as Halder plunged forward, narrowly avoiding a toppled barrel spilling grain and debris across the path. To the left, a skirmish raged, a soldier's dying scream piercing the air. To the right, a wall of fire licked at the sky, its heat searing even at a distance.

"We run!" I shouted, my voice raw.

Halder's hooves pounded against the shattered cobblestones, each strike echoing in my ears like a drumbeat. The chaos around us softened—not fully, not all at once—but I could feel it easing, the cacophony fading into the distance as the Fief Lords' commands cut through the din. Soldiers turned from their fights, falling into step behind their lords. Others, still caught in the fever of battle, ignored the shouts and continued their brutal work. The air still rang with steel and screams, but the tide of it shifted, narrowing its focus on us.

Halder pushed forward, his powerful strides cutting through the ruin of Riverhalv. He jumped a smoldering pile of debris, flames licking dangerously close to his legs. As we landed, a sharp cry escaped him, and I felt the shudder through the reins. My chest tightened as I caught sight of the blood streaking his dark coat. Small cuts and scrapes, but each one told a story of how close the chaos had come to taking us.

Niklas clung tightly to me, his breath coming in ragged bursts against my back. "They're not stopping," he said, his voice barely above a whisper.

"They won't," I said, though my voice felt hollow. "Not until they have you."

A narrow alley opened ahead, barely wide enough for Halder to pass through. Soldiers blocked the path behind us, their shouts rising in pursuit. I pulled the reins hard, sending Halder into the gap. His flank scraped against the jagged stone, another cry escaping him as we burst onto the next street. Men scattered, startled by the sudden arrival, and Halder surged past, weaving through the wreckage like a shadow.

Behind us, Cedric's voice rose above the clamor. "Don't lose them! To the gates!"

I could feel his presence pressing closer, his fury a tangible weight on my back. Ahead, the gates of Riverhalv loomed, framed by the broken remains of the town's wooden walls. The bridge stretched out beyond, a wide span of timber arching over the rushing waters of the River Halv. It should have been freedom. But it wasn't.

Spearmen stood at the far end of the bridge, their ranks tight, shields interlocked. Their spears gleamed in the firelight, a wall of death waiting for us. I pulled Halder to a stop, his hooves skidding against the slick wood as he spun, his dark eyes flashing with confusion and exhaustion.

I gripped the reins tightly, my chest heaving. Around us, the Fief Lords surged forward with their soldiers, Cedric at the forefront, his face a mask of cold determination. Behind him, banners swayed, tattered but still standing tall, a cruel reminder of the power that chased us.

Halder stamped the ground, his cries cutting through the air, searching for direction. My mind raced, every possible escape route collapsing in on itself. The water below surged and churned, a dark, endless expanse broken only by the reflection of the noon sun. It roared against the wooden supports of the bridge, the sound rising like a warning, relentless and unyielding.

We were trapped.

Halder shifted beneath me, his muscles quivering with exhaustion, his dark coat streaked with blood. The wall of spears at the far end of the bridge gleamed in the firelight, the soldiers behind them unyielding. My grip on the reins tightened, my fingers slick with sweat. The thought of forcing Halder through that wall, of risking him, Niklas, and myself against the forest of sharpened steel, twisted my gut.

But going back wasn't an option either. The chaos in Riverhalv churned and boiled, and behind us, the Fief Lords had gathered, their soldiers forming ranks that closed off the wooden bridge. Cedric stepped forward, flanked by the white-haired man with the snowflake emblem and a tall woman clad in battered armor, her gaze sharp and assessing—a fighter, no doubt, another lord.

Cedric's red hair was slick with sweat, his angular features twisted into a mask of mock concern. "Enough of this foolishness," he called out, his voice carrying above the din. "Hand over the prince, and no one else needs to die."

Halder snorted, his hooves striking the timber of the bridge as if echoing my defiance. Niklas gripped my waist tighter, his breaths coming fast and shallow.

"Not a chance," I spat, my voice hoarse but steady. "You're not taking him."

Cedric's smile curved into something thin and sharp, his green eyes gleaming with calculated malice. "He is the heir to the kingdom. Do you think you'll keep him safe, boy? Against armies? Against fate?"

Niklas spoke then, his voice cracking but resolute. "You'll not have me, C—"

Cedric's head snapped toward him, his expression darkening. "Enough," he barked, cutting the prince off. "I am here to protect the heir, nothing more."

The lie hung in the air like smoke, heavy and suffocating. I felt Niklas tense behind me, his hands digging into my sides, a silent plea to keep going, to resist. My chest burned with the weight of it all—his fear, Halder's labored breathing, and the looming wall of enemies that pressed in from all sides.

Cedric raised a hand, his voice cold and commanding. "Grab them. Pull them down."

Soldiers surged forward, their boots thudding against the wooden planks of the bridge, the gleam of spear tips catching the sun's rays. Halder snorted, his breath hot against the chill air, and shifted beneath me. His ears flicking back, his powerful muscles coiling as he sensed the encroaching threat. I could barely see out of my left eye, blood still clouding my vision, turning the world into a red haze. My grip on the reins was slippery, my arms aching as I pulled sharply to the side, guiding Halder to dodge a thrusting spear.

The circle tightened with every step. Niklas clung to me, his breath sharp against my back. I felt his desperation, his fear, cutting through the chaos like a blade. One man lunged closer, his spear aimed low, and Halder reared, his hooves striking out. The soldier stumbled back, his weapon skittering across the planks.

"Hold!" Cedric's voice rang out, sharp and imperious. "Get me the prince!"

But before they could act, a sound cut through the chaos—a clash of steel from the other side of the bridge, followed by shouting. The soldiers nearest us hesitated, their heads turning toward the commotion.

Then, out of the haze, they appeared. The Forsworn.

A break formed in the wall of soldiers as fighting erupted behind them. Through the gap, I saw her. Sanne stepped forward, her presence sharp and commanding, her light hair catching the light of the fires like a banner of gold. Commander Crosse strode beside her, his face grim and set, a blade in one hand, his other resting on a bloodied Wulfric who stood tall despite the wear of battle. Just behind them, Oliver followed, looking sheepish and slightly exasperated, clearly having failed to keep Sanne back with the Forsworn as ordered. Behind them, Forsworn soldiers advanced, their darkened steel glinting like shadows made real.

The woman at Cedric's side stiffened, her sharp gaze narrowing. Her lips parted as if in disbelief, but her voice came steady, carrying across the tension of the bridge. "It's her," she said, a mix of awe and frustration in her tone. "Princess Sanne."

Cedric's face twisted, his composure fracturing for the first time. "Damn it all," he hissed under his breath. Halder shifted beneath me again, his dark eyes flicking toward the reinforcements, his powerful body trembling with anticipation.

For a moment, the world seemed to hold its breath.

Princess Sanne stepped forward, her presence commanding despite the bloodied chaos surrounding her. Not a single soldier moved to stop her, as if some invisible force held them back. Her light blonde hair, like Niklas's, caught the firelight, gleaming like a pale halo against the darkness of war. She stopped just short of the tightening circle of soldiers around Niklas and I and spoke, her voice steady and carrying over the din.

"My uncles," she began, her words cutting through the silence that had fallen. "They thought they could play this game, weaving us all into their plans like pawns. They sought to use my brother and me as tools, nothing more, to secure their thrones and their power."

Cedric tensed, his hand tightening on the hilt of his sword. I could feel his anger, his frustration radiating like heat from a forge.

Sanne raised her chin, her tone unyielding. "But I am no pawn. I am a princess of this kingdom, born to its blood, and I will not stand by while it tears itself apart. I will do what I was born to do. I will take control of this kingdom and unite it under one name."

Cedric sneered, stepping forward, his angular features twisted with disdain. "Your uncles are dead. Whatever plans they had for you died with them. And you—" He pointed a finger at her, his voice venomous. "You're not fit to lead anything, much less this broken kingdom."

Commander Crosse, standing beside her, gave a low, humorless chuckle. "And you think you are, Cedric? Spirits save us all if that's true."

Sanne's expression shifted, a flicker of shock crossing her face at Cedric's words. "They're dead?" she said softly, the weight of the revelation settling like ash in the air. Her voice was distant, thoughtful. "They were men of ambition. Not kind men, not fair men. But they were family." She drew herself up again, the fire returning to her gaze as she strode forward through the circle of soldiers to her brother, Halder and I. "And now, who is left? Who is fit to lead? My brother?" She turned her gaze upward, toward Niklas.

Her hand extended toward him, her palm open and steady. "Niklas, come."

Niklas hesitated for only a moment before sliding off Halder's back, his boots hitting the bloodied ground with a dull thud. I followed him down, feeling the weight of the moment pressing against my battered body. We stood together, shoulder to shoulder, as Sanne regarded Cedric.

"Or perhaps you, Fief Lord Cedric?" she said, her tone sharp as a blade. "You, who orchestrated this chaos? Who has played both sides, pitting family against family? Is this your throne to claim?"

Cedric's jaw clenched, his arrogance crumbling under her words. "I've done nothing but protect this kingdom," he spat, his voice rising. "You think your uncles were paragons of virtue? They would've destroyed this land with their endless scheming!"

"Scheming?" Sanne's voice was cold and sharp, cutting through the chaos like a blade. "And what do you call this, Cedric? The war you manipulated, the lives you've thrown away—all for what? A throne to kneel beside?"

Cedric's face darkened, his composure snapping as he sneered. "You know nothing, girl. Without me, this kingdom would've fallen long before your uncles died. I've held it together. I've orchestrated every move to ensure its survival!"

"Survival?" Sanne's voice was ice, laced with disgust. "Look around you, Cedric. This isn't survival. It's ruin."

Cedric's lips curled into a cruel snarl, the veneer of control shattered. "Enough!" he bellowed, spurred by the princess's words as he lunged toward Sanne, sword raised.

The world slowed, every sound muffled beneath the pounding in my ears. My battered body screamed in protest as I reached for the axe at my side. Pain blurred my vision, but my fingers found it, the worn handle familiar, grounding. Grief, anger, and every raw emotion Cedric had cultivated through his schemes surged through me. My parents. This war. Every shattered life.

Cedric's eyes met mine as I raised the axe, his expression shifting from fury to something darker—realization. He knew.

I threw.

The axe spun, end over end, a dark blur against the firelit chaos. Cedric faltered mid-charge, his lips parting as if to curse me, but no words came. The axe struck true, the head burying itself deep in his chest.

His knees buckled, and he staggered, his sword slipping from his hand to clatter uselessly on the blood-soaked bridge. His eyes remained fixed on mine, wide and disbelieving, as he crumpled, a crimson pool spreading beneath him like the weight of all his sins laid bare.

The Fief Lords around him froze. Their faces were a tapestry of shock, confusion, and uncertainty. No one moved, no one spoke, as Cedric's body slumped forward onto the bridge.

The silence was deafening.

The lull that followed Cedric's collapse was heavy, broken only by the faint rasp of his labored breathing, until that too was silent. The axe jutted from his chest, the dark stain spreading across his fine tunic, his once-commanding figure reduced to a heap on the bloodied ground.

A murmur rippled through the gathered soldiers and Fief Lords, a mixture of shock, confusion, and raw tension. One of the lords, a man with dark, slicked-back hair and a crimson sash across his armor, pointed sharply at me. "This boy is a murderer!" he shouted, his voice trembling with fury. "Execute him, here and now!"

The soldiers hesitated, their weapons half-raised, uncertain. Princess Sanne stepped forward, her voice cutting through the commotion like a whip. "You will do no such thing."

The man's face twisted in outrage. "He—"

"He just saved your queen," Sanne interrupted, her voice steady but sharp, leaving no room for argument. "Unless you wish to defy the crown, lower your weapons."

The soldiers exchanged glances, their grips loosening as they slowly obeyed. The unspoken question had found its answer. In that moment, Princess Sanne was more than a title—she was a ruler.

She turned to face the gathered Fief Lords and soldiers, her pale blonde hair catching the faint light of the dying fires. "This war has cost us everything," she began, her voice carrying across the bridge. "Not just the lives lost today, but our unity, our purpose, our pride as a realm. We have been divided too long, torn apart by ambition, greed, and old wounds. No more."

Her words settled like the first snowfall of winter—cold, quiet, inescapable. "There will no longer be fractured kingdoms under the illusion of one. No more petty wars between brothers. We will be one realm, under one crown. Together, we will rebuild what was broken."

She let her gaze sweep over the assembled lords. Five remained, their faces a patchwork of doubt, exhaustion, and flickering resolve. The white-haired man stepped forward first, his eyes weary but clear. "I served your grandfather, the last true king. And now, I will serve you, Queen Sanne."

The woman beside him, her armor battered but her presence commanding, nodded in agreement. "As will I. We cannot afford to be divided any longer."

Another lord, younger but worn, raised his sword in salute. "For the realm," he said simply, his voice like steel.

The man who had called for my execution and another woman at his side exchanged tense looks, their hesitation hanging in the air like a storm cloud. "This isn't what the princes wanted," the man said, his voice uncertain but defiant.

"It's what the realm needs," Sanne replied, her gaze cutting through his resistance.

He faltered, his lips pressing into a thin line. The Fief Lady at his side lowered her head but said nothing.

Commander Crosse stepped forward, his armor scuffed and his expression grim. He dropped to one knee before Sanne, his voice ringing out as he spoke the words that would change everything. "All hail Queen Sanne Vognsen."

The others followed, one by one, until the bridge itself seemed to bow beneath the weight of their submission. My legs felt weak, not from pain but from the enormity of the moment. Halder stood steady beside me, his dark coat streaked with blood and ash, his breathing heavy but resolute. Niklas stepped forward, his hand trembling but finding strength in his sister's outstretched grasp.

    I dropped to one knee, my fingers brushing the cold, splintered wood of the bridge. My heart pounded as I bowed my head, a gesture not for a royal, but for the hope that her words carried. For the first time in what felt like an eternity, the realm had a monarch—and a fragile, flickering hope.

Epilogue

Weeks had passed since the last echoes of battle faded from Riverhalv's scarred streets. The wounds left by war were still raw, but the city had begun to stitch itself back together. The morning air was cool, laced with the faint scent of damp earth and freshly hewn wood. The ruins stretched out before me, no longer lifeless but alive with the determined rhythm of rebuilding. What had been a battlefield was now a patchwork of scaffolding, bricks, and sweat-streaked workers. Wooden walls gave way to stone reinforcements, and the vision of a new keep had already taken root in the minds of the masons and builders who toiled tirelessly to shape it.

Princess Sanne moved through it all like a steady current, her presence felt in every decision, every quiet nod of approval. She worked with precision, her light blonde hair pinned back as she spoke with the Fief Lords, their soldiers, and the people of Riverhalv. There was no grandeur to her now, just a relentless drive to rebuild what had been lost.

Commander Crosse stood beside me, his broad shoulders hunched as he leaned on the handle of a shovel. He had traded his armor for simple work clothes, though the sharpness in his eyes hadn't dulled. Wulfric was further down the line, directing a group of Forsworn as they hauled timber toward the riverbank.

"It's clever," Crosse said, his voice low. "Keeping the fief lords here, tying their soldiers to the work. Forces them to look each other in the eye, to remember what this cost."

I nodded, wiping the sweat from my brow with a dirty sleeve. "She's building more than walls. She's making allies."

"She'll need them," he muttered, his gaze flicking toward Sanne as she laughed softly at something the white-haired lord said. "This is only the beginning."

"Speaking of beginnings," Wulfric's familiar gravelly voice cut in as he approached, his arms crossed over his broad chest, "what about you, lad? You staying on with us here? Or have you had enough of our lot for one lifetime?"

I smirked, shaking my head. "I'll leave after the ceremony tomorrow. Too much road ahead to settle just yet."

Wulfric grunted, his expression softening. "Fair enough. But don't think you can just disappear without a word. We'll be keeping an eye out for you, Tomi. Halder's taken a liking to you, and that doesn't happen often."

"Nor does Wulfric admit it," Jory's voice chimed in, light and sharp as always. He emerged from a nearby group of workers, his hands smeared with grease or sap—possibly both. His face split into a grin as he looked me over. "You'll visit, won't you? Spirits know what trouble you'll get into without us."

I raised a brow at him, grinning despite myself. "You just want me to check up on whatever it is you're tinkering with."

Jory spread his hands innocently. "It's not tinkering. It's engineering. Besides, you taught me well—thought you'd want to see what a good student can do."

"Dangerous, more like," I said, but the grin stayed. "I'll visit. Just to make sure your traps don't take down half the woods."

Crosse stepped closer, resting a hand on my shoulder. His grip was firm, his expression harder to read. "You've done well, lad. More than well. I'm proud to call you Forsworn."

"Same here," Wulfric added, nodding. "You've earned it."

The words hung heavy, and for a moment, I wasn't sure how to respond. My throat tightened, and I settled for a simple, quiet, "Thank you."

The group fell into a comfortable silence, the sound of hammers and saws filling the space between us. For the first time in a long while, I felt something solid under my feet—not just the ground, but the sense that I belonged, if only for a little while longer.

My gaze moved back to follow the Princess.

I could see it—the way she moved among them, the once-proud lords who had fought tooth and nail for their princes. Now they followed her lead, their voices quieter, their pride tempered by the scars of war. It wasn't perfect; I could still see the tension in their movements, the wary glances exchanged when they thought no one was watching. But they stayed. That was something.

We stayed too. To help after the battle while our own wounds healed. The Forsworn had settled into the rhythm of rebuilding, lending their strength and skill where they could. It was strange seeing Wulfric and Blae joking with townsfolk, or Peter and Svend helping children carry water from the river.

Riverhalv was changing, and so were we. The work was hard, unrelenting, but there was a sense of purpose to it. A new keep rose from the ashes, its foundation carved deep into the heart of the city. It was to be the new capital of Velmira, a symbol of unity in a kingdom that had been fractured for too long.

I looked out over the city, the sounds of hammering and sawing filling the air. For the first time in years, there was a strange, quiet hope that maybe, just maybe, we could build something worth keeping.

The next day I found myself in a grand hall, the beginnings of the new keep as the scar across my face itched. My fingers traced the jagged line from my temple down to my chin, rough and new, a reminder of what the battle had taken—and what it hadn't. My other hand played with the edge of the leather eye patch that now covered my injured eye.

Healers had worked on me with practiced care after I was brought in, but I didn't make it easy for them. I'd never liked healers—not their probing questions, not their pitying looks, and certainly not their leeches. What they'd done to my mother had left scars deeper than the ones on my face. Still, they'd done their best, and I endured it in silence. Whether my eye would recover or not was still an open question, one I wasn't ready to ask myself.

The clanging of tools and distant chatter faded as the city stirred for another reason. Riverhalv's streets grew quieter, the workers pausing to join the growing procession heading toward the square. Today was not just for rebuilding—it was for a crown. The coronation of a new queen would mark the first steps of a fractured kingdom finding its footing. I lingered for a moment longer, letting the weight of it all settle over me before turning to follow the crowd.

Wulfric stood beside me, arms crossed over his chest, his face unreadable as he watched the scene ahead. The others were nearby—Oliver, Blae, and even Niklas, his posture straighter now as if the weight of his sister's words had settled into him. For the first time in a decade, there was calm, and I wasn't sure how to feel about it.

The ceremony began with the white-haired Fief Lord—Sigrid Frostborn, as I'd learned—stepping forward, his voice strong and steady as he called for silence among the gathered crowd. The other lords flanked him, two on each side, their expressions varying from pride to reluctant acceptance. The crown itself glinted in the midday sun, a simple yet striking piece of silver and gold adorned with carved leaves and the faint shimmer of inset emeralds.

Sigrid raised the crown high, his voice ringing out. "By the will of the spirits' and the unity of this realm, we crown you Queen Sanne Vognsen."

The cheering erupted like a wave, crashing over the square, voices lifting in unison. I glanced at Sanne, standing tall despite the exhaustion etched into her face. Her light blonde hair gleamed, and for a moment, she didn't seem like the same girl who had stood beside me, handing out rations to the Forsworn after a battle just a few seasons ago. This was someone new—someone the realm needed.

The crown settled onto her head, and the cheering grew louder. Queen Sanne raised her hand, and the sound softened, the crowd hanging on her next move. Her voice carried with purpose. "My first act as queen is to recognize those who have given everything to protect this realm."

She turned to Commander Crosse, who had stepped forward, his weathered face stoic but his eyes sharp. "Commander Crosse, you have led the Forsworn through impossible odds. You have defended the people when others turned away. It is my will that Kyrne and the surrounding woods be yours to govern, not as a warrior, but as a Fief Lord."

The crowd erupted again, cheers mingling with astonished murmurs. Crosse didn't bow—he simply nodded, a warrior accepting another burden. I caught the faintest hint of a smile on Wulfric's face, the kind of pride he didn't often show.

As the crowd cheered, I let my fingers drop from the scar. The crown glinted in the sunlight, a fragile, flickering thing, much like the hope that came with it. For the first time, I thought maybe, just maybe, it could hold.

After the ceremony, as the crowd began to disperse, I lingered only long enough to take it all in—the cheers, the crown gleaming in the sunlight, and the weight of what it meant. Wulfric had clapped me on the shoulder, his grin sharp and full of something that felt almost fatherly, before shoving Halder's reins into my hands. "He's yours now," he'd said simply, and that was that. The horse shifted beneath me, eager to move as the road stretched ahead. I had almost reached the edge of the square when I heard my name, clear and deliberate, cutting through the noise like a sharp arrow finding its mark.

"Tomi."

The voice pulled me from my thoughts. I turned to see Sanne approaching, her silver hair catching the midday sun, with Niklas close behind. They both looked so young and yet impossibly old, their faces marked by the burden of the crown and what it now meant. Sanne's expression was calm, a quiet strength in the way she carried herself. Niklas's was more hesitant, his blue eyes searching mine.

"I wanted to speak with you before you left," Sanne said, stopping a few paces away. "To thank you."

"For saving us," Niklas added quickly. His voice was steady but softer than his sister's, more tentative. "And... for the mountains."

The mention of the mountains hit like a stone dropped into still water. My throat tightened. "You don't have to—"

"We do," Sanne interrupted, her tone firm but kind. "We were children then, and there was so much we didn't understand. But now we do. What happened was never your fault, Tomi. Or your father's."

I looked away, the words I wanted to say caught somewhere in my chest. "I appreciate that," I managed finally, my voice low.

Sanne stepped closer, her gaze unwavering. "You are always welcome at the palace. Once it's built that is and whenever you're ready. You've earned that place." She hesitated, then smiled, a faint curve of her lips that held something real. "I was hoping you might accept another offer, though."

I raised a brow, already dreading the formality that was sure to follow.

"Royal Hunter," she said, the words carrying weight. "For the crown."

The offer hung in the air, heavy with meaning. I glanced at Niklas, who gave me a small, hopeful smile. My fingers brushed against Halder's reins, the leather grounding me. "That's an honor," I said, my voice slow, careful. "But not yet. I think I've had enough of crowns for a while."

Sanne's smile didn't falter. If anything, it softened, understanding in her eyes. "The offer stands, Tomi. Whenever you're ready."

I nodded, grateful for the grace in her words. "Thank you. For now, I just want to go home. Back to Elkswood. To my friends."

"And the book," Niklas said, a hint of a grin playing on his lips.

"And the book," I admitted, smiling faintly. "There's still a lot of it left. And maybe it's time I wrote some stories of my own."

Sanne extended a hand, and after a brief hesitation, I took it. Her grip was firm, steady, a promise in the gesture. Then she let go, stepping back with Niklas at her side.

I climbed onto Halder's back, the horse shifting beneath me with the same restless energy that had carried us through the storm. I glanced down at the siblings, their silhouettes framed by the fractured ruins of the city. "Good luck, both of you."

"And to you, Tomi," Sanne said, her voice steady.

I turned Halder toward the open road, the reins firm in my

hands. The city faded behind me, the echoes of war giving way to the quiet rustle of the open countryside. Ahead, I spotted Oliver waiting with his new horse, his hand raised in greeting, his grin unmistakable even from a distance. We'd agreed to make our way back to Elkswood together, where the forest promised its familiar embrace and the scattered pieces of our lives waited to be gathered.

As Halder's steady gait carried me forward, my thoughts drifted—first to my parents, their faces vivid in my memory. My mother's laughter by the river, my father's quiet strength in the woods. They had taught me so much about survival, about the bonds that held us together even when the world tore us apart. Their absence still ached, but their presence lingered in every step I took.

I thought of Anni, waiting in Elkswood, and the book she still held. A part of me was eager to see her again, to pick up where we'd left off—not just with the book, but with the fragile thread of something more. And Oliver, at my side, his loyalty as steadfast as the trees we once hunted in together. They weren't just friends; they were the family I'd chosen, the ones who made the road ahead feel less daunting.

The sun broke through the clouds as Halder and I approached Oliver. He greeted me with a steady nod, his calm presence grounding me more than words could. The scars I carried were heavy, but the promise of what lay ahead felt lighter—something I could carry, step by step.

With a final glance at the fading silhouette of Riverhalv, I turned my focus to the path before me. The road stretched wide and open, the promise of home etched into its winding curves. Whatever waited in Elkswood—in the woods, in the book, or in the life I'd build—I would find it.

And this time, I wouldn't be doing it alone.

The End.

DISCOVER MORE

If you enjoyed this book, please consider leaving a review.

If you'd like to be kept up-to-date on the status of the final book and new releases by Simon Shugar then please consider joining my newsletter!

www.simonshugar.co.uk/newsletter

ABOUT THE AUTHOR

Simon Shugar, a native of Oxfordshire, England, currently resides in North Carolina, United States, with his awesome young son, Thomas and adored dog, Jasper. As a voracious reader, Simon found inspiration in the captivating works of Robin Hobb, Brandon Sanderson, and Patrick Rothfuss throughout his childhood.

Originally pursuing a degree in game design at the University of Wolverhampton, Simon was drawn to the art of world-building and the endless possibilities it offered. However, he later transitioned to a career in software engineering, seeking stability and practicality.

This change of direction ignited a new creative spark within Simon, kindling a passion for writing. It wasn't until years later, with some spare time and unwavering determination, that he began translating his vivid imagination into words on paper. With every story, Simon continues to enthrall readers as he brings his unique worlds to life.

www.simonshugar.co.uk
www.facebook.com/simon.shugar.author

Printed in Great Britain
by Amazon